DEATH
ON THE
DANUBE

STEVEN M. MOORE

Death on the Danube
The Third Novel in the
Esther Brookstone Art Detective Series

Steven M. Moore

Copyright 2020, Steven M. Moore

Print ISBN: 978-1-77242-122-4

Carrick Publishing

Cover Art, Sara Carrick

Praise for the Previous Two Novels in the Series:

Rembrandt's Angel (Penmore Press, 2017)

"*Rembrandt's Angel* is a complex thriller with several plots intertwined throughout the story. It is recommended for serious mystery fans who are looking for not only a challenging read, but also one that allows readers to become an armchair adventurist and detective, along with Brookstone and van Coeverden, spanning many different parts of the globe."—Lynette Latzko, *Feathered Quill Book Reviews*

"A deftly crafted and consistently riveting read from beginning to end. 'Rembrandt's Angel' showcases author Steven Moore's genuine flair for originality and his impressive mastery of the Mystery/Suspense genre. While unreservedly recommended for community library collections, it should be noted for the personal reading lists of dedicated mystery buffs that 'Rembrandt's Angel' is also available in digital book format."–*Midwest Book Review*

Son of Thunder (Penmore Press, 2019)

"…an exceptionally well-crafted and well-researched novel. Even though I haven't read the previous novel in the series, I had no trouble becoming invested in the story and getting involved in the protagonists' lives. I enjoyed the connection between Esther and Bastiann and how they seemed to balance each other out. While Esther is a firecracker, Bastiann is the calm soul that brings her back to earth while helping her fly. I also enjoyed how Esther seemed to bring a lot to the story. From her quirky personality to her great sense of humor, she made things work while having a grand time. The development of the story was great, the plot was incredibly rich and the characters were super entertaining. It is a great story and I cannot wait for more." —Rabia Tanveer, in her *Readers' Favorite review.*

"Practiced mystery author Steven M. Moore creates three tales in one, from different historical plateaus, blending elements of a modern thriller with myth and fact from two earlier centuries in his newest offering, *Son of Thunder.* Moore has written about Esther and Bastiann previously; the interest about and between the two is deepened in this latest exploration of their vibrant partnership. Though Esther seems at times the more assertive of the two and quite capable of taking care of herself, she needs someone like Bastiann—a plodder, an observer, and a good man to have on one's side when the chips are down. Moore offers an abundance of stirring intrigue related to the current political climate, against a background of historical speculation…Moore's deft interweaving of history, religion, fable and fact makes for a fascinating read, highly recommended for readers who favor a thriller that makes them think beyond the page."—Barbara Bamberger Scott, in her *Feathered Quill* review

Summary of *Death on the Danube*

Esther Brookstone, ex-MI6 agent in East Berlin in the Cold War and ex-Scotland Yard Inspector in the Art and Antiques Division, is on her honeymoon with Interpol agent Bastiann van Coevorden. Their idyllic cruise down the Danube is interrupted when a reclusive and mysterious passenger is murdered. Why was the victim alone on that riverboat filled with couples, in a stateroom by himself? And who killed him? Esther and Bastiann were often called Miss Marple and Hercule Poirot by wags at the Yard, and this addition to the series might remind readers of Christie's *Death on the Nile* and *Murder on the Orient Express*, but this mystery/thriller is very much a story set in the twenty-first century. So tour the Danube with Esther and Bastiann…and enjoy the ride!

Esther and Bastiann's Danube Tour Itinerary

Friday, Vilshofen: Arrival, check-in, and welcoming party
Saturday, Vilshofen: 12 p.m. departure for Passau
Saturday, Passau: "City of Three Rivers" walking tour—
    10 p.m. departure for Linz
Sunday, Linz: Austrian lakes tour—overnight departure
Monday, Weissenkirchen: Dürnstein walking tour, Melk
    Abbey visit—overnight departure
Tuesday, Vienna: "Imperial Vienna" tour, Schönbrunn
    Castle—overnight departure
Wednesday, Bratislava: "Coronation City" walking
    tour—8 p.m. departure
Thursday, Budapest: "Queen of the Danube" tour
Friday, Budapest: Departure

Cast of Principal Characters

Maxim Dragavei = the victim

Linda Santos = Maxim's girlfriend

Esther Brookstone = ex-MI6 agent, ex-Scotland Yard inspector, and current art gallery owner

Bastiann van Coevorden = her husband, an Interpol agent

Elise Mayer = art history professor at the Universität Wien

Gazsi and Maja Kertes = Hungarian couple #1 from Budapest

Ken and Kayla White = Short Hills, NJ couple

Sander Janssen = the riverboat's captain

Marisol Salazar = the riverboat's staff member who discovered Maxim's body

Dr. Amy Peterson = the doctor from San Diego who signed the death certificate

Judith King = Amy's spouse

Hal Leonard = Bastiann's Interpol colleague

Caitlin Marshall = the riverboat's cruise director

Fritz Reiner = inspector from the Austrian *Bundespolizei*

Viktor and Luynhen Demyankov = Bulgarian couple from Sofia

Robert Winston = Scottish insurance inspector from London

Razvan and Ihrin Culianu = Romanian couple from Dresden

Janos and Ester Rakoczy = Hungarian couple #2 from Dresden

Security Agencies: Acronyms and Comparisons

Internal security: British MI5: US FBI & DHS : French DGSI : Russian FSB

External security: British MI6: US CIA : French DGSE : Russian SVR

Notes: The MI in MI5 and MI6 signifies "Military Intelligence"

FBI = Federal Bureau of Investigation

DHS = Department of Homeland Security

CIA = Central Intelligence Agency

The DGS in DGSI and DGSE signifies "Department General of Security...," while I means "Interior," and E means "Exterior"

FSB = Russia's Foreign Intelligence Service

SVR = Russia's Federal Security Service

Bundespolizei is used in both Austria and Germany and means "Federal Police." In the text, their personnel have just been called "Inspector" and SOCOs ("Scene of Crime Officers"—US CSIs) or "officers." These are approximately equivalent to the FBI in the US.

Glossary of British Idioms for US Readers

Note: These are often used by Maxim, Esther, and even Bastiann (because he's with Esther so much.) Some are slang (which Esther tries to avoid in more formal conversation) and others just expressions not often used in American English. The list below contains the most obvious ones used in the novel, but no subtle differences like towards vs. toward, etc. Please keep these in mind if you want to call the "blues and twos" because you're "gobsmacked" by perceived copy-editing errors. Some of those might still remain, of course, but then again, they might just be more evidence supporting Shaw's statement that "England and America are two countries separated by a common language"; or, perhaps in more pedestrian terms, that there's American English and there's British English, and the two languages are separated by a very large pond!

aggro--aggravation
Auld Reekie—Edinburgh, Scotland

barney—verbal skirmish
blaggard—scoundrel
bloke—guy
blues and twos—emergency vehicles, or patrol cars in
    general (for blue lights and two people)

car park—parking lot
chap—fellow, guy

chappie—fellow, guy
chat up—flirt
chin wag--conversation
CID—Criminal Investigative Department
copper—police (man or woman)

DC—Detective Constable
DCI—Detective Chief Inspector
DI—Detective Inspector
DS—Detective Sergeant
do a runner—disappear
dosh—money (wad)
droll—boring, irrelevant

fag—cigarette
fiver—five-pound note

give stick—beat up, verbally or physically
gobshite—mean or contemptible person
gobsmacked—astonished, astounded (a "gob" was a wad
     of tobacco)
goolies--testicles
GP—General Physician

hire-car—rental car

Iron Lady—Margaret Thatcher

kerb-crawler—prostitute (kerb is curb in the US)
knackered—exhausted

do a lie-in—sleep late
lorry—truck

monkeys—500-pound note
MPs—members of parliament

nick—steal (verb); police station (noun)
niggling—trifling, annoying
nutter—crazy person

old chestnut—adage or saying

pillock—fool
pish-tosh—only a trifle
PM—prime minister (who's also an MP)
prat—a stupid or foolish person
publican—owner of a pub

SCO19—Specialist Crime and Operations group (SWAT
    group in the US)
scrote—lowlife
SOCO—Scene of Crime Officer (CSI in the US)
sod—annoying person (noun); deprecate or disparage
    (verb)
stunner—pretty woman

telly--television
tipple—imbibe an alcoholic beverage
tosh—a trifle
trainers—sneakers (US East Coast) or tennis shoes (US
    West Coast)
trawl—search

wrinklies—elderly people

yob—rude or aggressive person

Introduction

The great detective Sherlock Holmes had his Dr. Watson, who observed and recorded his many adventures; art detective Esther Brookstone has yours truly. Unbeknownst to her at the beginning, I started to chronicle her many cases, many of them more interesting than my own when I started at the Yard. She was running the Art and Antiques Unit at that time, a position I inherited from her when she had her fill of bureaucracy. Even in her retirement, she manages to find trouble.

When my wife and I left Esther and Bastiann van Coevorden at the old priest's mansion outside Lyon (actually, it's his sister's place), it seemed incredible to me Esther had just said her wedding vows for the fourth time. Bastiann always appeared to be an upstanding gentleman, of course, and we knew both old lovebirds well, so we expected them to enjoy their golden years traveling back and forth between Amsterdam, London, and her old castle near Edinburgh.

Of course, a honeymoon was in their immediate future, and they took a Danube cruise to celebrate their vows. I can say trouble found Esther this time, I suppose, because she didn't look for it, and they certainly had an unexpected adventure, which I chronicle in the following pages. They were a bit more forthcoming about details in this case, and Bastiann even let me borrow the notes he made on fiches while interrogating crewmembers and passengers during his investigation. I have added some reasonable guesses about some people's backgrounds where neither he nor Esther had data to offer.

George Langston, London

Part One: Germany

"God hath given you one face, and you make yourself another." *Hamlet*, Act 3, Scene 1

Chapter One

Friday Afternoon: Vilshofen

Vilshofen, the largest town in Germany's Passau district, has a history going back to at least the year 776, with twelfth-century documents showing its current name. With flooding from the river a constant problem, they began to construct dams in 1957. A new bridge was finished in 2002, and Vilshofen became a popular port for passengers beginning or ending their riverboat cruises on the Danube. Today visitors are attracted to the town not only for its old world charm, but also as being an excellent place for art, museum, and festival lovers.

Maxim Dragavei threw his suitcase on the large bed and collapsed onto the stateroom's little sofa. *Safe at last, I hope. At least for the time being.*

He knew he looked like a funeral director from America's Old West, with his gaunt cheeks, sideburns, mustache and goatee, and piercing dark eyes, but he liked black suits and often even wore black casual wear. His girlfriend Linda had liked dressing in black too, although she'd been much shorter and always looked more jovial than he did. She'd been good for him in that way and often made fun of his serious nature. She always saw the glass half full; he always saw it half empty.

He'd always survived by his wits. They would be looking for him everywhere now but perhaps not on a river cruise among its gawking tourists. Once in Budapest, which he knew well, he would do a runner, taking a new name and making a new life for himself. Its proximity to Russia didn't worry him too much. There were plenty of Hungarians who hated Russians, even the fascists there who were so much like them—the Russians had abandoned any ideological underpinnings even before the Soviet Union's fall. He would blend in, maybe find a nice Hungarian woman to marry, and be free from his past. *And perhaps live the life of a rich man?*

His problem would be financial security. Accessing his considerable savings in Zurich might be a problem, but not because of bankers or authorities. The Swiss hated Russians too, but the bankers sometimes collaborated with authorities now, if it suited them. Yet his secret bank accounts weren't as stuffed with ill-obtained gains as some dictators and other criminals' multiple accounts, which would set off anyone's suspicions, so he would have less leverage with the bankers. But he was a master of disguise, so Maxim Dragavei could appear there at the bank in any form.

Every opera singer is an actor, no matter how good the singer or how bad the actor. He could become anyone for a time. Most Swiss had never seen this Maxim Dragavei face to face—the name's original owner was in a grave in an obscure Romanian village—and the bank's clerks likely wouldn't pay much attention to what he looked like as long as he had proper identification for the bank to record, which he would have. Any disguise he wore would keep whomever might be following him guessing. The problem would be traveling to Zurich when Russians might be looking for him there. *And maybe Americans?*

But he first needed some time in Budapest to catch his breath and plan for his future. And killing his long-lost relative would be a satisfying prequel to all that. Her traveling on the river cruise had given him the idea to use it to withdraw from his previous life. It would be an added bonus to settle accounts with her on the way to Budapest. Or in that city, for that matter. Not a requirement, of course. He didn't even know her personally. He only had her picture taken from a newspaper article. He would have to be careful, though. *Once a copper, always a copper!*

In accordance with his glass-half-empty attitude, he prepared himself a drink using a small bottle from the minibar, took two sips, and then carried the glass to the deck to enjoy the remainder, watching the sun's bright rays glinting off the Danube's ripples and eddies.

***

The first night's welcoming party was boring; he would have enjoyed it much more with Linda. Many passengers were old, although they rarely acted their age.

The next morning was quiet, but he still avoided the lecture and socializing, staying in his stateroom most of the time. He was glad when the riverboat departed for Passau at noon.

There had already been some tours; he'd skipped all of them. He'd seen too many towns like Vilshofen and Passau, and walking in the open made him an easy target for a sniper. *Play it safe,* he told himself, *until you're far downriver.*

After dining on pre-dinner cocktail snacks in the riverboat's lounge and admiring the pianist's playing for a few moments, he left. He also avoided the crowded dining lounge and returned to his stateroom and its comfortable deck. The boat wouldn't leave until ten p.m., so it would take its nap along with Maxim at the river's edge until then. The ripples and eddies of the Danube were still mesmerizing, so he fell asleep with the whiskey doing its job as soporific.

A noise awoke him. He became instantly alert.

"Housekeeping." *A woman's voice.* He smiled at his overactive nerves. *But I have a right to be nervous!*

It had become late afternoon while he dozed. He knew staff would be preparing passengers' cabins for the evening while they were dining.

While he'd avoided the prying eyes of curious diners by snacking, not dining, he knew some passengers had already observed earlier that he was traveling alone. Some had even questioned him. *Busybodies, all of them! Everyone wants to know where you're from, what you do for a living, and so forth.*

Although he would now be considered rich even compared to them, their lives had likely been a lot more comfortable than his had been. He hated them all. *Especially my relative!*

"Come in. I'm on the deck." He glanced over his shoulder and saw an older woman carrying towels. *Some dolt treats her well enough, but silver earrings? Linda always requested gold.* Still, this one's man was obviously not part of the staff if the earrings were truly silver. Of course, he had no idea what staff members were paid.

"Do what you have to do. I'm only enjoying the scenery."

"The light's going to be gone, sir. Just some lights onshore soon. May I turn on some more lights and stand your suitcase at the foot of the bed for a moment?"

He wasn't familiar with the accent. But it was there. *Certainly Slavic, but not Russian, thank God!* The cruise line hired staff from everywhere. He supposed they were good jobs, especially for younger people from poorer EU countries wanting to see more of Europe, which passengers were also set on doing.

He was accustomed to living out of suitcases. Now he had to pretend to be a rich tourist. *I have the deluxe stateroom, after all.* There was plenty of room at the foot of his bed for his suitcase.

"Of course. Whatever you need to do. But be quick about it."

He took another sip from his third glass of whiskey. He drank it neat, but it had cooled a bit while on the little table next to him on the deck. *Not great, but it's free.* Taking the deluxe stateroom had been a whim, the best choice of those offered to him, but he would enjoy its comforts—rooms on the lower decks were small. He liked quality travel arrangements, but most in his life had been inexpensive with corresponding trips often rushed.

His weariness, the riverboat's slight motion, and the strong drink made him groggy again. *I'm tired. Tired of running, tired of hiding.* He hoped it would all end soon with a new life in Hungary. Switzerland could wait until things cooled off.

He barely felt the pinprick in his neck but grabbed at the woman's hand. He missed and hit her ear instead, before succumbing to the drug.

***

The woman wrapped the syringe and drug bottle in a wash cloth and put the little package in her cart. She reached into her pile of towels to find the dagger. It looked like an expensive artifact, but it was a fake. *No matter. It's sharp and will do the job that needs to be done.*

She'd been chosen, more for her ability to dress as a cleaning lady and look inconspicuous. They had plans B, C, and so forth, just in case—they were professionals, after all—but they needed to hurry. She wouldn't fail. Her training was too good.

She wasn't tall, and she looked the part of a woman who'd once been a lovely girl but subsequently had a life of hard work. She wore her black hair laced with gray short, and her face was somewhat puffy. One had to look carefully to see her blue eyes because her eyelids made her squint even when she was laughing and happy, which was actually often the case in recent years because of her chosen profession. She fed off the exciting, dangerous assignments…and they allowed her to enjoy various men, sometimes before she killed them.

They'd only known about the target's cruise plans at the last moment—she'd admired his scheme—but they had quickly regrouped and created their own plans. They didn't need detailed orders. All they needed was the general order they'd all received: *Kill Maxim Dragavei.*

She didn't know much about the man, but she knew what he'd done to make everyone mad at him. It wasn't her place or the others' to think about such things in detail, although she suspected the Hungarian couple knew more about him. *No matter. We have a mission. Period.*

She knew exactly where to stab her victim. He wouldn't be her first kill. Presumably he wouldn't be her last either. She was a professional mercenary-assassin. She wondered if he was. *At least once.*

She left the dagger in her victim's back and didn't bother cleaning up. There would be no prints—she wore the standard rubber gloves and Tyvek booties riverboat cleaning staff wore.

Time to go to dinner and celebrate with some of that free wine. To sleep, perchance to dream, Maxim Dragavei!

Chapter Two

Friday Evening: Vilshofen

As the musicians and singers warmed up, Esther Brookstone patted the end place on the bench she'd saved for Bastiann van Coevorden, her new husband. He arrived and took his seat, giving her a weak smile; he looked lost. A busty woman dressed in traditional Bavarian garb placed a bowl of large pretzels and steins of beer in front of them.

"You know I'm not into festivities like this," he groused after the woman left.

"Raise a pint and you'll get into the spirit. Or spirits, in any case."

She watched him take a tentative sip. She knew he preferred Dutch beer, but he had to be thirsty because he'd been a good sport about tending to all her luggage. For dinner, she'd change again. *A lady must always be presentable in public.*

After a quick trip to London, she'd met him in Paris where he'd gone after their wedding near Lyon. The plane trips from Paris to Frankfurt and then on to Munich were uneventful, but the long bus ride from there to Vilshofen had put both of them in a surly mood. She thought the festivities were exactly what they needed to perk up their spirits.

She wore a serious purple dress with a gold chain resting nicely in her cleavage; he was dressed more casually. Her dress showed off her still slim, youthful figure—*an old woman borrowing a younger woman's body,* she thought with a smile. *Just like Jane Fonda. You wish, Esther!*

She'd continued her gym sessions even after she retired, and all the exercise recently in Turkey trying to find St. John's tomb had whittled off some pounds too. Her natural auburn curls only showed a few streaks of gray, and her girls still might turn some heads with the help of a bra. But she knew time was her enemy, although Bastiann didn't seem to mind a few wrinkles here and there, mostly on the back of her hands.

He was a barrel of a man, a bit shorter than she was, an older version of David Suchet who had played Agatha Christie's detective, Hercule Poirot. His mustache and demeanor often reminded people of that incarnation of Poirot; his piercing blue eyes appeared to see into her soul. *And maybe everyone else's?* But her Dutchman won her approval more as a quiet romantic, albeit often far too involved in his work. The strength in his arms complemented the agility in hers in a good fight, but he'd never boast about his skills and eschewed any publicity about his cases.

Some passengers were already fascinated by their age difference, but Esther didn't see a problem with it and thought the two of them were equally active. She studied the muscular men in the entertainment troop, dressed in their leather shorts and *lederhosen*, and wondered about her habit of chatting up the fellows. *You have to become accustomed to living with a man again,* she told herself. *They can become jealous.*

She had buried her three previous husbands years earlier. Bastiann was completely different from any of them. In fact, they were all different. *There are certain arguments to be made for polyandry. One can legally sample different men at the same time and at a younger age.* She smiled at the thought and decided there was also the alternative. *A whore could do that too!* She knew that wasn't their motivation, but she'd been amused by *Fanny Hill* when she read it secretly as a public school student. Not nearly as funny as Benny Hill had been on the telly, but still better than that *Four Something-or-Other* story.

***

Esther managed to pin Bastiann's name tag on his shirt pocket. She'd encouraged him to attend the festivities in a polo shirt; he always insisted they have a pocket, though, where at least one pen lived like a kangaroo's joey. Outside he might have felt a chill, but in the tent and with the beers, his bare, hairy arms would allow him to be more comfortable. The only jewelry he wore was that special gold wedding band and a gold watch.

That pinning backfired. One young dancer stopped at their table, her flirty eyes sparkling.

"*Herr* van Coevorden, come dance a polka with me." Bastiann looked daggers at Esther, but he went with her and gave it his best.

And I was worried about chatting up men? That slut is thrusting her girls at him!

She'd wanted the first dance on the riverboat, of course. In spite of their ages, they were newlyweds and maybe the only recently married couple onboard. They'd danced the first dance at their wedding, a more sedate Viennese waltz, and she wanted to continue that tradition to let the world know he was hers now. *Definitely not a traditional wedding. Bastiann did a marvelous job organizing that ceremony.* She'd reserve her judgment about the riverboat cruise, though. She'd only done large cruise ships before. *Still, it's the romantic Danube!* The whole tour was planned to a T—food, drink, entertainment, and land tours. *What could go wrong?*

While Bastiann danced his first polka, Esther surveilled the crowd. She noticed a tall, gaunt man was doing the same thing. She could tell he was tall because he was a head above his bench mates, a couple on either side of him. While those at his table were having a great time, he was alone and appeared not to enjoy the festivities at all.

Their eyes locked for a moment, but then his moved on. *He seems too intense for someone on vacation!* Sunken cheeks, small mustache and goatee, and dark eyes gave him a sinister appearance. *Like an old silent film villain.* If the mustache were longer, she could imagine him twirling it like Bastiann did sometimes when deep in thought, but her husband wouldn't be wearing a villainous scowl or leer when he did it.

Prepare to die, my dear! She smiled at the memory of how her father had liked Hollywood's old villains more than its heroes and heroines. Vincent Price had been a favorite. She'd had a lot of arguments with the old vicar, but with age she'd mellowed, realizing he could have been far worse as a father. He wasn't a religious fanatic, after all, but he'd thought tending to his flock was an important business, more important than most anything else, including his family. *Considering that flock's tithes put bread on our table, he had a point!*

Reminiscences ended when one man in the traditional Bavarian leather shorts asked her to dance. *Now it's time for me to chat him up a bit!*

Seated again with Bastiann later on, she looked across the tent from where the creepy fellow had sat, who now had disappeared—*we outlasted him at any rate!*—and saw another loner sitting between two couples. Not creepy, but urbane and dashing, and dressed similarly to

Bastiann, casual male dress *à la mode*. He met her gaze, smiled, and winked.

She thought those two loners cancelled each other out. Yin and yang, although she couldn't remember the distinction between the two. She took hold of Bastiann's hand. *You're no longer in the hunt, Esther, so neither matters!*

A pair of women appeared to be having more fun now, their explosive laughs causing Esther to watch them and smile. *Hispanic? They always love a party.* They sat between two men, so they probably weren't alone—*and maybe why they're having so much fun?* Another pair was more serious. *Academic types?* They were unaccompanied.

It was surprising how diverse the international crowd seemed to be. *Are all the company's riverboat cruises like this?*

She continued to study the crowd as the night wore on, but she noticed Bastiann was tiring. She was too. *Can we discreetly do a runner?*

***

Professor Elise Mayer also surveilled the crowd from the tent's back corner, wishing her fiancé was with her. She too was alone, although the boat's captain, a proper fellow, sat beside her ramrod straight. She was his special guest because she was on the riverboat to give an art lecture the next morning, but her mind was on her painting, not the handsome captain.

Is it a Caravaggio? Jörg, her colleague at the university, thought it might be. But copies of famous paintings were as common as fleas on a mongrel dog. Even a Renaissance maestro's students copied the maestro's paintings as fast as he produced them.

She became involved in the evening's festivities, at one time even dancing with one woman from the entertainment group who dressed in German folk costumes. After doing her share and sitting down tired, she took a long pull from her stein and thought of her grandparents' tales of horror, thoughts motivated by every trip she made to Germany. She didn't understand why that occurred, for those thoughts were completely opposite to that Bavarian *joie de vivre* so evident at the party.

She was somewhat frumpy and didn't pay much attention to how she dressed, a reaction to her mother's long-term badgering her about her apparel. Franz, her fiancé, told her she was sexy. *Isn't that all that matters?* she wondered. She brushed back her blond hair and adjusted her thick glasses to see the crowd better. She never wore them to bed. It made the sex more mysterious and fantasy-like.

Her paternal grandparents had grown up in Salzburg, her grandfather a professional violinist and her grandmother an English teacher in a public school. Both parents were World War II orphans, both sets of grandparents refusing to become members of the Nazi party after the *Anschluss*, which had caught them by surprise. She knew there was truth in the statement that Austrians had been more fascist than Germany's Nazis themselves—after all, Hitler was Austrian—but she also knew many people who supported him initially, including her grandparents, had second thoughts…often too late to save themselves.

Now fascism was returning to Europe. She didn't know what to make of it, and it depressed her. *If my fiancé and I decide to have children, what future will they have?* Fortunately the festivities began to take her mind off such things. She even laughed as an older barrel-shaped passenger tried to keep pace with the German showman in slapping his knees. *That old fellow is a bit tipsy, but he's having a great time!*

Chapter Three

Saturday Morning: Vilshofen

Early next morning, long before the riverboat pulled away from the Vilshofen dock at its scheduled 12 p.m. departure time, the pale promise of a beautiful dawn was beginning to rob darkness of its power as Esther took a seat on the boat's prow. Her sweater was adequate even in the crisp air, and the tea and warm scones she had carried from the boat's large, comfortable lounge finished warming her. Twinkling lights on one shore of the Danube made her think of Roman soldiers in bivouac waiting to confront Goths or Huns.

These were natural thoughts for a woman who long ago had reached that mature age when she knew she had more years behind her than ahead. Unlike the Danube so full of history, though, her own history, albeit full from the perspective of one human being's brief time on the planet, was much shorter. The river would flow on while her days with Bastiann would come to an end. *Happiness is so fleeting!*

She had to be fair, though. Her life had generally had many good moments. Losing three husbands before ever meeting Bastiann wasn't particularly good, but before those dark moments there had been many good times. While she knew some people called her a Black Widow behind her back, which she generally ignored—Britain had only false black widow spiders that weren't as venomous as their American cousins—she sometimes wondered if she was the wife who brought a dowry of bad luck to a marriage. She had welcomed Bastiann's proposal, even dragged it from him, but that niggling fear often entered her thoughts.

Like many people as they age, she'd become more forgetful. But her sojourn in East Germany as an MI6 spy during the Cold War was as clear in her mind now as her more recent cases during her years in Scotland Yard's Art and Antiques Division, years that hadn't been all that dangerous, with only some exceptions like pursuing that missing Rembrandt stolen by Nazis in World War II. But her retirement from the Yard had also started out with Death hanging around too as she searched for St. John's tomb.

This is our honeymoon. Why does Death now seem so near? She stared at the river, but that ancient flow had no answers for her. *Pish-tosh, old girl. You're in a foul, dark mood!* She wanted this trip with Bastiann to last forever, though, and she wanted to relish every eternal minute. She'd faced Death many times before, and she would spit in his face if he dared make an appearance anytime soon. *I will make the most of our time together.*

The noise of the lounge door sliding open and shut and the sound of footsteps caused her to turn to her left.

"Tea and scones, how typically English," Bastiann said, sitting his coffee atop the same table as her tea service and plopping into a chair beside her. "I was half-expecting you to try to join me in the shower. You were a she-devil last night. Maybe it was the beer and schnapps at the welcoming party providing too many calories you decided to burn?"

"*Au contraire, monsieur.* It was dancing a polka with that handsome captain. I'm attracted to Dutchmen, I suppose, present company included. And for your information, the two of us wouldn't have fit in that little vertical coffin they call a shower stall unless you shed a few more pounds." She patted his belly.

He grabbed her hand and kissed it, and he then thought about what she'd said. "Yes, Captain Janssen might be Dutch. The name sounds like it could also be Norwegian or Swedish, depending on the spelling. I'll admit the fellow was in a festive mood, along with everyone else. Tonight we'll have to pop the cork of that bottle of complimentary champagne they left for us in our stateroom."

"If there are other honeymooners onboard, we're definitely the oldest among them. Even some of the fifty-year-olds were prancing around like twenty-year-olds in heat. Absolutely slutty compared to me, I dare say."

"Thank you for saving your lust for me, my dear." Bastiann stared at the river for a moment. "To make a droll change of topic in comparison, think of the history of this river."

"I was thinking about that. Now I'm thinking about breakfast. A nice English-style breakfast: rashers, eggs, and toasties, as common folk might say in Eire. Shall we go below and queue up with the other old-timers who arise as early as we do?"

"After I finish my coffee."

"Don't dawdle then. I finished my tea, and I don't want to get a chill."

***

After breakfast, which had been a lovely one in the riverboat's dining room with its full buffet, they reentered the community lounge where they found optimal seating before the day's lecture.

An old gentleman approached Esther and Bastiann. She appraised him even before he spoke, as was her custom. He appeared to be harmless enough, although he looked like that banker logo for a Monopoly set with his spiky eyebrows, bushy mustache, jowls, and protruding belly, only lacking the monocle. She'd always disliked that icon, so his appearance was somewhat disturbing, but she also knew first appearances could be deceiving.

"Gazsi Kertes, madam. My wife over there's Maja." Esther waved hello to a mousy women in a pale green dress with bright yellow flowers, a summer dress not all that appropriate for October. The wave wasn't returned. "I've read all about your escapades, Mrs. Brookstone," her husband continued. "I want to congratulate you on teaching those migrant bastards a lesson there in London."

Esther looked towards the ceiling, not even pretending to hide her displeasure about those comments. Those escapades had brought her much more fame than Andy Warhol's allotted fifteen minutes, and she could have done without it. And she hadn't even been there in London when MI5 went after the terrorists!

She glared at him. "Sir, they weren't migrants. They were ISIS sympathizers who became terrorists. We most likely have more ISIS sympathizers in Britain planning more activities like that one, especially with our economic problems, but perhaps they'd be less prone to sympathize if people like you treated them more fairly instead of feeling enabled by the PM to attack them verbally, if not worse. That goes for most of Europe, by the way."

She wasn't sure about the old man's country of origin, but the name sounded Hungarian, and their treatment of migrant refugees still was deplorable. Hungary's ex-PM Orbán had used it and that awful pandemic to put a stranglehold on Hungary and ensure the one-party hegemony of Fidesz. Her visitor seemed about to respond but only returned her glare instead, made an approximate military about-face, and returned to sit with his wife.

"Justified, but a bit caustic, my love," Bastiann said to her in a whisper. "That's not the way to win friends and influence people. He and his wife are Hungarian, by the way. Obviously a supporter of the right-wing government there. That shouldn't affect us at our final destination. They're still in the EU and love to take euros from all the tourists."

"But now there's no possibility for any other type of government there. The Fidesz controls everything. Hungary is basically a dictatorship, even if it's still in the EU. I'd avoid that Gazsi bloke. Can you imagine having dinner with such a fascist? I might throw my soup in his face."

Her anger diminished and her face returned to its natural color. A black couple then approached them.

"Ken and Kayla White. May we join you?" said the husband, flashing a winning smile.

Just enough silver in his hair to look like a handsome rake, or perhaps a bold and good-looking highwayman ready to snatch a damsel and carry her away, thought Esther. *Now here's a couple that would make for a more interesting dining experience!*

"Absolutely," she said. After they sat, Esther asked, "Ready to cruise? Where are you from?"

Harry James, her Jamaican handyman at her gallery and also a great friend, was black too, but she knew most of those onboard were Yanks.

"Short Hills, New Jersey. It's not far from New York City." Kayla leaned forwards. "That fellow talking to you before is a bigot. Don't ever tell him you vote Labour."

Aren't all hills short? But the last warning made Esther suspicious.

"How did you know I favor Labour?" Esther said.

"We read all about you in the New York Times," Ken said. "We came through London and heard a bit more. Some BBC documentary. We're celebrating our twenty-fifth anniversary by seeing some of Europe."

BBC documentary? Esther's anger returned, although more muted now because she tried to hide it from the couple. It wasn't their fault that obnoxious BBC producer who'd badgered her at her castle had gone ahead and filmed his documentary.

Bastiann caught on to Esther's discomfort, but he laughed. *Will he try to make light of that BBC bloke's invasion of our privacy?*

"We're celebrating ours too." He winked at Esther. "Number one. Or is it zero? We're on our honeymoon, to put a fine point on it."

"I bet you have stories to tell," Ken said. "I mean, about that incident in London. We should do dinner sometime during the cruise so you can tell us all about it."

"Count on it," said Esther. *Sounds like a better time than we'd have with the Hungarians!*

Bastiann looked at Esther and raised his eyebrows. She understood his message: They couldn't talk much about anything relative to that incident, especially about MI5's involvement.

"Here's our speaker," he said. "She looks young."

***

Because the riverboat would soon be cruising down the Danube to its first stop in Passau, they'd have some introductory presentations in the lounge, their first of many scheduled. The first lecture's title, "Modern Art and the Danube," didn't exactly thrill Esther. She sold modern art in her London gallery, but she didn't understand most of it. She liked some early twentieth-century impressionist works, but artwork predating that appealed to her more.

She perked up when the lecturer, Professor Elise Meyer from the University of Vienna, went somewhat off track, though.

"And, if Gustav Klimt is a bit too modern for you, here is a famous Botticelli you can see at the Louvre in Paris," said the lecturer, passing to another slide. "If you take the company's Rhine tour, you can plan time to see it in Paris, the 'City of Light,' and all the rest of its wonderful art. Of course, my Vienna also has something to offer in that respect." There were some chuckles among the crowd.

Esther didn't mind the professor inserting the cruise company's marketing ploy into her talk, but the incorrect statement bothered her. She raised her hand. Bastiann had recognized Botticelli's painting too. He tapped her on her knee and shot her a warning glance, but she ignored him and brushed his hand aside.

Elise lowered her glasses onto the bridge of her nose to peer at Esther. *They make her look too old. She should use contacts,* thought Esther.

"Yes, ma'am?"

"I'd like to make a tiny correction, if you don't mind. That painting is a recently discovered Botticelli now displayed in the Uffizi Gallery in Florence. It hasn't had enough time to become famous, I dare say."

"Are you sure?" said the lecturer.

"Absolutely, my dear. I authenticated and appraised it shortly after it was discovered. A dear friend of mine owned it and gave it to the Uffizi."

"And who might you be, ma'am?"

"Esther Brookstone, owner of the *Masterworks Gallery* in London. The previous owner of the painting in

22

question, before the Uffizi and my friend, was Botticelli's parish priest, so it enjoyed a centuries-long hidden history."

There were murmurs circulating around the thin crowd—some people were still doing a lie-in, or enjoying a late breakfast, after the previous evening's festivities, so the crowd wasn't that large—but other people had recognized her name and whispered to their neighbors. The Hungarian glared at her and shook his head.

The lecturer looked around the crowd and then back at Esther.

"We can talk afterwards, Mrs. Brookstone. For now, we'll just have to agree to disagree."

Esther didn't wait for afterwards. She wanted to ascend to the top deck with Bastiann and return to viewing the peaceful and historic river, taking it all in, especially when the riverboat was ready to depart Vilshofen.

They bid adieu to the lovely black couple, went to the boat's prow, and climbed the stairs to the top deck.

***

After the noon departure from Vilshofen, Esther and Bastiann spent time acquainting themselves more with what would be their next week's home on the water. Unlike a big cruise liner, which was more a floating city, their riverboat had fewer passengers and crew and was more lengthy than wide, but its different levels could be confusing. She soon had it all mapped out in her mind, although she had to consult their little map of the boat's layout at times to figure out what things were called.

They started on the top deck, where they spent some time watching the departure, and then they worked their way below. That top deck had a pool no one was likely to use in the cooler October weather; lounge chairs, both covered and uncovered; and an oval track for walkers or runners. Stairs to it from the level below could be found fore, aft, and mid ship.

Their stateroom was one level below the top deck and a half floor above the community lounge and reception area, and the cruise director's station was located in front of the elevator on that same level. Passengers often gathered there as she tended to their needs. A large bowl of candy was on her desk to sweeten the crowd if it became too large and impatient. Esther had already noted that awful Hungarian took a handful every time he passed.

The main dining room was one floor below the community lounge, with its kitchen located beneath the prow. There were two dining areas, that main dining room, which could hold all the passengers; and the Chef's Table, where reservations ahead of time were needed. She knew Bastiann had planned some more formal events for their cruise experience, among them dinner at the Chef's Table, but the first night's dinner would be in the main dining room, a comfortable place with its central station for buffet service and drinks of all types, except for wine, which was offered at the table. Various tables seating four to six allowed people to socialize during their meals.

Because many meals would be in that room where most passengers would dine, she didn't want to dress the same for dinner every night. She figured the same people would often see her, so she wanted to be more chic compared to her usual work-a-day attire, appearing there every night in a fresh and different dress. That had added to Bastiann's woes when hauling the luggage into the reception area, but the boat's staff had then placed it all in their stateroom.

Chapter Four

Saturday Afternoon: Passau

Passau is a town in lower Bavaria near Germany's border with Austria; it's also known as the "City of Three Rivers" because the Danube is joined there by the Inn from the south and the Ils from the north. It was once an ancient Roman colony, but today it's the last stop before Linz for riverboats cruising downriver.

After docking at Passau about three, Esther and Bastiann took the short walking tour. Other more energetic souls hiked to the castle or took a bike ride.

Neither Esther nor Bastiann had visited the quaint town previously. They both thought it was charming, even more so after they took the brief walking tour, but they had always liked Bavaria more than the rest of Germany. Ignoring the anomaly of East Germany under the Soviets, there were two German regions, Bavaria and Prussia. Esther often equated Munich to London and Manchester to Hamburg for that reason, and Bavaria was a logical stepping stone to Austria.

They had lunch in town and returned to the riverboat and an afternoon of leisure for her while Bastiann spent some time answering email in their stateroom. She went to the top deck and found a seat where light was good and at the right angle to read a book. She couldn't focus on the book, though, a novel about a Nazi spy in England before D-Day and her love affair with a SIS agent—the Secret Intelligence Service, now more commonly known as MI6, had employed Esther during the Cold War. The book was too near the truth at times, but that still couldn't focus her.

"Grüss Gott, meine Frau. Might I interrupt?"

Esther looked up from her novel. She could barely make out the professor's face with the bright sunshine, which was at her back, but the Austrian equivalent of *guten Tag* gave the woman away, as well as her Viennese German accent.

"Professor Mayer, I presume. Can I help you?"

"Yes, but first I want to apologize. You were correct. I misspoke."

"No need to apologize. If I had a fiver for every time I've made a mistake, my husband and I would have this cruise already paid for and then some. I didn't want your listeners to assume they could see that painting in Paris, though. Now, please sit so I can see you better. In what way can I help you?"

Esther waved at Amy and Judith who were using the walking track for some exercise. Other fitness addicts were toddling along too. The top deck was the place to be that afternoon with its surprisingly good warm October weather.

***

After Elise sat across from her and Esther could see her better, even through her companion's sunglasses, which appeared to be prescription Polaroids and not as dark as some, she could see from the professor's eyes that her companion was troubled. Esther said as much.

"That's perceptive of you. I suppose an ex-Scotland Yard agent is trained to notice such things," Elise said. "But as for helping me…you see, my fiancé and I might have discovered a Caravaggio. Own, I should say. I can't pay you much, but I'd like you to authenticate it. I've heard about your expertise."

"I see. Authentication is a tricky business. Same for provenance. Even experts make mistakes. Not long ago, the Met in New York City had to correct the provenance of 'The Rape of Tamar' by Eustache Le Sueur. I might not be your best choice for authenticating a Caravaggio. Besides, Bastiann and I aren't only on a cruise; this is our honeymoon trip. I won't be free when you return to Vienna. I'm sorry. I'm guessing that's where the painting is."

"Correct. In my apartment." She removed her sunglasses.

She was plainly dressed in trainers, white shirt and shorts, and wore no makeup, but without the glasses, Esther could see she was a stunner. *I knew she'd look better without those professor's glasses. Use contacts, girl!*

"As you know, I teach art history at the university."

"And you're doing what the Yanks call moonlighting by giving lectures on these cruises. As compared to moonshining, but I suspect the origins might be common to the two terms. So…good for you. However, like I said, while you'll be heading home when the boat docks in Vienna, I'm afraid I won't have time until after the cruise. Maybe not even then."

"Actually I'm leaving even earlier, in Linz. I have to give another guest lecture in Salzburg, my home town. I'll travel there in one of the tour buses."

"That's convenient, but it only reaffirms my point: I can't help you. I must return to London soon after the cruise. It's not wise to leave my gallery alone for too long. I trust my employees with the routine things, and my ex-employer and his wife check on things from time to time, but there are always not so routine problems where they might need some help."

"I'm sad I can't have you and your husband over for dinner or tea so you can look at our painting. We can only admire it and wonder."

"You have to be careful with Italian Renaissance painters. Your Michelangelo, for example, Michelangelo Merisi da Caravaggio, was no different from the better known one, or Da Vinci or Botticelli, for that matter. They say Henry Ford invented the assembly line, but Italian Renaissance painters should receive all the credit. Their students popped out copies like crazy." Esther thought a moment. "You should contact a friend of mine, Sergio Moretti, the man who owned that Botticelli. He lives in Vienna now. I was only one of four experts who authenticated that painting for him. He can give you one of the others' names, and that person can authenticate the Caravaggio for a reasonable price, I'm sure, or I'll never forgive Sergio. He must be a distant relative of Ebenezer Scrooge; he paid me nothing except airfare and hotel. But he's my friend, so I wouldn't have accepted anything from him even if he offered."

"Do you have his card?"

"No, but I can give you his address and number." She rummaged around in her purse and took out her mobile to access that data. She wrote the information on the back of one of her own business cards and handed it to Elise. "Mind you, he's not available right now either. He's off on a jaunt to New York City. Wait a few weeks to call him. Will that do?"

"Marvelous. I really appreciate that."

"So…do you only teach art history, or do you also do research?"

"Both. For my historical research, I focus on Roman art but dabble in art from the Danube region through all the centuries, Viennese and other Austrian art in particular."

"Hence the title of your lecture. University life is sedate and disconnected from the world most of the time. One of my husbands taught and did research at Oxford."

"One?" the professor said with a smile.

"Bastiann is my fourth. But don't get the wrong idea. I do miss them all, you see. The first three unfortunately passed on, a traumatic occurrence each time. The only thing good about that, besides being loved by them for a time and my loving them all forever, is that they left me wealthier each time one passed on. Bastiann has replaced the excitement in my life, though, maybe too much."

Mayer gave Esther a sly wink. "A man should do that on his honeymoon, I suppose."

"Not only in that way, my dear. The first three were quite lusty when I encouraged them, but Bastiann's kept me alive a few times too during some criminal investigations."

"That terrorist thing wasn't only about you then?"

Esther sighed. Elise Mayer had likely used the internet to find out more about Esther, not limiting herself to what Esther had said about the Botticelli.

"Bastiann always tries to downplay his participation. Interpol, you know, doesn't like their coppers to be on the Times's first page, or in any other media rag, for that matter."

***

Elise was happy she'd accepted the cruise line's offer to lecture. She'd met some nice people, including Esther Brookstone, although their first interaction had been a small clash between two strong artistic personalities. She now had someone to authenticate her painting. Her fiancé Franz would be pleased.

Among the passengers, she'd also met an American physicist. They'd spent some time talking about the Danube's locks and flood control. His attention was more focused on the issue of climate change, though, not art, which tied in nicely with flood control as extreme weather events became more common, but he seemed to know enough about music and was a fan of Gustav Mahler, often called the last Viennese romantic composer.

The only people she'd found obnoxious were the Hungarian couple, Gazsi Kertes and his mousy wife, Maja. Both turned out to be bigots, although the wife was so meek she often appeared to be embarrassed by her husband. *Maybe he'd brainwashed her?* Elise detested such people. Austria had also been veering to the right in recent years. As a historian, she couldn't understand it. *Why did people forget so much so soon?*

She was looking forward to her time in Salzburg. She was a fan of Mozart. Her favorite evenings were filled with wine and cheese and the music that genius had composed, and her fiancé, Franz the cellist, was a willing participant until young hormones took over. She smiled. *Sometimes Mozart leads to more active pursuits! He was an incurable romantic as well.*

She wondered about Esther Brookstone. She was a lot older than her husband. *Yet here they are, on their honeymoon!* Was it time to talk about a wedding and honeymoon with Franz? She spun the diamond engagement ring on her finger. *Maybe I should have asked Esther for her advice about that too?*

That discussion with Franz might lead to talk about children. The old fear gripped her. *What kind of world will today's children have?* They'd arrested the neo-Nazi university student who had thrown red paint on her, but that experience had taught her a lesson: There were still people out there, often among the young, whose memory of those dark times was nonexistent, yet were convinced the old fascist ways in Austria had been better!

Universities were supposed to be havens for reasoned discussion and debate, not violent and emotionally disturbed right-wing activists. *They had to be disturbed, right? What sane person would want to return to such dark days?*

She knew Esther Brookstone must have seen some dark days too. She wished she had more time to spend with her. Duty called her to Salzburg, though. *Sometimes life gets in the way of creating strong, personal friendships.*

***

After talking to Elise, Esther had cocktails in the lounge with Bastiann where they listened to the pianist for a while. They also took the opportunity to meet some other couples, most a lot more pleasant than the obnoxious Hungarian. It was a pleasant way to work out some of their soreness from the night before and the walk-about tour in Passau.

They went to their room where they dressed for dinner and then returned to the dining room to find a table. The right-wing bigot and his wife passed them by without a glance. Esther breathed a sigh of relief. *That bigoted old man would surely cause me indigestion!* Kayla and Ken White joined them after asking politely. She welcomed them. *Some people are uncouth, others not.* She liked Kayla and Ken.

Esther decided they'd be spoiled by their evening meals. Wine was free, and passengers could sample some of the best Europe had to offer. She went for a merlot because she was having *filet mignon*; Bastiann opted for a dry chardonnay to go with his salmon. The riverboat's serving staff also offered them various appetizers along with a sampling of freshly baked breads. They both chose the mixed greens with a light dressing. Three soups were also offered; Esther chose lentil and Bastiann lobster bisque. Entrees came with roasted potatoes and a vegetable medley. Esther decided she should have chosen the salmon when she saw lovely dessert trays pass by their table several times. In their stateroom earlier, she had read the boat's chefs made use of local, fresh products as much as possible, and those desserts bore local names too.

Kayla was a light eater, but Ken had a good appetite. She also chose salmon, and he opted for *filet mignon.*

While neither Esther nor Bastiann went into much detail when the couple inquired about their escapades, they all enjoyed a lively conversation while eating dinner. The black couple had done well as entrepreneurs and their oldest son had just received a Rhodes scholarship. She wondered if they'd have had that much success in the South. *Maybe in Atlanta?*

She'd never spent much time in Yankee-land, but she'd heard bad stories about people who would make the Hungarian fellow seem like an angel, people mostly from what Yanks called red states. She wasn't sure about the veracity of such tales—even in England, regional prejudices abounded, so she generally preferred to reserve judgment. She didn't exactly know what those monikers meant either, but she knew blue and red were the colors of the two major political parties. *Their version of Labour and Conservative.*

The honeymoon couple and anniversary couple were having after-dinner coffee and perusing their dessert menus when they heard screams.

"Go," Esther said to Bastiann. "Something's happened!"

Chapter Five

Saturday Evening: Passau

Bastiann dashed from the crowded dining room, nearly knocking over a waiter, and took the stairs two at a time to the corridor leading to their stateroom. The screams had come from that direction but had now stopped. He guessed the location of the problem, though, when he noticed some boat's personnel and a few passengers milling around toward the narrow corridor's end nearest the elevator and stairs, not far from the cruise director's station. He strode to where a stateroom door stood wide open and pushed through the mixed crowd in front of it.

"Who are you?" said the captain, stopping him with a palm placed on Bastiann's chest. "No passengers are allowed near this stateroom until after authorities come onboard at Linz." He looked at his watch. "Or Passau. We'll be disembarking in two hours for Linz."

Bastiann peered around the captain and saw the body on the room's balcony, slumped forward in a deck chair with the head balanced against the safety rail. He studied the scene for a moment, his practiced eyes registering details, including the knife in the back, just left of center, and then flashed his Interpol credentials.

"I can help," he said. "And perhaps we should wait for Passau authorities together?"

The captain ignored the question, examined the credentials, and then handed them back. "You're the older fellow on his honeymoon. I didn't know you were with Interpol. Yes, we probably should wait for

34

authorities together. This is a new experience for me. Any more advice?"

"Indeed. I can take over policing responsibilities until some authorities come onboard."

The captain nodded. Bastiann eyed the body on the narrow balcony again. There wasn't much blood pooled on the floor.

"Did any crewmember examine the body?"

"I-I saw the knife when-when I entered," said a nearby woman. "I came to prepare the stateroom for the evening, knocked, and then went in when there was no answer, figuring the passenger had gone to dinner."

Bastiann studied the woman for a moment. Either she had a good tan, or she was naturally olive-skinned. Most personnel taking care of passengers' staterooms were affable and hardworking East Europeans, white for the most part, but he couldn't place this woman's accent. *No matter.*

"How far did you enter?" he said, trying to determine if the crime scene was compromised.

"Only far enough to see the knife and blood. That's when I started screaming." She was emotional, almost in tears. "I saw a lot of trouble in my homeland as a child, but I've never-never seen a dead-dead body before."

"You found him like that?" Bastiann said. She nodded. He turned to the captain. "Do we know who the passenger is? He looks familiar from the back side, so maybe I've seen him around. Not on the walking tour, though. Maybe at the party the night before?"

"If he was waiting for Vienna and Budapest, he's surely disappointed," mumbled the captain.

Noir humor? Nerves? Bastiann saw the captain was stone-faced, though. *Maybe somewhat in shock as well?* Bastiann knew a murder couldn't be a common occurrence on a riverboat. The captain hadn't needed to say that.

"We need to preserve the crime scene," Bastiann said, after deciding that was still a possibility. "Can you tell the crew and other passengers to return to their usual business? Then this door should be locked and you and I need to talk."

The captain gave a hug to the woman and told everyone things were under control, so they should go back to their usual activities. Bastiann knew they would be gossiping about what had occurred when they could, but that could be done away from the crime scene.

"Let's go to your stateroom," the captain said to Bastiann. "We can talk things over there."

***

Bastiann gestured for Sander Janssen to take a seat on the small sofa. He sat at the counter that served as a makeup table for Esther as well as a desk for him, with its keyboard and monitor at one end.

"Both passengers and crew showed ghoulish curiosity," Bastiann began, "and added to Marisol's distress."

Sander shrugged. "It's human nature."

"One of its less attractive aspects."

Again a shrug and then a surprising change of topic. "You're from my country. Shall we speak Dutch?"

Unlike Bastiann, the captain was tall, slim, and looked like Michael Douglas in his prime. His blond beard and curly blond hair belied that comparison, though. Bastiann thought there might be some Viking blood in his past. He stood straight as a military man but slumped a little when he sat. *From the stress?*

Bastiann switched easily into his native language. "Fine with me, captain. I'm sorry this crime has occurred on such a lovely cruise."

They spent a while talking about Amsterdam and a changing Europe. In spite of the difference in ages, their backgrounds were surprisingly similar. Both talked about skating on the canals in winter, for example, and how narrow houses and steep stairways made it difficult for renters all across the city.

Bastiann had an ulterior motive: He was trying to calm the man. But the Interpol agent had to admit he enjoyed the camaraderie with this chap who knew Holland and Europe so well.

At one point, he heard the deep thrum of engines.

Sander looked at his watch. "We're pulling out, with no word from Passau authorities yet. Saturday is one hell of a night for a murder. They're all probably in the pubs."

"I'd call them again and say they'll need a patrol boat if they want to catch us. Or we can just wait for Linz authorities. That's a change of countries, though."

Sander made the call. When he put his mobile away, he sighed. "They'll see if they can send someone. There are some things I must do now, so I should end our lovely discussion. On a small boat like this, rumors will spread like wildfire, and most will be unfounded. Some passengers will also surely wonder if they're safe. And with reason. I can use your help, if only temporary."

Bastiann gave the man a quelling look. "I agree. I can't blame passengers. As for feeling safe, perhaps a circular placed near the registration desk will serve to mitigate passengers and staff's fears. I add the latter because that poor woman was almost in a state of shock."

"Marisol. She's Filipina. And a good employee." Sander looked out the open door to the corridor. "I'll do that. What's your plan? How are you going to handle this?"

"Discreetly, I assure you. I would like to use your ship-to-shore equipment to talk with both Passau and Linz authorities. Linz will be our next stop, but I'd like to forewarn them, if it's not too much to request."

"I already informed both Passau and Linz, although Passau is somewhat slow on the uptake. They'll likely put me through the gantlet because I allowed my boat to leave Passau. Time got away from me."

"Make me the heavy," Bastiann said with a smile. "I don't see a problem. Like you said, it's Saturday night."

The captain shrugged. "Linz authorities will be waiting when we dock, but sure, it would likely be more productive to discuss things with them. Passau is small, and that means a small police force." He looked to the corridor again and then stood. "You must understand my sentiments. Here I am, the authority onboard, responsible for over a hundred passengers and many crewmembers, and we have an assassin on my boat."

Now we're down to the gruesome details, Bastiann observed. *But he appears to be doing it more calmly.*

"Quite the violent event. The knife in the back certainly excludes suicide. Was the victim traveling alone?"

The captain nodded. "Maxim Dragavei. He had that large deluxe room all to himself. He purchased his ticket at the last minute."

"Curious. Many passengers reserve their trips well ahead of time, like I did. How did he pay for it?"

"I can check. We'll sort those things out by the time we dock in Linz. It's for the better we didn't delay departure. I'd prefer not to involve Passau authorities now if we can avoid it. As I hinted, the Linz crew would be more competent. Thank you for stepping forward, Agent van Coevorden."

"No problem. And call me Bastiann. Is there a doctor onboard? Someone who can write a death certificate at least, even if it's a temporary one."

"I can sign that too, and confirm the doctor's qualifications, but I'll be damned if I'll examine the body. The doctor should do that and then help me write the report. I'll check the passenger list. Are we done here? I need to write that circular calling for calm."

"For now we're done," Bastiann said. "Go to it, Sander."

***

Earlier that evening, Dr. Amy Peterson was enjoying a late dinner with her partner. They'd had a busy day. The castle tour in Passau had taken a lot from them, so after dinner they returned to their stateroom and were soon in nightgowns and comfy in their bed. They had opened the shades, although there wasn't much to see except shore lights, and they were awake when the boat left for Linz. Soon after that, there was a knock at the door.

"I'll get it," she told Judith, turning on her side's lamp.

She threw on a robe, went to the door, and opened it to see Captain Janssen standing there. She'd danced with him at the welcoming party in Vilshofen. A pleasant man, he'd appeared overly preoccupied at the time. *Or had he realized Judith and I are a couple?* If so, maybe that was the worry. *Everyone wants to be so politically correct these days!* But now he really seemed to have a lot on his mind.

"Excuse me. I apologize for invading your privacy. I understand one of you is a doctor?"

"Pediatrician," Amy said. "Dr. Amy Peterson." She gestured toward the bed. "My spouse, Judith King." Judith waved from the bed, not smiling nor frowning, and Amy held out a hand. "We danced a polka or two at Vilshofen." He nodded and shook her hand gently. "Is someone sick?"

"More than sick. Deathly ill, to be precise. I suppose you haven't heard because it just happened. One of our passengers has been murdered."

"Oh my Lord," Amy said. "We stayed up for the welcoming party, slept late, and still weren't recovered enough for that castle hike. After our late dinner, we decided to crash. No wonder we missed all that excitement, although that might be a good thing."

"Whether for your late dinner or early retreat to your stateroom, or, depending on where you were sitting, for all that noise made in our kitchen. you might have missed out on all my crewmember's screams." He glanced at Judith and then smiled at Amy. "I'd like to ask for a huge favor. We have an Interpol agent in charge of the investigation, at least temporarily. He'd like a doctor to provide him with a preliminary cause of death, although that should be easy enough."

"And why is that?" said Amy.

"The knife stuck in the victim's back makes it fairly obvious."

Amy heard Judith gulp. Amy only swallowed, her mouth then becoming dry as she wrung her hands.

"I'm not a medical examiner, captain. I'll do my best, but a specialist should really do the job, don't you think? And maybe I can get one of the retired RNs to help. I met them at the welcoming party."

"I'd prefer you do it alone, if you don't mind. Keeps it clean, as it were. It's still a distance downriver to Linz, with several locks, and I expect a thorough job will only be possible after we arrive there. Between the two of us, we can at least create a temporary death certificate."

Amy glanced at her partner. "You'll be okay?" Judith nodded. "Let me dress then," she said to Sander. "I'll be with you in a moment."

Sander thanked her, retreated to the corridor, and closed the door.

***

Five minutes later, Amy joined the captain. She had pulled on a sweatshirt bearing a UCSD logo, blue jeans, and tennis shoes, and tied back her black hair to make a pony tail. Her blue eyes were still filled with sleep, her white skin nearly translucent.

She grabbed her purse and followed the captain to the victim's stateroom. The pediatrician took the proffered gloves and booties and slipped them on. "From the cleaning personnel?"

"That's right. Any port in a storm. The woman who was supposed to prepare this room tonight won't need them or her cart for a while, I'm sure. We've given her a sedative."

"I suppose I should check on her. Or maybe one of the RNs can do that. Authorities will want to question her when she's recovered. They'll want her first impressions, how the body was situated at the time of discovery, and so forth."

"You're sounding like a crime scene pathologist."

Amy smiled. "I read a lot of mysteries. I loaded my e-reader with several for this cruise. Can't say I've been able to read much, though. The trip itself has been such a lovely distraction. Until now. This isn't a lovely distraction, anyway you cut it." She eyed him. "You're not accompanying me?"

He handed her some plastic bags that were made available to passengers who wanted laundry done. She stuffed them part way into the jeans' hip pocket.

"I'll skip the up-close inspection, if you don't mind. I saw enough dead bodies as a young soldier. Never thought I'd see one here on my boat. Most any riverboat captain would consider it an exceptional circumstance."

"Very well. We should really have a recorder." She remembered fictional autopsies where the ME would do his thing, speaking into a microphone. She liked the one in Tess Gerritsen's books. As a substitute, she pulled a notebook from her purse. "My travel diary. I might be compromising the crime scene somewhat, but I'll use it to jot down my observations and transcribe and edit them later."

There wasn't a convenient morgue to do an autopsy. She couldn't even do a decent job with the cursory exam usually performed at the scene of a crime. *Am I wasting my time?*

She nodded at the captain and then walked through the stateroom to the balcony. Cold air now blew in from the river through the open sliding door—the victim's internal body temperature was now irrelevant—and the thrum of boat engines was more apparent.

The body was leaning forward with the man's forehead resting against the guard rail. *Where to begin?* She first examined the knife in the victim's back. It had a curious and ancient-looking handle and had been precisely placed just left of center to pierce the heart. *Not hard to accomplish if you know what you're doing.* She shuddered once and then became more professional. *Had the victim been pushed forward to make that thrust with surgical precision? If so, how was that accomplished? TBD.* After removing the knife and putting it into one of the plastic bags, she pulled the victim back in the chair and lifted an arm and recorded its rigidity.

"Rigor is just beginning, although the cool air might have speeded things up. I'm not taking his rectal temp. That's disgusting and would be inaccurate for the same reason. From the arm, I believe this man was killed recently, though."

"Our man in the lounge bar saw him around five, so we know the approximate time of death already. Do what you need to write a preliminary report."

As she continued with her tasks, she imagined she was taking a time machine back to her medical school days where labs for anatomy courses required examinations of dead bodies, both inside and outside. Not the most pleasant aspect of her education, but a necessary one. Fortunately she now only had to examine the outside.

She noted a series of light bruises on the wrist and one on the left jaw. *Were there two assassins, one pushing and then holding the victim, the other plunging the knife into his back?* She only recorded the question, not having an answer at the moment for that question or her previous ones and refusing to make conjectures.

She then noticed the needle mark on the man's neck. *Maybe the answer?* The bruises might be from trying to get maximum force applied to the knife. If drugged, pushing the victim forward slightly and stabbing him would have been easy. Plunging the knife in that far, maybe not so much, because that required force, and that's where the bruises could have occurred too, for leverage.

Returning to the captain, she said, "It's possible he was restrained and then sedated, or vice versa. It's hard to determine the exact sequence of events. There are some light bruises and a needle mark. In any case, the injection probably sedated him, allowing his assailant to plunge the knife into the victim's back. A toxicology exam is required. I recommend we put the body on ice and wait for a proper ME."

"Just one assassin did all that?"

"Possibly a team of two, like I said. The outcome was the same. The victim died from his knife wound. I'd need to do a full autopsy to be one-hundred percent certain, but the knife most likely entered the heart. The victim bled out, although most of the blood likely remained in the abdominal cavity. Probably painless, except for a few seconds, as if that would be any comfort to him."

"Can you write all that up?"

"Of course. Obviously a full autopsy is impossible here."

The captain took the last as obvious. "And talk to Agent van Coevorden?"

"Is he the gentleman you mentioned—I'd forgotten his name; maybe too much wine—or will another inspector be coming onboard at Linz?"

"No, talk to Bastiann first, regardless. He's onboard now. He's one of our passengers who's likely lamenting he chose this cruise, as are you, I suspect. He's on his honeymoon. I'll tell him to expect you."

"Tomorrow, if you don't mind. I'm beat. I can write things up before breakfast." She sighed. "This trip has been lovely up to now, ignoring this unpleasant business. But there's been a lot to do and see already, and frankly, both Judith and I are still adjusting to the time change. I'm sure you understand."

"We try to keep our passengers busy," said the captain. "That keeps them happy and out of trouble." He gestured toward the body. "At least most of them."

"And pretending to be an ME isn't exactly my preferred activity on a vacation cruise, helping in a murder investigation, you know."

"I appreciate that help. I'll see you tomorrow. Good night, doctor."

She walked toward the elevator, feeling that his eyes were following her. *I'm not bi, captain!*

Chapter Six

Saturday Evening: En Route from Passau to Linz

Esther Brookstone was propped up in bed reading a mystery, that novel by another new author she'd discovered, when Bastiann entered their stateroom.

"All sorted out, love? Some passengers are fussing, you realize, most likely talking about it all the way to their rooms and beyond."

"Captain Janssen will hand out a circular calling for calm. He's also trying to find a doctor who will examine the body. I'm in charge of the murder investigation for now, at least until we dock in Linz. We might have a visit from Passau authorities as well as some from Linz, if the first are so inclined to pursue the boat. We'll be crossing from Germany into Austria, so we'll have a tale of two cities in that case, and probably an international incident if the media have anything to do with it. I can see their sensationalist articles now."

"An unusual event, and not exactly the honeymoon you planned."

"No, and I'm sorry. I venture no one on this boat expected such an event to occur, except Dragavei's assassin. Or assassins. Tomorrow could be a busy day."

"Anything I can do?"

"Your contacts might be helpful later on, but being your usual supportive self will suit me just fine and motivate me to hand the investigation over as soon and in as good a shape as I can. The sooner the better, I say. Hopefully in Linz. Did you stay for the entertainment?"

"With a murder investigation going on involving my sweet husband? Not likely. Besides, I was still recovering from our welcoming festivities in Vilshofen and our little walking tour in Passau. Too much beer and too many polkas, in addition to sore muscles. I prefer Viennese waltzes to polkas."

He smiled. "The festivities were enjoyable. But I wasn't very good in my efforts to match that old Bavarian in his knee-slapping routine, nor swirling around with that young woman and dancing a polka. I shouldn't have sat on the end of the bench. I was an obvious target."

"You were a good sport, but if we're going to have a busy day tomorrow, perhaps we should get some rest."

"Just snuggling then?"

"Suits. Unless you have the urge."

***

Sleep or the urge to do anything else in bed had to wait because the Passau inspector and his SOCOs caught up with the riverboat long before the 5:30 a.m. arrival in Linz, even before they reached the border with Austria because of the Danube's locks. Bastiann hastily dressed in a Queen plus Adam Lambert T, khakis, and trainers, and met the captain and inspector in the Chef's Table, which was now empty.

"It seems to me," the inspector, a large chap with a belly likely indicating his love of beer, said to the captain, "that you only have two choices: You can turn your boat around and dock in Passau until this crime is solved, or we can release the boat en route, so to speak, so you can continue on to Linz. In any case, you have to realize the murderer is probably still onboard. *Herr* van Coevorden could remain in charge in the latter case, even when the riverboat crosses into Austria, which might be for the best because of the case's international nature."

"Sorry, captain," Bastiann said to Sander after recognizing the truths in that pretentious spiel. "I know those aren't terribly good choices, and Linz authorities might not allow us to continue even if our Passau inspector here gives his okay."

Captain Janssen nodded at the inspector. "We've already decided Bastiann will be in charge of the investigation, due to its international nature, as you say…if Interpol approves, of course."

The captain winked at Bastiann. They had only talked about that possibility. *Does the captain consider the Passau inspector incompetent?* Bastiann was ambivalent, knowing local law enforcement was often underestimated. The man hadn't risen to his rank without any skills, after all.

"And I know the inspector would prefer us to continue downriver," Sander continued. "Out of sight, out of mind."

The inspector smiled at that perception, his bulldog jowls making the smile appear broader. *He only lacks lederhosen and a Bavarian hat with a feather,* observed Bastiann, whom the inspector's jolly attitude had won over. *Is he like this with all murders? Or is it his manner of coping with a difficult job?*

"I presume your company would prefer that too," said the inspector. "All your passengers might request a refund otherwise." He looked at his watch. "If I give the okay now, you will even be on time." He inclined his head toward Bastiann. "Considering this agent's record, you will be in good hands. And it's not out of sight, out of mind. sir. There are some loose ends to tie up here. The medical report, for example, although the good doctor's will likely be confirmed for the most part after you send it and we've examined the body. But I agree it's best to let Interpol handle the case. The murder occurred on international waters, after all."

"Since the Treaty of Paris in 1856," observed the captain. He sighed. "Those were precisely our thoughts." He winked again at Bastiann. "This might seriously affect your honeymoon, Agent van Coevorden."

"On the contrary, my wife is ex-Scotland Yard. With her connections, she'll be a tremendous help, if permitted, and will probably enjoy returning to some investigative activity for a time. But you're the man in charge, captain. I'm good with whatever you decide."

"I see. My first priority is my passengers, your wife and you included. I believe I can limit the damage and their discomfort by moving on. It will be work for you, though."

"All the same, it will be a pleasure to continue the voyage. We can observe passengers and crew as we travel. We'll be discreet with our inquiries, I assure you."

"Thank you." The captain stood, palms still on the table, his arms supporting his weight. "This meeting is over, gentlemen. Thank you, inspector, for your attendance and assistance."

***

"Keep me posted," Bastiann told the inspector as he and his crew were about to climb aboard the police speedboat to return upriver to Passau.

"Does Interpol have any particular interest in this case you haven't mentioned? I thought we didn't even have an ID beyond the passenger manifest."

"*Domnule* Dragavei's passport might not be genuine," Bastiann said. "but that's the information on the manifest. He spoke German and English as far as anyone knows, but Dragavei is a Romanian name, and his passport agrees with that perception."

"Aha, a spy!" The policeman from Passau seemed proud of his conclusion.

Bastiann sighed. "A man with an old or even fake passport is *not* necessarily a spy, sir. He told several people he was an opera singer, but I'll have to confirm that gossip in my interviews, of course. As such, he could also be an actor, and he could be playing the role of anyone and have many enemies onboard this riverboat. In particular, he could be an international criminal well known to Interpol. I'll have to sort all that out as soon as possible."

"Yes. I see."

The inspector glanced at the body bag they were now loading on the speedboat. Bastiann hadn't wanted to wait for Linz, and the inspector had appeared eager to at least make that contribution. Of course, it wouldn't be much work for him. And Bastiann knew Esther likely wouldn't approve of storing a body in cold storage in the kitchen until they reached Linz!

"He did have a sinister air about him, even in death."

Bastiann sighed again and handed the man his Interpol card. "Would you be so kind to send a copy of your ME's report to my email account even if it only corroborates the doctor's, the one who performed the preliminary exam. I'm also interested in a toxicology report if he can perform one, no matter how long it takes, but, in any case, I'll pass the information on to Linz authorities when we dock there, just as soon as we make contact. If he was rendered unconscious before he was stabbed, that could mean he knew his assassin, which could give us a clue about his true identity if the Dragavei one was false."

"Or assassins. Like Comrade Putin's assassins in England. No knife needed in that case, although they failed, but not without killing some innocents in the bargain."

Spies again? "Yes, SVR and its minions, official or otherwise, use special methods, but there are other assassins in Europe besides the SVR's."

Bastiann recalled the case he'd worked on with his NYPD friend when Castilblanco's own European vacation had been interrupted. Although the terrorist-assassin in that case used more direct methods, even terrorists might use poison, especially if it was to keep their victim from screaming as they stuck a knife into him…or worse, like beheading him.

Chapter Seven

Friday before the Cruise: London

When Edward Morgan AKA Maxim Dragavei walked away from Esther's gallery, paranoia had gripped him. *I shouldn't have queried the help,* he observed. *They will tell her, of course.*

He knew it would also provide another clue about his whereabouts to the SVR or whomever Putin would send after him. And he couldn't ask for help from the CIA either. They might know by now some of their own had been killed by his girlfriend Linda or him.

After leaving Esther's diverse staff—the two English women and that black chappie were probably suspicious of him—he'd driven a hire-car through the Chunnel and into France and on to Germany after he'd learned about Esther's honeymoon plans. He met the riverboat at Vilshofen, along with many others, passengers coming from both Munich and Prague in buses, all of them appearing knackered from their long trips. The first-class stateroom was forced upon him—it was the only one left on the top level of rooms, so that was luck—and he didn't mind the extra comfort. He would miss sharing it with Linda, though. That woman always liked luxury.

Some other passengers had also obtained rooms at the last moment. He'd overheard some couples bragging about it during the boarding process. He knew that wasn't uncommon, especially among rich Europeans who could often take seven days off at a moment's notice— the cruise line often offered reduced prices to fill the boat—but he didn't understand why a tiny room in steerage halfway below the waterline was anything to gloat about, no matter what the price reduction might be.

He mostly avoided everyone once onboard, only caring about knowing which cabin Esther and her new husband were in. He surveilled them as if they were only another assassination target, which they were...especially in Esther Brookestone's case.

There were several couples who made him nervous besides Esther Brookestone and Bastiann van Coevorden. His distant relative and her husband alone caused him aggro because she was ex-Scotland Yard and he was Interpol, but he knew all about them. When he'd looked for background information about Esther, he read about her escapades with Bastiann where they thwarted an ISIS terrorist attack on London. That meant the crone wasn't helpless. It also meant he would enjoy the challenge of killing her even more.

The other couples he had his eye on were East Europeans. Of course, Putin's avengers could assume any disguise, but old Soviet networks in Iron Curtain countries of Eastern Europe had members who'd morphed into SVR agents or mercenary-assassins like Maxim. And many spoke English and Russian as well as their native tongues. Not knowing the backgrounds of those couples only heightened his paranoia.

He went over in his mind what he'd learned about those other couples during the boarding process and welcoming party that evening. Part of being a good assassin was being a good observer. He spent a half-hour at the boat's polka-and-beer fest watching everyone, including Esther and Bastiann, who managed to make fools of themselves.

One would think they were irresponsible, pubescent teenagers. Esther might be older than Uncle Angus if he were still living!

***

With the ship's on-again-off-again Wi-Fi system, Maxim was able to find out more details about Esther and Bastiann from media coverage of their exploits. He decided both were competent, even if they were wrinklies. He also decided the Interpol agent could be an effective shield for his new wife, although the Bernini bust incident in Italy proved she was a spry old bag who knew how to fight.

I wonder how she learned those skills. He had learned his from Linda. He couldn't find anything consequential about Esther's past before her days at Scotland Yard, though. And she'd been in that backwater Art and Antiques Division at the Yard, where such skills would play only a minor and occasional role. He still suspected she'd had another life in law enforcement before her days at the Metropolitan Police.

And she had said wedding vows before Bastiann! He read about the three previous husbands too. *She's not the typical taciturn, emotionless Scot.* Her last before Bastiann had been an Italian count.

He also studied how she was repairing his uncle's castle, thinking he would have sold the rundown place in a flash, considering Uncle Angus hadn't taken care of it. *Some real estate developer could build a nice hotel on that lake!* He'd visited it often in his teens, throwing wild parties to make himself popular with other teens, especially the lasses.

He supposed Esther was comfortably wealthy after wearing out three husbands before Bastiann, but she wasn't among what Yanks called one-percenters, a thought carrying him back to that ominous day when Linda and he took on a new assignment, their last....

***

"He's a target because he's wealthy?" Maxim asked the CIA agent, in reference to their new mission to assassinate a Russian oligarch.

"No. He's a target because he's a murdering SOB who does Putin's bidding, runs a sex-trafficking ring, and provides arms to terrorists. It's a new program: stop terrorism by removing their suppliers. We work with many agencies around the world. That he's become a rich bastard doing it is irrelevant."

"Like weeding an English garden," Maxim said.

"Call it what you want. Will you take the job?" Linda and Maxim both nodded. "Great. We expect complete deniability, of course."

"I already assumed Leo wasn't your real name," said Linda. "But I thought the CIA didn't assassinate its enemies."

Maxim by that time knew his lover well. He knew she was uneasy about this new mission. *Why?* They had been successful so many other times. *And who is she to question this CIA bastard?*

"We prefer to have proxies do the dirty work, like long ago in Iran and Chile, but what do you think the attack on Qassem Soleimani was? Even bin Laden? Those and others are only the ones who make the news. And if our president hadn't boasted about Qassem so much, we wouldn't have so much congressional oversight now. Thank God that president's long gone."

Maxim smiled. "I'll forget I heard that."

Inwardly, he had cringed. He had done some work for Qassem in Paris.

It's a shithole world…

Part Two: Austria

"Listen to many, speak to a few." Hamlet, *Act 1, Scene 3*

Chapter Eight

Sunday Morning: Linz

Linz is the capital of Upper Austria and where the Traun flows into the Danube. It's the third-largest city in Austria and the center for Austrian steel and chemical production. It's in the country's north-central region, approximately nineteen miles south of the Czech Republic's border, and it spans the Danube. Long before it became one of Hitler's "Führer Cities" and the proposed site for his new art museum (he spent nine years of his childhood there), Mozart spent a productive four days there composing the famous Symphony in C Major, now named to honor the city.

The next morning after their arrival in Linz, Esther and Bastiann went early for breakfast, which they expected to be another elaborate if informal affair with choices to suit any passenger's predilections for that early meal. As they dressed, they discussed the case.

"A knife, you say?" He gave a positive nod to her question. "That's primitive but effective, I suppose. It beats a gun—very silent, although that hunk Harrison Ford as Indy didn't worry about that in *Raiders of the Lost Ark* when confronting the sword-waving Egyptian. Guns lack finesse, though, and I do hate them. I'd rather break a man's neck than shoot him."

"I see guns as a necessary evil in the military and law enforcement," he said, "but not in the hands of private citizens, who often don't have proper training and are stupidly careless. But you're not going to take me off on a tangent, are you? There's not really much to discuss here."

She ignored his question and plowed on. "Yanks have problems with guns, and some there are always prattling on about their damn Second Amendment rights. As if our Magna Carta were a piece of paper nicked from an old-fashioned WC."

He now knew a Brookstone diatribe awaited him. If she were in Washington DC, she might be speaking or picketing against the conservative US Supreme Court that rejected attempts at reasonable gun control more often than not. He knew the reasons but didn't know if she did. *Oh well, a new discussion,* he thought, pulling on his khakis. He hadn't worn them since that night with the Passau inspector; they felt loose. *Did I pack suspenders?* He cinched his belt tighter, ignoring the wrinkling of the pants, and added a polo shirt and trainers to complete his holiday garb.

She continued. "America's founding fathers only wanted to keep their militias armed because they beat the pants off our stupid King's soldiers, who made themselves into easy targets with those ostentatious red coats. At the time of the American Revolution, the phrases 'bear arms' and 'keep arms' were used almost exclusively in a military context. I trawled a database collected by Brigham Young University a few years ago; it proved that conclusively. Some old judge on their Supreme Court selected only those references from it where private gun ownership was mentioned. He then used them to make his case that military assault weapons were justified. Imagine! Typical fascist trickery. Fortunately that bloke passed on, but not before he did a lot of damage."

"You don't like Americans much, do you?"

"Not anymore, at least not those kind, who are basically Nazis. And not when someone is going to kill me in Florida near one of those swamps filled with alligators because he becomes angry with me and 'stands his ground'! As if there were any solid ground in Florida. When we went through Texas that time on our way to Lima to visit that cartel leader, I feared for my life, but more for the Texas cowboys riding around in their macho trucks equipped with gun racks, than for that cartel leader Ernesto. Castilblanco and your sometimes partner Leonard are okay, but they'd likely be among the first to limit private gun ownership in America."

"See, you did go off on a tangent, my dear."

"Sorry. But if our assassin had used an automatic weapon with a high-capacity magazine, he could have popped out of that stateroom, gone down to the dining room, and blown most of us away!"

"With that pleasant thought in mind, let's go to breakfast. Are you ready?"

***

Breakfast was again mostly buffet, everything available around that central island, including coffee, tea, and juice, but a cook was also there preparing omelets made to order. They offered a large variety of delicious breads and pastries on a separate table. The dining room was sparsely populated, but there was already a buzz. Other passengers stared at them, more at Bastiann than Esther.

In the omelet line, a woman behind Esther introduced herself. "Hello. I'm Dr. Amy Peterson. I need to talk with your husband about the murder."

Good thing she said why! Amy was too pretty to let her talk one-on-one to Bastiann otherwise, although Esther thought it would take more than a pretty, youthful face to wrest him away from her.

"You can join us at the table," said Esther, scowling a bit.

"I apologize. I guess it's a bad time?"

"Just don't be too graphic. I'm experimenting with this omelet. My stomach's still somewhat abused from all the beer I drank at that Vilshofen bash, and the street food yesterday in Passau didn't seem to help settle it much."

"Understood," said the doctor. "I have the same problem with any change in diet, which always happens when I'm traveling. Is this your first river cruise?"

"I only cruised in big cruise ships previously, and only those in a professional capacity. You?"

"We did their Rhine trip a few years ago. It's hard for me to get away from my practice."

"American?"

"We're from San Diego, California."

"Oh my, that's a long trip. Too many time zones. We just toddled over from Paris after our wedding, but I live in London. Correction: I had to go back there to check on my gallery. I met Bastiann in Paris afterwards, before coming here. I'm English, but my new husband is Dutch."

"Yes, I know all about you two. Word gets around fast. You were responsible for foiling that terrorist attack in London a few years ago."

And other things since, observed Esther, studying the ceiling and rolling her eyes. They'd never found that Rembrandt painting, and she had yet to come to grips with her frustration over the Vatican's continuing cover-up about the tomb of St. John the Divine.

"Yes, I'm that Esther Brookstone. My husband is still with Interpol, but I'm retired from Scotland Yard."

"I'm sorry this terrible event is ruining your honeymoon."

"I will work diligently to save what I can. Bastiann spent a lot of time planning. I was busy with other things, so that's the least I can do for him. Follow me."

She took her mushroom and bacon omelet, the doctor following with her cheddar cheese and green pepper one. Amy's companion soon joined them.

***

During breakfast, and after several coffee refills, the doctor described her *post mortem* of the body and handed Bastiann some handwritten papers. Upon reading about the needle mark, Bastiann wondered if it could be for administering poison as the Passau inspector had suggested. But then the knife didn't make sense, so it had to be a drug used to subdue the victim long enough to finish the job in a more violent fashion. *Is that symbolic?*

"This will do until the Linz CID team can take over," Bastiann said after his brief examination of what the doctor had written. "I shall send copies to both authorities, in Passau and here in Linz. Could you have the captain also sign the original and copies? And thank you for helping out. Where did you store the body until the Passau contingent took it?"

"It was on ice, in the galley. The boat is too warm."

Esther gulped, stopped eating her omelet, eyed the kitchen door, and covered her mouth.

"Easy, love. Sorry. And he's gone now. I should have discussed this whole thing with Amy offline."

But Esther's frown grew. Bastiann knew something more than the idea of a cold cadaver in the kitchen was bothering her. *Maybe I shouldn't have used the doctor's first name?*

They didn't discuss the case much more. A new tour awaited them.

Chapter Nine

Sunday Morning: Linz

When they returned to their stateroom after breakfast, Bastiann took some time to write out some fiches where he'd summarize information gleaned from interviews he planned to do with crew and passengers. They contained names, ages, places of birth, citizenship, current residences, occupations, and locations at the victim's time of death. They also had a place for notes, and he could continue those onto the back of the cards.

His first ones were all too obvious:

> Name: Esther Brookstone
> Age: 67
> PoB: Kingston-upon-Hull
> C: UK
> Res: London
> Occ: owner of the *Masterworks Gallery*
> L@TOD: dining lounge
> Notes: Helps B

> Name: Bastiann van Coevorden
> Age: 55
> PoB: Amsterdam
> C: Dutch
> Res: Amsterdam
> Occ: Interpol agent
> L@TOD: dining lounge
> Notes: Leads murder investigation

Name: Maxim Dragavei
Age: 35
PoB: Bucharest
C: Romanian
Occ: opera singer
L@TOD: D's stateroom
Notes: Victim! Purchased cruise ticket at last
minute.

Bastiann was familiar with crime or murder boards, from both his work and his fiction reading. Many investigators liked to use them if the number of suspects and persons of interest was small enough. Even in that case, he'd often found paper versions written with pencil more useful because they were portable and correctable, but also in his present investigation there were too many people. The fiches would allow him to review and sort through them quickly. *If I had an old-fashioned Rolodex, I'd have a new system!*

Of course, his idea wasn't an original one. As an avid reader, he paid attention to interviews his favorite authors made, and he had noted how some used those fiches to keep track of characters: names and other essential data on their front and character descriptions on the back. It was an ideal system for his large number of interviewees. *Anything to simplify the work!*

In any case, he knew he had a lot of work ahead. *What a honeymoon!*

While Esther finished dressing, he went to the lounge. He was staring out the tall windows at the Danube when she joined him.

***

"You appear to be deep in thought," Esther said.

She sat by him and surveilled the lounge. People were there waiting for their tours. They were mostly chatting, but some glanced their way. It was still early.

"That Passau inspector is probably happy to wash his hands of the problem. We'll see how it goes here in Linz. I'm trying to keep damage to our honeymoon trip to a minimum. I'm looking forward to the tour, in fact. I called Hal for some database help at Interpol, by the way."

"Pish-tosh. I know you feel our honeymoon is in trouble, but it won't suffer too much." She leaned against him. "And I shall call Jeremy, maybe even from our first stop. One can never have too much information." She patted her husband's arm. "But you should consider all this an omen. Our marriage means we can continue to be a crime-fighting duo more often. Working as a team. Nora and Nick Charles. Or Miss Marple teaming up with Hercule Poirot, as some wags in the Yard would have it, in an intimate way like those other famous couples of crime fiction."

"Oh, please. Only your old boss gives credence to those gossip mongers."

"As a joke, love. George Langston lives vicariously through our exploits. As an administrator, he doesn't see much action. I'm so glad I offloaded that awful job on him. It never sat well with me."

"And he likely wants you back to make him look good."

"Everyone is replaceable, dear man, and frankly I became tired of internal politics and higher-ups always wanting me to retire. You know all about the first and maybe not enough about the second."

"Yes, your bureaucracy was nothing compared to Interpol's. Comrade Putin even tried to put in his own man a while back, you know. Our ties with UN bureaucracy can work against us. We mostly serve at the whim of the EU and UN's budget bureaucrats, and local police forces often consider us meddlers."

"My, my, the inspector was that bad?"

Bastiann shrugged but smiled at his bride's deductive reasoning. "Not really. Maybe I'm ready to retire too."

"Forget about all that for now. Look out the windows at the wonderful scenery. Isn't it lovely? Early morning on the world's most famous river!"

"It's almost as if we were in a time machine and have now materialized on a Roman barge parked on the Danube's shore."

"There's your peculiar taste in science fiction again. There are no Goths or Huns on the bank shooting fiery arrows at us, thank goodness." She thought a moment. "Maybe today they're Russian oligarchs and right-wing fanatics."

Esther and Bastiann dropped into a period of silent contemplation of the river's beauty. As she relaxed, her mind turned to her goodbyes at her art gallery during that quick return trip to London. That event had started off with some strangeness...

***

Esther entered the gallery and spotted the "Madonna with Child" she had restored not long before. Her handyman Harry had found the perfect place to display it. Anna and Dorothy, two artsy women who also helped her at the gallery, came running towards her.

Anna, a stunner, was thin and often smiling. Dorothy, with her plumpness and thick glasses, looked to be more serious, and she was. Both girls knew art, even the modern schools and their artists where Esther was weak.

After some pleasantries, Anna said, "Dracula was here to see you yesterday morning, Esther."

She looked from Anna to Dorothy and then back at Anna. "Is this like my friend Sergio being the elf from *Lord of the Rings*, who was really a dwarf, mind you?"

Anna smiled. "Your visitor's name was Edward Morgan. A tall, skinny fellow dressed in a black cape as if he had just stepped out of 1890s London into our time. Top hat, too. Mustache, goatee, and sunken cheeks. Lacked only fangs, mum."

"You might be thinking of Jack the Ripper. Dracula was from Transylvania. And he didn't like the light of day." Esther couldn't recall anyone with the mysterious visitor's name or description. "What did you tell him?"

"Maybe I shouldn't have," said Dorothy, looking first at Anna and then back at Esther, "but I mentioned your honeymoon and the river cruise. We're so happy for you, Esther."

"Thank you for that. I hope to have a still-functioning gallery when I return. So this fellow was creepy?"

"Absolutely," said Anna. "The creepiest."

"Good thing I was here, mum," said Esther's trusted Jamaican handyman, Harry James, with a wink and a smile. "The young ladies might have bared their necks for him otherwise. He wasn't that fanged chap from *Twilight* that all the women swoon over, either—that includes my wife, by the way."

Esther returned the smile. She could imagine Harry's Cockney wife as an incurable romantic. She and her employees were a tight group now, and she enjoyed the camaraderie. She still felt guilty about Harry's encounter with a knife-wielding thief, but she now counted the Jamaican and his wife as good friends who fortunately held none of that against her.

"I don't know anyone named Edward Morgan, so I can't tell how much the girls' imaginations have run wild again. Did he leave a note or business card?" Anna and Dorothy shook their heads while Harry shrugged. "Okay, I have other things to worry about, so I'll have to put Dracula out of mind unless he pops out of his coffin and returns to bite us. Keep me informed. I have to go and finish packing now. I only wanted to make sure everyone was okay and prepared to do without me for a while. The Langstons will be checking in on things once and a while, so be prepared for surprise visits."

"Sounds like you'll have a great trip," Harry said.

"I'm going Dutch with Bastiann," she said, enjoying the pun. "He's put a serious dent in our combined finances by choosing that top-of-the-line suite, but I forgive him. It's his first honeymoon, after all, so I suppose I must indulge him." She winked at Harry. "And that deluxe suite might come in handy if we spend a lot of time in it, as we shall, I'm sure."

"You'll have great fun," said Dorothy. "A true romantic cruise down the Danube. We all envy you."

"And it's a vacation you both deserve," said Anna.

Edward Morgan? The description of the visitor to her gallery seemed to match the picture of Maxim Dragavei on her mobile Bastiann had sent her, that same creepy fellow whom she'd seen at the welcoming party. *Should I mention that to Bastiann?* A frisson went down her spine.

Chapter Ten

Sunday Morning: Paris Suburbs

Interpol agent Hal Leonard had no idea why the man they'd searched for had taken an apartment in the Muslim slums in the Paris suburbs. *Perhaps he was trying to approach ISIS sympathizers once again?* Arms dealers sold to anyone, this one in particular.

Ernesto Felipe Lopez Diaz, a Colombian cartel leader but also active in Peru and elsewhere, made money in sex trafficking and the illegal arms trade as well, most of the latter selling weapons and ammo to terrorists, especially to those in Afghanistan who sold him cheap, raw opium in return. Halting the illegal arms trade had become Hal's specialty. It was an endless task. When one arms dealer was brought to justice, another would pop up to take his place. Hal had no love for cartel leaders either. The goons of one in Texas had nearly killed him.

A mix of *gendarmes* and DGSI agents accompanied him. "*Tres bien, mes bêtes,*" said the DGSI agent in charge over their com system. "*Allons-y.* Let's go. We have him."

The last was for Hal, although everyone spoke French. He smiled.

Before they could obey the leader's command and enter the building, three of Ernesto's thugs appeared, saw the good guys starting to move in, and opened fire.

Hal had been in firefights before. He hated them, and now he had someone to care about, someone waiting for him. *That makes one hell of a difference!*

Two thugs fell. The third, the man with a big hooked nose and pox-scarred face, tried to escape by running straight at and then around the old truck Hal had been using for a shield while he fired at the thugs. By then the hulk had tossed his gun, its magazine depleted. Hal put his gun away and stepped in front of Ernesto's bodyguard, ready to tackle him and slap the handcuffs on.

Wrong move! The thug straight-armed him like he was a defensive tackle who had just enjoyed his first pass interception against a famous but careless opposing quarterback. After Hal fell hard on his butt, the hulk ran right into the waiting arms of three *gendarmes*. It took all three to put the handcuffs on him.

"Get Ernesto!" Hal said into his mike to his comrades.

***

Hal watched the *gendarme* push the handcuffed cartel leader's head down to put him into the patrol car's backseat. Esther and Bastiann's information had been instrumental in bringing Ernesto Felipe Lopez Diaz to justice. Hard work on Hal's part had completed that chore.

He was disheveled—brown hair in disarray, fashionable salt-and-pepper stubble, and rheumy blue eyes—his appearance not completely caused by the run-in with Ernesto's wild rhino. Hal was dressed in his usual work clothes—Hawaiian shirt, Levis, and sneakers.

He pulled out his smart phone from his jeans' back pocket and realized it was crushed. *I'm not surprised.* The hard fall on his butt after the goon had pushed him would be difficult to live down. His companions would rib him all the way back to HQ. That thug now was lying on the grass with handcuffs pinning his arms behind his back.

Hal stopped the lead DGSI agent who was passing by.

"Can I borrow your cellphone a moment?"

"You have five minutes. I have to file my report with it."

"*Merci.*" He called Bastiann. "*Bonjour*, bro. Guess what? We finally got the SOB!"

"Which SOB?"

"Ernesto Felipe Lopez Diaz, *mon ami*. Only for illegal arms dealing, mind you, but that's better than Capone's tax evasion, and it will be good enough to put him away for some years."

"He'll just run the cartel from his cell. Where are you? Sounds like Paris."

"You can tell a city from its sound?"

"Paris and some others. Smell too, but that doesn't transmit well on the mobile. *Très bien*, Hal. Ernesto Felipe's threatening look can chill your soul. I know that from personal experience."

"Yeah. We received some of those looks from him while he sat in the patrol car. A true psychotic sociopath. I thought you might enjoy the good news. Where are you?"

Bastiann sighed. "In the middle of a murder investigation."

"So you abandoned your honeymoon orgy. What's the matter? Did the old girl wear you out?"

"The victim was a passenger on the same riverboat we're on. I decided to call you, but you beat me to it. Are you returning to Lyon?"

"Eventually I'll have to. I'm staying in Philippa's apartment for now, here in Paris. She might get worried if I'm late. But I should return to Lyon before Karl has a fit. What's the favor?" Hal knew Bastiann well. His friend was always serious.

As if to contradict that thought, Bastiann became more social. "How's that romance going? And how's Philippa?"

"Hot and heavy. And she still isn't ready to return to work. I'm not sure she wants to return."

"She'll become antsy. Give her my best. But back to business. If I text you a list of names, can you check them out in our databases? You probably don't have to be in Lyon to do it."

"If I can't, I'll find someone there who will. Call me at home tomorrow evening." He rattled off Philippa's number, although he expected it to be on Bastiann's speed dial. "If I'm not there, Philippa will be."

"Thanks. *Ciao*. Don't celebrate too much. There's always another criminal to apprehend."

***

Hal opened Philippa's apartment door with the key she'd given him and spotted the only woman he'd ever been serious about. Her *petite* frame, short, blond hair, and intense blue eyes always reminded him of a porcelain doll his sister once had, not that this doll couldn't liven things up a lot more.

She put her novel open but face down onto her lap, those eyes now questioning. He recognized the book as one Bastiann had recommended titled *The Mensa Contagion,* or something similar, by some obscure US author. He wondered if it was about that group of geniuses, but the cover screamed sci-fi. Hal didn't like that genre; Bastiann did.

He knew the woman had a thing for Bastiann. He wrote it off to his friend's saving her in another firefight, but he sometimes wondered. She seemed somewhat envious at Esther and Bastiann's wedding where Philippa and Hal had first met. *Was it envy for the bride, that is, most women's desire for a fancy wedding, or because Bastiann was no longer available?* Those questions weren't easy ones at the beginning of a relationship.

"I was worried," said the DGSE agent, who was still on medical leave and in recovery mode from the gunshot wound that had almost killed her. While Interpol agents often didn't do the heavy lifting when bringing a criminal to justice, they could, and DGSE agents even more so. "Any success?"

"*Mais oui, ma cherie.*" He handed her the bouquet. "Picked these up for another woman, but thought you deserved them more."

She laughed. "You should know by now I can always tell when you're lying."

"Careful. You might make me into an honest man, and then who knows what will happen?"

She stood and hobbled toward him. "I'll put these in water. I have a roast in the oven. Started it only twenty minutes ago. It will take a while."

"Any hors-d'oeuvres on the menu?"

"Me and wine. Go to your stall, my stallion, while this mare checks the roast. We have plenty of time before dinner."

***

Not much later, Hal was propped up on three pillows sipping wine when he said, "I talked to Bastiann today."

"How is that man who saved my life?" said Philippa, who was snuggling next to him and enjoying how his free hand played between her legs.

"Very busy."

"I imagine. Esther is one hot lady. She doesn't act her age. And at their wedding, the two seemed like lovesick teenagers going to their first dance."

"Don't let your lurid imagination go crazy now. Maybe not so busy in that way. And I seem to remember we were hot and heavy at that wedding too. Love at first sight, *mon amour.*" He pointed to the flowers atop the chest of drawers, their splendor doubled by the attached mirror. "I didn't know if you had any allergies. I need to get to know you better." She laughed and he smiled. "To answer your question: Bastiann's in a murder investigation."

"And the honeymoon?"

"Exactly what I asked him. Still in progress, I guess, but with some extracurricular activities on that riverboat now added. Bastiann is swamped with investigative bureaucracy, the kind I hate—he prefers good old-fashioned detective work. And here you envied them."

Hal had been his friend's best man. He wondered how they were doing on the riverboat in general. He knew Bastiann hadn't planned that trip nearly as well as he'd planned the wedding. He hadn't even known details he'd normally have considered important. Hal was surprised his friend and colleague had done as well as he did. *There wasn't much time, especially not for that meticulous Dutchman.* Of course, that was what made his friend such a good Interpol agent. He preferred crime details and associated puzzles to action. Hal needed both, and perhaps more of the latter.

"It would be a way to distract you from your work."

He rolled toward her a bit. "You know DGSE would welcome you back."

She sighed. "Of course. They'd better, but when I'm ready. Right now I'm enjoying all the pampering."

He kissed her. "We're both lucky. And the pampering works both ways."

They both had suffered through near-death experiences in their jobs. His was in Texas where the NYPD cop Castilblanco had saved his ass; hers was in Casablanca where Bastiann had saved hers.

Two white houses kept us alive so we could be together. It's a strange world.

Chapter Eleven

Sunday Morning: London

"Good work, gentlemen," Jeremy Brand told his MI5 crew gathered in the dark counterterrorism center. The tension in the room had left.

He wiped his brow and smiled at them all. The air was heavy and musty, and electronics equipment, from panels with blinking lights to computers and video monitors, challenged the AC system. Com units chirped to each other. Most monitors on the walls now showed no action, only an area sealed off with police tape.

The dozen or so agents had swung around from their workstations. Most were smiling, more for the successful mission than his praise. All looked tired. They were a diverse and mixed crew of smart women and men, and they'd been working hard in a stressful situation. He gave them a hearty round of applause.

Sometimes we're successful, he observed to himself as he clapped.

The Irish terrorists had encountered a barricade when they entered the narrow street with their car bomb. They tried to back out, but SCO19 trucks blocked their retreat. The two terrorists who didn't surrender died; the other two who did would be in prison for a long time.

Ever since Boris Johnson closed the border with the Republic of Ireland a few years earlier because of Brexit, there had been unrest in Northern Ireland. Not as much as during the Troubles, but a lot of Catholics were mad about being cut-off from their southern brethren as a consequence of the UK's leaving the EU. The Irish

Republic was still in it. That situation had led to some violent acts, including organized bombing attacks in London and other major British cities. *Déjà vu*, he thought, remembering other bombers like the Price sisters who long ago had nearly died in a hunger strike after being caught.

And now we have more terrorists to worry about than just ISIS sympathizers. Thanks, Boris!

He waved a hand and showed an upturned thumb to all the operators at their consoles and left the room. His office was two floors up. He took the stairs for some exercise, even though he was tired. Worrying about an op was always exhausting.

***

"Congratulations, sir," said an aide ensconced in the little room near Jeremy's office that also was home to the secretary pool supporting Jeremy and his colleagues in the counterterrorism unit. "You had a call."

"Anyone important?" said Jeremy, thinking maybe the current PM had called to congratulate him. Jeremy knew the bloke and didn't like him much, but he would have accepted some praise. *Although we're only doing our jobs!*

"A civilian. She sounded sassy and seemed pushy, so I got rid of her. But she insisted on leaving her name."

Jeremy frowned. "And? What was her name?"

"Esther Brookstone."

Jeremy now grimaced. "Can you do a trace and call-back for me? I'll chat with her in my office."

"Sorry, sir. Girlfriend?"

"No need to know. But no, she's not, as if it were any of your business. She's generally a pain in the arse, so you might have done me a favor."

Jeremy returned to his office, plopped into his chair, and sighed. *So much for MI5 being an easier posting than MI6!*

He had been one of Esther's MI6 handlers in East Berlin during the Cold War. Like many men in her life, she'd chatted him up a bit, which he now saw more as boredom on her part. Most spy work was boring—often a waiting game both sides played, looking for the chance of a coup, no matter how small, against the other side. There were no licenses to kill, a myth perpetrated by endless James Bond movies, but the game could be deadly all the same. Esther had done as well playing it as anyone had. *Unsung heroes of the realm*, he thought.

He'd transferred to MI5, assuming it would be less stressful work, but the counterterrorism unit had soon taken over his life, although it also led to his involvement in several ops in response to Putin-directed assassinations. *We can never let our guard down!* That guard was more expensive now, which also made it a target for budget-slashing MPs. The royal family had needed to intercede a few times. *Sometimes the old witch did some good. His Majesty seems a bit more modern in performing his kingly duties.* And all the stress had affected his waist and hairlines. His two stents were less obvious consequences.

Like Sergio Moretti, Esther's handler before Jeremy, he'd been disappointed when Esther chose men to marry he considered even more boring than the two of them. He didn't know much about Bastiann van Coevorden except that he was much younger than Esther, Sergio, and he were.

More power to the old girl, he observed. *She lost her first three husbands.* He smiled. *Maybe she wore them out?* A younger one might outlast her.

He wondered what she wanted from him this time.

***

Jeremy had just started his short report on the terrorist incident—the secretary pool was an anachronism he only used for much longer reports—when his aide put Esther through.

"Hello, Jeremy, are you being a good little boy and saving Great Britain from Johnson's many mistakes?"

"Cheeky as usual. Are you still gloating about your new PM? Labour could mess things up for our country even more, you know."

"Tosh, Jeremy. All politicians do anymore is create chaos. Nothing new there under the sun, or fog, as the case may be for you in London right now. And it all gives the press something to write about when there's no scandals involving the royal family to keep those vampires sated with royal blood."

"You called me to discuss something else, I hope. I have a report to write."

"*Da, tovarishch.* My honeymoon has become more of an adventure, to put it mildly. Thank you for the wedding gift, by the way. When I return, I'll send out some formal thank-you notes." She cleared her throat. "But, to the point: Poor Bastiann is in the middle of a murder investigation, a case local authorities have passed off to Interpol because it involves several EU countries. Well, two for now."

"It always amuses me that the EU wants to be the United States of Europe but is incapable of resolving such procedural issues, or maybe unwilling to do so."

"That sounds like old Boris, I dare say. And I'm not sure the Yanks do a very good job of it, at least not in the twenty-first century."

"No, it's all me. MI5 ignores politics. And what I said is true. Before Brexit, it became hellish at times. Now we can at least thumb our noses at the EU some."

"But you and I were in MI6 at one time. They can't do what you say, at least not too often. They have to pretend to collaborate. Couldn't do much otherwise. But I digress. I want to help poor Bastiann, and you're my man on the inside."

He was immediately suspicious. He thought Esther often abused their friendship.

"What kind of help?"

"If I send you a list of names, can you have someone trawl MI5's databases to see if there's any correlation?"

"That's illegal. You're a private citizen now."

"That never stopped you before."

"You were at Scotland Yard, so you did have an official capacity. But you're right. That's also being a private citizen as far as MI5 is concerned, because we'd take over the case if it truly affected the entire nation."

"But London would have suffered its worst terrorist attack in history if Bastiann and I hadn't passed that important intel to you."

Yes, and it would have been even worse than the one they'd just stopped. Jeremy sighed. "Okay. Whose names? And how many?"

"No more than two hundred. Crew and passengers from our riverboat."

"You'll receive your information, Esther, but in batches. I'll have some people work on your list during downtime. I'm not taking them away from critical missions."

"Understood. I'll prioritize the list for you. The first name on it will be Maxim Dragavei, the victim."

"Sounds Eastern European. Why will I be checking on a dead man?"

"Because he might be a bad character whom someone wanted to kill. That's mostly Bastiann's idea, not mine, but he could be right. In my opinion, he might only have been a second-rate opera singer. I only wonder if there's something in his past we need to know about."

"Okay, send the list. You'll need MI6 or Interpol for the EU and beyond, you realize. If your victim is only an international player, for example, MI5 might have nothing on him."

"Bastiann is working on Interpol, but I don't have MI6 connections anymore."

"I do. Maybe I can do something there. No promises, mind you. And Esther?"

"Yes?"

"Don't let this ruin your honeymoon." Jeremy laughed. "It might be your last one."

"That's a bit harsh, old friend. You owe me a curry dinner for that awful comment."

"We'll go Dutch then. You'll owe me one for your list."

Chapter Twelve

Some Months Earlier: London

John MacDonald was only a skinny lad when he moved in with his uncle Angus MacDougall, the original owner of Esther's castle. At fifteen, his uncle evicted him.

My own fault. His uncle was loving but strict and demanding, and John was rebellious, more so than the typical teen. Afterwards, he didn't try to stay in touch either, although he wrote a few letters over the years. He savored his freedom. School became a thing of the past. Weed and sex took precedent…and the money necessary to finance those habits.

Nicking items here and there had led to something bigger once, a black Jaguar some rich prat had left running. His friend Edward died in the fiery motorcar crash outside Manchester; John was a passenger in that stolen car. Before he escaped the burning vehicle, he had the presence of mind to slip his own personal documents into Edward's coat pocket and nick those of his friend.

Media reported the motor accident involved a single driver, who was Edward but reported as John, a man who they said died after stealing the Jaguar and crashing it. The only witness to the theft said there'd been only one person driving, so John was home free, an omen causing him to think he led a charmed life.

Because he wasn't that good at stealing cars, he found a new trade. He became a self-taught opera singer—not a good one, but an improving one and good enough to make a living in small productions around Europe. He'd always had a good voice. After his voice changed at fourteen, Uncle Angus had even suggested he become a singer. He knew his uncle wasn't a music critic, but John liked to sing, and steadily improved.

That new trade also offered him opportunity to hone his skills in his old trade, which he was also good at, burglary. He soon knew every pawnshop in Manchester, many more than the few Edward and he had originally frequented. Burglary provided him with a steady income.

He longed for more, from moving beyond small theater groups in his singing career to more lucrative heists in his burglaries. He went international. His fortunes improved a lot after he met Linda in Frankfurt. She became an insatiable lover and almost as good as he was at breaking and entering rich people's homes to nick their expensive belongings. The couple's Zurich bank accounts started to swell.

"I have a confession to make," she said one night in Prague.

She also admitted to having another trade, assassin for hire. Her suggestions for performance sites and target mansions around Europe, which he had believed were only because of her business acumen, came from clients who hired her to kill someone at that locale. He began to participate in that even more lucrative business.

Everything went swimmingly until that day their victim had many important and powerful friends. He was a thug, oligarch, and SVR collaborator, and the contract for that hit was with the CIA. John hadn't known about the SVR connection until after Linda was killed in a shootout, and John as Maxim went into hiding. He had contacts in Romania where he stayed for a few months, working again as an opera singer in small productions and lying low otherwise.

When he learned his uncle had passed on, he wasn't surprised the old man didn't leave him anything. *He believed I was dead!* But he resented that Esther Brookstone, a distant and unknown relative, inherited the Scottish castle. His mind snapped. A wild, insane desire for revenge made him leave hiding and pursue her.

Maxim had other reasons to dislike his distant cousin. For example, she had enjoyed a life he'd never had—a solid family life as a child, although he mightn't have done well with a vicar as father; financial comfort and stability, mostly inherited from her three previous husbands, especially the last, who had been a Swiss banker as well as a count; and respect, even fame, as a Scotland Yard inspector. Jealousy was another powerful drug leading to that addictive and mad desire for revenge.

She was also an art expert, as he'd observed while visiting her gallery. He traveled enough to appreciate the quality of paintings she sold there; and, in his walk-around, he saw a lab where she probably authenticated and/or restored paintings. His art was his music, and it had led him to more lucrative pursuits, to be sure, but it was also solace as he became even better at his singing. He supposed it was the same for Esther Brookstone and her gallery full of paintings.

Uncle Angus had been frugal and never bought artwork—all the dark portraits of glowering ancestors in the old house came from previous generations—so Maxim didn't experience good art in Edinburgh except for some random school trips early on. He remembered that first experience with fine art, though…

***

"I can give you a few monkeys for it," said the pawnbroker. "Say twenty."

John turned to Edward and smiled, "See. More than he gave us for the Rolex."

Edward shrugged, picked up the little green statue, and examined it, rubbing its fat belly. "What's it made of, mate?" he said to the pawnbroker. "Looks corroded, like old copper." He dug John in the ribs. "Get it? Corroded copper?"

John nodded but rolled his eyes. Edward's quips weren't as clever as his friend thought they were.

"We steal that sometimes too," Edward said to the old man. "Usually good for a few pints."

The pawnbroker smiled upon hearing the admission. "This is jade, and the statue is the Buddha, a common subject in Asian art. A nice little piece, I dare say."

John grabbed the pawnbroker by his shirt collar. "You wouldn't be scamming us, would you now?"

The man freed himself and glared at John. "Take it or leave it, yob! I don't have time to waste on the likes of you two blokes."

"It's good money," Edward said to John. "Or are you going to start collecting artwork now? Count me out if so."

"The watch and statue might be worth ten times what he's offering."

"It's a pawnshop run by a damn Jew. They all are. What do you expect? We're in the wrong profession."

"We have no profession, but we need the money for pubs and lasses."

"And he's offering that, no questions asked. Agreed?"

John shrugged.

"If you're finished with your philosophical debate," said the pawnbroker, "can we finish this up. I won't pay any more. Period."

John shrugged again. "Okay. Give us the money."

He walked from the pawn shop scowling...

That's how he learned his artistic sensibilities should always take second place to making a real living. And he liked the money better than singing.

Chapter Thirteen

Sunday Morning: Linz

"Hal Leonard sent some information from Interpol," Bastiann said to Esther.

"Anything in particular? I'm still waiting on Jeremy."

"Nothing, except for a confirmation that Interpol and other authorities conjecture Dragavei might have been a mercenary-assassin. Too many victims in places where he was at the same time and locale. There might be some woman involved too."

"He was alone here on the riverboat. I wonder if his luck ran out and someone evened scores."

"Only problem with that theory is that someone is probably still be onboard," Bastiann said. "Someone on this boat is a murderer, unless he was a stowaway and managed to jump ashore. All passengers and crew are accounted for."

"The police cannot possibly interview all passengers here at Linz, love," Esther said. "The Austrians will have to send a team onboard, and we'll be stuck here if the ship is detained."

"Boat, ma'am, it's a riverboat, and that's not possible," said Caitlin Marshall, the cruise director, whom the honeymooners had met earlier soon after boarding. She had been observing the interesting exchange with an amused expression. "Bastiann, you agreed to continue investigating the case as we go along."

"I'm having second thoughts," Bastiann told her. "We're on our honeymoon, after all."

The cruise director shrugged and smiled. "Can't you mix business with pleasure?"

"Pish-tosh, it will be fun, dear."

Esther then smiled at the cruise director, a pleasant woman similar in appearance to herself, only thirty years younger. She had that Celtic look, with a little more red in her hair and a fuller face with only a hint of past childhood freckles. She wasn't nearly as tall as Esther—more Bastiann's height. No, not like me at all! *My same sparkling personality, though.*

"We've been working together and will continue to do so," Esther continued. "I'd like to review all passengers' documentation, especially the victim's, now that we have some solid data to compare it to."

"Esther, you should stay out of this," Bastiann said. "I still might have to let the German and Austrian federal police handle the case. I'm not even sure if Interpol will approve of my participation. Lyon hasn't yet done so. If I have to hand it off, why become involved?"

"From those passport stamps he received—now everyone visiting the continent does because of Brexit—we already know Mr. Dragavei spent time in England," said Esther, "and he claimed to be Romanian. This is an international crime. Right up Interpol's alley. And it's your own time too. They can't tell you what to do when you're on vacation."

"Agreed. Authorities at the homicide location usually take over. But I repeat: For God's sake, we're on our honeymoon!"

"This lovely woman is correct, dear Bastiann. We can mix business with pleasure. We can add to our fun aboard by finding an assassin while the boat floats down the Danube, with Dame Agatha looking over our shoulders."

"Fun? Are you obsessing again? Your fun has nearly killed us at times." But Bastiann knew he'd lose the battle with two women ganging up on him. "Okay. While you review passenger and crew records, I'll start interviewing crewmembers. Can you help with all that, Mrs. Marshall? After the tour today?"

The woman smiled again at their banter and added some of her own. "So it's Mrs. Marshall now? Before we all agreed you can call me Caitlin."

"I apologize. I put my Interpol hat on. I don't want to upset either crew or passengers, but we might as well start. I'd like to commandeer the Chef's Table during the day if possible. Otherwise I'll use Dragavei's stateroom after it's cleaned. Can you arrange all that?"

"The Linz authorities might do your interviews all over again," said Esther, as if she were changing her mind about Bastiann's managing the investigation. She was only making an observation about a possible waste of their time, though.

She noticed Caitlin looked worried about that comment for some reason.

Bastiann shook his head. "Not if I'm still in charge. Personally, I think most crewmembers don't know much about our victim or have any idea who could be his murderer. They'll be the easiest to clear of any suspicion, if only from being a small number compared to the number of passengers."

"Let's do it then. After the tour, though."

Bastiann soon updated Dragavei's fiche:

> Name: Maxim Dragavei
> Age: 35
> PoB: Bucharest (?)
> C: Romanian (?)

Res: Bucharest (?)
Occ: opera singer; assassin for hire?
L@TOD: his stateroom
Notes: Victim! Purchased ticket @ last minute.
   Possible   mercenary-assassin   is   Interpol's
   guess.

***

Esther spotted Elise Mayer when everyone waited for their tour buses to arrive. She was in the queue for one heading to Salzburg. Esther noted the young professor was teary.

"Hold my place in the queue," she told Bastiann, and then joined Elise. "What's wrong, Elise?"

"Oh, hello." She took off her glasses and dabbed at her eyes with a handkerchief. "I guess I won't need your friend's reference for someone to authenticate our painting after all. I just learned a thief broke into my apartment and stole the painting!"

Oh my, this woman is emotional. Poor fiancé. And she seemed to have such a strong personality! Esther did a quick bit of profiling. *Austrians are more emotional than Bavarians, and most everyone's more emotional than Prussians.*

"My dear, you must keep a stiff upper lip, as my compatriots often say. Look on the bright side: That heist means someone believes your painting is valuable. Where did you find it?"

"Franz and I go on weekend trips around the area to buy antiques. It's amazing what you can find. We bought a house in the Vienna suburbs, and we're trying to decorate it as tastefully as possible. He plays second cello in the Philharmonic, and I have a professor's salary, so our future family finances are usually in poor condition."

"Which one of you liked the painting?"

"We both did. Franz thought it was at least a good copy, and no one would know it wasn't real. I thought it might be the real thing after a guest at my apartment, a fellow professor, said there was a high probability it's authentic."

"He'd be my prime suspect." Esther's tour bus was the first to pull in. "I have to go now, Elise, but let me give you another name." She jotted down on the back of another one of her business cards the name of a friend in the *Bundespolizei*, Austria's federal police, whom she'd once worked with on a case. "He's a bloodhound for sniffing out stolen art and art thieves, take my word for it. My mobile number is also on the card. Same card as the other one, of course, so you can give that one to your fiancé. Keep me informed about how things go."

"I was too harsh with you, Esther. You're a nice person. I had you all wrong." She blew her nose.

I hope that fiancé marries this woman. She'll be in terrible shape if he doesn't.

"People often do that. Maybe because I'm very blunt. Maybe it's my distant Scottish ancestry, which I only recently learned about." *Those people aren't emotional either!* "I most likely need to buy one of those popular DNA kits, but I resist because I don't want to find out Daddy wasn't really my father, or something similar. *Ciao*. Have a good lecture in Salzburg."

***

Neither Esther nor Bastiann had been to Austria's lake district. They'd chosen that tour over the two Salzburg tours for that reason. The trip leaving Linz was interesting in itself but became somewhat tedious once on the main highway, so the two talked about the case. When the bus pulled off, the scenery started to change, and the tour guide's descriptions became more colorful.

Gretchen the guide had been born in the lake district and was wearing an Austrian peasant's costume for the tour. Black hair in pig tails added to the look. She had an effervescent personality. She was also a big woman; her commanding voice boomed through the transceivers they all used.

At one point, when they were passing through a small village, Gretchen pointed out her family home. Although the modest dwelling fit right in with that *Salzkammergut* hamlet, it reminded Esther of the vicarage where she'd grown up in Hull. For a long time, though, she'd been a big city dweller, whether on missions for work or only for day-to-day living. She thrived in an urban environment, but there was something to be said for the simplicity of the countryside.

Her Hull home, nestled not far from the ocean, wasn't purely rural—Hull was a large town in Yorkshire—and neither was her school chum's mansion near Wantage in Oxfordshire— but both areas were provincial compared to London. And both were restful for her for only as long as it took to become bored.

Is the countryside only a place for rest and relaxation? she wondered. She believed she and Bastiann could achieve that with her castle near Auld Reekie after some more improvements. But he was also an urban dweller. She could imagine needing more of that rest and relaxation as she grew older. *Will he?*

Why did life seem so more complex as one aged? So many questions, so few obvious answers.

Esther understood Gretchen's pride. One's birthplace was often special. Her handyman, Harry James, still sang reggae and ska hits from his homeland; and she knew Bastiann, though he had a French mother, was proud of being Dutch. Her own upbringing—her father had been a vicar—had influenced her in many ways too, including the artistic sensibility she had inherited from her parents.

Their tour followed E55/E60 to Mondsee, where they visited St. Michael's, the church where *Sound of Music*'s wedding scene was filmed. She'd never liked that schmaltzy Broadway megahit, although she liked some songs. "Edelweiss" was her favorite, but she thought it might be an Austrian folksong. She also liked Julie Andrews's voice, especially in the musical *My Fair Lady*, so she'd become sad when she heard doctors had ruined it.

The tour continued to Seewalchen, then onto Weyregg am Attersee, where they stopped for a while. Then on to Bad Ischl, where Emperor Franz Josef summered, and finally through St. Wolfgang and Fuschsee.

The lakes were beautiful. Their stop in Weyregg was near the end of a huge lake, the Attersee, partially blanketed in fog that day with sun peeking through the mists in spots, causing beautiful mirrored images of the Alps' foothills in the turquoise waters. The sparkle was hypnotic at times. They were given a lot of time to have pastries and coffee and walk about, taking in all the scenery.

Indeed, the mystical landscape was a spiritual experience, perhaps explained by the guide's story about a monk, Wolfgang, who had settled across the lake so long ago. *If I were going to become a recluse, this might be a nice place to do it.*

Walking back from their coffee and pastry snack, they found a bench at the edge of the car park where they cuddled to protect themselves from the cool October breezes coming in from the Alpine foothills across the lake.

"You know," Bastiann said, "about three hundred kilometers from here, near the border, there's another lake, Weissensee, where the ice is always thick in winter, not like here."

"Sounds truly cold. That's not a romantic topic, considering you're not holding me close enough to warm me."

"I apologize." He drew nearer and held her more tightly. "Only some nostalgic reminiscing about my childhood. I skated when young and thought I might want to participate in the *Elfstadentocht* someday."

"That sounds like an orgy of elves. What is it?" Because she knew German and its penchant for compound words, she could guess, but she wanted Bastiann to become a bit put out. She liked to tease him.

"It translates to 'Eleven Cities Tour,' and it's about two hundred miles of ice skating. A skaters' marathon. The winner is famous in Holland throughout the following year. It's like Manchester United versus Manchester City, or the finals of Irish Rugby. It's the thing to do in Holland."

"So why didn't you do it? I take it you skated."

"Of course. No Dutch boy would be without ice skates."

"Were they silver?"

"You're making fun of me. I wanted to be a long-distance skater, but my legs are too short."

"Your legs are fine, as well as the plumbing between them."

"Not for long-distance skating. One needs long strokes."

"I see. Can I ask a dumb question?" Bastiann nodded. "How is this Weissensee related to that elves' orgy?"

"They haven't been able to run the *Elfstadentocht* in Holland since 1997 because of global warming—it's too dangerous. They moved it to the Weissensee here in Austria."

"That's a roundabout way to arrive at the greatest existential problem human beings now face, climate change. And my head hurts from thinking about it all. I'm no longer a young activist beating on the doors of 10 Downing Street. Time for quiet, my Dutchman."

"Sci-fi often features global calamities."

"I prefer elves to ETs. Quiet."

They lapsed into quiet contemplation of the scenic Alpine hills meeting the lake waters. In the depth of that romantic interlude, she thought of her Austrian federal police contact…

***

Esther had spent her years in Scotland Yard's Art and Antiques Division recovering stolen artwork; arresting art thieves; embarrassing or taking into custody those who bought what art thieves stole; identifying art scams, where she'd learned she had a talent for authentication; and foiling black marketers in general. Inspector Fritz Reiner focused on the same thing for Austria's *Bundespolizei*. She had first met him, though, at a concert in Lugano she'd attended with Alberto Sartini, her last husband before Bastiann.

Her Italian count and the Type-A Fritz connected over too much wine at intermission. Afterwards the three enjoyed a late dinner together.

The two men, one Italian and the other Austrian, looked similar. Both were good-looking—black, wavy hair with enough gray to be interesting, small mustaches, and intelligent blue eyes. Fritz's cheekbones were more pronounced, and he was thinner in the waist. Both men laughed a lot, and she felt left out of the conversation at times.

"I can't believe you haven't married," Alberto remarked to Fritz when the conversation lagged somewhat. He hugged Esther. "Aren't you afraid you'll spend your last days alone in this world?"

"Who said I'm alone? I'm the type of fellow women love to have fun with. I'm independently wealthy, so bad pay for my work in the Federal Police doesn't matter, although that work is more than just an interesting hobby. And, because of my cases, I often meet wealthy, cultured ladies like I described. If you kicked the bucket, Esther might be among them." He smiled at Esther; she smiled back, knowing their must be a punchline. "You'd be surprised, Count Sartini, how many widows have had enough of marriage and only want to have some good fun. I can offer that."

"Interesting," Alberto said. "Many would call you a gigolo, although you're not in it to marry the widow and steal her money. Interestingly enough, the word comes from French for 'dancing partner', and not from Italian. The age-old dance of courtship and sex makes that origin appropriate. The implication is the man is younger than the woman, though, but you're as old as I am."

Fritz laughed. "I can only add one fact to that synopsis: The widows often want an experienced lover without commitments."

"You both are in the presence of a lady, so you can change the topic anytime now," Esther said.

Alberto nodded, accepting her mocking chastisement. "What are you doing here in Lugano, Inspector?"

"Chasing down stolen art, of course."

The ensuing discussion piqued Esther's interest in a possible future career...

After her count had passed on, Esther remembered Fritz's stories about his widows, so she avoided him. But they'd had one case together she would always remember, one establishing the focus for her later years and her obsession for recovering stolen artwork, especially paintings stolen by Nazis, and returning them to the rightful owners, or, failing that in the cases of many Jews who'd died in concentration camps with no living relatives, having them displayed in a museum with acknowledgement of their past owners and their fates. She never wanted anyone to forget the evil of the Third Reich, especially when it came to Jews and stolen art.

***

Bastiann heard the tour guide's voice booming out before he saw her. "*Herr* Bastiann, *Herr* Bastian!*" He turned to see her running toward him, some of her traditional Austrian garb flowing behind.

"What is it, Gretchen?"

"There's been an accident! One of our tour couples has fallen into the lake."

He stood and looked down from the safety railing in front of their bench to see two locals pull one Bulgarian tourist from the cold water into a rowboat.

"Are there witnesses?"

"They went part way down to the lake—" The guide gestured, indicating the steep path. "—so people only saw them when they were already in the water. Maybe they were taking a selfie?" She used the English word "selfie"; he wondered what the accepted German equivalent was.

Bastiann descended the path a bit with Gretchen and studied the spot where she said the couple had fallen in. The safety railing appeared to be sturdy enough there as well. *Were they pushed?*

"That's only a five-meter drop from here," Bastiann observed. "I'm surprised they didn't survive. The plunge isn't much different from one taken from a swimming pool's high board, if that much."

"They're dead?" Bastiann nodded because the locals had pulled out the second Bulgarian, and one local had looked up and shook his head. "Good Lord! What will become of me? I've never had an accident on a tour."

Once people die, thought Bastiann, *the living often soon succumb to self-interest. Gretchen was worried about her job. Relatives would be worried about inheritances. Or am I being too cynical?*

Esther joined them. "That railing is more than waist high," she observed as the small rowboat approached the dock with the tourists' bodies. "Perhaps someone pushed them?"

Bastiann smiled. *Great sleuths come to the same conclusions.*

"It's a selfie, I tell you!" Gretchen wailed. "They used their smart phones all the time as cameras, even shooting pictures through the motorbus's windows when they'd only photograph reflections. It's an insult to this beautiful and mystical scenery that requires profound meditation."

I'll give her that. Bastiann paid more attention to Esther's comment reinforcing his observation, though. *Had this Bulgarian couple become a danger to Dragavei's assassin?*

He wondered who would be next.

*****

Another person had been watching when the Bulgarian couple's bodies were pulled from the cold lake waters. He knew the person he'd been following was good at his trade. That person had proven how good he was by taking a role in a macabre reality show when he pushed his compatriots into the water.

STEVEN M. MOORE

The agent analyzed his mistakes. Number one: He'd lost sight of the man. Two: He hadn't expected him to act so boldly, not on a tour, for God's sake! And three: HQ hadn't suggested to the agent the man might still be dangerous. *Maybe Dragavei hadn't been the only target?*

He wrote off the whole incident as collateral damage and an item to add to the man's many crimes. At some point they would turn him over to Interpol. But HQ wanted to gather them all up, not just pick the low-hanging and rotting fruit.

Sometimes this job sucks!

Chapter Fourteen

Sunday Morning: Vienna

"Yes, yes, I am Inspector Reiner. Yes, I'll hold." Fritz Reiner winked at his colleague at the neighboring desk. "Some lovely professor at the university wants my body."

"You wish," his neighbor said.

That professor finally came to the phone and said, "Thank you for chatting with me, *Herr* Inspector Reiner. I am Professor Elise Mayer. Our mutual friend Esther Brookstone gave me your name."

"*Fraulein* Brookstone? How is my favorite art detective doing?"

"The last time I saw her, she was on her honeymoon."

"Ah, then *Frau* van Coevorden? So she jumped on the marriage carrousel's pony and won that fourth ring. Never met her Interpol agent, Bastiann, but I knew she was quite smitten with him. Nice enough fellow, I suppose, but I didn't consider him her type." She coughed. "I'm guessing your call has something to do with an art heist, though, not Esther's many husbands."

"*Ja,* someone took my Caravaggio, and your office sent an agent to my apartment to interview me who had no art knowledge whatsoever. I was about to have the painting authenticated."

"If it's truly a Caravaggio, it could be worth some euros, to be sure. If it's a copy by one of his students, not so much. It's too bad you didn't authenticate it first."

"We bought it from a farmer. I had to give a lecture…never mind. I met Esther and asked her to authenticate it."

"She'd do a good job for you, that's for certain. Look, I'm off at noon. I'll first check on who has the case file here and then drop by your apartment, say about three. Don't worry, professor, I'll be thorough. I value Esther's faith in my work. By the way, what do you teach?"

"Art history."

"And your husband?"

"He's my fiancé, and he plays cello for the Vienna Philharmonic."

Fritz jotted down the information. After obtaining the woman's address and confirming her phone number, he hung up and turned to his next door neighbor again.

"Just my luck. She's not after my body after all because she has a fiancé. I can still help her, and maybe manage to change her mind." He rattled off the names of the professor and her fiancé. "I want a background check on them. Can you help?"

"Isn't that your job if you take the case?"

"You can help some, won't you? We both have to work on Sunday, so let's make the most of it. Besides, I have to find out who our clueless colleague was, the policeman who went and took this lovely lady's statement. Or find his notes, at least. I hope he bothered to make some in spite of his lack of art knowledge. This could be an interesting case. Imagine, a Caravaggio!"

The woman shrugged. She thought Fritz might be more interested in the professor than in the painting. She knew his reputation.

***

Elise opened the door, leaving the chain in position.

"Fritz Reiner, *Bundespolizei*," Fritz said, showing his credentials. "*Fraulein* Professor Mayer?"

"Right on time," she said, removing the chain and opening the door wide. "Thank you for coming, *Herr*

Reiner. Please follow me to the living room where we can talk." Once there, she gestured to a wing chair and took a seat on a small sofa. She pointed to the bare wall to her left. "That's where we hung it."

Right to the point, observed Fritz. I like that. *She should lose the glasses, though. Makes her look like...a professor!* "The painting that's possibly a Caravaggio. A perfect spot for it."

"Not really. You can call me Elise, by the way. Neither daylight nor distant city lights favored the painting when it was on that wall. And, if I were certain it was truly a Caravaggio, I would be worried about controlling temperature and humidity. In our new house, we could put it in the music room and control the environment there. We'll do that in any case for Franz's instruments."

"Franz is a musician, a cellist. I take it he owns other instruments besides a cello?"

"Both of us play the piano, and we have an old upright I inherited from an uncle. Franz also has a violin. None of those instruments is particularly valuable, but a controlled climate helps keep them in tune. He can tune the cello and violin, of course, but the piano is more difficult."

"Interesting. But back to business. I've read my colleague's notes." He jerked a thumb back the way they had come and said, "The front door was the one damaged? He didn't say."

"No. That was the bedroom slider. The fire escape also serves as a small balcony. Come, I'll show you."

The apartment was small and typical housing for living near the *Ringstrasse*; the single bedroom was straight down the entrance hall. It appeared small with the double bed in it. Fritz ignored the clothing on the bed, although the black undies and lace bras peeking out from under a washed load caught his attention. The professor, like many Austrian women, was likely not as serious as she looked when it came to bedroom activities.

The multi-purpose balcony had a single wicker chair on it, but at its side was the fire escape. Unlike the view from the front window in the living room, the view here was only of an alley.

"May I?" he said, indicating the locked sliding door.

"Be my guest. We fixed the lock and alarmed the door. The front door too. One keypad's in the hall coat closet, the other's in the bedroom closet here."

He nodded. "By we, you mean you and your fiancé?" Her blush was faint, but he held up a hand. "Only asking. Where does your fiancé practice his cello?"

"When not with the orchestra or in its associated practice rooms, he practices in his studio apartment nearby. A cello isn't that portable."

So he's moved in but keeps the old studio. Interesting.

"Better than a bass viol, I suppose." Fritz released the top and bottom deadbolts and opened the sliding door. He stood on the balcony and stared down through the rusty iron grating at a garbage bin. "The thief probably hopped atop that bin to reach the ladder and pull it down. The sliding door likely didn't come with a good lock." She shook her head. "You were smart to add the deadbolt mechanisms."

"Too little, too late, of course. My only excuse is I have to request permission from management here to do anything. In this case, they were only too happy for me to add the upgrade."

"I would like to talk about who else knew you had the painting."

"Let's return to the living room then."

***

"Let me see now," Elise said as Fritz waited to learn whom she had told about the painting. "My mother knew we bought it. She told me it was a waste of money."

"Would she tell anyone else if that were the case?"

"I don't know. You're not writing any of this down. I think your colleague only pretended to do so, by the way."

"Probably." Fritz tapped his forehead. "All here, *Fraulein*. I'll organize everything and record it all later in my report, together with other facts and my hunches, and so forth. Now, about your mother?"

"Interesting. You must have a good memory. I'm even terrible with names." He nodded. Elise folded her hands in her lap. "I don't know if she'd tell anyone. She doesn't like to spend money on frivolous things or anything fake, so she might be embarrassed I did, which represents my own feelings and my reason for not mentioning the painting before or after the theft to any friends, or to confide in someone about what fools Franz and I have been about security."

"Maybe she's practicing to become a mother-in-law?" Fritz said with a smile.

"Perhaps. She often drops hints about grandchildren. She's a bit complicated. We're not that close anymore."

"Father still living?"

"Deceased."

"What about someone Franz knows?"

She thought a moment. "He has an artist friend who believed the painting was only a good copy. Wilhelm paints modern works, so I'm not sure his opinion is worth all that much. It was my colleague at the university, Jörg, who said it could very well be a Caravaggio."

"With that opinion, he could be a suspect. I suppose I should speak to him. Is he the gossiping sort?"

"Hardly. He's brilliant but extremely shy. I always feel sorry for him, so Franz and I often invite him to dinner. He's comfortable enough conversing about art and music with us. The last time was mostly a disaster, though. I burned the roast, and the woman we invited to be his blind date came on too strong. I embarrassed…well, never mind. He knows his art, though, so I valued his opinion."

"Did that woman overhear his opinion?"

Elise pondered the question. "Maybe. Vilma is flighty and chatters away at anyone who will listen. She's a definite possibility for gossiping about the painting. How are you going to move forward? There are so many people you might need to track down."

"Three basic steps: First, I'll chat with Wilhelm and Vilma and see who they talked to about the painting. Same for Franz, who might have said something to one of his fellow musicians, for example. It's like tracing one's family tree. It's often surprising what I can turn up. That's how I'll start."

"May I ask you a question about your work environment?"

Where did that come from? "That depends. There are things I can't mention to civilians."

"Your colleague never asked any of these questions."

Yes, because he was just going through the motions. "He was pulled off to another case." Fritz couldn't say he was the one who'd made that happen. "It happens sometimes. We're very busy, you see. I'm here because Esther Brookstone gave you my name. I'll do my best for you because, one, I love chasing art thieves and recovering stolen paintings, and two, we did a disservice to you. It

105

might take me a while because I'm also multitasking, but if I can't find your painting, not many could do better."

She smiled. "I appreciate your candor. I'll find addresses and mobile numbers for the three people you mentioned. You could go crazy, I warn you, because, like you implied, one person could lead to others, and so forth. That's where that Kevin Bacon game came from decades ago, I suppose, but it's more like multiplying microbes."

"You sound like an epidemiologist."

"That, sir, is my mother. She's an expert on infectious diseases. She worked on that COVID-19 pandemic a few years ago."

"I remember. That was a bad winter, with the flu and that awesome gift from the Chinese, like we needed another virus like SARS, MERS, and the swine flu."

Chapter Fifteen

Sunday Evening: Linz

Bastiann started interviewing after dinner. The Chef's Table was still in full swing with its multi-course meal prepared by the riverboat's principal chef, so he used Dragavei's stateroom, which had been cleaned and was now empty. He made himself at home and set up the computer system to his liking, as he'd done in their own stateroom.

He thought doing the interrogations in Dragavei's cabin might make the unknown assassin nervous when interviewed. If he'd escaped earlier, everything would be a waste of time, but that would also mean the murderer had to be a stowaway. All passengers had been accounted for multiple times. And the incident in the lake district seemed to indicate the assassin might have been on that same tour bus, if that incident was truly a case of murder and not an accident. He would focus on the passengers from that tour first.

To be complete, though, he first interviewed Marisol Salazar, the woman who had found Dragavei's body. Earlier on one of his many trips along the corridor from their stateroom to the victim's, he'd noticed her talking to a man he recognized but couldn't place. Her confidant was dressed in a waiter's uniform. *That should have been a clue!* Upon entering Dragavei's stateroom, Bastiann remembered...and knew why it had slipped his mind. Omar Dushey had cleared dishes the night of the murder when Esther and he dined with Kayla and Ken. *That had been a hectic night!*

Omar had seemed like a decent chap, albeit a little nervous. Bastiann had always admired how waiters could stack many dishes together and carry them all away, a juggling act that for him was on a par with skills found in Cirque du Soleil performers. Omar was no exception, but he had jostled the diners' plates a bit, earning him a frown from the head waiter.

As a child, and like many children, Bastiann had wanted to be many things. First on his list was to be a long-distance skater, motivated by his clandestine skating on ice-covered Amsterdam canals. Second was to be a waiter, something his mother had found amusing.

Is it my imagination, but did Omar look at me with a fearful expression as I passed by?

Bastiann initiated the interview with Marisol, putting that thought on hold. He now knew she was Filipina, and her face framed by short, black hair, exhibited that lovely Asian-Spanish mix he should have recognized when he wondered about her accent. There were several Filipinos among the crew—all amiable, hardworking staff.

Somewhat recovered, she was still nervous. She wrung her hands, and he noticed they were rough. *Can they be the hands of an assassin?* He doubted it.

With his first questions, he didn't learn much more than he already knew from the crime scene and doctor's reports. Marisol had a glowing record of three years of service with the cruise company. Bastiann already knew she was also well-liked by other crewmembers, including the captain and cruise director. Maybe her nervousness implied no guilt; she must still be traumatized by the whole incident. But he continued.

"I saw you with Omar. Are you his friend?"

"All staff members are my friends."

That answer didn't suit Bastiann. "Okay. He appeared skittish. Do you know why?"

"I don't know that word, *Herr* Bastiann. You talk like *Frau* Esther."

"I suppose so. I'm married to her, after all." He smiled. "And English isn't my maternal language, so I probably tend to copy her British expressions. Skittish means nervous, frightened about something."

"I see. Omar is nice, not skit-skittish."

But she was. He saw the continued wringing of hands. *Poor woman!* He left the interview at that.

> Name: Marisol Salazar
> Age: 27
> PoB: Manila
> C: Filipino
> Res: Munich
> Occ: riverboat cleaning staff
> L@TOD: D's stateroom
> Notes: Probably strong character, but now traumatized; discovered D's body.

> Name: Omar Dushey
> Age: 28
> PoB: (?)
> C: Greek (?)
> Res: Athens (?)
> Occ: riverboat wait staff
> L@TOD: (?)
> Notes: Relationship with Marisol?

***

Bastiann next interviewed the man who'd been at the reception desk when the murder occurred. Reception was located in front of the elevator, a modern device with mostly glass walls, like the kind that might scale the sides of a modern hotel. And the boat's reception area served the same purpose it did in a modern hotel—check-in, information, and attending to guests' problems, which mostly reduced to referring passengers to the rack of pamphlets and lists of daily tours, or to the cruise director for more difficult problems.

Bastiann wanted to know if the chap had noticed anyone climb the short staircase on either side of the elevator, or if anyone took the elevator, up the half-floor to that critical corridor where the victim's stateroom was located. That corridor passed the cruise director's desk, but she was often not there, but instead out and about the boat taking care of passengers' questions and needs as well as sending everyone off on their tours.

The receptionist had seen or heard nothing out of the ordinary before Marisol's screams, but it became clear he didn't pay much attention to the elevator or stairs surrounding it because he was usually busy with other chores. His job wasn't unlike a hotel receptionist's, because the riverboat was like a small hotel. *Or B&B, considering most of our meals are taken aboard!*

And so it went. By the time Bastiann quit for the night and before the boat departed Linz, he had finished with all crewmembers except for the captain and cruise director, most of the interviews with the crew being short, and he'd started with the passengers who had been on the tour bus to the lake district.

First up were Amy and Judith. Neither had much to add to what he already knew, so their interviews were also short.

Maria Ramirez and Cecilia Cruz were new to him. He'd seen at least one of them but hadn't met either one. He shuffled papers and then smiled to put them at ease.

He'd decided to interview them together because they shared a stateroom like Amy and Judith. He'd been surprised when they entered Dragavei's cabin. They looked like clones.

After introductions, he said, "You two must be related. Maybe sisters?"

"She's my twin sister," they both said…and then they burst out laughing.

He now remembered seeing one of them at the welcoming party. *Maybe both?* He could have seen one and then a different one later and think they were one and the same woman, especially if they were similarly dressed. Now one wore a red sweater, the other blue.

He checked his two fiches. "Both of you were born in Las Cruces, New Mexico, and are now living in Albuquerque, correct?"

They both nodded. "And both retired RNs and living in the same retirement village. I'm Maria Ramirez, by the way. She's Cecilia Cruz."

Maria has the red sweater, Cecilia the blue. That maybe wouldn't help him tomorrow, but for now it did.

"I take it Ramirez and Cruz are your husbands' surnames."

"You've got it, Mr. van Coevorden," Cecilia said. "Ex-husbands, to be precise."

"Call me Bastiann. RN means 'registered nurse'?" Both nodded. "Are you living together in that retirement village." Both nodded again.

"You ladies appear too young to be retired." The women giggled. "Did I say something funny?"

"Our retirement village is for people fifty-five and over," Maria said. "We're not elderly and are still fairly active. We'd had it with the bedpans and so forth as we basically supported our abusive, good-for-nothing husbands for many years, so we retired."

"Mama always told us Latino men make good fathers but terrible husbands," Cecilia said. "She was somewhat biased, considering she kicked Daddy out, but she was right in our case."

"So you have children?"

"I have three and Cecilia four," Maria said. "We shut down the factories after that. The Church has to come into the twenty-first century about such things, you know, birth control and divorce, in particular. Juan and Ricardo continued with their philandering, so we dumped them. I was the first one to get smart."

Cecilia smiled at her sister. "But I hooked you up with Jake."

Maria shrugged and winked at Bastiann. "Jake and Elliott are bunking in the next door cabin to us. They're from the same retirement village."

"Nothing serious," Cecilia said. "Only fun and travel."

Bastiann's head was spinning after trying to keep the twins' romantic problems and family histories straight, a feeling exacerbated by his perception he was seeing double. *Okay, let's focus.*

"Did you ever meet the victim, Mr. Dragavei?"

"He was sitting on the tent's other side from us at the welcoming party," said Maria. "I can't say he was an attractive man. Creepy is a better description. He was looking around at everyone. We only noticed him because he's tall. Jake and Elliott are short, like you."

"Was he looking at anything or anyone in particular?"

"Admiring the German girls' boobs at times, but mostly only noting who was there, I guess," said Cecilia. Maria nodded.

"Where were you when he was killed?"

He never expected an honest answer to that question if the person interviewed was the killer, but if there was an answer, he could check it to confirm. And, in contrast, the assassin's body language might give him away.

"Sitting right behind you and your wife and that nice black couple," Maria said. "We heard the screams."

Bastiann thought a moment. *Of course, four of them, Maria, Cecilia, Jake, and Elliott.*

After some pleasantries about the cruise, he let them go.

Name: Amy Peterson
Age: 32
PoB: Santa Barbara, CA
C: US
Res: San Diego, CA
Occ: pediatrician
L@TOD: top deck
Notes: King's partner; served as temporary ME

Name: Judith King
Age: 34
PoB: Monterrey, CA
C: US
Res: San Diego, CA
Occ: runs nursing home and assisted care facility
L@TOD: top deck
Notes: Peterson's partner

Name: Cecilia Cruz
Age: 56
POB: Las Cruces, NM

C: US
Res: Albuquerque, NM
Occ: retired nurse
L@TOD: dining lounge
Notes: Maria Ramirez's twin sister

Name: Maria Ramirez
Age: 56
POB: Las Cruces, NM
C: US
Res: Albuquerque, NM
Occ: retired nurse
L@TOD: dining lounge
Notes: Cecilia Cruz's twin sister

***

Bastiann next chatted with Luynhen and Viktor Demyankov. They were good friends of the Rakovski couple, also on his list of lake district tourists to interview, but this Bulgarian couple didn't offer anything to help his investigation.

She wasn't tall and was probably a stunner when young, as Esther might have said. Her black hair laced with gray was worn short, as if she might have the role of a page in some Shakespearian production at the Globe in Stratford-on-Avon, and her face was somewhat puffy. One had to look carefully to see her blue eyes because her eyelids made her squint a bit.

Her husband looked scruffy and somewhat like an overweight Yul Brynner. His bald pate with its age spots made his bushy eyebrows appear less pronounced. And he didn't smile a lot. *Of course, in these circumstances, interviewees have a right to be unhappy.*

Luynhen had been nervous, reminding Bastiann of a cat purring but swishing its tail in pent-up anger; Viktor was defensive and confrontational. He wrote both his observations off to their suspicion of authority.

He'd checked off six names for a later conference with Esther to recall more details about their pasts before their interviews. All six were East Europeans—Viktor and Luynhen Demyankov, the Bulgarian couple he'd just interviewed; Janos and Eszter Rakoczy, the other Hungarian couple; and Razvan and Ihrin Culianu, the Romanian couple. Interviewing the Rakovski couple was less urgent because they walked with canes and were older friends of the Bulgarians who were killed and the Demyankovs. Bastiann was afraid he was profiling, but the other American, British, French, and German couples didn't set off any particular alarms, in their documentation or otherwise. Those couples did.

Citizens of those East European countries had only recently shaken off the yoke of Communism after the Soviet Union collapsed along with the Berlin wall, and they might still be justifiably wary of any authorities because some of their countries were returning to fascism, as if Soviet Communism and fascism were somehow different. He expected those interviews to be more interesting, if not confrontational. Esther and he had already experienced the old Hungarian's acerbic nature before the art lecture, and he'd just experienced Viktor's.

He decided to call it a night although there were still many more passengers to interview.

At that late hour, and before he made an escape to his own stateroom, the Linz authorities came aboard, led by Inspector Hans Becker from the local police.

Name: Luynhen Demyankov
Age: 47

PoB: Sofia
C: Bulgarian
Res: Prague
Occ: nurse
L@TOD: lounge
Notes: Friendly with Rakovskis. Somewhat
    nervous; reaction to authority?

Name: Viktor Demyankov
Age: 51
PoB: Sofia
C: Bulgarian
Res: Prague
Occ: pharmacist
L@TOD: lounge
Notes: Friendly   with   Rakovskis.
    Confrontational; reaction to authority?

***

"We should search all staterooms," the Linz inspector said to Bastiann when he finally made his appearance and they had time to talk about the case. "We'll have to delay the boat's departure."

Not practical, thought Bastiann, *when we don't have enough manpower combined to perform such a search.* He decided to go easy on the gruff copper in his rebuttal, though.

"Good luck on finding a judge to issue search warrants for that, Hans."

The Linz inspector, typically officious like many local authorities, wasn't the worst he'd met with his obnoxious blustering and posturing—the Passau inspector had been worse, for example, albeit a bit more amiable.

"And for that," Bastiann continued, "it would have been a lot easier if we'd stayed in Passau."

"Why didn't you insist on that?"

Bastiann had been thinking that the spirit of Bavarian cooperation from nearby towns would have made the manpower problem easy to solve in Passau. Linz was a big city, so coppers had a lot more to do there. That presumption didn't take into account the quality of the searchers obtained from Passau officers and friends, of course, but he felt he could have given them easy-to-follow instructions. He was assuming that Becker would want to run the show yet accept none of the responsibility. He could say none of that, of course.

"First, it's questionable whether I had the authority to do so, especially now. Second, both crew and passengers would be terribly upset, along with the cruise company, I suppose, if we'd stayed in Passau."

He was simply reminding the man of what he already knew, or could guess.

The inspector nodded. "Murders have been committed. Weren't they already upset?"

Bastiann shrugged. "More upset then. Third, I saw no reason to delay the voyage, seeing as how we could investigate the murder on the boat en route to Budapest, taking the crime scene along with us, as it were, and your people could investigate the murders in the lake district, if indeed they were murders."

"We can do that. It puts us in a bind, though. Not exactly Linz's jurisdiction."

So they're either shorthanded or there's competition, observed Bastiann. "If that's the case, I then suggest you hand your task off to the Austrian federal police. As you say, the crime in the lake district didn't take place in Linz, after all, so that's justified. I wouldn't let authorities in Weyregg am Attersee handle it, though. I observed it to be a sleepy little hamlet. Of course, the murder on the riverboat took place on international waters."

Becker had already dismissed the riverboat murder apparently, because he said, "And we and they might be happy to hand it off to Interpol again. No one wants to rock the grand riverboat of tourism, if you'll pardon the pun."

Bastiann smiled. "Including me." He leaned toward the Linz inspector. "Let me state that these crimes likely won't be solved by either interrogations or searches here onboard, the latter being impossible anyway. Someone, maybe multiple someones, onboard this riverboat has or have something in their past that's incriminating. We have Wi-Fi on board—at least most of the time—and I can connect to various public databases and social media sites using it, some of them inaccessible to you. My wife also has connections via Scotland Yard. We've already gathered a lot of information." He avoided the mention of their consultations with Hal Leonard and Jeremy Brand, which weren't officially sanctioned.

"I see. But do you have any hunches? If so, let's hear them. Simple curiosity on my part."

"The injection preceding the stabbing is an unusual MO. And the stabbing itself was very precise. All that makes our crime into a more professional hit, or the perpetrator had skills the usual tourist doesn't have, at any rate. Perhaps medical experience of some sort too."

"What about the doctor who performed the preliminary exam?"

"Doubtful. But yes, she would have the necessary skill to make a little neck injection. I doubt she has the strength to plunge a knife in someone's back to the hilt, though."

"And precisely hit the heart. You never know."

Bastiann noted that added detail indicated the inspector had perused Amy's report already. "Oh, that she could do with her knowledge, and with precision. Any good doctor knows anatomy backward and forward. In any case, I already interviewed her as well, and we'll be checking more into her background." He gave a little shrug and smiled. "But back to our discussion. I prefer to continue the cruise so I don't have to rush our investigation. Or, do you think the assassin will strike again, like in the lake district?"

Hans frowned. "We don't know if he or she has, or they have, more targets in mind. We might have a serial killer or killers, for all we know, so these murderers become crimes of opportunity and essentially random."

"Oh, please. Serial killers usually have consistent MOs, and the two MOs used aren't consistent." Bastiann didn't have much experience with serial killers, but he'd discussed the Hindley case of the moors murders with his NYPD homicide detective friend Castilblanco, who had some experience with killing sprees. "They're often crimes of opportunity, as you say, but the MOs are usually consistent. If there's another murder, I suspect that the victim or victims will be related to the other victims in some way and not the MO. I'd be willing to bet on it. I'm not a great believer in unrelated coincidences, although, contrary to popular fiction, they often occur, making our jobs even harder." *Why am I lecturing this pillock?* "And I intend to find out the connection between the victim here and the Bulgarian couple in the lake district murders, if there is one, although I suppose there's still always the possibility the last was indeed only an accident. We'll be studying all the passengers and how they're related too, even whether they've made friends, or enemies, with other passengers while onboard."

Bastiann sensed his weariness had made him ramble on when he should be trying to rid himself of his pest so he could sleep.

"If you move on, I can't help you much in that regard." Hans thought a moment. "And how is your wife taking all this?" he said. "I surmise she must be chomping at the bit to put her hoof more into your pond?"

That metaphor annoyed Bastiann. He eyed the Austrian. If he was married, Bastiann felt sorry for the wife. "I assure you she's as displeased as I am about having our honeymoon affected by a murder investigation, although she's also very understanding. I can't quite interpret the meaning of your second question."

Hans shrugged. "She's acquired a bit of a reputation here on the continent for bringing those neo-Nazis near here to justice, and for apprehending that Roman art thief. I imagine that's just the tip of the iceberg. It must be hard when she steals the spotlight from you, so to speak."

Bastiann frowned. "Media controls the spotlight. Neither of us looks for it." *Especially me!*

"I suppose. I'd still like to meet the old girl. One can't help admiring a strong, smart woman, although I would never marry one." Hans coughed politely. "Are we through here, Agent van Coevorden?"

Bastiann nodded. *He does have a way with words!* "A follow-up in the lake district is all I request, either from you or the *Bundespolizei*." He waved a hand, indicating the long hallway visible from the open door to Dragavei's stateroom. "Considering we've now lost three passengers, we could have at least one more stateroom available for you or some of your officers to help me finish interviewing. You're welcome to stay here if you like."

"Wasn't this where the victim was murdered?" Bastiann nodded. "No, I'd better return to the city. I'll get the land investigation rolling early tomorrow."

Chapter Sixteen

Sunday Evening: Linz

There were abusive, misogynist men who looked for submissive women to marry. Esther was certain Gazsi Kertes, who wasn't nearly as much fun as Henry Higgins's Hungarian competitor in *My Fair Lady*, was one of those men, and his poor wife Maja was one of those women. As Yanks would say, "That's one strike against him!"

Castilblanco would like that baseball metaphor, she decided. She'd never met the man, but most Americans loved their game as much as old Commonwealth countries loved cricket. For example, G.H. Hardy, the British mathematician more famous for discovering Ramanujan than for his own mathematical research—a movie was made about that—had been obsessed with cricket. She'd seen some of that Cambridge-versus-Oxford competitive spirit when she was at Oxford.

Some men would abuse their wives verbally, others physically, and some did both, and yet they would still expect their women to be subservient and tend to their every need. Some would even attempt to justify that with verses from the Bible. She doubted Gazsi was religious, though. Better said, she surmised his religion wasn't one leading to a moral life. She decided to find out more about that man's "religion." While most passengers on the riverboat were well-to-do, his imperious scowl led her to believe he was used to ordering people around. She would look for evidence of that too.

Unlike some older people, Esther was computer literate—maybe not as good as Bastiann, but good enough. She'd also taken courses both inside the Yard and remotely at home, mostly to keep up-to-date, but others were on subjects that interested her. She liked the logic and order one needed to effectively use the technology.

She sat at the keyboard and monitor located at the end of her makeup table Bastiann also used for a desk, logged on to the internet, and started a search for Gazsi Kertes. There were some references—it was a common enough Hungarian name—but she found his picture on a company site, and that alone made the search worthwhile. He was the CEO of a large chemical manufacturer of questionable agriproducts sold in various European countries—questionable because she also found news about litigation pending against the company. *He's poisoning the environment! Strike two!*

She copied the picture and went to a social media site she often visited because it had a facial recognition tool she liked. She found more on Gazsi. Much of it was troubling, He was a big contributor to Fidesz, giving both time and money to Hungary's right-wing party, which was still in control, and he supported several right-wing organizations given to rants against anything not Fidesz. *Strike three!*

None of that was against EU law, of course, and certainly not in violation of any present Hungarian law in that one-party country. Because countries like Hungary and Poland were still technically democracies, she'd decided a while ago that if their citizens wanted a right-wing government, that was their masochistic choice. Of course, one had to be careful: That acquiescence was what brought the Nazis to power!

But now she had dirt on Gazsi Kertes she could throw in his face if the two of them had another tiff.

She had seen on the big cruise ships, those floating cities, the whole spectrum of human behavior generally covered, from arse to angel. It was interesting to see that in the much smaller statistical sample aboard the riverboat. People were polite, but she was a good judge of human nature. As with Gazsi, words and body language were telling. And Gazsi was towards the arse-end of the spectrum while Maja was possibly towards the angel-end. *Poor woman!*

She doubted Gazsi was Dragavei's murderer, though. The man might bully people, especially women, with biting words while flashing that Il Duce imperious scowl, but he most likely didn't have the goolies to stick a knife in Dragavei's backside. *Or does he?* He had seemed to back off when she had stood up to him.

No, there must be others beyond Gazsi at the arse-end of the human spectrum where the dark evil of sick human souls lurked. Dragavei himself could have been such a person. Such evil tended to become cannibalistic, feeding off good and bad persons alike.

She returned to her thoughts from the day before. She'd been right. Death was riding with them on the riverboat, using someone to do his bidding to commit a murder, possibly three. She shuddered. *Will there be more?*

She put her notes in order so she could leave them for Bastiann's perusal, deciding to wait up for him. He might be able to use them if he interviewed the Hungarian couple. *Or if he has a barney with Gazsi Kertes!*

***

"Done for the night, love?" Esther said when Bastiann entered their room.

He first used the cruise-supplied keyboard to bring up his playlists on the Apple monitor. He picked one, loosened his tie, and tossed his sports coat onto a chair. He gestured toward Esther's notes.

"You've been busy."

"Only some notes on Gazsi Kertes. Read them tomorrow. That's nice music. It sounds terribly difficult to play and sing, though. What is it?"

"A Sibelius song called 'The Tryst.' I just finished interviewing some passengers and dealing with that Linz inspector. Cecilia and Maria might be modern versions of the main character in the song, so I thought it appropriate. Let's only say it relaxes me and leave it at that."

"Now you have this cat's curiosity piqued. I shall have to look up that song."

"It's Finnish. My mother read a translation to me years ago. She did things like that."

"Quite *la grande dame, ta mère.* I would have liked to meet her."

"You can, through her son."

"That's almost poetic." She went pensive. "You have interesting playlists."

He pulled off his shirt and pants. "To answer your question, yes, I'm through for the night and very much regretting this job. Perhaps you can contact George Langston to see if Scotland Yard has any information we don't already have. We have a lot, but I'm still groping around in the dark."

"You poor man. Perhaps you need another kind of groping." She pushed him back onto the bed. "You've been a bashful 'Enry 'Iggins far too long for this ole Liza. And you're all tense and in need of some rest and relaxation." She sat beside him. "If I can't get a rise from

125

you, we'll have the speediest divorce outside Beverly Hills."

Bastiann eyed Esther. Her robe was now open, showing the panorama of delights awaiting him.

"You were planning this?"

"Call it my reward for my research work on that awful man, or a distraction from what I found. A lady has needs, after all. Or what's a marriage for?"

She burrowed into his boxers with one hand and twiddled with what she found.

"That's better now. Let me open the blinds and kill the inside lights. It's more romantic that way when we get down to business."

Although at first she seemed not as energetic as her words implied, he could hardly keep up with her as "business" progressed, but he enjoyed every moment.

Chapter Seventeen

Monday Morning: Attersee

Inspector Heidi Schweiger walked up and down the steep path at the Attersee's edge without discovering anything new her SOCOs had missed. She hadn't expected to find new evidence; they were thorough.

On her last upward climb, she stopped at the point where the couple had gone over the railing. She stared at the cold, deep water. *People should learn how to swim.* She then regretted that thought. Her main exercise was swimming laps, but she did it in a heated pool. The shock of the lake's cold water might have been too much for the old-timers, especially because they'd been fully clothed.

With her tall, supple body, short blond hair, and brisk, energetic steps, she could have passed as a student in any university's athletic program. She had been that, as a swimmer. Her first love was police work, though. Her father had been a cop, her mother a forensics specialist. Police work was in her genes.

She was also motivated, more so than most at her sleepy station, so she was somewhat disappointed a crime hadn't occurred in this case. The travel guide's theory hadn't panned out. Mobiles had been found in the victims' coat pockets. That meant they either had an accident or were murdered. And selfies weren't a possibility for the former. But there wasn't any other evidence of foul play. She couldn't imagine how anyone could go over that waist-high railing by accident, but she also didn't have anything to prove they were pushed. *This case is a waste of our time!*

She returned to the car park where the path began and saw Nicky waving to her from their patrol car. She joined him.

"Our office received a call," her patrol companion said. He pointed across the lake. "We need to go over there. A fellow watched it all happen. Had the presence of mind to whip out some binoculars."

"So it was an accident?" Heidi said.

"No, they were pushed. He couldn't see whether the culprit was a man or woman—our witness might be elderly, but the couple could have also blocked his view—he claimed a hand to each back at the same time pushed them both over the safety barrier, though."

She beamed. "Let's go, Nicholas. Have your recorder ready. We now have a double-murder case."

"Shouldn't we call that Bastiann fellow?"

"After we interview the witness and confirm his story. That won't solve the murder case, but it will confirm there is one, which would be useful information to him."

***

The witness was a man who looked to be in his fifties. He was alert enough and quite charming. He focused on Heidi more—*and not just because I'm the principal officer,* she observed—but shook both their hands. He led them to a sitting room and motioned to some rustic chairs, removed a rubber apron spattered with paint, and sat opposite the two *Bundespolizei* inspectors on a sofa with frayed upholstery. After explaining why they hadn't just called, and giving their usual warning a recording would be made of the interview, Heidi asked their witness to tell his story.

"I often watch the lake, you see. It's amazing how its colors and the sky's colors change through the day and seasons."

Heidi admired some paintings on the small sitting room's wall, more abstract versions of the vista seen from the witness's front porch. "Extreme impressionism, but I can see what you mean. So you were painting the lake then?"

"No, only studying it. Imagining how I'd paint it that day, if you will. That day was an interesting one, with both fog and sunlight. That couple across the lake distracted me. They appeared to be pointing right at me."

"Maybe they saw sun reflecting off your lenses," said Nicky.

"No, at the time I wasn't using the binoculars. Wrong angle too. The sun was behind me. And I still have good eyesight. I don't know what I'd do if I didn't. Beethoven could still write music even while deaf, but can an artist paint if he's blind? I don't even want to think about it." He paused to refocus. "I used the binoculars to study them and determine what they were pointing at—better assessing their line-of-sight. Curiosity, you know. Tourists provide a lot of laughs sometimes. For all I know, they were only pointing at the Alpine foothills, which are so beautiful and mysterious, especially now in the fall. It looked like that might be the case."

"That's when you saw someone push them over the railing?" said Heidi.

"Absolutely. No doubt about it. I couldn't see the face of who did it, though, because the attacker turned. I nearly dropped the binoculars when that occurred. I tried to call your office twice but was put on hold. I gave up until this morning. I don't suppose you folks have many murder cases."

"Our office said you couldn't determine if the attacker was male or female," Nicky said.

"If female, she'd be wearing a pants suit or jeans and sweater, from the barest glance I obtained, or something similar. I didn't see the face. A wide body, though, so maybe male? The assailant had spun around and run down the path. I only saw the back."

"Down?" said Heidi. "Did she or he leave in a boat?"

"Couldn't tell. There are little inlets along the shore and lots of shadows there. That might be the case. You'll have to ask around. When there aren't so many tourists here at the lake, locals like to fish. You can do that in summertime, but you won't catch anything. Now you might have better luck."

"We'll have to go back," Heidi told Nicky. "The path keeps going. I didn't follow it all the way down to the water." She stood. "Thank you for coming forward. We have some more work to do now, so you'll understand why we're off." She glanced again at the artist's paintings. "What do they sell for?"

He told her, she gulped, and she and Nicky found their way out of the small cottage.

Chapter Eighteen

Monday Morning: Weissenkirchen

The Danube valley between the towns of Melk and Krems in lower Austria is called the Wachau. The river flows north-northeast from Melk to Dürnstein, curving southeast and then east past the city of Krems. In the Wachau, the town of Spitz lies on the Danube's western bank and the town of Melk on its eastern bank. The whole valley is known for its vineyards and other agricultural products, particularly apricots.

The riverboat left Linz at 4 a.m. and would arrive in Weissenkirchen at 2 p.m. After breakfast, the cruise director would give another lounge lecture.

Kayla and Ken White were eating breakfast in the dining room when Captain Janssen breezed by.

"From what I've seen, I like the captain," she said to her husband as the man disappeared into the boat's kitchen. "He's quite the dashing figure in his uniform."

"And I like the cruise director," he said, "and I haven't seen enough of her, in uniform or without."

They both laughed.

"I bet the captain's ex-military," he added. "I can tell. The Interpol agent might be—he's tight-lipped enough and reminds me of my old lieutenant, but his wife might be the general in that marriage."

"My dear, you already know very well you're only the king of the castle until the queen, namely me, arrives. Esther and Bastiann are recently married. If he doesn't know it already, he'll learn soon enough women rule the roost, if not the world."

They laughed together again.

"The cruise director isn't overbearing, but she keeps things moving along," he said, "so maybe she rules the captain?"

"Different domains, dear. His job might be the easier one too. I wouldn't want to have the cruise director's."

He thought about that while he toyed with his omelet. His mind wandered to consider the murder investigation Bastiann was conducting.

"I wonder if Bastiann will interrogate any Americans."

"I bet he knows everyone's background by now. He'll know you're an out-of-shape ex-Marine, for example. It's unlikely he'll believe you came all this way from New Jersey to kill that poor man."

"Hon, there's not a passenger on this ship that's poor. That victim was only unlucky…or somebody was on his trail for something he did."

"I suppose. Will you hurry up? Forget the omelet and eat your muffin. I want you to take a walk with me on the top deck. That stent was a warning. You should heed it."

"I know, I know. Don't worry. I'll be around for a while, I promise. Say, there's Bastiann." He waved the Interpol agent over. "How's it going, Bastiann?"

Bastiann put down his coffee and joined them at the table. "If you mean the murder investigation, I'm getting nowhere fast. If the killer is onboard, he has a good cover."

"Onboard?" Kayla looked around the dining room, at Ken, and then back at Bastiann. "Are we in danger?"

"Maybe…if you knew the victim well, or who killed him." Bastiann smiled. "I doubt the victim was ever in New Jersey. Hard to tell about his assassin. And he or she or they might still be onboard."

"So the captain's 'stay calm' message was misleading?" said Ken.

"No, calmness is the best policy right now. Let me do my job. You two old lovebirds should enjoy your cruise and forget about the investigation." He smiled at the amiable Ken. "You don't have anything to worry about unless you murdered Mr. Dragavei."

"While that sourpuss might have quite a few enemies," Ken said, "I'm not one of them. I can hardly pronounce the fellow's name."

"He's kidding you," said Kayla, winking at Bastiann.

"Actually anyone on this boat could be the murderer," Bastiann said, "which makes my job difficult. I'll interview all the passengers and crewmembers by the time it's over with, if only to find out if they saw or heard anything."

"And what about Esther while all that's going on?" said Kayla.

Bastiann pondered the question. "She's fine, doing a lie-in this morning. She's ex-Scotland Yard, so she enjoys being in pursuit of a criminal once again. I'm not sure I'm keen on it, though."

"That's maybe true," said Ken, "but you're on your honeymoon. You should be—er—celebrating your nuptials in a carnal way too."

"Ken!"

"What? I thought I said that in a civilized manner."

Bastiann blushed and then laughed. "We'll have plenty of time to play. We're participating in as many cruise activities as I dare, and I'm running the investigation as we go. That's what the cruise company wanted, according to the captain and cruise director."

"Makes sense to me if you can be discreet," said Ken. "Both with bedroom activities and the investigation. I bet most passengers won't even notice what you're doing for the second if you don't interrogate them."

Bastiann shrugged. "We have data on all of you, and maybe more to come. It will be easy to prioritize, even skip interviewing some passengers and crew, I hope."

"Are you ex-military, Bastiann?" Ken said.

"No, but I know you are. I've had a long career in law enforcement, that's all." He thought of some firefights he'd been in during that career, most of them unexpected because Interpol usually only worked with local and national police who did the heavy lifting. Most of his service was plodding investigation just like he was doing. "I trained for that because of my mother. She was in what became the French DGSI."

"What's that?" said Kayla.

"Like your FBI and DHS combined," Bastiann said. "Look, I have to run. You two lovebirds have a good day."

***

"Nice guy," Ken said after Bastiann left, "although somewhat intense. I don't envy him. Talk about ruining a honeymoon. Hell, Esther might divorce him. What would you have done in similar circumstances?"

Kayla thought a moment. "I guess I'd let you do your job during the day and not let you get much sleep at night. And remember, you were overseas a lot and often in danger, which was no fun for me and our sons." She smiled but then frowned. She leaned forward to whisper. "Did you see the sadness in his eyes when he talked about his mother?"

"You're better at reading people than I am. Always have been. I know you have a theory. Let's have it, old woman."

"He said he went into law enforcement because of his mother. I bet something really bad happened to her. I'm going to ask Esther."

"Oh, for God's sake, leave it alone, Kayla. Let them have some privacy. They're on display enough because of the investigation."

"I suppose. But I'm curious. Those two have a history too. I'm curious about that as well. I mean more than we know about from the media coverage."

"You live vicariously through other people's lives and adventures. Me, I'm happy with the boring routine in my life. I happy with my peace and quiet."

"And with boring work that's bad for your heart."

"I suppose that's a hint for a trip to the top deck." He pushed the omelet to the center of the table. "I had that chef fellow make it too complicated anyway. Let's do it then, but a walk will only make me hungrier."

Chapter Nineteen

Monday: Lyon, France

Sr. Agent III Karl Schuster, Bastiann's direct superior at Interpol, had decisions to make. First, he had to decide whether Bastiann was looking for a way out of the investigation. *Is he only going through the motions?* When Hal Leonard told him about the database requests, Karl okayed them—such requests could have come from the German or Austrian *Bundespolizei* in any case.

Second, he had to decide whether Interpol should handle the murder investigation, through Bastiann, of course. That was easy to justify. A riverboat on the Danube is on international waters. *But Bastiann is on his honeymoon!* Yet he didn't have free staff available right now, so his agent was in the right place at the wrong time.

And that was the third decision: He had to decide whether the chance of ruining Bastiann's time with his new bride was worth it. He wasn't afraid of Bastiann, but Esther could be difficult. He'd chatted with George Langston, her old boss, so he knew she could be abrasive and rebellious. *And vengeful?*

From Hal, he knew both agents were thinking about retiring to spend more time with their women and take less risks in pursuing criminals. Any jobs Karl could imagine them taking would potentially be more dangerous than their current ones, though. Interpol agents usually worked with local authorities, so risk to life and limb was often minimal. But, in the riverboat case, there was none, although Bastiann would have to do most of the job. It seemed both the Austrian and German *Bundespolizei* had used the international aspect as an excuse to assume minor roles in the investigation, nearly washing their hands of the case.

Maybe I have no choice? Until they confirmed who the victim was and what he was doing on that riverboat, it was also hard to pass the case on to spooks like those in the CIA, MI6, or SVR in a way that satisfied his UN masters. Of course, the SVR probably wouldn't even touch it, considering the Russian leader's man had been rejected as Interpol head. Putin was a vengeful bastard. Or would they snap it up in a second to create a cover-up for their own dirty business dealings with Dragavei? Putin's security agencies were like those Russian dolls: open one and there was another one inside, down to the special units dedicated to interfering in democratic elections. FSB, SVR, and GRU were all bad actors as far as Karl was concerned, and he was often happy Interpol wasn't in the same business as Western intelligence agencies.

He leaned back in his chair and patted his stomach, thinking he should go out for a walk. He popped his suspenders and straightened his tie. He stood, thought a moment, and grabbed his sports coat. A walk meant passing by support staff, after all, so he had to dress a bit smartly. He'd take the coat off after exiting the building and carry it.

***

By the time Karl returned from his walk, he'd made his decision. He found the number, picked up his phone, and keyed it in. It took some time to connect to the riverboat, which was a moving target for mobile phone towers, he supposed, although probably not as fast as cars on French and German highways.

"Agent Schuster, you're up early," said Bastiann. "I suppose you and Hal chatted about my requests. Captain Janssen wants formal authorization for my investigation, probably more to fend off any media that might want to make his life miserable."

"And you? The investigation will take time away from your honeymoon, time Esther and you undeniably deserve."

"Thank you for your concern. I'm okay doing the investigation, and Esther can help out a bit with her own connections."

"Langston is a good man, but I doubt Scotland Yard has the extensive databases we have."

"You're likely correct. But Scotland Yard isn't her only connection."

"I'm familiar with some of her past history. Be careful with that. We don't want to create an international incident, or reflect negatively on Interpol."

Bastiann laughed. "Spoken like a true manager. Do you have any suggestions beyond that?"

"Are you sure the murderer is still onboard?"

"Except for the dead passengers, they and all crewmembers are accounted for." He chuckled. "And with the Danube's current, it's not likely an assassin came and left like James Bond in a tuxedo under a wetsuit."

Karl smiled. He had been about to mention something similar, more as a joke to lighten the discussion.

"Just be careful. If the murderer's still onboard, the investigators, namely Esther or you, could be in danger. Any news about the lake district victims?"

"The Austrian *Bundespolizei* have confirmed those two passengers were murdered. They have that case. Part of my job, of course, is to see if there's a connection."

"Too much of a coincidence, I'd say. Do be careful. Tell Esther that too."

"I'll keep you informed."

Chapter Twenty

Monday: Weissenkirchen

Esther had more reasons to flag the East European couples Bastiann had already selected. And some others, even from the group not on that tour to the lake district. All couples she flagged had blurred passport photos of young people not matching the passengers' ages and current physical characteristics, and some of the passports were old too.

She too had thought the Bulgarian couple's deaths at the lake might be an accident, but it was too coincidental to completely ignore it. She was surprised to hear the *Bundespolizei* had a witness and had opened a murder investigation. *Fat chance they'll have of solving that case if it's related to ours. The couple's murderer is probably back onboard with us!*

"There are too many names," Bastiann complained. "Did you find anything peculiar in the background for the ones you flagged?"

"Not a lot. The husband of the Korean couple from Manchester works for a pharmaceutical company—I always suspect South Koreans because that madman is right next door—and the Russian couple lives in Oslo where the ex-patriate husband, now a Norwegian citizen, is a civil servant—at least he didn't flee to next-door Finland. Googling names doesn't help much either. I found that information on Gazsi, but there's nothing there with much relation to the investigation. Or for anyone else. I can send some names to Langston, my old boss, like you said, but I hate to do that. Maybe Jeremy's overtures to MI6 will produce something."

"I made my inquiry to Hal more official by requesting more information from Interpol, after obtaining permission for the investigation from Karl. We *are* running this investigation, after all. By default, I dare say, because other authorities washed their hands of it."

She ignored her husband's editorializing. "Yes, what Hal sent wasn't that much, but you said he and Karl chatted about diving deeper. Jeremy might be our man, though."

"I'll talk to Hal again. A personal touch often helps. All we know about our victim is Maxim Dragavei was a suspected assassin-for-hire, without any proof, mind you, but he was an opera singer as well. If the first was only a cover, maybe someone was out for revenge. Or wanted to stop him before he could act again."

"Interesting. Or someone didn't like his singing." Her joke fell flat. Bastiann didn't even smile. "Any information about the people who hired him?"

"I repeat, suspected assassin-for-hire. Computer-detected patterns exist that made Interpol flag him. And he was in Paris when a hit was made on a Soleimani agent."

"I hadn't heard that one. Ancient history, I suppose."

"Keep that in confidence because it might have been my slip of tongue. Be a jewel and forget about it." Bastiann thought a moment. "Maybe authorities can learn something from the murder weapon."

"A cheap knockoff from your description, but no stone unturned, as they say. I'll follow up on that. Send a picture to my mobile."

"We each have more work to do. I'll continue my interviews."

"I'll pass for now. I want to take the tour. You should come."

"I've seen many an abbey and enough little hamlets full of tourist traps. I'll start touring again with you in Vienna."

She examined the list he was perusing. "You should interview this man next," she said pointing to a name.

"Robert Winston? He's from London, born in Glasgow."

"I saw him at the welcoming party. Another loner, like Dragavei. Very mysterious, but not as creepy. In fact, he looks like Sean Connery in that movie *Entrapment* with Catherine Zeta-Jones. Hard to say who looked better in it, I dare say. I see him a lot in the library or reading poetry in the lounge. Usually American poetry."

"That sounds awfully suspicious," Bastiann said with a smile.

"Seriously. You must find out why he's traveling alone. Maybe he's MI6?"

"Or maybe he's looking for a girlfriend. Maria Ramirez or Cecilia Cruz would be good candidates, but they have Jake and Elliott respectively. Or is it Elliott and Jake?" He scratched his head. "Let me take a look at the Interpol data." He found what he was looking for. "Your suspect served a while ago in one of those weird regiments you people have...in Afghanistan. Helicopter pilot. Say, I wonder if he knew Harry. It's the same regiment."

"You knew that ahead of time. Admit it."

He laughed. "Look, I don't know why he's traveling alone. When I interview him, I'll make the query."

***

Robert Winston entered Dragavei's stateroom as if he had rebar for a backbone. "I looked for you at the Chef's

Table, old chap. Nice, welcoming place. If I had a companion, I'd try it. I suppose you can't see as much at night from there, though. Some chap named Ronaldo said you were here."

They shook hands. He took a seat near Bastiann, who was at the keyboard. He shuffled his papers and then turned again to face the man. *This is likely a waste of time.*

While nervous, the man's record was impeccable. He didn't look much like Sean Connery except for his debonair worldliness, but Bastiann could understand Esther's observation. The sleek, salt-and-pepper hair and chiseled facial features were set off by a whiter beard. *That would attract any woman!* The crow's feet at the corner of his eyes gave him a worldly, wise, and mysterious look too. Unlike some, he didn't think that the old chestnut, "You didn't stop looking until you're dead," only applied to men.

After more preliminaries, Bastiann went on to his usual questions, confirming name, age, place of birth, citizenship, current official residence, and occupation, which was now insurance investigator. He also confirmed the firm's focus, mostly insuring rich people's homes and tracking their burglaries.

As Bastiann went through his routine, he noticed body language: Robert was becoming increasingly nervous. *Is he the killer? A helicopter pilot doesn't strike me as someone who's practiced at assassinations! Or nervous person, for that matter.*

"We're just about finished," Bastiann said after a moment. "One more question: Where were you when Maxim Dragavei was murdered?"

"That's a bit complicated, Bastiann. I have no one to vouch for me."

"Those traveling as couples don't have any advantage over you in that regard. One partner might be covering for another. It's a simple question requiring a simple answer. I can confirm your veracity later."

"Most people were dining," he said.

"Including my wife and me. Were you?"

"No. I was elsewhere."

"Where?"

Robert stood and walked to the room's corner, hands clasped behind his back, and looked out. "It was a spur of the moment decision. I visited Dragavei's stateroom. I was here, and the door was slightly ajar. I only wanted to frighten him, show to myself he wasn't worthy of my sister." He turned, fists now clenched and exhibiting an angry, red face. "He raped her, Bastiann!"

"I beg your pardon? So you killed him?" *Could it be so simple?*

"I wanted to. I tracked him and found he was a suspect in some burglaries my firm had covered years ago. They were itching to get something on him, but he then disappeared."

Maybe we didn't go back far enough? observed Bastiann. *But neither the Yard nor Interpol would have had those records if Dragavei wasn't convicted.*

"I tried to tell my sister he was no good. She became a nun because of that SOB. It's weird she'd become obsessed with an opera singer, but that's what happened. She was only eighteen. When I entered the stateroom to confront him, he was already dead, that horrible Italian knife in his back."

Bastiann nodded. "That proves you were there, at least. Look, lovesick teenagers are taken advantage of by rock stars...and it seems opera singers can get in on that act as well, if you'll pardon the pun. No one can do anything about that if they're two consenting adults, and that's sixteen or older in the UK. But about the knife: how did you know it was Italian? Not too many people know about that ornate knife. And is it really Italian?"

"Most likely Venetian—Venice wasn't part of Italy at the time—but it's a cheap copy. I know collectibles."

"Why didn't you come forward before?"

Robert hung his head. "I knew it wouldn't look good. Like I said, I had no one to vouch for me." He looked up and met Bastiann's eyes. "I didn't murder him, and I have no idea who did. Otherwise, I would congratulate the assassin for a job well done and give him an expensive bottle of cognac. I couldn't have done it, even for our family honor."

"You're a strange man, Robert Winston, but I believe you." *He wouldn't have admitted to being here otherwise!* "How is your sister now?"

"Quite happy the last time we talked. Maybe it's true that God works in mysterious ways."

"One more thing before you leave: How did you know Dragavei would be on this particular riverboat?"

"I was shopping in London for a new painting and saw him leave a gallery three doors down. Pure coincidence, but I never forget a face. I followed him, of course. I have a bit of training for that."

Why did he do that, if he wasn't going to confront him? Or kill him? Some doubt returned, ergo.Bastiann decided he'd have to watch the fellow. But then a thought occurred to the Interpol agent.

"Do you happen to remember the name of that gallery he visited?"

Robert thought a moment. "If memory serves, it was called *Masterworks Gallery.*"

Esther's gallery! Bastiann frowned. *Does that connect Dragavei to Esther?*

The Interpol agent struggled to be objective. If there was a connection, several questions had to be considered: Had Dragavei been after Esther? If so, was that related to her past espionage work? And had she realized he was a threat and taken preventative action when she discovered she was in danger? He knew his new wife could defend herself, but could she have stabbed the man in the back to do so? He didn't think there was a high probability for that—he'd once seen her scoop up a spider and release the arachnid outside, and she hated spiders!—but he couldn't ignore the possibility.

Of course, he would have to check Robert Winston's story. If false, the chap would still be a prime suspect in the case, no matter how affable he seemed to be. And, even if true, that didn't mean he wasn't pursuing Dragavei for other reasons. It was hard to imagine any American passenger was pursuing Dragavei, but the victim had been based in Europe, so any European passenger might have been. The only American who made him suspicious was the doctor from San Diego, but anyone with some medical knowledge that would guide the placement of that knife could have been a killer. But a professional hit man would have that knowledge too. *Was that Robert's real occupation?*

He decided he'd have to leave all the Americans and some of the least suspicious characters to Esther. Her chores should be more restricted to the safer interviews because he thought they would be less dangerous.

What a way to start a marriage!

***

There were several Bulgarian couples who'd taken the cruise. One couple were the victims at Attersee. Another

146

were on the tour with Esther. And yet another Bulgarian couple was next in line for an interview. Esther had told him all three couples were chummy, understandable for compatriots. They all had been on that lake tour.

He had to take what Esther told him with a grain of salt, though. She was into reporting on onboard dalliances, for example, and knew a lot about who was chatting up whom, as she would say. Considering his wife could also be a big flirt sometimes herself, all that amused him. He'd told her six Californians looked like a partner-swapping religious cult in his opinion, not that anyone's sexual mores bothered him anymore as long as people left him alone. Some years ago, a gay man had run for US president, and a lesbian was now in the running for Holland's PM, a sure sign the world was growing more diverse and tolerant, both of which he believed were major improvements.

After the Rakovskis came into Dragavei's stateroom, Bastiann explained to the couple why they were there: It was only a part of the general investigation into the crime.

"My wife is helping me some, but she couldn't be here right now. I'm from Interpol, by the way, and she's ex-Scotland Yard."

"How convenient," said the husband, although his face made it abundantly clear he didn't think it was. "Will this take long?"

"No. It's only a preliminary interview, more to get to know some passengers better."

"I suppose we're all suspects," the wife said.

She was taller than her husband, the two having heights comparable to Esther and Bastiann's, respectively. They looked like they were in their late forties or early fifties.

"Everyone on the boat is a person of interest, ma'am, but not necessarily suspect."

After confirming the basic data he already had on them, including their ages, he cleared his throat and continued. "I've observed you're chummy with that other Bulgarian couple." That was basically Esther's observation, but why complicate the question?

The husband glanced at his wife and then studied Bastiann's face. "So what? We're friends with other cruise couples too. We eat dinner with a different couple every evening." He frowned. "We were friends with the couple that drowned too."

The wife nodded. "As for the other couple who went on that lake district tour, Luynhen and I began chatting not long after we came aboard. We have a lot in common." She took her husband's hand. "Boris, my husband, and Viktor, Luynhen's, are old, boring men who need social organizers like Luynhen and me. We both had to work hard to convince our husbands to go on this cruise." She smiled at Boris. "We should have gone on the tour this morning."

Bastiann learned more about the women's plans to reform their husbands than he did about anyone's possible involvement in crimes, but he kept them on his list along with Luynhen and her husband Viktor.

> Name: Katrina Rakovski
> Age: 56
> PoB: Sofia
> C: Bulgarian
> Res: Sofia
> Occ: accountant
> L@TOD: lounge

Notes: Tough woman, trying to reform her husband?

Name: Boris Rakovski
Age: 58
PoB: Sofia
C: Bulgarian
Res: Sofia
Occ: dentist
L@TOD: lounge
Notes: Somewhat confrontational

***

Next, Razvan and Ihrin Culianu made themselves comfortable on the little sofa across from Bastiann. Ihrin looked around Dragavei's stateroom. *Is she admiring it?* Their own room was one of the riverboat's smaller ones.

All the couples Bastiann had asked to come in had agreed and were skipping the tour, and for basically the same reasons as Bastiann: Europeans were surrounded by centuries of history and religion; Americans, Australians, and Canadians not so much. Only those curious about what used to be beyond their reach behind the Iron Curtain were keen to go sightseeing through history.

Ihrin was thin and nervous; Razvan was bald and fat with a monk's tonsure. Razvan joined his wife in surveilling the room like birds of prey looking to nest.

"We should have signed up for this, Razvan," she said to her husband, indicating the large stateroom with a wave of her hand. "It's much nicer."

"We only use ours to sleep," the surly and jowly man said.

There are a lot of old blokes onboard who aren't having much fun, Bastiann observed. He wondered about their reasons. His were clear: The investigation was a damn nuisance!

"I won't keep you long," Bastiann said. "Your documentation brought you here." He slid the ship's records across to them. "You should update these photos. Your passports too."

"I told you," Razvan said to his wife. He turned to Bastiann. "Throwing out the Soviets and joining the EU didn't change a damn thing. Police are still nosing around, only different ones now. Sometimes." He sighed and appeared to force a smile. "We haven't changed those documents since we sent the damn Soviets packing. No need to do so. I travel for business and sometimes Ihrin tags along, but it's all within the EU. She wants to visit Yellowstone and Yosemite someday— those are parks in the US, in case you didn't know—but the Swiss Alps are good enough for me. Damn Americans started demolishing all that was good and let us do away with the Iron Curtain, and Boris Johnson added his bit in England with Brexit. We don't need either America or Britain."

A nervous rant? Or is he trying to appeal to my international perspective? In any case, Bastiann thought that little speech was insincere. Coming from Romania, he supposed it was a diatribe a Romanian might spit out.

"I'm not here to debate politics or the international situation. Did either of you know Maxim Dragavei?"

"He's the victim?" said Ihrin.

The husband glared at his wife. "Of course, he's the victim! I told you that."

She shrugged. "I forgot. We only saw him when he came aboard. I recognized him."

Razvan shook his head at that, and Bastiann perked up.

"Oh? From where?"

"On one of Razvan's trips, we went to see him sing. A university production. My husband hardly ever pays for tickets, but they were only ten euros apiece. What university was that, Razvan?"

"You remember the price of the tickets but not the university?" The husband shook his head again. "A university in Berlin, I believe. *Frei Universität* maybe? I might be wrong. I do remember Dragavei had the role of Iago in Verdi's *Otello*. Not a bad singer, perfect voice for it, and the price was right."

"You didn't see him anymore once you came aboard?" said Bastiann.

"We tend to eat a late dinner," Ihrin said, "and we never saw him on tours. We hadn't done that many yet, I suppose, before...well, you know. He seemed to be a shy man, maybe something of a recluse? I suppose opera singers are like actors in that way. Their stage presence often belies their shyness."

Nerves again? Her answer provided far too much information.

"Did you ever speak with him, in Berlin or otherwise?"

"If we didn't see him, how could we speak to him?" said Razvan.

That confrontational answer surprised Bastiann. He frowned but plowed on. "In these interviews, I also like to learn about the interviewees." *As a cross-check to data we have,* he didn't add. *And there's always a chance of catching someone in a lie.* "What's your profession, Mr. Culianu?"

"I was trained as a medical doctor, but now I sell medical supplies and instruments for a Dresden company. All around the EU; Scandinavia too."

"In your training, I suppose you learned about anatomy?"

"Of course. One unpleasant aspect about that profession is cutting up cadavers to see the insides. I'd have preferred something else less ghoulish, but the Soviets micromanaged everything. No freedom to choose, you know."

"I suppose micromanaged is one word to describe it," Bastiann said. "I'm guessing, Ihrin, you started your gift shop after the Soviets left?"

"Maybe five years later," said Ihrin, looking at her husband.

"Trinkets for tourists," he said. "Lots of fake, cheap junk. You can see some inventory on the website. Give him a card, Ihrin."

Bastiann pocketed the card. "Thank you for coming in. That will be all for now. I know where to find you if I have more questions."

He would make a request to Interpol for more information because he believed the couple, especially Ihrin, were hiding something.

Name: Ihrin Culianu
Age: 42
PoB: Bucharest
C: Romanian
Res: Dresden
Occ: gift shop owner
Res: Dresden, Germany
L@TOD: lounge
Notes: Not a dutiful wife, and met D before

Name: Razvan Culianu
Age: 44
PoB: Bucharest
C: Romanian
Res: Dresden
Occ: medical supplies salesman, Dresden
company
L@TOD: lounge
Notes: Somewhat confrontational, tries too
hard, and met D before

***

Janos and Eszter Rakoczy, the other Hungarian couple onboard, had some problems with English, and Bastiann didn't know Hungarian. He believed it was an impossible language to learn. But they were fluent in German because they lived in Germany, so the Interpol agent switched to that language.

Unlike the thin and tall Culianu couple, Janos and Eszter looked more like Bastiann, especially the husband, with his short arms and legs and large head on a short neck, all those parts stuck on a barrel-like body. The wife knew how to make the most of what she had, but the husband didn't seem to care much about his appearance. *Of course, they are on vacation.*

Whereas Bastiann was still muscular, they appeared to be somewhat flabby. They were also younger than the average passenger. They were having great fun on the cruise and said as much, even with the adventure of being interrogated about a murder.

After introductions and confirming what data he had on them, he started his interrogation in earnest.

"Are you visiting relatives at the end of the trip?"

"That's the plan," said Janos. "Both sets of parents live in Budapest. But we're celebrating our anniversary onboard."

Bastiann smiled. His married life was barely starting.

"My mother becomes all gushy," added Eszter, "and keeps telling me to give her some grandchildren. It's our fifth wedding anniversary. Our careers are our priorities right now, so she'll just have to wait."

"And from all the onboard gossip, you probably already know it's our honeymoon," said Bastiann with a smile. "I guess that's why this riverboat tour is called 'The Romantic Danube.' And what are your professions?"

"This is about the murder, right?" said Janos. "We never met the victim, you know."

"Yes, it is. I believed that was clear. And you can still know something that might shed light on the case without being directly involved. However, the reason you are here is because pictures in your documentation records are blurry. From your birthdates, you were born after the Soviet Union's fall, and Hungary is in the EU now. I wonder why you don't have better photos."

"They're cheap passport photos. No one in the EU pays much attention to passports anymore."

The Dutch do. But Bastiann knew the more one went southeast in Europe, the sloppier documentation became. And Hungarians likely only worried about documenting migrants!

Janos shoved two drivers' licenses toward Bastiann. "These are better pictures and newer as well. We had passport photos taken in a street booth a while ago. I also thought they were horrible. The license photos were recently taken in the department of motor vehicles.

Although not flattering, as one would expect, they're better."

Bastiann compared the sets of photos and nodded, handing back the licenses. "You mentioned the importance of careers. I'll repeat my question: What are your professions?"

"Janos is a manager at a pharmaceutical company in Dresden, and I teach anatomy at the *Hochschule fur Technik und Wirtschaft.*"

Two more people based in Dresden in the East German state of Saxony, observed Bastiann. *One with access to drugs, and another knowing anatomy. Strange that bad passport photos led to two couples with such backgrounds.*

"Tell me about your parents," said Bastiann. "I suppose they were glad to see the Soviets leave?"

Janos sighed. "What many people around the world don't realize, especially Americans and British, is most people in old Soviet bloc countries hated the Soviets." He glanced at Eszter. She gave him an encouraging smile. "It pains us our country is now turning to the right over the continuing migrant situation, which has only become worse, but our right-wing leaders aren't nearly as bad as the Soviets were. Our grandparents were nearly killed during the 1956 revolution and badgered during the crackdown that followed, and our parents' political proclivities were formed by their upbringing. Need I say more?"

Bastiann shrugged. "Some of my ancestors, Dutch and French, felt the same way about Nazis; Hungary's and Poland's current right-wing leaders often remind me of them—or at least what I know about them from reading history. Too many people saw Soviet Communism as different from fascism, when it really wasn't. Your country's pain is more recent than my country's, of course. But let's focus. If you never met Dragavei, do you know any other couples that might have?"

"I was expecting that question," said Janos. "Passengers were gossiping after the murder. No one seemed to know the fellow. Hard to imagine someone wanted to kill him because of his antisocial behavior, though. Someone mentioned he was alone onboard. People usually travel in pairs on these cruises." Janos smiled. "This whole affair is an adventure neither Eszter nor I could have imagined having."

"My Esther and I neither." He handed them his card. "Keep your ears and eyes open and let me know if anything, and I mean anything, looks out of the ordinary. Thanks for coming in."

He put the couple on a standby list as possible suspects. Body language could be a powerful indicator of guilt or innocence. Theirs has been a bit contradictory— youthful, exuberant behavior even toward the interview without any curious glances around the room, like many other interviewees had made. That aroused his suspicions. *Or maybe others told them already about the scene of the crime?*

Name: Eszter Rakoczy
Age: 33
PoB: Budapest
C: Hungarian
Res: Dresden
Occ: anatomy professor
L@TOD: top deck
Notes: Furtive—hiding something?

Name: Janos Rakoczy

Age: 34
PoB: Budapest
C: Hungarian
Res: Dresden
Occ: pharmaceutical firm manager
L@TOD: top deck
Notes: Too affable?

Bastiann interviewed eight other passengers before arriving at the two cruise company employees he was planning to leave for last. Esther had found them suspicious. He thought she might be temporarily insane, but he decided to get those interviews over with too, hoping they would be as brief as the other crewmembers' interviews had been.

Chapter Twenty-One

Some Months Earlier: Toulouse, France

Linda Santos first had seen Maxim Dragavei as a dumb jerk she could manipulate. He grew on her, though, especially after he became a willing accomplice. Her lover had his dark side, though. Sometimes even when they were hot and heavy in bed, he'd go off to a faraway place. After that happened a few times, she decided he was as crazy as she was.

He didn't talk to her about his uncle much, and she only learned about him when Maxim seemed to be debating with himself in his sleep about plans to kill that relative. She counted two or three personalities in that debate. She queried Maxim about his uncle later. His response: "Just a stupid old man. Forget about him."

With every contract, she wondered whether he would fail her at some critical moment. That was on her mind as they surveilled their target's apartment building from across the street as they hid just off it in a shadowy alleyway.

If the pay wasn't so good, I'd retire. She smiled at the thought. She realized she was kidding herself. She'd welcome contracts even if they paid next to nothing. The kills were like sex for her, both an ecstatic rush no drugs would ever duplicate.

***

Linda and Maxim saw lights come on in the apartment. Their target was home. He adjusted his cap and shirt—blood from the delivery man's knife wound didn't show as Maxim tucked it in and looked at the takeaway chain's trademark and the name Pierre to refresh his memory. *Get into the role, lad!*

She stretched to give him a kiss. "I'd order takeaway from you any day, *mi amor.*"

He sensed the familiar stirring in his loins. God, what a woman! *But is the stirring in anticipation of the kill or the sex that will come after?* With her, each mission was like a double *espresso.* He wasn't sure what motivated him more. *Maybe the money?* He definitely enjoyed fattening his bank accounts.

To business! "If there's a door chain, we can both break in," he said, refining their plan's details. "Otherwise, wait at the side of the door until I'm in."

She agreed. He knew she would ably adjust as their mission continued, and her adjustments always were successful.

They entered the building and climbed the stairs. She easily dispatched the target's two bodyguards. The silencer meant the two shots wouldn't be heard by anyone, but they would have to take care of the bodies soon before anyone happened along. The burn mark on the floor from a dropped fag might be a problem. He glanced along the hall. There were others on the worn carpet. *Not exactly an elegant place for a rich oligarch!*

"Takeaway delivery!" he called out after knocking at the target's door. His French wasn't that good, but delivery people were often not native French speakers.

"Go away! I didn't order takeaway. Get rid of him, Volodya!"

The last was in Russian, but Maxim knew it as well as French. *Volodya must be one of the dead bodyguards.*

"It says Apartment 4G on the order, *monsieur.* I'll still need your signature if you don't want the takeaway. I have to show I tried to make the delivery, or I'll be in trouble."

The door opened wide; Maxim faced a burly man who examined his uniform—faded blue jeans and dirty trainers completed Maxim's deliveryman disguise. He turned the bag on its side so the target had a firm place to sign, placed the receipt on the bag and its takeaway carton underneath, and handed the Russian a pen.

Fortunately the target didn't look for his men. The fool took his eyes off Maxim to study the receipt.

"Different phone number, you idiot. I won't—"

The bullet from Linda's gun cut the complaint short as it ripped into the Russian's skull.

***

"Not a bad little place, and much better looking than outside," Maxim said, looking around the target's apartment, "but you'd think an oligarch would live a richer lifestyle."

The apartment was in a newer but somewhat rundown building and large for lodging in Toulouse, but the stylish furnishings appeared to be Victorian or older and a bit faded. The two of them had dragged the two bodyguards inside earlier and cleaned the hallway. The spatter wasn't too bad—bullets were still rattling around in the brains of all three.

Maxim knelt and examined the contents of the liquor cabinet. The target had a good supply of red wine, so he supposed the white must be in the refrigerator.

After cleaning some more, hand-shampooing the carpets in the corridor and entranceway enough to remove any sign of blood or brain material, all in haste in case someone came, they had a decent feast in the dining room, making good use of the takeaway meal and bottles of both red and white wine.

Afterwards, and true to his past as a burglar, Maxim couldn't resist prowling around more to see what he could steal. They wanted to make it look like a bungled burglary, after all. Linda took some jewelry maybe destined for female visitors, and he nicked some male trophies—gold money clip, ruby ring, and a Jerry Garcia tie. *What was that about?* The target's thousand-euro loafers were too big for him. *Too bad!*

They left via the backdoor that led to the building's car park bordering on an alley. They put Linda's gun, their rubber gloves and Tyvek booties, and rug shampoo bottle and brush into the takeaway bag along with two bricks and tossed the entire mess into the twilight shadows on the Garonne as they crossed over a bridge. Night-crawling students were out and about, so they fit right in.

"Know what I want to do when we return to the hotel?" she said as they waited hand-in-hand for a light to change so they could cross the street.

He eyed her. She licked her lips and then winked. He understood her perfectly.

"We'll need more wine."

***

There was no need to report the success of their mission—all the news the next morning carried the story: "Russian Dignitary Murdered." They both laughed at the word "dignitary." Their victim had been as much a thug as Putin. By the afternoon, their blood money was equally divided and deposited in their two new secret Swiss bank accounts in Zurich. Each of them now had two, one for American contracts and one for Russian ones.

"I guess we can exist on that and what's in our other accounts until the next contract," she told him before he fell asleep again after their lusty morning exercise.

A few days later, Linda and Maxim traveled to Oslo where he would sing in a small and abbreviated production of *The Magic Flute* for Christmas, similar to the one at New York City's Metropolitan Opera every year. He didn't classify that opera as particularly Christmas-like, so he didn't understand the New York tradition, and the cold in that Scandinavian city was nearly unbearable, but Linda had a New Year's date with an uncle in Copenhagen upon their return to slightly warmer climes. It was also nice to sing without any assassination plans to worry about.

The SVR would surely learn about his appearance at the event, of course, but he figured Linda and he would be long gone by the time they organized anything. And he considered their trip to Denmark a trial run to see whether they might be safe in making a short side trip to Zurich afterwards.

"You were better than the other singers," Linda observed as they finished a late dinner before returning to their hotel.

"Sarastro's role isn't that difficult," he said. "Dessert?"

"Only coffee, *mi amor*. I have to keep in shape for you."

"Your shape is just fine, plus all your other qualities."

After coffee, they left but skipped the taxi. Even with the cold, their hotel was just three blocks away, only a short walk. In spite of their riches, Maxim insisted on being frugal. They walked at a brisk pace with arms locked.

She surprised him. Hearing the speeding car first as it came around the corner they'd just passed, her reflexes took over. She let go of his arm and reached into her purse for her gun, spinning to face the oncoming car. Her cat-like reflexes didn't help her this time. The car wasn't the weapon. As she raised the gun, three bullets ripped into her body, two of them lethal hits as he soon learned.

They fired at him from a bad angle, so he was able to save himself by diving into the stairway entrance to a basement apartment. His own gun out, he peered at the street in time to see the car disappearing around the next corner.

He rushed to her and cradled her head, tears streaming down his cheeks. *Damn the Russians! Damn the Americans!* But he recovered quickly. He dragged her body into an alleyway where he removed all her clothing. He left her there, taking her purse, gun, and bloody clothes with him. *Not a proper burial, my love, but I must do a runner!*

He was afraid of going to Zurich to retrieve some of his funds. And there was no way to access Linda's either, there or elsewhere. Fortunately he had his own money in several other accounts in several countries to tide him over for a bit, but not nearly the amount he had stashed in his retirement account in Zurich…

He'd often had chin wags with his aliases. That one when Linda had asked about his uncle had been particularly bad. Edward often egged him on in his burglary schemes with her. Maxim justified the later killings they did, as well as that thrill obtained by taking another person's life. Now those alter-egos seemed united in a common cause: Make Esther Brookstone suffer for stealing from him what remained of the life he'd enjoyed with his uncle.

He had spent some time in Transylvania. Its dark history perhaps made the three personalities coalesce into one amalgam, a strong alloy that could vanquish any enemy. He'd set out to pursue Esther, even knowing the Russians were probably after him. Putin's minions often sought revenge, but he believed he could handle them when they found him. It would take them some time, especially if they thought they'd killed him along with Linda, so he had time he could use to pay back Esther Brookstone. And then, only then, would he figure out how to get on with the remainder of his life.

Chapter Twenty-Two

Monday: Weissenkirchen

Before leaving on the tour, Esther had reminded Bastiann he still needed to interview the captain and cruise director to complete the process for the crew. She had detected a problem she thought her husband must resolve to make that process complete.

She had noticed by then that Caitlin Marshall had a bit of an Irish brogue. As she performed her background checks, she put together some of their cruise director's history. Born Caitlin O'Hara in Dublin, she'd gone to Trinity College and received a degree in sociology and then married the Englishman Edwin Marshall, who'd worked with teams to help new countries enter the EU. She later become a tour guide for the cruise company, working her way up to cruise director. There weren't many facts available beyond those. Esther had found some of them on web pages associated with the river cruise industry and the cruise line's website, but most were discovered by using an app particular to their cruise, in a section title "Meet Your Crew."

Esther generally liked the Irish. She believed they'd been treated unfairly over many centuries by her country, especially during the famines, and never blamed George Bernard Shaw too much for making fun of England's uppity aristocrats and politicians. Her father, the vicar, hadn't liked either Irish or Catholics; he'd given Esther and her brothers tongue lashings when they teased him about how they'd all be Catholics if Henry the Eighth hadn't wanted a divorce. By the time those two Price sisters nearly starved to death in their hunger strike, Esther'd had it with Britain's policies that had caused so many deaths as the Queen's government tried to hold on to Northern Ireland (the Republic had gone their own way years earlier, and, like Switzerland, had been non-aligned during WWII).

Many Irish like Caitlin had risen above all those centuries of bickering and bloodshed and shown their mettle. *A thumb in the eye to past PMs and the rest of Parliament, I'd say.* More than that, Esther had found Caitlin to be someone she wanted to call friend. The cruise director was willing to listen to any passenger's problem, and then she would take the necessary steps to solve it if she could. Esther was sorry she and Bastiann hadn't made that extra land package some had added to visit Prague before the cruise. That would have given her three more days to get to know one of the most pleasant persons she'd ever met.

Sander Janssen might be that same class of person. Esther didn't know him as well, more because she saw him less. Bastiann knew the captain better and had confirmed the man was a good egg, albeit somewhat withdrawn. Bastiann had worked more closely with the cruise director and captain because of the investigation.

Esther's problem was simple: The other crewmembers couldn't account for Caitlin's whereabouts when Dragavei was killed. It was time for someone to query her...and Sander Janssen, directly.

***

Bastiann called the captain and cruise director in separately, with Sander going first. By then, he knew them both well, and both had contributed to the investigation. But that nagging doubt still remained. *Leave it to Esther,* Bastiann thought. *We make a good team.*

"Isn't this interview somewhat anti-climactic?" Captain Janssen said after taking a seat across from Bastiann.

"You appear to be nervous, Sander," Bastiann said. "Let me be direct then. Other crewmembers have said you were the first person at the murder scene after Marisol screamed. How'd that happen? I'd expect you to be off somewhere being invisible and doing captain-like things in the navigation bridge on the top deck."

Captain-like things? Were those Esther's words? Now I'm talking like her!

"I don't know. Yes, I happened to be in that corridor. Let me think." Bastiann waited as the captain collected his thoughts. "Oh yes, I was heading to the Chef's Table at the corridor's end. As captain, I occasionally drop in to say hello and praise the virtues of our chef."

"I see. But Ronaldo was only two cabins forward readying a stateroom when he saw you pass. You must have been nearly at the entrance to Dragavei's room."

"I suppose so."

"Which would put you farther away from the Chef's Table and nearer the elevator, shall we say?"

"That's where this stateroom is. Like yours, it's one of the deluxe staterooms on the boat. They have easy access to the reception area and lounge and are only a level and half up from the dining room using the stairway or elevator."

"Precisely. They're also near the cruise director's desk." His expression was blank, but he eyed Sander, ready to see any hint of duplicity via a facial expression or other body language. "How long have you known Caitlin?"

Although a segue to her seemed logical, Sander seemed surprised at the mention of the cruise director's name and hesitated. "For a while." The imprecise answer wasn't accompanied by any revealing body language.

"Could you be more precise?"

Sander shrugged. "Maybe five years now. We've been together on cruises maybe two or three times that number. Possibly more."

"In spite of her last name, she was born in Dublin. Marshall was her English husband's name, who's now deceased. I'm sympathetic to that, of course. Esther has lost three."

"Really? I'm sorry for her."

"Not a pleasant experience for her, to put it mildly, and not for Caitlin either, I imagine. Did you comfort her?"

"Her husband passed just before our second cruise together. This same route, Vilshofen to Budapest."

A detailed memory for five years ago, mused Bastiann.

Sander continued. "I arranged for a replacement and for her to disembark in Vienna and fly back home to take some time off to mourn him. She should never have come on that cruise so soon after that tragedy. She was a wreck."

"But she did return to work soon after?" Sander nodded. "Did you continue to comfort her?"

The captain raised his eyebrows. "I beg your pardon! I don't like what you're insinuating."

"I'd like to believe we have a growing friendship, Sander. Are you protecting Caitlin? Did she murder Dragavei?"

"What in God's name would make you think that?"

"No one knows where she was at the time the murder occurred. Perhaps she was still here, in Dragavei's stateroom? Witnesses not only said you were the first on the scene besides Marisol, but you were holding that poor woman and trying to calm her. Was that done to let Caitlin slip by and leave the stateroom unseen?"

"You've cooked up quite a theory, Bastiann."

"Detectives develop theories that fit all available facts. When new evidence appears proving a theory wrong, they reject that theory and look for another. All very scientific, you see. Prove my theory wrong, Sander."

Bastiann wasn't about to admit that it wasn't his theory. It wasn't Esther's either—just a prod so the interviews of the crew were complete. Neither believed that Caitlin could be a murderer.

The captain sighed and hung his head. "Okay." He then looked Bastiann straight in the eyes. "Caitlin was waiting for me in my cabin. I was going along that corridor, but the reason she wasn't at her station and couldn't be found was exactly what I said. Are you satisfied?"

"Why didn't you say so earlier?"

He shrugged. "We were waiting for the opportune time to announce our romance to the world. I for one didn't know how the cruise line would react. I gave her an engagement ring on our last cruise together."

"She wears no rings."

Sander smiled. "Very observant. We're keeping it all secret. Silly decision, I suppose."

"But a bit exciting for you too, I'm guessing. Clandestine romance and all that sort of thing. By any chance, did you name this cruise?"

"You mean—?"

"'The Romantic Danube,' yes," Bastiann said with a chuckle.

The captain smiled. "Will you keep this quiet?"

"It will only be between you two and Esther and me, I assure you. But please consider making an announcement."

"There's no rush."

"While I hope not, you two might be on another cruise like this one. Not likely, but you never know. Maybe similar circumstances where crew and passengers must be interrogated. Your interrogators might not be so friendly and understanding the next time as Esther and I are."

> Name: Sander Janssen
> Age: 40
> PoB: Antwerp
> C: Dutch
> Res: Amsterdam
> Occ: riverboat captain
> L@TOD: near D's stateroom
> Notes: Works well with others, though somewhat aloof; company man; affair with Caitlin; not a suspect!

***

With this new information, Bastiann decided to cut short his interview with Caitlin Marshall.

"We had a little problem," he began, "with figuring out where you were at the time of the murder. Just to confirm, where were you?"

Caitlin thought a moment. "I can't recall. There's always so much to do at the beginning of a cruise. You saw how it was."

He stood, went to the door, looked into the hallway, and shut it. Returning to his seat, he said, "I'll get right to the point. I've talked to Esther via mobile. She wants to see your engagement ring. I still owe her one. Our marriage was a bit rushed. There was a lot going on then as well."

She looked around the room as if searching for eavesdroppers.

"Sander told you?"

"He had to. You'd be under suspicion otherwise."

"I see." She smiled. "I'm not sure I should show my engagement ring to Esther. Between you and me, Sander went overboard, if you'll forgive my saying that, considering where we are. You'd be spending far too many euros to compete."

"It's not a competition. I'm sure Sander considers you worth it."

"No doubt Esther's worth it too. She seems like a wonderful lady. Will you keep all this to yourselves?"

"If at all possible, and that's a guarantee if we catch the assassin. Are we good here?"

She sighed. "I knew I'd come under suspicion. Sander knew it too. We never imagined being in this situation."

"You'll make a wonderful couple. How do you manage cruises where he's not riverboat captain?"

"It's hard. But you have a more complicated situation, don't you? Isn't Interpol HQ'd in Lyon? I doubt there's a direct flight between London and there."

"You have a point. Yet we even manage to meet at her castle near Edinburgh."

"Esther has a castle?" Bastiann nodded. "Then she will want a really expensive diamond!"

> Name: Caitlin Marshall nee O'Hara
> Age: 32
> PoB: Dublin
> C: Irish Republic
> Res: Munich

Occ: cruise director

L@TOD: Sander's stateroom

Notes: Pleasant, great social skills, great organizer, affair with Sander...not a suspect!

Bastiann returned to his own room to organize his notes and wait for Esther.

Chapter Twenty-Three

Monday: Vienna

Elise's fiancé Franz informed Fritz Reiner the he'd only told Walther, his artist friend, about the painting. Fritz observed Franz's German was like reading a book—sentences far too long for normal human speech and loaded with many erudite words with Latin roots. *Classical studies?* Fritz himself had suffered through those and had taken a lot of ribbing when he started to work for the *Bundespolizei* after specializing in criminal justice, something a lot more practical. *But I still ended up pursuing the classics,* he mused.

Franz looked like a musician, though, with his long hair and pale skin indicating he spent too much time inside. Fritz couldn't understand what Elise saw in him.

Walther was the next one on Fritz's list.

"The owner of the gallery that sells most of my paintings here in Vienna sent his aide to pick up some new ones," Franz's friend said. "I told him about Elise's painting, the only person I can remember telling about it. I asked him how much a Caravaggio might be worth. He said priceless if it was truly a Caravaggio, and maybe five hundred euros or so if it was a good copy complete with frame. Because Franz told me they'd only paid fifty euros for it, I figured it wasn't even a good copy, in spite of his opinion."

"What's the aide's name?"

"Giovanni. He's Italian and a gentle soul who's touched." Walther tapped his forehead. "Simple fellow. Wouldn't hurt a fly. Tries to learn as much as he can at the gallery, though, and he knows almost as much about pricing artwork as Arturo, the gallery owner."

Fritz then visited the gallery to talk to both Arturo and Giovanni. Neither appeared to be physically equipped to jump on a bin and climb a fire escape to steal a painting. Arturo was in his seventies and used a cane, and Giovanni was short, fat, out of shape, and witless. *No, wrong word. Spacey*. The lad was intelligent enough when talking to him.

Elise's friend Vilma was Polish, a bubbly, cheerful woman who couldn't remember who she'd told about the painting, if anyone. She went to the bottom of Fritz's list, only because she had no information. He had already discounted Elise's colleague Jörg, whose position as suspect was now ranked ahead of Vilma's. The man was so heavy he was a ticking time bomb for a heart attack. Jumping on a trash bin wasn't in the cards for him either, although Fritz remembered most Sumo wrestlers were surprisingly agile, strong, and energetic.

Fritz wasn't having much luck and might soon be called to task for spending too much time on the case. *Yet, if I solve it, the VIPs will take all the credit!*

***

Fritz returned to Elise's building to study the fire escape from below. He left his car on the street in front of the building and walked through an alley to reach the back. To confirm his opinion about Jörg and some of the others, he was gauging how hard it might be for even him to climb to Elise's sliding balcony door when he heard a noise in the alley, He peered around the building's corner and saw a drunk weaving and stumbling into the alley and knocking over trash cans as he did. He collapsed. Fritz rushed to him.

"Are you okay, old man?"

Rheumy eyes stared at him. "That you, Hans? Can you spare some euros for an old friend? I need to eat something."

"I'm not Hans," Fritz said. "Who is he?" The inspector wasn't all that interested; he was only trying to determine the drunk's health condition by his ability to answer.

The old man looked around as if he were trying to recover his bearings. His eyes then focused on Fritz. "Street, not this alley. Building across the street from this one. Apartment 2B. That worth some euros, *guter Freund?*" Two bloodshot eyes stared at him with hope.

Fritz handed the drunk a five-euro bill. "Go find some food, *mein Greis.*"

He knew the drunk would probably sleep it off and then spend the money on more liquor. Normally Fritz would take him to some eatery, sit him down, and pay for the food, which was always the better, more humane strategy. But he needed to return to the station.

He went back to his car. As he pressed the button on his key fob, he paused. *2B? That's Elise's apartment number too. Building across from Elise's?* He looked up and smiled. *Thank you, old man.*

The drunk's occasional benefactor Hans Gelb had a clear line-of-sight across the street and through Elise's front window to the wall where the painting had hung. Fritz climbed the stairs and knocked at apartment 2B. No one was home. Or they didn't answer. He looked at his watch.

Tomorrow morning, I'll return with a thermos of coffee and stake out the place.

***

Fritz began his stakeout by sipping on the evil office coffee while studying Hans Gelb's photo. *This fellow is so plain he could lose himself in a crowd in a moment. Or maybe the driver's license photo doesn't do him justice?* Fritz had found no police records on Gelb. He wondered if his hunch was wrong.

He was an investigator who mixed hunches with facts. The latter could only take one so far, but by pursuing them one could often generate hunches because the human brain often made intuitive leaps. At least, his worked that way. He surmised scientists often experienced those same leaps. And, like them, he still had to gather more evidence to support the theories built from those few facts and hunches.

His suspect came out with a large, flat package he put in his car's backseat. Fritz already had checked the plate; the car belonged to Gelb. When he drove off, Fritz followed.

He has the painting. And I bet he has a buyer! Like Esther Brookstone, his goal was always to recover the painting and return it to its rightful owner as first priority, and put behind bars both seller and buyer as a second one. He lived for the first, but always wanted to do both.

After some twenty blocks, Hans's car turned into yet another alley. Fritz knew most of them in Vienna, but this was a new one for him.

He parked on the street and went into it, hunkering down behind yet another trash bin after spotting the approaching Mercedes-Benz entering the opposite end of the alley. Using his government-issued smart phone to trace the plate, Fritz found the Mercedes belonged to Boris Lagunov, an oligarch and one of Putin's biggest supporters. *Thank you, Federal Police database.*

He frowned. *The man might have diplomatic immunity.* Austrian authorities, considering their country in general and Vienna in particular as a center of the diplomatic universe just like the French, often handed that out too freely sometimes. That could be a complication if he tried to make an arrest.

But Labunov is most likely the buyer. Is an oligarch a fascist? he wondered. There wasn't much difference in his mind's eye because they both had histories of dealing in stolen artwork. The Nazis had stolen many works of art, many of them from Jews; Russian oligarchs were known to do that too, and not just from Jews.

Years ago, Esther had helped him return one painting where the buyer was a diplomat…

***

"Shall I hit the thief high and you low?" Fritz said to Esther, not wanting to put his new friend and co-art lover in too much peril.

"That's a good way for one or both of us to be shot," she said. "And we might damage the painting."

Strange priorities: she considers the painting more valuable than her life!

He summarized what they knew. "The provenance is now clear, *liebchen*. The *SS-Obersturmführer* steals the painting from that old Jew in Paris, he sells it to that VIP in the Vichy government, and it ends up with the VIP's son in Köln where it's stolen again by this female art thief, who's waiting now for the Hungarian military attaché to bring her money."

Esther nodded. "Anyone who says the black market in artwork is simple needs his head examined," she said. "I only want to grab the painting. Once it's returned, perhaps we can convince its rightful owner to lend it to a museum so everyone can view it."

"But I'd like to put both thief and buyer behind bars. You know you do too."

"Fat chance of doing that with this buyer," said Esther as this black Mercedes stopped near the female art thief. "He might even have diplomatic immunity, although the plates aren't diplomatic."

The diplomat stepped out of the car.

"Our Hungarian has the money in a briefcase." Fritz watched as the Hungarian pointed to first the small case and then the painting wrapped in its protective carton.

The thief gestured toward two trash bins up against the building's wall. The two, thief and buyer, went there, and the thief placed the package on top and peeled back some of the carton. The buyer smiled and nodded after his inspection and handed the briefcase to the woman.

"One briefcase full of money for a Renoir. Not quite a fair—where are you going?"

Esther had stood. "I have a plan."

She walked toward the two who were closing the deal. "You might want an authentication," she told the Hungarian, "because this thief often sells forged paintings."

"Who are you?" said the woman.

"I authenticate paintings. And I happen to know where you stole this one. I tried to authenticate it two weeks ago for its owner, but discovered it was a copy. The owner still wants it back, though. Sentimental attachment, I suppose. He sent me to negotiate its return."

"Is this true?" the Hungarian asked the thief.

"How the hell should I know?" She took a gun from her purse. "You can do what you want with the painting, but I'm taking the money."

"You are mistaken," the Hungarian said.

The sound of the shot echoed in the alley for seconds after the bullet hit the art thief's chest. Esther dove for the pavement. Before the thief fell, she got off a shot, hitting the buyer in the head. The Mercedes took off, burning rubber, and then quiet returned to the alley.

Fritz walked over and offered Esther a hand, pulling her to her feet.

"Was that all planned?"

Esther glanced at the two dead bodies. "Actually I was creating the plan in real time. But no, none of what happened was in my plan. The results still work for me, though. What do we do now?"

"We close the case and return the painting to its rightful owner."

Fritz later heard that the old man wept when the police returned his painting to him. As a young child, he had survived Terezin and was the last living relative of the original owner...

I wonder if Esther's trick will work here.

***

Hans, the art thief, approached this newer model Mercedes. Fritz watched as its passenger-side window lowered. *Gun!* Two shots. One bullet hit the painting. *No!* The other spun the thief around after he dropped the painting.

The window went back up. Boris exited from the driver's side, walked around the back of the car, and picked up the painting. That was when the thief shot the oligarch. The window lowered again. This time a bullet in the head finished Hans. There was some activity inside the Mercedes, and then it roared off.

Fritz approached the two bodies. *Almost déjà vu,* he observed. *Who could have guessed that art thievery could lead to such violence? Twice!*

He was happy he hadn't had to offer to authenticate the painting. He kicked the oligarch onto his back. *COD:*

one shot in the eye. Pistol caliber: TBD. He flipped over the thief's body and saw the bullet-proof vest. *That's a new wrinkle.* The thief hadn't trusted the Russian, and justifiably so. *In this case it's not clear there was any money!* From the beginning, the oligarch had possibly planned to take the painting without paying. *1956 proved Russians are more murdering bastards than Hungarians,* he mused with a frown. *And it continues!*

Fritz lifted the Caravaggio with care, fearing the worst. But only the old wood frame had been hit. *The good professor can certainly afford a new frame!*

Chapter Twenty-Four

Monday Afternoon: Dürnstein and Melk

As the riverboat had entered the Danube valley known as Wachau, Esther spotted vineyards on the slopes of the steep hills surrounding the river, hills that nearly became the walls of a canyon the river had formed. She loved vineyards and once had taken a course on oenology, although Great Britain couldn't compete against Austria, California, France, Italy, or Spain. Even wines from Argentina, Australia, Chile, and New Zealand did well in London compared to anything British. Unlike a total connoisseur, though, she believed any wine a person thought went well with a dish was the one they should serve. She avoided dessert wines with dessert, though, preferring sherry or port.

Wine had been part of her upbringing, although her parents limited themselves to bargain continental varieties they only imbibed on special occasions, her father giving her a taste every so often. The old vicar often quoted the American polymath, Benjamin Franklin, who said once that wine was "a constant proof that God loves us, and loves to see us happy." Esther had considered that ironic because her father all too often was a sour and dour old gentleman. *Maybe he didn't drink enough of God's gift?*

Those ramblings led her to think about how prehistoric human beings might have discovered wine. *Probably by accident?* She'd have to query some of her erudite friends about that. *Or maybe Bastiann will know?* Her husband was more a trivia collector. He even knew some chemical secrets: for example, how to make window cleaner and hand sanitizer. Some of his chemistry lessons had stuck with him, but not her. She only remembered pure alcohol was an essential ingredient of both, although she didn't know if it was the drinkable kind.

Those rambling associations accompanied her through narrow streets and into a small shop where she picked up a bottle of her favorite fragrance at a greatly reduced price compared to what it would cost in London. *Damn Brexit!* She almost bought aftershave for Bastiann but remembered he might have enough to last until the end of the trip. While inside, she saw Robert Winston walk by the shop. *What's he doing here? He wasn't on the bus.* She soon put that out of mind, though, discovering another shop with some interesting scarves.

In general, she had a great time in Dürnstein visiting shops and taking in the charms of the quaint old town. It was like many small, charming towns in Europe, though. Austria was full of charm. She had enjoyed the charm of the lake district more, but her afternoon tour had started off swimmingly.

Amy, Judith, Maria, and Cecilia were all on the tour too. They chatted up a storm on the bus. They went their separate ways in town, but everyone was due back at the bus for the continuation of the tour. Most made it on time. Those who didn't caused a delay of only five minutes.

There were other tourists, and local guides shepherded their flocks well. Then again, the town wasn't big enough for people to get too lost. She wrote her group's delays off to other things, like haggling over the price of items in little shops, an art she had mastered long ago.

Like the other women, Esther had worn trainers, always wary of cobblestoned streets. Europe was full of them. Could old-world charm be found in the ubiquitous threat of breaking a leg or an ankle? Prague, the land part of the cruise line's tour they'd skipped, was known for its cobblestones, for example. Called the "Golden City of a Hundred Spires," that old capital, largely undamaged by the Soviet occupation, even had an ancient castle full of cobblestones. She would have loved to do that land package before arriving at the riverboat, but things had been so rushed.

Once, before the Soviets left Czechoslovakia—the country's breakup into the Czech Republic and Slovakia occurred later—and in her capacity as an MI6 spy behind the Iron Curtain, she'd made a drop at a vendor's kiosk on the Charles Bridge in Prague, an easy task compared to some others she'd had. She even bought a sausage wrapped in rustic bread there. Not wanting to be obvious, her treat served as camouflage to take in the old bridge built over the Vlatava in 1357. It was named after Charles IV, Holy Roman Emperor, and had not suffered when the Soviet Union fell, as so much had.

That mission was a success, for both the drop and the sausage. She didn't like most types of sausage.

***

The next stop on the tour, *Stift Melk* AKA the Melk Abbey, also had historical significance. Esther knew her history, but seeing it—or what was left of it, as the case might be—made touring Europe all the more appealing.

She'd enjoyed Dürnstein but didn't have enough time on the bus to recover from her walk-about and prepare herself for the climb up the steep stairs to the abbey grounds. The small tour bus's driver had used his satnav to wind through the town's narrow streets and finally climb the steeper road to the visitors' car park. She then lugged herself up that awful staircase to the former garden and orangery. The other women left her behind, but she made it with calves protesting. It was some comfort to know the walk all the way from the town of Melk, with its long climb on the "Beggar's Stairway," would have been much more demanding.

From April to October, one can wander around the abbey's grounds and interior. After eating an acceptable pastry, a fast-food approximation to apple strudel, and drinking some hot tea in the outdoor café, all enjoyed as the other women babbled on about everything under the sun except the tour and, thankfully, not the murder investigation, they all started wandering. Entering the building and walking around was easy in comparison to those stairs. Now she was the one who left the women and other tourists behind as certain details grabbed her attention.

Although the building was like an assembled jigsaw puzzle, it was an example of Baroque architecture in its purest form. Many of its features were centuries more recent than its founding date of 1089, but the atmosphere of ancient political struggles and religious intrigues still prevailed. It had served as the setting for the movie *The Name of the Rose* based on Umberto Eco's book by the same title. *Hmm. Another good Sean Connery movie!*

In the *Stiftkirche* AKA the Abbey Church, she tried to resist the urge to cross herself. King Henry the Eighth's Anglican Church wasn't Catholic, but nearly so, and her father had been a vicar, so she finally gave in to the urge in front of the main altar. She then chose to visit the Altar of St. Benedict over St. Kolomon's because the monks in the abbey were Benedictine, even though the

Irishman Kolomon had been the patron saint of Austria until the newly sanctified St. Leopold, dead Bavarian royalty, took over that role. She had no idea what an Irishman had been doing in Austria, leaving his body and jaw bones at the abbey with his skull elsewhere. She couldn't wait to say to Bastiann, "Don't lose your head like St. Kolomon."

She was admiring St. Benedict's ornate altar when she heard a noise behind her. Across the way, standing in front of St. Kolomon's altar with its own nave, a man pointed a gun in her direction. She hit the floor, and the bullet smashed into the wall. The noise from the gun reverberated around the church.

She jumped up, but her assailant had done a runner. Three monks were now trotting towards her, their robes flowing behind them.

"Hide behind some pews!" she called out in German, not knowing if they understood English. They, along with her, followed that advice. *Will I ascend to heaven to join St. Benedict?*

Another shot! The bullet tore through the old wood above her head. Silence then reigned in God's house.

***

The agent was already at the abbey and watched the bus load of tourists unload. She spotted the woman she'd been following, the only pageboy haircut in the group. *Why the knapsack?* The riverboat passengers did a lot of walking on their tours, even the so-called easy ones, so most didn't weigh themselves down like that. Some women didn't even carry purses, using instead those little tourist pouches strapped around their waists.

The tourist group moved up the long flight of stone steps from the parking lot, so she followed...and then had to pretend she was interested in the gardens as most from the tourist group snacked at the little outdoor café.

The old English woman was holding court with the four American women, but they went their separate ways after finishing, first the English woman and then the two pairs.

Will I be as spry as she is at her age? She knew the woman's history in MI6 and admired the courage she'd shown performing her duties behind the Iron Curtain. *Was it all wasted effort?* Many people thought the Cold War was won because the Soviet hegemony couldn't compete economically with the West. She thought efforts like those of Esther Brookstone and many others had at least hastened the Soviet Union's collapse. *But isn't Russia just as bad? If not worse?*

The agent had been so intent on studying the English woman she hadn't realized the one she was supposed to follow had disappeared. Most everyone was now inside.

I'll find her in here somewhere, she thought as she followed.

But the agent wasn't familiar with the abbey's interior. She was still wandering corridors when she heard the shots.

It appeared no one was hurt, though, so the agent was glad she had resisted running to help. She'd backed away. She hadn't blown her cover. *And the old woman proves yet again she's resilient.*

The agent had a good idea about who'd done the shooting. *But why?*

***

"I understand you're involved in a murder investigation on the riverboat," said the pudgy inspector from the town below with the abbey's same name.

Although Esther had wanted to leave enough time to sample the abbey's excellent wines, she and others had waited in the car park along with the three monks and her four new friends, and watched his small patrol vehicle struggle up the road. *With his pounds onboard, no wonder.*

Other patrol cars soon followed. Everyone had gone inside except for the monks and one officer, and the remainder along with the tourists were now sitting around a long wooden table that filled a small room, although the inspector's youngest aides were standing as stiff as old statues of saints, taking in the discussion.

The words "murder investigation" had caused Esther to go through in her mind the list of everyone from the riverboat who'd been on the tour and when she'd last seen them. She even included the tour guide who had traveled with them all along but had left them alone at each stop. That list had all the characteristics of the investigation at large—anyone could have taken those shots. But no one in her mind's eye matched the mental image she had of the shooter. She then focused on that mental image, knowing the inspector would be asking for her description.

Not the usual small-town copper, Esther decided. *He's found out some things already.*

"That's correct, Inspector Schmidt."

Their conversation was interrupted when the officer who'd been with the monks entered and saluted the inspector. "Sir, we have searched all the grounds," he said in German, "but we found no signs of the shooter."

But definitely someone from our tourist group, observed Esther, looking around the table. *I shall avoid saying that, though.* A frisson went down her spine. *Someone who wants to kill those in charge of the investigation! Even my four friends are suspect because they weren't with me.*

With that realization, Esther said to the inspector, "Could I excuse myself for a moment? I must warn my husband. He's the Interpol agent in charge of the investigation on the riverboat. There are two other presumed murders, by the way, that took place on a tour to the lake district."

"The federal authorities, the *Bundespolizei,* have that case." He waved a hand. "Yes, please go and warn your husband. But I'll need a description of the shooter when you return."

"I'll make a visit to the WC too, if you don't mind."

"Too much information, but please do so. We're going to be here for a while."

But it didn't take that long because the inspector finished with her first, focusing mostly on the shooting and what the shooter looked like. He also released all the riverboat passengers and other tourists who'd seen nothing, including her four friends, who had only heard secondhand about what had happened. *Claimed to see and hear nothing,* thought Esther. One of them is lying.

***

In the little bus on the return trip, she had some pain in her chest and some vertigo even while sitting. *Lunch indigestion? Stress from what happened?* She asked Amy and Judith about her symptoms.

"You should see a doctor, someone who can do an EKG," said Amy. Judith nodded. "Just to be sure."

Esther had studied Judith's body language carefully. Amy's partner was a bit acerbic at times and seemed too possessive, but she'd known plenty of heterosexual couples where one partner attempted to micromanage the activities of the other. *Do I do that to Bastiann?* She thought not, because her affable Dutchman could be so stubborn at times. *Maybe he gives in more when there's not too much to lose by giving in?* She loved him. From what she observed, Amy and Judith were in love too. That always meant partners had to have a meeting of minds in a relationship. *But is it possible either Amy or Judith knew Dragavei before?* They'd been in Europe before, after all. *Maybe many times?* She'd have to check on that!

Esther agreed with the doctor's advice, though. When the bus stopped for a light, she exited. She'd decided to error on the side of caution. She waved at the concerned Amy, pointed to her left breast, and then at a sign along the street. *No way am I going to broadcast this all over Weissenkirchen.*

She popped into the walk-in clinic she'd spotted.

"What's the verdict, doctor?" she later asked the GP when he came into the exam room with the EKG results. She didn't care for him all that much. He had cold hands; so had the tech.

"Your BP's fine and your panel shows no abnormalities. Do you have a cardiologist, *Frau* Brookstone?"

"Do I need one?"

"There are some irregularities in the EKG. You should have an echocardiogram. We can't do that here, only in a hospital. Old women often don't have the same symptoms as old men."

Esther only paid attention to his statement about the EKG results, or she would have made some nasty comments about his use of the words "old women." Instead she said, "What kind of irregularities?"

"A bit hard to explain. EKG's are complicated and difficult to interpret, and harmless irregularities are common."

"Stop blathering in your medical mumbo-jumbo. If I can play Scarlatti, I should be able to understand an EKG. Am I going to have a heart attack?"

"You might only have some gas putting more pressure than normal on your heart, which is why they call it heartburn." *Lunch indigestion?* "Or a scare recently." Stress from what happened at the abbey? "And traffic can be hectic in Melk's narrow streets, you know." *I wasn't driving!*

"I live in London. Melk could fit in Piccadilly Square."

"Return to your riverboat, *Frau* Brookstone. We can call a taxi. But see a cardiologist when you return to London, just to be on the safe side."

"I'll do that."

What a waste! They had traveler's insurance, but the inconclusive exam results left her worrying. *Should I tell Bastiann?*

As she walked by the receptionist on her way out, Esther glared at her...only for the sin of being young.

Chapter Twenty-Five

Monday: Weissenkirchen

In the late afternoon, Esther provided Bastiann with details about her deadly adventure at the abbey.

"Definitely someone from the boat," he said. "Only authorities know you're assisting me." He thought a moment. "Correction: I told one of the Bulgarian couples."

"Hopefully not the one on my tour. I could have been killed, Bastiann. Or one of those nice, handsome monks would have gone to heaven to wear his halo sooner than expected." She emitted a nervous laugh.

"First Dragavei, then the drownings at Attersee, and now this," mused Bastiann. "Too much violence. I'm going to try to convince the captain to tighten security both onboard and on tours."

"If we discover who killed Dragavei, everything will be resolved. There must be something in his past that will offer a clue. People don't murder someone for no reason."

Bastiann thought of Robert Winston's sighting of Dragavei at Esther's gallery. *Is Esther somehow connected?* She would have told him if she knew, of course, but he didn't want to alarm her by asking, especially when he feared what her answer might be.

"Terrorists do," he reminded her.

She nodded. "This doesn't smell like terrorism in the modern sense of that word. I'll admit I was terrorized, but I was in more delicate situations when I was in MI6."

"You'll have to tell me about them sometime."

"You know I can't. The point is: We're going to have to work our arses off and find out what's going on *tout de suite*. I want to see some of Vienna, after all. I have fond memories of the place."

"Before I was around, or after?"

"As Bertrand Russell might say, that's not an exclusive 'or,' love. But we digress. It's not only about who killed Dragavei. It's about who killed the Bulgarians at the lake."

"Two different MOs, to be sure. By the way, I forgot. After my interview of the Culianu couple, I checked some of their background, including the website of Ihrin Culianu's gift shop." He showed her on the Apple monitor.

"All cheap junk. Oh, I see what you mean. Some of those knives look like the one stuck in Dragavei's back. But remember Robert Winston said it was a cheap copy. Every gift shop in Europe might sell trash like that to tourists."

"Knock-offs or not, all those knives are lethal. I added 'gift shop has similar knives' to her fiche."

"And Winston's presence in Dürnstein," she said, "without being on the tour."

"Interesting. Could he have taken the shots?"

"Too tall. And he was in a sports coat and tie. Maybe he had personal business there?"

"And maybe I'll ask him what that was."

***

After her report to Bastiann and leaving him to his work, Esther went to the lounge to chat with people. Maria, Cecilia, and their significant others were now there playing bridge, so she introduced herself. Bastiann had told her about their story. *The name for the tour, "The Romantic Danube," seems to be taken literally by many passengers!*

She smiled. Even with the investigation, Bastiann and she were squeezing a bit of romance in.

In the boat's lounge, there were also two holies sporting their dog collars: one chatting with the Californian group, and another alone with his wife. She decided she'd save Bastiann and herself some time and use the second to screen the first. *They must know each other.* She was waiting for her target's wife to leave when she heard a raspy whisper.

"It seems you're more interested in the passengers than the scenery, Esther," said Captain Janssen.

She looked over her shoulder to see a smiling face.

"Sander, you're very perceptive. I'm helping Bastiann. I'm sitting here trying to decide who here will be the first people I interview."

He came around the small sofa and took a seat beside her. "It's odd, you know. If one were to believe media reports, you should be running the investigation." She frowned. "Don't get me wrong. Bastiann has some positive press too, although it's mostly in association with you. I did read one report about how he helped save a kidnapping victim in Casablanca, for example."

"There's no such thing as positive press, at least not for the person in the news." She then thought he might take that the wrong way. "Please don't misunderstand me either. Solid, fact-based media reports are absolutely necessary to keep the public informed, but I deplore sensationalism and the use of false data. And backstory and follow-up are absolutely necessary so readers have all the information."

"All I'm saying is that the investigation is in good hands, no matter who's running the show."

"That person is definitely Bastiann. I have no authority, and I shall be very careful not to leave the door open for accusations that my amateur's status tainted the investigation when the murderer comes to trial." She paused to take another quick look around the lounge. *Is the reverend's wife preparing to leave?* "And rest assured, Sander, that neither Bastiann nor I seek attention from the media. We want this investigation to end probably more than the cruise line does."

"Because it's your honeymoon?"

"Yes, that to, but mostly because we have no desire for fame. And heaven forbid the public thinks we're some strange sleuths who must solve a murder even on their honeymoon."

Sander stood but thought a moment. "If Bastiann can end the investigation without a lot of fanfare, the company will surely show their appreciation by giving you two a discount on another cruise. They're already very grateful that this cruise could continue." He gave her a little salute. "Have a good day, Esther."

***

After the captain went on his way, Esther turned her attention once again to the cleric. She studied him at a distance. He appeared uncomfortable in a sports shirt with the clergyman's collar, wore pleated khakis making him look like an Oxford student, and sported black trainers that clashed with it all. He was likely in his mid-forties with some white in his perfectly combed hair. *In spite of the apparel, a truly handsome man who might turn some heads among the younger ladies in his parish*

She hadn't met the wife, but the woman seemed comfortable with her station in life and could be an acceptable ornament next to the vicar as the congregation left the church. She approached the cleric after hearing his wife announce she was going to visit the gift ship. Esther had already done so; she'd bought some jewelry.

"Do I detect a fellow Anglican?" she said as a way to announce herself, interrupting his perusal of the list of activities for the remainder of the tour. "My father used to be a vicar. My name is Esther Brookstone." She offered a hand.

He stood and greeted her, his hand warm and smooth. *Not a day's hard work in this bloke's history,* she observed. He had a pale, pasty look, and thin lips. His face was as expressive as a store window's mannequin, complete with a few cracks from age.

"Reverend Madison, ma'am. Arthur Madison. Are you enjoying your cruise?"

She sat, and he followed suit. "It's become more interesting than I'd bargained for. As you know, my new husband finds himself in charge of a murder investigation. I'm helping. I have some questions for you, if you don't mind."

He nodded and smiled. "No spiritual problems, then?"

"Perhaps one: a troubling religious experience," she said, thinking of that cave near Ephesus, Turkey. "But we can discuss that later. Did you know Mr. Dragavei?"

"At the welcoming party, I made the remark to June, my wife, that he appeared to be a troubled chap. Body language is telling, and I'm used to employing it when comforting my flock."

Like a detective. And like I'm reading you now. "Did you chat with him?"

"Some people, like you, have approached me, Esther, but we're on vacation like you and your husband. I won't approach people who appear troubled but aren't from my congregation.

I know them well, so that's different. Otherwise, privacy rules."

"No proselytizing then?" she said with a smile.

"Anglicans don't proselytize."

She nodded, not willing to debate the point. "Do you know the other man-of-the-cloth aboard?" She didn't point, but Arthur looked at the Californian group.

"Reverend Tom?" She nodded. "He's from our American side, the Episcopal Church. I've chatted with him. He's the leader of that Californian group, but he's travelling alone…for obvious reasons, if you know what I mean."

Esther did: *Code for Tom's being a gay man.* That wasn't obvious to Esther, but she knew a major difference existed between Anglicans and Episcopalians. She'd never understood the big deal, as long as one was open about it. And it might mean the English vicar was a bigot. Not every Episcoplian priest was gay, and she often surmised some Anglican ones were but hid it. *We live in a strange world!*

"He's part of that large group of Californians, right?"

"Mrs. Dawson in their group is a travel agent who helps organize tours for church members." Arthur chuckled. "They call them religious study tours. The current one's purpose is to study and compare the parallel development of Protestant and Catholic movements in Europe. In particular, Martin Luther's Reformation. Sounds very academic, I must say."

"And as good an excuse as any other to go abroad and have some fun. I'd guess Henry the Eighth's break with the pope was likely more motivated by his desire for a divorce than anything Martin Luther did."

Arthur inclined his head in partial agreement. "Episcopalians are probably closer to Luther's ideas than

Anglicans. Except for our allegiance to the British monarchy, we're more Catholic. But you know that."

Esther wasn't going to debate that point either. "So all the Californians are filled with God's spirit?"

"Reverend Tom is. The others are likely more often filled with spirits." He smiled at his own joke. "But they're all young and healthy. They go on the level three tours and do a lot of biking. Perhaps they're the future for a more moral America."

"Indeed. Yanks are questionable in that sense at times, especially certain politicians. But ours aren't saints either, by a long shot."

"The Empire is fading, ma'am, and we're still struggling with the aftermath of Brexit. The EU is in decline too. China, Russia, and the US are the new bullies on the world stage right now." He laughed. "Call brat-like behavior what you like, but I see it as a lack of a moral underpinning in general." He eyed her. "Where was your father a vicar, Esther?"

Going to check up on me, are you? "Hull...in Yorkshire. I grew up there. It's strange how much you sound like him."

"Accent-wise? I hope not. You don't have that accent either."

"I've had a few years and spoken enough foreign languages to lose it."

She spent the rest of their time discussing the vicar and his wife's backgrounds as well as those of the Californians, including Reverend Tom.

She then moved on to the American physicist to continue her chatty, informal interviews to complement Bastiann's more formal ones, especially with persons he believed were beyond suspicion. She didn't mind meeting new people, and who knew? Maybe she'd ferret out a clue or two in the process. *One never knows what people might have seen or heard.*

Name: Beatriz June Madison
Age: 62
PoB: London
C: English
Res: Alfriston
Occ: housewife?
L@TOD: lounge
Notes: No interview—not a suspect.

Name: Arthur Madison
Age: 63
PoB: Leeds
C: English
Res: Alfriston
Occ: vicar
L@TOD: lounge
Notes: Esther interviewed him—not a suspect.

***

Jackson Ford, the physicist, had the scruffy appearance of an old man with his Scottish shepherd's cromach, a person whom Esther imagined she might encounter on a hike near her castle. He looked up from his book.

"Can I help you?"

She offered a hand. "Esther Brookstone."

He nodded, stood, shook it, and then took his seat again. She sat next to him on the small lounge sofa.

"I earlier saw you chatting with Professor Elise Mayer."

"Yes. A charming, intelligent woman." He leaned into her. "My wife might have been somewhat jealous, but we were only talking about the Danube's locks. Some on the river are more than a century old. Mostly me talking to her, I suppose, but we also talked about Viennese composers."

"But you're reading a Deaver paperback now? Not exactly non-fiction, I dare say."

"I found it in Dürnstein. It's well written. Historical fiction, or at least a historical setting, a thriller about Nazis. The title is the translation of the German word for zoo. It's much better than that long series he has."

"About the paraplegic forensics specialist," she said with a nod. "I visit out-of-the-way used bookshops too. You can even find stands in some marketplaces."

"I had this dream of owning one when I retired…a bookstore, I mean. But then reading went out of style in our country, and bookstores started to close their doors. That virus a few years ago did them no good either. Everyone started buying online."

"Maybe in your country. In England, there are still many around. In the rest of Europe too, as you know." She eyed her fellow booklover. "You know I'm helping my husband?" He nodded. "Did you ever meet the victim, Maxim Dragavei?"

"I had no idea about what had happened or who he was until my wife told me. Martha's more gregarious than I am, so she's met a lot of passengers."

"Did she meet him?"

"No, and she told me about your husband's taking charge of the investigation. Makes perfect sense to me. All his suspects are here onboard, right?"

She smiled. "Not everyone onboard is a suspect. But someone might have seen or overheard something that could help Bastiann in the investigation."

"My wife said many saw Mr. Dragavei at the welcoming party, their *Oktoberfest* in miniature. I'm sorry to say we can't confirm even that. We weren't very sociable and went to bed early. All my information about him is secondhand and not too reliable."

"I understand." Esther stood. "If you or your wife think of anything, please let me or my husband know."

What a nice, odd man, Esther observed as she moved on. *And definitely not a suspect.* He wouldn't have needed a knife. He could have beaten Dragavei to death with that cromach! His personality reminded her of Nicholas Greenly, the erudite Oxford professor who had given her information about Bernini and his sculptures. *Old academic types. They can be good lovers— cuddly, stuffed toys to play with!*

Name: Martha Ford
Age: 73
PoB: Lowell, MA
C: US
Res: Cambridge, MA
Occ: retired schoolteacher
L@TOD: lounge
Notes: No interview; not a suspect.

Name: Jackson Ford
Age: 74
PoB: Schenectady, NY
C: US
Res: Cambridge MA
Occ: retired professor
L@TOD: lounge
Notes: Esther interviewed him; not a suspect.

Chapter Twenty-Six

Tuesday Morning: Vienna

Vienna isn't typically Austrian; it's as cosmopolitan as London and Paris. It's the capital of Austria and its largest city, containing nearly one third of the country's population. It has the sixth-largest population within city limits among EU cities. Until the beginning of the twentieth century, it was the largest German-speaking city in the world. Today, it's the second-largest German-speaking city after Berlin, and still a cultural center reflecting its rich history as the capital of the Austro-Hungarian Empire, where many composers and artists became famous...and where modern psychoanalysis began with Freud.

The riverboat docked in Vienna around 8 a.m. Esther and Bastiann had their breakfast and waited for their tour in the lounge. She knew he wasn't accomplishing much in the investigation and was frustrated as a consequence, so it would distract him.

It was another example of the standard city tour the cruise company offered, with bus rides and walking involved. Esther saw Cecilia and Maria with the Californians and others on their bicycles ready to take off on another tour of more difficulty. She waved and they waved back. *Oh, to be young again!* She'd rode a bicycle as a child, but hadn't done so for years. *Maybe I'll have Bastiann buy me one for riding around my castle.* Considering the hills around her property, though, maybe that wasn't such a good idea, but she still thought it might be good exercise. *I'd be risking life and limb in the city.*

Once again Esther and Bastiann used the tap-to-pair feature with the wooden lollipop the guide was holding for all to see. The chip inside it synched their transceivers with the guide's. From then on, they could hear everything she said. *Ah, the wonders of modern technology,* Esther mused. *How much simpler her spy work would have been with it!*

The guides were usually locals provided by local tourist agencies. They weren't permanent employees of the cruise line, which hired them to run the tours at the various ports of call along the Danube. Some dressed in traditional costumes like their guide for the lake district tour had done. All knew the local area and customs and spoke excellent English as well as the local vernacular, and they often spoke some other languages.

They climbed onto the tour bus and took seats towards the middle.

"Look, we have that doctor and her partner as fellow passengers," Esther said to Bastiann as she spotted the couple also climbing aboard.

"You don't have to whisper," he said. "They're probably married, you know."

"I'm not whispering because of that. The doctor fits my profile of the assassin."

"Oh, please. Am I to suppose she came all the way from San Diego to kill Maxim Dragavei?"

"Maybe it's only a question of his insulting them sometime in the past. Remind me of what the partner does."

"I don't carry all the facts of the case in my head."

"Most are on your mobile."

He sighed, pulled the smart phone from his coat pocket, and checked.

"She runs an assisted care and nursing home facility in La Jolla. My, that does sound suspicious, doesn't it?" He seemed to be saying that a lot to her. *I'm not getting early dementia!* That never worried her; the advice to see a cardiologist did.

The couple took seats opposite Esther and Bastiann. Amy, who had the aisle seat across from Bastiann, reached over and tapped the Interpol agent on the shoulder.

"Hello, Agent van Coevorden. Are you and your new bride enjoying your honeymoon? I hope so. Judith's and mine was such a disaster."

"Oh, why was that?" Bastiann gave Esther an I-told-you-so wink and nod.

"We were in California's wine country when those awful brush fires broke out. All hands on deck, as they say. Judith has EMT experience, and I'm a doctor. We volunteered to help."

"God put us there to help," Judith leaned over to say.

"Were you working in a hospital?" said Bastiann.

"Mobile ones. Made me think of *MASH*. We kept pace with the firefighters."

Amy shook her head and made a moue. "We were treating smoke inhalation, burns, and broken bones for the most part. We were well supplied, but the fires were just too much. An entire town was destroyed."

"Yes, terrible," Esther said, remembering the news. "Australia had it worse, though. Practically a whole continent burned."

"It's not a competition," snapped Judith.

Amy patted her partner on her knee. "Easy. You're misinterpreting what Esther said."

I have the idea Judith doesn't like me, thought Esther. *Oh well…*

"But your honeymoon was ruined," Bastiann said, eyeing Esther.

Judith leaned over Amy again to say, "We made up for it with a later cruise on the Rhine. Lovely trip. I do hope the weather holds for us now. A lot better than London fog, right Esther?"

Attempting to wave the white flag, are you? Esther recalled her reflections on wine and vineyards upon entering the Wachau. California's wine country might be a nice place to visit sometime with Bastiann, but that state was so far away from London. Of course, Australia was even farther. She still would mention that possibility to Bastiann. *If he retires, we can do more traveling.*

"English weather isn't our best tourist attraction," she said. "When I lived in Oxford, which is northwest of London, we sometimes had better weather. Enough gloominess to keep a Londoner happy, though. It's interesting how the good days often occurred during exams. You'd think the good Lord wanted to punish the poor students even more. I have an old school chum who lives near Wantage, not far from Oxford. That whole Thames Valley can have nice weather at times, although winter tends not to be."

"Did you teach there?" Amy said.

"My husband at that time did. And he did research. I was but an academic's dutiful housewife."

"And ardent picketer in support of unions, pound animals, Alan Turing—"

Judith interrupted Bastiann. "The gay mathematician?"

"The hero of World War II," Esther said through pressed lips. "Her Majesty's government then wanted to reward him by curing him of his gayness."

"When were you picketing for all that?" said Amy.

"When I was at Oxford. I don't remember the exact year."

"He was treated so badly," said Judith.

"And Oscar Wilde too, to name another victim of the Commonwealth's justice. And Bastiann exaggerates. I didn't want to cause too many problems for Albert."

"British royals were whacking off heads before the French Revolution did it in assembly-line fashion to their own royals," Bastiann said, "both figuratively and literally. Torture, even gay bashing, is an English tradition as old as Yorkshire pudding."

"Which is more like quiche," said Esther, playing along with Bastiann's teasing of the Yanks. "but it's a side dish. I have good recipes for both."

But Judith made a more serious turn in the conversation's path. "Waterboarding of those suspected terrorists by the CIA was awful too."

That took the four into politics. Because their political predilections were similar, Esther didn't consider it all that much fun. She was happy when the tour bus started on its journey.

***

They went around the *Ringstrasse*, seeing stately old buildings and dodging new trams all appearing to go the wrong way next to the bus. Their transceivers received the guide's descriptions, which Esther enjoyed more when she was talking about art and music related venues. During the walking tour, they had a chance to enjoy coffee and chocolate *Sachertorte*, a decadent snack. Esther doubted the walking compensated for the calories, but she also took the opportunity to pop into some galleries along the way. The artwork on sale was overpriced. She mentioned that to Bastiann.

"Maybe one has to get away from areas with all the tourist traffic," he said. "Your gallery has much more reasonable pricing compared to those chic galleries in central London."

She refrained from asking why her gallery wasn't chic. Knowing her husband, he was only using "chic" as a synonym for "overpriced," which was all too often the case.

Back on the bus, Bastiann mentioned Sergio Moretti, Esther's friend; Bastiann knew he lived in Vienna. He thought Esther might want to give her fellow art lover a ring. Bastiann had last seen him in that city.

"I thought we might visit him while we were here," she said. "Now that we're married, you no longer have any reason to be jealous. And his wife is a pip. But he's now in New York, of all places, working with the FBI as a consultant as they try to find out who used a kidnapping to do an art heist."

"Did the kidnapping victim survive?" Bastiann said, remembering all too well the case where Philippa was shot.

"Yes, although the poor dear is traumatized. She lost three valuable paintings, after all. They're still trying to find them."

"That sounds like a case you'd do well on."

"Don't tell Sergio, but they requested me first. Our friend Castilblanco reminded the FBI about my expertise, and I recommended Sergio because of our upcoming river cruise."

She didn't mention her retirement from the Yard had made the FBI lose interest. Sergio no longer had an official connection either, but he was a man. *Oh well...*

She snuggled closer to him. "I knew I'd be occupied with higher priority items."

"Their loss, my gain. Ah, Amy and Judith again."

After the couple took their same seats, Amy leaned across the aisle again and said, "I don't suppose you've found out what they injected into that poor victim."

"Diprivan. It's often used in day-surgeries as an anesthetic."

"It's called Michael Jackson Juice in the States," said Judith. "Of course, Moonwalk Michael's doctor was prescribing it incorrectly. Sometimes it doesn't pay to have a personal physician."

"Michael and Prince found that out the hard way," Esther said.

"And it would have made it easy to stick a knife in the back," said Bastiann. "I mean Dragavei's back. You were right, Amy, about that, and that the assailant successfully aimed for the heart."

"Couldn't have done it better myself," said Esther. "A very professional job, I dare say. Amy, you might have needed Judith's muscle, though." Esther enjoyed their shocked expressions. "Only joking. I can't imagine why two such lovely women would do such a thing. Unless—" Bastiann lightly elbowed her. "—unless he insulted you both sometime in the past. People can be terribly homophobic."

"We never talked to him!" Judith said.

"Easy, girl," Amy said to Judith. "Esther's not homophobic, are you, Esther?"

"Heavens no, my dear." Esther smiled, more because she was remembering the thief who had stolen the Bernini bust. "The Labour Party has a huge umbrella that welcomes everyone. We've grown up a bit in Britain since that Turing incident, thank God."

The guide's voice came over their transceivers again, ending their chin wag, and the tour continued.

***

In the afternoon, they visited *Schönbrunn*, the summer castle of Maria Theresa, the last Hapsburg, a family that dominated East European politics for centuries. When Bastiann made a comment to Esther about that, she wondered about the empress being the last Hapsburg; she'd had sixteen children, after all.

"I suppose that might be an explanation for all the rooms here, although it was more likely only an ostentatious display, braggadocio about having the castle with the most rooms among all her inbred royal cousins. And that 'last Hapsburg' bit only means Napoleon put a stop to all that royal nonsense when he declared himself emperor. It's sad the French Revolution's equality, fraternity, and liberty went by the wayside with the Little Corporal, much to Beethoven's chagrin. Give a leader too much leeway and he becomes a despot. Or she, in the case of the Iron Lady."

"I agree with your mishmash of history for the most part. The US's decline began with her friend Ronald Reagan, Thatcher's conservative partner. They both might be better than some recent fascist personalities, though. Just my opinion, of course, worth about as much as the success I've had with my investigation. Shall we wander in the gardens?"

They wandered a bit and then found a nice bench. For October, the day was splendid. It was sunny, air a bit crisp, and the sky was an intense blue. Esther supposed the more south they went, the more warmer the days would be. Would Budapest be stifling? Enough leaves were turning in the empress's park to challenge any painter's palette.

Other tourists were wandering about. Esther spotted the Hungarians, Eszter and Janos. She waved but the pair didn't see her. *They appear to be in a hurry to go somewhere!*

She mentioned them to Bastiann. "Some nationalities go overboard with spices," she said, making small talk while enjoying the ordered landscape. "The Hungarians believe paprika needs to be on everything, Mexicans even put chili on papaya, and Indians go overboard with the cumin. And so forth."

"Now that would be an interesting combination— Hungarian *goulash* and Indian *tikka masala*, all accompanied by Mexican tacos. Because I'm half French, I prefer cuisine with more subtle flavoring. The riverboat's kitchen doesn't do too badly in that regard. I must compliment the chef when we meet him at his Table. That's tomorrow, right?"

She nodded. She was surprised he remembered because she thought he'd lost track of days. She was happy to see him relax. He hadn't done much of that since Dragavei was murdered.

"You can take me to your favorite Parisian restaurant to sample fine French cooking," she said. "I can't imagine finding a suitable French restaurant in London that's reasonably priced, especially now during the downturn. Of course, almost anything is better than plain British dining."

He smiled. "You haven't tried haggis yet. We'll go through Edinburgh on the way to your castle, although the best might be found there in January."

"Your castle too now, my dear old fellow. But you will never find me eating haggis, in January or otherwise. Scots make some strange gastronomic choices. If we ever turn the castle into an inn, I'll serve only Indian food. I'm fond of it."

"I'll take you to a fine restaurant in Paris on our tenth anniversary to try to change your mind."

She made a moue. "I might not make that date, love. I might be singing with angels by then. One never knows."

Bastiann frowned. She knew he was depressed by such talk. She was saved when he also spotted the Hungarian couple striding along at a brisk pace.

"Power-walkers, aren't they?" said Bastiann. "And when these lovely gardens should be enjoyed while strolling slowly through them. In their case, to celebrate their anniversary, they should be holding hands like two young people in love." He thought a moment. "Aren't they young for this cruise? But they're legit. I checked. Like East Germans, Hungarians kept good records during the Soviet era. Their grandparents were given a hard time after the 1956 Revolution. I doubt if their grandchildren now have much love for the right-wing politicians in charge of Hungary either."

"The grandparents certainly wouldn't see much difference between their current lot and the Nazis, nor between them and the Soviets, for that matter. Say, they're acting a bit strangely."

They watched as a runner passed by the pair and appeared to receive something from Janos Rakoczy, as if the two were in a relay race.

"Did he pass something off to that jogger?" Bastiann said. "I needed some binoculars."

"And perhaps vice versa? My, that jogger runs well. Even in my youth, I couldn't run like that. I always had to turn about and kick my brothers in the goolies when they chased me for being a brat."

"It could only be the case of an accidental jostle," said Bastiann, "but I'll query them this evening. The other couples I have my eye on are out and about too. I saw them inside, but I lost them here in the gardens. Have you seen them?"

"The gardens are huge. And they could still be inside. I wouldn't have minded taking a nap in one of those old beds. Princess on a pea, as it were. And frolicking with you before the nap, as the empress must have done to produce all those children."

"I know you're tough, Esther, but sometimes you're a sweet, incurable, and lecherous romantic."

"It would be fun to time-travel back to that era, but with my luck, I'd be the empress's maid, washing out her knickers every blessed morning. Or her brats' nappies."

***

The agent had followed the tour group inside the castle. It wasn't hard for him to feign interest in old tapestries and furniture—his checkered sports shirt, bow tie, and khakis made him look like a nerdy tourist, and it was easy to keep an eye on the two couples they were tracking.

His female counterpart was doing the same thing, but she had joined the guided tour group. Other tourists not from the riverboat had joined that group too, taking advantage of the free descriptions. The riverboat's transceivers weren't allowed. *Completely nonsensical,* he observed, *considering the cacophony of many languages from Arabic to Zulu.* Pictures weren't allowed either. *Maybe the tapestries and paintings should have glass covers like the Mona Lisa?*

He noticed the Interpol agent chatting with one man. He thought the agent might be incompetent but gave him the benefit of the doubt. It wasn't like he had much information to work with. Interpol's databases couldn't compare to theirs.

When the tour finished inside the castle, everyone went outside on their own, mostly as couples or families, to enjoy the well-manicured gardens and sunshine. His female colleague joined him there.

"I'll take the Bulgarians," she said, "and you take the Romanians. Watch them carefully. Someone might contact them."

"How do you know that?" he queried.

"It's logical. It's the ideal place." She smiled. "And HQ just informed me to expect it. They're stuck on the boat until it reaches Budapest, but their handlers probably won't let them run without a leash for that long. We can scoop all of them up if contact is made."

Unlike Esther and Bastiann, they didn't have the Hungarians under surveillance. The Bulgarians and Romanians played their roles of tourists to perfection.

They met again in the parking lot.

"We need to tell HQ they had it wrong," he said.

"Or they missed someone," she said.

Chapter Twenty-Seven

Tuesday Afternoon: Vienna

When they returned to the riverboat, a reporter was waiting for Bastiann. Jana Graf looked like she'd just entered college—a small blond-haired young woman with sparkling blue eyes belying her predatory expression. A bounce in her step and other attributes made Bastiann feel old. The captain introduced them and then left them in the nearly empty lounge except for two passengers who were reading in the little side library. Now Bastiann was the interviewee.

She fired off a machine-gun blast of questions. *Maybe she's nervous?* He was too, because he didn't want to divulge too much about the investigation.

He had worked hard on his German over the years. Most of his difficulty stemmed from its similarity to Dutch, but he believed he'd mastered the language. He was surprised he didn't understand a lot of what the reporter said, but Austria's German was somewhat different from Berlin's. And she spoke it like an auctioneer. He held up his hand.

"Slow down, please. One question at a time. German isn't my mother tongue."

"Sorry. I'll start over. First question: If you can't arrest anyone, what will you do if you find the killer?"

She's likely referring to Interpol's tradition of working with local authorities and letting them make the arrests. That had changed somewhat because of necessity, mostly because of terrorism.

"If there are local police around, they'll arrest him. If not, I'll make the arrest. Interpol agents can do that now."

"Do you have a gun?"

"I usually don't carry one, and I certainly didn't pack one for this trip."

"But how will you arrest the murderer then?"

Bastiann sighed. *This is tiresome.* "*Fraulein* Graf, do you have any other questions?"

"*Ja.* And it's *Frau* Graf. As of three months ago." She laughed and showed him her rings. "What can you tell me about the victim?"

"I can't discuss that."

"Do you have any suspects?"

"I can't discuss that either."

"I'll take that as a no. What does the cruise line think about this case? Don't they want to squelch it?"

"You'll have to inquire with Captain Janssen. I have no official relationship with the cruise line."

"I already asked him. He was circumspect too, but more informative than you are. I gathered the cruise line has no official opinion. I only wanted to compare your answers." She turned to the next page in her little notebook. "It can't be good for them."

"Our cruise continues in a normal fashion. I'm making as few waves as possible. For the most part, the only passengers affected are my wife and me."

"But the rest of the passengers must be shocked."

"I suppose. Please don't ask them, though. That would only remind them of that horrible event that evening."

"Have you had a case like this before?"

Good question. Goes to my experience. He decided it was best to be honest.

"No. It's unusual. Riverboats are a safe mode of travel."

"What about that incident in Budapest a few years ago?"

Bastiann recalled the accident occurring there during a nighttime sightseeing cruise on the Danube. An optional nighttime tour by minibus was now offered.

"You should ask the Hungarian authorities about that."

"You said your wife is affected. Is that because you spend a lot of time on the investigation, or is your wife helping you?"

"Not officially."

"But she's ex-Scotland Yard, correct?"

"I won't deny it."

Jana smiled. "Only checking. I don't want to get anything wrong."

"Of course not."

Bastiann spent another ten minutes with the reporter. He hoped his interviews with passengers and crew caused less aggro for them...but not if one of them was the assassin.

***

Esther had left Bastiann alone with the reporter to go and listen to the cocktail-time pianist again, a clever chap who played everything from classical to Beatles' songs, which were also now classical in a sense. He played everything from memory. She only knew some short classical pieces by memory. This fellow had an immense talent for storing all that music in his head, although she knew the secret for the popular songs: memorize melody lines and ad lib chord progressions, riffs, and rhythms. That kind of improvisation was a skill she couldn't quite master because, at least for her, it all too often reduced to melody in the right hand, chords in the left.

She then noticed Arthur Madison was having a heated discussion with Viktor Demyankov, who had become red in the face trending towards purple. *Maybe the Bulgarian has high blood pressure?*

"It appeared you were having quite the barney with our fellow passenger," she said, approaching the vicar after Viktor had left the lounge. "Can I help with anything?"

The vicar stood, invited her to sit, and sat himself.

"That bloke is a complete nutter. He believes prostitution should be legalized in the EU. I was just giving him some stick."

"How'd you ever become involved in that discussion, Reverend Madison?"

Now it was the vicar's turn to become red. "I objected to a comment he made about our cruise director. He has a low opinion of the Irish."

"I see. I suppose I shouldn't say anything, but I must defend poor Caitlin as a citizen of the world because our country left the EU and hers didn't. I shall speak my mind. In many countries, police often look the other way when it comes to prostitution, mostly because there aren't enough of them, meaning the police, even to handle other crimes. The women shouldn't be prosecuted, only those who exploit them. I'd like more social workers and politicians to work on the conditions leading to prostitution too."

Arthur thought a moment. "Isn't that what is done?"

"Not enough. Gobshites turning runaways into kerb-crawlers is common enough, and sex trafficking is often as lucrative to blaggard entrepreneurs as the gun trade."

She recalled Ernesto, the cartel leader both she and Bastiann knew.

"Isn't it like the drugs? There's a demand, so providers meet the demand."

"Perhaps." She winked at him. "Women don't create the demand, Arthur."

"I can feel a sermon forming in my mind."

"It will be a difficult one to write, especially for the men in your flock."

***

The newlyweds ate an early dinner and then decided to eliminate the nighttime tour into Vienna, preferring to leave the evening for more detective work. After all, they had enjoyed Vienna at night before, although Bastiann still owed Esther an evening's spring or summer trip to Grinzing to dance waltzes and drink wine. And she had enjoyed the time spent visiting her old friend Sergio when authenticating his Botticelli, although that had all started before lunch.

All three couples Bastiann had labeled as more than persons of interest—Bulgarian, Hungarian, and Romanian—had been on the morning and afternoon tours with Esther and Bastiann, along with Amy and Judith. All three couples left for dinner and a concert featuring music by Mozart, making for a long day.

He couldn't help studying the couples on the day's tours but had learned nothing. He had other suspects in mind as well, but the Eastern Europeans were his focus. *Only because of their documentation? Or because they are Eastern Europeans?* Again he had guilty thoughts about profiling. Searches in Interpol databases had turned up nothing so far. *But a successful assassin wouldn't be in one of our databases, would he?*

Once Eastern European countries threw out the Soviets, Bastiann had known it was only a matter of time before they'd go back to being fascist, and Hungary, Italy, and Poland had only confirmed those predictions. Right-wing politics had been increasing in Europe since 2015, making those three not the only countries in the EU following that trend. France's presidential election had a right-wing candidate—fortunately she lost—and Germany's PM had been faced with right-wing protests, even violence. Even the US was still controlled by a right-wing minority. Everyone gave lip service to democracy, though, even China and Russia, and would continue to do so as long as the right won control in elections and could satisfy all their hunger for greed and power.

Is the GOP in America any different from Fidesz in Hungary or Law and Justice in Poland? Had Great Britain's Johnson been any different from Trump or Netanyahu? He didn't know. He also wondered what his old NYPD cop friend Castilblanco thought about what was going on in his country and around the world. His friend had fought to preserve democracy and freedom. He must be disappointed with how things turned out.

I can't get away from the case, but I must. It's unfair to Esther if I don't.

Chapter Twenty-Eight

Years Earlier: Edinburgh

Angus MacDougall's house in Edinburgh was old but not nearly as rundown as his castle. In the few good months of weather during the year, it possessed stately splendor and represented the best of what the city on the Firth of Forth had to offer. In bad weather, it became a grim reminder of the city's worst, where fog rolled in from the seaport to blanket it in gray, tattered tarps, and where evil taibhse might be found roaming around in such houses waiting for anyone who dared to venture inside. And that inside had always been gloomy and foreboding to John, with its heirlooms from the past, including swords, crossbows, and battle helmets along with old, dark oil paintings of his ancestors glaring at him in nearly every room.

Both Angus and John's bedrooms were on the second floor, their doors facing each other at the landing's opposite ends after ascending the stairs. Two more bedrooms and a single bathroom in the middle sat off it too, facing the large open space continuing up more than two stories from the parlor below to heavy oak beams, a space providing the landing with some light from the large front windows, albeit anemic illumination during bad weather.

As John searched under his mattress and at the side of his bed where it met the wall, he heard his uncle's footsteps upon the stairs and the squeak of the landing's floorboards long before he knocked on John's door. The old man didn't wait for an invitation to enter. He burst in and showed John the money roll.

"Looking for this, me lad?"

John grabbed at it. "That's my dosh!"

The old man pushed John onto his bed and then threw the money roll onto his chest.

"Tell me where you got it. Tell me, or I'll turn ye pretty face into pulp!"

John looked at his uncle's hard fists. He'd never beat John. He'd been more than tolerant of his nephew's bad behavior. John knew he often tried his uncle's patience. But John couldn't help himself. Now he wondered, *Will this be the first time?* Angus MacDougall was a giant of a man, but he looked twice as big when John looked up at him...and those hammer-like fists! He cringed. He had no choice to take it if it if his uncle lost his temper. To prevent that, he answered.

"Okay, okay, I'll tell you. I stole some things and sold them to a pawnbroker."

Angus glared at his nephew. "I'm disappointed in ye, lad. And myself, for that matter. I've failed your parents. You aren't my kin anymore. When I return, you'd better not be here. Take what you need and leave. And keep your damn dosh. You'll need it on the mean streets. And maybe get a real job! Stop stealing what people have worked so hard to obtain."

Angus stomped from John's room.

***

The publican plopped Angus's pint onto the bar and knifed off its head of foam. His burly customer quaffed half of it.

Bobby studied his friend. Dark curls mixed with gray were wet, but the face was dark red. *Is Angus having a heart attack or a stroke?* The city was nearly as dark with mist, the darkness always settling early that time of year.

"Yer drinkin' like there's no morrow, Angus. What's troublin' you?"

"My nephew John. He's a thief. But I kinna turn him in to the coppers, can I? Seems it wouldnae be right, me being his uncle."

"Might be good for what ails that lad, though—he has the Devil in him, like many our young that age. My old man's solution when I became something of a rebel was to make me enlist. As Her Majesty's toy soldier, war put the fear o' God in me. That might work well with your nephew too."

"He'd never do something so worthwhile, I wager, if soldiering is worthwhile. His Majesty dinnae care if you live or die, mate. Always been that way. That's why we need our independence. To hell with him and that whole royal lot. The lad too. Good riddance!"

Bobby ignored the statements about Scottish independence. His customers were evenly divided on that issue, although Brexit had been a bitter pill for some and turned their minds. They'd been debating the issue even before Brexit, though.

"What's your plan then, Angus?"

"No plan necessary, mate. I kicked the lad outta my house. O'er and done with, 'tis, and better for it."

"Aye, maybe better that way. He'll have to grow up some, I imagine. Hey, slow down, man!"

Angus had swallowed the rest of his beer in one gulp. "'Nother pint, Bobby. I'm not going anywhere for a while. And I walked here, so I can stagger home the same way."

As Bobby went to the tap with the empty pint glass, Angus eyed the lass serving beer to four men in the corner. They were all admiring what gifts nature had given her. *Sometimes you need more than beer to forget your problems.* Years ago was when he could go all night, drinking and whoring around the city.

He wondered if John would return for his funeral. Not likely.

He'd miss the lad. He knew John wouldn't miss him. *Yes, I failed.*

The drink didn't seem to mitigate that failure.

***

John didn't miss Angus at first, but the old house had been the center of his universe for so long, he missed having it as a base. Life became a blur, and he couldn't focus and often felt lost.

Everything had changed when the young thief met Linda. With all the robberies and then the violent assassinations, he'd been on a huge thrill ride ever since. Life was exciting, and the two lived it to its fullest.

Their histories were similar. Both sets of parents were gone. He'd lived with his uncle, and she'd lived with her grandparents in Chevy Chase, Maryland, where the old Cubans had made a new home after fleeing Castro's Cuba.

More from rebellion than political convictions, Linda had told the son of a Russian embassy worker she was twenty-one when she was only fourteen. They had two dates before he raped her. Diplomatic immunity freed him to return to Russia without prosecution. Since then, she'd hated authority figures and most men. Especially Russians. John was one male who was an exception. It was ironic she worked for other Russians, and for many others.

He knew she was crazy, but he was crazy in love. He remembered that first kill when she scared him more than usual, though.

"You're a crazy slut," Dragavei called out as Linda kept shooting into the body until her high-capacity magazine was empty.

She dropped the gun and clutched one breast with one hand and her crotch with another. "Makes me all wet, Maxim, just like you do!"

"Get your kicks, babe, in any way you like, but I never want to be on your bad side."

"I have no bad side, amorcito. You can do me however you want, whenever you want, and I'll come. You know that." She spit on the corpse. "I see that awful Russian in my mind's eye and can't control myself. But you're right. Never cross me, you bastard. I'd cut your balls off and choke you on them. Let's get out of here."

He got used to her blood lust and enjoyed her sexual lust. That old goat Angus MacDougall was mostly forgotten.

He didn't think she'd ever forget the Russian rapist.

The beginning of one mission still bothered John, though...

***

Maxim followed the hulk from the hotel's bar to the elevators. *Could I take the scrote?* He hoped he wouldn't need to try. They went to the fifth floor, turned right in the hall, and stopped in front of room 511. The big man frisked him.

"Wait here," said the bodyguard.

Soon the door opened. "He will see you now," the giant said.

Once he entered the fancy hotel room, Maxim heard piano music playing interspersed with speech in Russian.

"That's nice," Maxim said.

His contact raised an index finger to his lips and gazed at Maxim with lizard's eyes as if Maxim were a dirty fly to be swallowed whole.

When the piece finished, the man said, "Tcherepnin's 'The Fisherman and the Fish,' based on Pushkin's fairy tale. The Imperial Guards' march is the best part, when the old woman becomes a *tsar*'s wife, but the entire piece is interesting. It's like *Peter and the Wolf* for adults. I'm glad you like it."

He turned off the music that had gone on to some other piece on his playlist and handed Maxim a brown manila envelope. "Ten thousand euros for each. Linda's deposited before, yours after."

"That's less than the previous mission."

"This target is only annoying to him, a buzzing gnat he wants to swat. The previous one did more damage. They're priced accordingly."

"I see."

The lizard smiled through thin lips. Maxim half-expected a forked, sticky tongue to pop out.

"You two do good work, but don't become too greedy...or sloppy. Or ask too many questions. The day one of your kills leads back to me, or any of us, for that matter, you're dead meat. Your bitch too."

If that goon wasn't standing at the door, arms folded, Maxim would have filleted the contact for insulting Linda. The big man hadn't found the knife in his coat lining.

***

Maxim left the hotel room, unaccompanied this time, and met Linda two blocks away. She examined the envelope's contents. "Seems too simple. Maybe that's why the pay is lower."

He frowned. "I hate that bloke!"

"Easy. As we say, el marano gordito da jamon para todos."

"What the hell does that mean?"

She laughed. "The fat pig provides ham for everyone."

"He's more than a fat pig." He eyed her. "You saw the target is an old Arab, right?"

"Who takes two wives to Paris to buy them clothes and shoes. Jewelry too, most likely."

"He also travels with a bodyguard."

"That never stopped us before. What kind of function can you do as cover?"

"It's August. Everyone's on vacation."

Maxim settled for volunteering for a benefit program for the ongoing reconstruction of Notre Dame. He wasn't particularly religious, but it was still a strange feeling to do a good deed once in his life. He would only have to sing some arias. He'd finish with "Largo al Factotum"—it was difficult, but the audience wouldn't be discerning and would enjoy it as a rousing finale.

The plan took shape. Maxim was the better shot—his uncle had taught him how to handle a rifle—so he had the sniper's duties, setting up on a roof across from the Arab's fancy hotel. His target exited with his family and stood with his hands around a little boy. Maxim hadn't counted on the child. One wife stood on each side of them, and the bodyguard stood in front of the old Arab. Maxim knew they were waiting for the valet to bring their car.

He sighted through the rifle's scope and decided the boy was short enough that he could hit the old bastard in the chest. The bodyguard was the problem; he was big and directly in Maxim's line of fire.

Leave it to Linda to find a solution to that problem. She went into action. She approached one wife and started to insult her in French expletives. The bodyguard stepped aside to move between Linda and that wife. Maxim took the shot.

They met at the hire-car parked two blocks away. Both were perspiring in the morning's heat, but Linda was laughing. She'd already ripped off her blond wig and blotted off the excess bright red lipstick.

"We're such a great team!" she said.

The image of the boy's frightened face would stick in Maxim's mind forever.

Chapter Twenty-Nine

Tuesday Evening: Vienna

Because they'd discussed the evening's dinner and performance long enough during the bus ride back, Ihrin and Razvan chatted about the murder cases in their stateroom after returning to the boat. They sat on their deck sipping white wine.

"Wasn't that Dragavei creepy?" said Razvan.

"Maybe he needed that huge stateroom so he could sleep in a coffin," Ihrin said with a smile. "I can imagine him flitting about the boat or over the Danube, looking for victims instead of bugs." She laughed. "Pity. He had a good voice. A bit flat on occasion, but, with more training, he could have done well on stage."

"Why did he come on this cruise alone? And why that stateroom? A smaller one would have served the purpose for one person. They haven't provided us with all the information."

She took her husband's comment as rhetorical. 'They' could be many people she'd prefer not to think about too much as she enjoyed putting a mellow touch on the evening. "I bet Captain Janssen is having a fit with all the murder inquiries going on. I wouldn't blame him if he did. Three murders and an attempted one are bound to upset anyone, and he's such a gentle man. Quite good-looking too."

"Don't get any ideas for wandering, Ihrin. We're supposedly a happily married couple."

"I want a divorce," she said with a laugh.

"We're not married." He stared at the dark Danube waters a moment, barely visible because of the boat's lights. "I'll wager the captain isn't the only one on the boat who's upset. People are nervous, and will continue to be so until the murderer or murderers are found. That doesn't bother me too much, but I can see it in the others."

"The Interpol agent is too stupid to find any murderers," said Ihrin. "And he's too much into his new wife."

"Most likely literally, every night," he said with a laugh followed by a wide yawn.

"Do you think so?"

"I believe she's what Yanks call a cougar."

"Well, good for her, I say. You haven't done me for a while, you old bastard."

But Razvan was already snoring. She rose, found the bedspread, and wrapped it around him. *If he falls over the rail into the water sleepwalking, that's his problem.*

***

Eszter and Janos also analyzed the recent murder cases while in the lounge waiting for dinner. They'd changed plans. They didn't particularly like Mozart, the composer featured at the concert for the tour the cruise company had arranged—more modern composers, especially Bartok, appealed to them more—but they also wanted to relax from the day's tours. They'd walked all around Schönbrunn. The ostentatious palace hadn't given their national prides any serious boost. A lot had happened in Hungary since the glory days of the empire—the Nazis and Soviets were two significant groups who'd been intent on quashing Hungarians' pride in their homeland.

"I might have seen Esther and Bastiann in the gardens," Eszter said. "You don't think they were spying on us, do you?"

"Possibly. I didn't see them. I only wish they'd finish with the investigation. What a way to ruin a river cruise! Here we have good weather, and someone commits a murder." He winked at her.

"Three. You didn't count the Bulgarian couple at Attersee, their deaths not an accident. And remember, Esther was shot at in the abbey." She said that with a smile.

"Those two could consider those events as only coincidences. Consider our old compatriots. It would have been better to eliminate them. At least, Gaszi. He's Fidesz."

"Janos!"

"Fascists like them give all Hungarians a bad reputation."

"Well, I'll have to admit I've considered throwing a plate of *goulash* in that awful man's face." She smiled. "And some other things as well. And he's sexist as hell. His poor wife is a mouse who meekly acquiesces."

"Not like you," said Janos. "How are you going to deal with your parents?"

"Like I always do. We'll have kids when we're good and ready. Right?"

"Agreed. I hope that argument works on my parents too. I'll throw in some aspirations about our careers. They're going to be all over us."

"Not a pleasant way to end our trip. But family must come first."

Especially ours, he mused.

***

Luynhen and Viktor had enjoyed the evening's performance but not the dinner arrangements. They'd wanted to avoid the obnoxious Dutchman and his quest to find a killer— they'd seen enough of the Interpol agent and his bride on the morning and afternoon tours—but they also couldn't help discussing the cases in their stateroom before retiring.

"There's more to her past than just being an art detective," Luynhen said as she removed her makeup. "That old battleax is tough…and sly. It's too bad both of them were on this cruise."

"And sexy." She studied Viktor in the mirror. He opened his arms. "Whenever you're ready, love."

"After that comment, you can pleasure yourself."

"Oh, please. You've always been my standby."

"Your choice of words isn't helping your case."

"Even if I wander, you still have to act the part of a dutiful wife."

"You're not acting when you go after me, and vice versa. Call it part of your benefits package, I suppose."

"Speaking of packages…" He pointed.

"Pervert."

"Slut."

"At least let me finish." She spread some moisturizing cream on her face and rubbed it in. "Would you really do Esther Brookstone?"

"Maybe…given a chance. Especially if in the heat of battle she gives up some key information. She and Bastiann aren't telling anyone too much. That old Hungarian's correct. We should request from the captain more transparency. Then we'd know who they suspect."

"That likely won't happen." She stood and turned to him, opening her robe. "Still thinking about that old whore?"

"At the moment, no."

Chapter Thirty

Tuesday Evening: Vienna

Bastiann had never had run an investigation like the present one aboard the riverboat. While Esther had investigated some interesting cases on big cruise ships where artwork was often sold, his Interpol work had all taken place on land. And while he could prioritize passengers according to how likely they were to be persons of interest or even suspects, there were so many people to consider, whereas she had always had only a few to worry about.

While he had his fiches to remind him of the results of his interrogations and extensive notes as well, he could still go through all the passengers and crewmembers in his mind. It was hard to maintain objectivity, though. For example, one Hungarian pair was affable and considered the investigation part of their entertainment on the cruise; the other pair, at least the husband, was irascible, obnoxious, and someone many people would want to be caught as a murderer. Experience had taught him it could be just the opposite, or neither one. Given the information he had, he could order everyone according to his perceived likelihood they could commit murder. That meant nothing, though, because many people might want to murder someone but never do it.

Yet someone had done an expert job on Maxim Dragavei, and that led to other doubts. What was the motive? What had the lanky chap done to become a target for an assassin? Their information pointed to Dragavei also being an assassin. Was this a case of pros versus pros where motives and actions took place in the netherworld of crimes committed because of international politics, said motives and actions he couldn't even imagine?

What would Hercule Poirot have done? Christie's famous detective also had a limited number of suspects on that steamship on the Nile and that train crossing Europe. For the riverboat he was on, there were hundreds. He could only completely eliminate Esther and himself. Poirot might have thrown up his hands! From habit, he twirled his mustache like David Suchet.

Even his friend Castilblanco often stated it: It's a great aid in an investigation when the number of possible suspects is small. But in most cases, finding the culprit even among a small number of suspects became more feasible with more evidence. Sometimes only one piece of evidence was all that was needed. But he had only a cheap dagger one could purchase anywhere.

The upcoming arrival scheduled for Budapest created a real deadline for him. He would either have to find the murderer before that, or turn over the case to someone else. He knew some people in the Budapest federal police, but it was a matter of professional pride to prefer closing the case himself. And, considering Hungary's present political situation, he didn't know if he trusted their federal police anymore.

With that, he revised his notes and decided whom to interview next.

***

Bastiann made two more interviews before the riverboat left for Bratislava the next morning. While they allowed him to meet their fellow passengers, they didn't shed information on the three murders.

The meeting with Liz and Ron Gross went well at first. They were a pleasant enough couple, although the heavyset Liz interrupted her husband a lot and often corrected him. *She's taken the role of Gazsi Kertes in this marriage!* After confirming their names and other data, he launched into a chatty session with the two Americans.

"I bet you didn't plan for this," Ron said. "A murder investigation on your honeymoon. Your new wife probably isn't pleased."

"Especially because she probably planned it," said Liz. "The honeymoon, I mean."

Bastiann, who had talked to Ron at *Schönbrunn*, didn't bother to correct her.

"I'm sure it's not a comfortable situation for anyone," he said. "I only have a few more questions." He consulted his notes. "You're an insurance broker, Mr. Gross. What kind of insurance do you sell?"

"Just policies from US companies. And we don't sell policies outside the US."

"He's not asking that, Ron. He wants to know what type."

Bastiann didn't particularly care. He'd just wanted Ron to talk more so he could observe the body language.

"Okay…we do a bit of everything. My agency uses the usual small town business model. Whole life, term life, property insurance, umbrella policies, all from multiple companies—you name it, we can get it for you. Not auto or health insurance, though."

"You were talking to some of the other Americans," said Bastiann. "Did they approach you or did you approach them?"

"He goes after any potential client," Liz said. "He tells them you can never have enough insurance."

"I suppose not," Bastiann said. He mentioned some names. "Any buyers among them?"

"No, and I don't see what that has to do with anything. I chat with people about insurance. It's my life."

"Besides me," said Liz.

"Yes, dear."

"That's precisely the point. You chatted with those people, and I haven't yet. Or I have and hope you can add more information. Did anyone appear preoccupied? Anxious? Anything that struck you as odd?"

"Well, that doctor and her partner were odd," said Liz. "Imagine. Two women going on like that. What's this world coming to?"

"They weren't odd," her husband said. "And I do business with people like that. I'll sell insurance to anyone. Who cares who they're humping?"

Bastiann looked toward the little deck, wishing he were sitting there with drink in hand, and then back at Ron. "Anyone else? You can save me some time, like I said."

"I'd talk to that doctor," Liz said. "She's most likely a man-hater, and that poor Mr. Dragavei was all man…in my opinion." She blushed a bit, perhaps realizing she'd admitted to having a wandering eye.

"Looked like a scarecrow," Ron said to Bastiann. "I used to play football for UTEP. That's University of Texas, El Paso, in case you're wondering. Can't expect foreign cops to know American universities." He paused, perhaps realizing that what he said had been a bit strong. "That skinny SOB wouldn't have lasted a minute on the field. Well, maybe twirling a baton."

"But he appeared to be sophisticated," Liz said. "Contrary to some men I know well. European types are sophisticated. Don't you think so, Mr. van Coevorden?"

He winked at Ron, remembering the words "foreign cops." Mrs. Gross had what he called an "otherwising" attitude, a nicer term than bigotry: Anything and anyone outside her small universe were questionable. *A small-minded human being,* he mused. "I prefer not to answer that question." He turned his attention to her, though. *Time to after you, lady!* "And do you work, Mrs. Gross?"

He was surprised at her answer.

"I write children's books. It's fun, so maybe it's not work? It's a steady income, though, unlike Ron's insurance business. Parents always want their little brats to read."

"That makes sense," Bastiann said. "Reading can be entertainment for them as well as a learning experience. I don't find enough time to read, but I enjoy it when I do. Are you also a reader? Maybe you can offer me some suggestions from recent titles?"

"I don't read that much. Authors shouldn't read. There's too much danger of plagiarizing. That even applies in my case. The text in a children's book isn't all that complicated."

"I'm surprised by your comment. Generally speaking, shouldn't authors at least want to read in their genres? Or even be avid readers? It seems that seeing what others are writing would also give them an idea what their competition is."

"Well, you're not an author. What do you know?"

Bastiann frowned. "Do you have children?" he said, trying to look for something positive in the woman. He couldn't help thinking of the difference between Liz and his own mother.

"No. I didn't want to bother with the little beasts. Children's stories should be written by objective observers. And they cover all sorts of adult genres, although they're not sold by genre."

Bastiann frowned again. "I'd supposed genres didn't really apply to children's books. They're stories for children, like William Elliot Griffis's tales."

"Who? Never heard of him."

Bastiann sighed. "'The Boy Who Wanted More Cheese,' 'The Goblins Turned to Stone,' and so forth. Dutch folk tales."

"Oh, no one reads those anymore. Little kids want picture books, the fewer words, the better. Parents are told to limit their kids' TV watching, so they put a picture book in each kid's hand."

"Don't parents read to their children anymore?"

"Nope. Modern parents don't have the time."

"So you write a story and have someone do the artwork?" *That type of collaboration might interest Esther,* Bastiann mused.

"Anyone can write the damn stories. I mean, you're talking stories for children here. They're all fluff. I spend most of my time setting everything up. I'm more of a production manager."

And here I thought you were an author. The woman was beginning to annoy Bastiann. He decided he'd heard enough.

"Thanks for coming in, Mr. and Mrs. Gross. If you have nothing more to add, I bid you good day. And enjoy the remainder of your cruise."

And that was a complete waste of time, Bastiann thought as the couple left. *I should have left that pair for Esther. She'd make mincemeat out of Mrs. Gross!*

He smiled, though. *It would be fun to put her away in a jail just for being such a witch!*

***

The next couple was even more abrasive. At least Gazsi Kertes was. The man lived up to Bastiann's image formed by their first meeting and Esther's notes, and his wife Maja could hardly get a word in. Between the two Hungarians, Gazsi seemed a likely candidate for someone who could murder and be arrogant enough to think he could get away with it. For some reason, that reminded Bastiann of a certain ex-US president and his boast about murdering someone on New York City's Fifth Avenue and getting away with it. Of course, arrogance and bluster didn't make anyone into a murder *per se*, or a lot of politicians would be in jail for life.

But Gazsi also dominated his poor wife. *Are Esther and I exceptional in establishing a balanced relationship?* He wondered if any student had ever done a sociology thesis answering that question, or at least studied the frequency of balanced relationships. *Out of so many relationships, how many are balanced?* Of course, they'd have to define "balanced" better. He believed Amy and Judith's showed balance; so did Kayla and Ken's. *Maybe Maja and Gazsi only prove that sometimes opposites attract? Human beings can be so strange!*

"Before we start, let me state you're going about this all wrong," Gazsi said.

"I hadn't planned for these interrogations, so I didn't bring my torture rack along with me on the trip," Bastiann said in a fit of biting levity. His attempt at humor didn't register.

"Forget the damn interrogations. You think someone's stupid enough to say, 'I did it'? Forensics is key nowadays. Hell man, if you torture someone, they're likely to say exactly that, even if they didn't do it."

"SOCOs made a thorough examination of this stateroom before it was cleaned. Medical exams were also performed. We also had two other victims on this tour where we have a witness. We've been collecting data, Urum Kertes. Passengers might not be aware of that because we've been discreet. Can you suggest any other improvements?"

"You see! We know nothing about any of that. You keep us in the dark. What did you find in the forensics sweep? What did the ME find? What did that witness see?"

"I'll refrain from defining 'discreet' for you, but in any investigation, authorities like to keep certain data from the general public. Sometimes a suspect knows more than he should; other times we can catch him by surprise when he contradicts facts. I've been doing this my whole professional life. How did you come by your opinions?"

"He reads crime stories," Maja said.

Gazsi reddened. "Shut up, woman! You embarrass me."

It went downhill from there. Gazsi left in a huff, threatening he was going to go after Bastiann's badge, which was something the Interpol agent didn't possess. Hal Leonard would be amused.

As a result of that interchange, Bastiann decided he needed to call it a night. He only had his notes left to organize.

***

Ronaldo stopped in the doorway when he saw Bastiann at the table reviewing and tidying his notes. The Interpol agent looked at his watch.

"You're early, *amigo*."

Bastiann had interviewed the crewmember some time ago and found him to be affable and smart. They seemed to understand each other well, belying their different backgrounds.

"I can come back to clean later, Mr. Bastiann."

"No, why don't you go ahead and start? I'm almost done here, and it's late. Has the crew recovered at all from this awful business?"

"Marisol might never be the same. Most of us won't recover completely until you collar the killer."

Bastiann smiled at that American crime-story chatter; he put down his pen. "That's understandable. I guess you need only give everything a quick once-over for now. We never make the room very dirty."

"I do a little bit every time, *sí*? You and your wife and people you interview are tidier than Mr. Dragavei was."

"How's that?"

"He was like a rich boy who expects his servants to always clean up after him. The room was always a mess, especially the bathroom."

If Dragavei wasn't his real name, could he have been a rich boy, someone born into a wealthy family? Bastiann asked himself. While the answer to that question would be interesting, he thought it would help little in the case.

"I see. Some people are messy. I'm sorry. That makes your job harder."

Ronaldo shrugged. "I'm paid well enough to support my family, so I'm happy to have this job. Many people in my home country don't have such an opportunity."

Good for you, thought Bastiann, knowing who the members of Ronaldo's "family" were.

"I've only been to Manila, so I don't know your home island. I suppose you speak Tagalog as well as English and Spanish. So many languages. It's an interesting world." My engine is running on vapors. "Let's shelve that discussion and finish our work, though, or we'll never be able to sleep tonight."

"I'll start with the balcony. I skipped it last time because it and that part of the room nearby had a major cleanup after...well, you know."

Bastiann resumed the organization of his notes until he heard the balcony's sliding door bang several times. He turned to see Ronaldo struggling to close it.

"Is there a problem?"

"It worked before, but I can't close it enough now to set the lock."

Bastiann went over to try himself. "It appears something is in the track where it meets the jamb."

"Excuse me?"

Bastiann pointed. "There's something there."

Ronaldo went down on his knees and probed with a pen. He soon found the problem. He held up a slightly damaged small silver earring.

"It seems Mr. Dragavei might have had a female guest even though he was alone on the cruise."

"Or it belongs to one of the women we interviewed," Bastiann said.

He couldn't remember that door being opened during any interview, though. He wouldn't have wanted the distraction. And the cleaning people only opened it to air the room as Ronaldo had done.

He took the earring and examined it in the palm of his hand. "There's some kind of residue on it. See these spots?"

Ronald took a closer look. "It might be cleaning fluid. Or maybe disinfectant. The stateroom was cleaned thoroughly after...well, you know."

"And after the SOCOs went over it and missed this earring. Or maybe it wasn't there then. That supports the theory it might belong to one of my interviewees." *But how did it get into the door track in that case?* He put the earring in his coat pocket. "Or it could even be from another cruise."

He knew it wasn't Esther's earring. She only wore gold, not silver. *Can it be the assassin's?* If so, he had no idea how to discover which woman onboard, if any, had lost a silver earring in the stateroom.

But that earring made Bastiann think of evidence that they did have, the ornate dagger. It had looked old enough to be a relic, although he believed the tarnish and pits in the fake silver handle and hard steel blade were only placed there to make it look old. Robert Winston had said it was modeled after a Venetian dagger.

Bastiann estimated the distance from the entrance to Dragavei's stateroom to the deck. The wall facing the bed had a length of four meters, the distance along the other side to the deck door was three, so the hypotenuse would be five meters. Add a bit more to go through the sliding door...

He had seen a knife from that distance—about fifteen feet in English units—but he had no idea it was an ornate dagger. Yet Robert had even determined it was a copy of a Venetian dagger. He must have been closer, as close as Amy had been in her examination of Dragavei's body.

Am I such a bad judge of character? mused Bastiann. *Even if Robert wasn't the murderer, he had lied about how close he'd been to the body! Maybe he just wanted to confirm that the man he'd wanted to kill was indeed dead?*

Bastiann decided he'd have to keep both pieces of evidence in mind. They were all he had.

Part Three: Slovakia

"Though this be madness, yet there is method in't." Hamlet, *Act 2, Scene 2*

Chapter Thirty-One

Wednesday: En Route from Vienna to Bratislava

Bratislava is Slovakia's capital. It is one of Europe's smaller capitals but still the country's largest city. Bratislava occupies both banks of the Danube and the left bank of the Morava. Bordering Austria and Hungary, it is the only national capital that borders two countries. The languages of the Czech Republic and Slovakia are similar, and many citizens in one country have relatives in the other.

Esther and Bastiann had a bit of a lie-in and went to breakfast late, arriving before the riverboat pulled out for Bratislava at eight a.m. While they'd decided to take the "Coronation City" walking tour in the capital of Slovakia, she also wanted to keep an eye out for silver jewelry, especially earrings. Bastiann didn't think that would lead to anything, but he agreed clues couldn't be ignored.

"You look depressed, love," said Esther, buttering a piece of toast while she tried to decide what else to put on it. "Right now you'd be a good model for Milne's Eeyore."

Her plate was heaped with food in the British breakfast tradition. He tended to start the day lighter, and often preferred a heavier lunch and not much for dinner. But he also foraged on her plate, particularly among the bacon slices.

"This donkey considers this case won't be solved before Budapest," he said, his mouth full of bacon.

"Sod those thoughts. That's nothing to be gloomy about. We have lorry-loads of data to pass on to whomever takes it over. You didn't solve every case that came your way. Neither did I. Some cases even go cold. Others solve themselves, like the case of that perverted old Nazi who eluded American and British authorities alike and ended up dead in that Amsterdam canal."

"Or when someone took out that American energy executive right before my eyes. I'll always wonder who that was."

"As our friend Castilblanco might say, someone who wanted a little street justice, perforce. Cheer up, love. One can only do what's possible and declare victory for what's achieved. It's like playing roulette at Monte Carlo."

"I never did that. Did you?"

"Why would I use that comparison if I hadn't? Back in the day, East German VIPs often played there to try their luck and sow their seed, as it were—hopefully nothing came of the latter, because we don't need any more monsters in this world. It was a convenient place to do some spy work for that reason, but not like James Bond. Those VIPs didn't like to be caught with their pants down, literally or figuratively, but they often were." She flashed him a wry smile.

"I feel like I'm missing knowledge about a large part of your life."

"Don't feel bad, love. Most people are. Oh, look. There's Amy and Judith." Esther waved and the couple came over to their table, glad for an excuse to change the topic.

"Sorry," Amy said. She and her partner were dressed in sweats and trainers. "We already finished. How's the investigation going?"

"It's moving along," Bastiann said.

"Swimmingly," Esther added, going along with his contradiction to what he'd said earlier. "We'll see you at the buses later on?"

"Better hurry," Judith said. "Caitlin doesn't like waiting for stragglers."

"And we shall not keep her waiting," Esther said. She looked at her watch. "But what's the hurry? We have plenty of time. The tours don't start until one."

"We're exercising some on the track on the top deck first. You can come and join us after your—" Judith eyed Esther's plate. "—feast?"

"Some of this is for Bastiann. He always nicks something here and there. I might have to return for some more bacon. And we have some sleuthing to catch up on this morning. Thanks for the invitation, though."

***

Both Esther and Bastiann worked diligently in their own stateroom for a few hours, going over notes, discussing what they knew about passengers, and creating theories about who the assassin might be. At the work session's end, nothing had been decided, but the facts and theories were clearer. They both agreed it was unlikely the three murders and attack on Esther at Melk Abbey were unrelated.

They grazed on the free sandwiches available in the lounge and then left the boat for their tour.

Like the one in Vienna, the "Coronation City" walking tour was again a mix of walking and bus rides, for there were a lot of odd ups and downs as they went around the hilly city. For example, the famous castle, which Maria Theresa remodeled for son-in-law Albert's coronation, hence the tour's name, sat high atop a hill overlooking the city. Their transceivers worked to perfection, and the guide was knowledgeable.

Their tour first stopped for a time, though, at the Old Market Hall, a place where fresh produce and bakery goods were sold. There were a lot of passengers from riverboats milling around within, theirs as well as others'. Bastiann thought he saw Omar and remembered the conversation with Marisol. *Time will make her bad memories about seeing Dragavei's dead body blur and be less traumatic,* he surmised.

Maybe Omar is looking for fresh produce for the riverboat's kitchen? There was plenty to be found throughout the marketplace. He wondered why one of the chefs didn't do the buying, though, expecting a chef to have a more practiced eye than a waiter.

Esther told him she'd also spotted Luynhen and Viktor in a heated conversation with Ihrin and Razvan Culianu.

"Those four make an interesting quartet," Bastiann said. "And they don't mix well with other passengers."

"Are they even more suspect now?"

"Less. Their attitudes probably only reflect their culture. They most likely distrust all authority, and with good reason, considering their previous lives behind the Iron Curtain. Where does all this produce come from, by the way?"

"Hardworking farmers must bring it in from the countryside. Traditions die hard in Europe, Bastiann. Only the Yanks have no culture."

"On the contrary, after many talks with Hal, I've decided they have far too much—the US is a country of immigrants. The advantage is they've had to learn to be more tolerant as a consequence. Castilblanco says over eight hundred languages are spoken in New York City."

"And he still owes me a curry dinner, where he could practice his Hindi."

"He speaks Hindi?"

"How would I know? If he doesn't, he'll have to practice a lot."

At another stop where Amy and Judith followed them onto the tour bus, Esther leaned into Bastiann and whispered, "Judith wears silver earrings."

Could Judith be Dragavei's killer? Bastiann thought the woman was somewhat abrasive, but that didn't imply she was a killer. He'd remember Esther's observation, though.

For now, he only nodded. "Silver and turquoise. Maybe southwestern-style jewelry. Not that unusual. California is near Arizona and New Mexico."

"Are you aware those western states are huge? Arizona alone could swallow five Slovakias, and one would still have to go from the California coast to reach the border." He shook his head. "I might go on a vacation there, but I certainly wouldn't travel from San Diego to Tucson to buy jewelry." As the woman neared them, Esther studied the earrings. "We'll have to check out her other jewelry."

"She could have bought it right there in San Diego. But you do what you want. I don't pay much attention to women's jewelry. Only yours on occasion, and I know you like gold."

"That's what drove all the conquistadors to America, after all. Not the English, though. They were obsessed with more business-like exploitations, stealing land from the natives and selling rum, for two." She thought a moment. "But you reminded me of something."

"What's that?"

"You owe me an engagement ring. You did everything backwards. You didn't carry me across the threshold either."

"Both IOUs I'll honor down the line. We've been busy, my dear."

She cuddled a bit. "That we have. Thanks for planning such a wonderful honeymoon, even though it hasn't turned out exactly as planned. No one can deny I t's been quite the adventure."

Chapter Thirty-Two

Wednesday Afternoon: Bratislava

Before Bastiann had to dress for the Chef's Table, he went to Dragavei's room to have some quiet time with his notes. Captain Janssen found him there.

"How is your investigation going?"

"Except for Gazsi's trying to organize a rebellion among the passengers, it's moving along. They often are slow moving until they're not. I suppose it's like long-distance skating where you shift into high gear near the end."

The captain took a seat on the small sofa near Bastiann. "Sorry about Gazsi. Some people are damn annoying. I've seen every type of human behavior imaginable, and my only sampling has been among passengers on boat trips, for the most part."

Bastiann turned away from the monitor where he'd been finishing the day's tasks by checking his email. "You didn't come to ask such a general question or console me for that bigot's behavior. What's bothering you, Sander?"

"Many things, but only one might interest you. For example, I'll only have about a half meter of clearance in the channel pulling into Budapest. The water level hasn't completely recovered from the dry summer."

"I understand sometimes you have to bus everyone around the shallows."

"Costly, so the company likes me to avoid that if at all possible. I'm somewhat worried, to put it mildly, but that's my problem, not yours."

"And what is mine? What thing should concern me?"

"We lost a man, Omar Dushey. He went to buy fruit in the marketplace for Marisol. Or so he told her."

"I saw him there. I assume he didn't return, so he lied to Marisol."

The captain winked. "Or she's lying for him. They're an item. Were, I guess I should say if he's truly disappeared. She seems upset by his disappearance. Finding a cadaver and losing her boyfriend all on one cruise—fate hasn't been kind to her."

"You're not suggesting Omar killed Maxim Dragavei, are you?"

"Unlikely, but I'd check his documentation again."

***

Back in his stateroom, Bastiann asked Esther to help. He pulled the records they had about crewmembers and passengers from their safe. He put her to work on documentation while he reviewed notes he had on Omar.

Esther used a magnifying glass to study Omar's passport photo. She knew Bastiann would wonder why she had the glass, although she'd told him her contacts were failing her. For passengers, the photo of the photo was only as good as the boat's machine that captured the images as people came aboard and registered, but the crew's were hi-res. Of course, crewmembers had already had their paperwork checked long before passengers appeared. All the employees' records were better than passengers', which helped in this case.

The cruise line doesn't skimp on security, she observed. *They have fewer crewmembers and passengers to worry about than those huge cruise ships.*

"I don't see any obvious flaws," she said.

"He has a passport but not a driver's license," said Bastiann, looking over her shoulder. "And the passport is Greek. Omar Dushey doesn't sound like a Greek name."

"I suppose he or his parents could have come from elsewhere. Omar Dushey sounds Turkish or Arabic to me."

"Could Maxim Dragavei have been a target for a terrorist? Maybe he discovered some ISIS plot."

"You're tired and looking to end the investigation, so you're ready to consider any conspiracy. And you have ISIS paranoia, maybe justifiably so after what they planned for London with the help of your irascible friend Ernesto. But lightning doesn't strike twice in the same spot."

"How is this riverboat in the same spot as London?"

"Figure of speech. I mean us, Bastiann. We'd be the ones where the lightning flashes struck twice. What are the chances we'd be involved in another terrorist plot?"

He nodded. "Not many. I suppose I should talk to Marisol again."

***

"Any idea why Omar disappeared?" Bastiann said to Marisol back in his interrogation room, formerly Dragavei's cabin.

He watched her lower her head and wring her hands. *She doesn't hide her nerves well.*

"Marisol?"

She jerked...and then raised her head and smiled at him. "I am skit-skittish."

"Sorry. Look, I have a murder investigation to run, and time is of the essence. I only need you to tell me your boyfriend didn't kill Maxim Dragavei. You must know why Omar has disappeared."

She glanced out the window to the left of the balcony. The curtain of darkness was falling on the Danube ending that day's play; similar shadows were crossing her face. Soon the riverboat would be leaving for Budapest.

"He is running from you, *Herr* Bastiann."

"Me? So he did kill Maxim?"

"No, no, no! Omar is gentle. He'd never do that. I'm going to meet him when we arrive in Budapest."

"Okay. That admission might help if we need to pick him up. If he didn't murder Maxim, why is he running?"

"He's Syrian…and an illegal. A migrant. From years ago, during that war there."

Bastiann sat back in his chair. "Interesting. When you see him, tell him I won't turn him in. That's not my job. You can go, Marisol."

He walked her to the door. "If it helps, I celebrate your romance. Relationships between people from different ethnicities and religions can still be difficult, but they give me hope for a future where everyone can understand and get along with everyone else."

"I-I don't understand."

"You're Catholic and he's Muslim, right?"

"No, I'm Muslim too." She smiled. "There are Muslims in the Philippines, *Herr* Bastiann."

Bastiann slapped his forehead. "Of course! I'm so sorry. Please forgive me."

"It's okay." She now laughed. "People make that mistake all the time."

"But your name?"

"In my teens, I legally changed it to Marisol Salazar to find better work. Please don't tell the cruise company. This is the best job I've ever had."

"I'm sure they wouldn't care about your faith."

"But they'll care about Omar being illegal."

"He was a good employee, so they might be willing to obtain a work permit for him and help him start the legalization process. Do you mind if I tell his story to the captain?"

"No. Captain Janssen is a good man. And he's always been so nice to both of us."

She kissed him on the cheek and left.

Chapter Thirty-Three

Wednesday Evening: Bratislava

Esther and Bastiann arrived at the Chef's Table venue fashionably late that evening. As they waited for the head waiter to seat another couple, they noted the main chef and his helpers were already busy in the small kitchen whipping up all the courses for the gourmet meals that would be served. Some diners were already seated, sipping on cocktails or wine, and many waiters were tending to their every need, delivering or clearing plates and filling or refilling glasses without being asked. The obvious goal was to provide passengers with an exquisite dining experience.

"Herr and *Frau* van Coevorden," said the head waiter, loud enough so the other passengers could hear. Some turned toward them because they were well known by then. "Welcome to the Chef's Table."

"Make that Esther and Bastiann, Sasha," Esther said much more softly with a sly wink. "Remember, we learned all about you and Ronaldo in interviews. And we're all among friends, so first names are called for."

"Yes, Frau Esther, the murder investigation is some excitement I probably didn't need in my otherwise dull but peaceful life." His voice now matched Esther's in volume. "A bit tense, I'd say, but an adventure. Follow me, please."

Sasha led them to a table for four where Kayla and Ken White awaited them. They both stood.

"Good evening, you two," Bastiann said. They all hugged and then sat, the two women next to each other as Sasha pulled their chairs to seat them. The two men seated themselves.

After some more pleasantries were exchanged, Kayla said, "I made Ken promise not to talk about the investigation, although some people here would want to hand Bastiann a megaphone and ask him tons of questions." She winked at Esther. "I'd like to talk about art instead, if you don't mind."

Is she used to controlling a discussion? Bastiann could imagine a confrontation between two type-A women. He didn't know Kayla or Ken that well. *Hopefully everyone just gets along.*

"You're on, my dear," Bastiann said to Esther with a smile.

She laughed. "Don't let him fool you. Bastiann likes to play the tough copper, but he loves art. I wouldn't marry any man who doesn't. He often visits two fine museums in Amsterdam, the Rijksmuseum and that strange-looking Van Gogh Museum. But, because I own a gallery, I suppose I'm the person to query about buying art without being scammed."

"Oh, Kayla doesn't want to buy art," said Ken. "Who can afford that? She wants to talk about painting. Her own, as a matter of fact."

"My, my. I'm not an artist. What's the problem, Kayla? I know artists can suffer from something akin to writer's block. Deciding what to paint might be a large percentage of the process. Is that the problem?"

The conversation was interrupted as several waiters served baskets of different breads, various appetizers, and wine—they'd enjoy a sample of varietals throughout the meal. After some tentative bites and a dainty sip, Kayla answered Esther.

"I have a problem focusing, which my instructors insist I must do. I like and paint in a lot of styles and love to paint still life as well as scenery."

Esther nodded. "Aha, that kind of focusing. I didn't hear any leanings towards the abstract, or portraiture, so hoorah for me." She popped a cherry tomato from her salad into her mouth and thought a moment. "What do you like to paint most?"

"Seascapes," said Kayla. "The play of light on waves, their spray, water dripping from rocks and rolling onto the sandy shore."

"That's what you should focus on then. Only make it interpretive, not like a photograph. An artist must put her soul into the painting, and that doesn't come out in a truly realistic painting passing for a photograph. Well, maybe in an Ansel Adams photograph, but otherwise no. And go to the real ocean and paint there if at all possible."

"We go to the Jersey Shore when we can," Ken said. "We love Spring Lake, for example. Lots of breakers, and a beautiful beach. I can sit and watch for hours while she paints."

"Good," said Esther. She pointed with her fork. "So is this, whatever it is." She'd indicated something looking like a strip of raw bacon. "Anyone know?" The other three shook their heads. "I must ask Sasha then. It's quite tasty."

***

Before the second entrée was served, Esther visited another table to say hello to Amy and Judith. They were sitting with one of the German couples.

"You look elegant tonight," Amy said. "Have you recovered from your experience?"

Esther put her index finger to her lips and glanced towards Bastiann, who appeared to be sharing a joke with Ken because the two men were laughing. Kayla looked bored, though, so she'd have to return soon.

"I want to request that you and Judith keep that quiet, please."

"You didn't tell Bastiann about your dizziness?" said Judith. "He should know."

"Not until I find out what caused it. I'll have a thorough examination when I return to London."

"What did that local doctor find?" Amy said. "I assume you saw one, not just a nurse."

"Absolutely. There were some irregularities in an EKG. For now, I'm writing them off to being shot at."

"You at least told Bastiann about that, right?" said Amy.

"Of course. It could have a bearing on the investigation. Shooting at me in the abbey, those two passengers killed at Attersee, and Dragavei's death are far too many coincidences for one riverboat cruise." Esther looked back at her table and then at her two new friends. "Remember now, mum's the word."

The pair of women nodded.

Esther waved at Bastiann, Kaylee, and Ken. Ken was pointing at her entrée. She gave Amy and Judith friendly hugs, nodded at the Germans, and returned to her table.

***

Upon returning, the foursome's conversation turned to Kayla and Ken's son.

"I heard somewhere or from someone you were at Oxford once upon a time," Kayla said, eyeing Esther over the rim of her wineglass. "Do you have any advice for our son? I think it could be something of a challenge for an American."

Esther thought a moment. *Is being "black" an implied part of that challenge?* She wondered if many black men had received the honor, although she could remember one.

"I don't see why that would be the case. Rhodes Scholars are treated like any other graduate students, although they tend to focus on the social sciences. What's your son's field of study?"

"Political science."

"For their program, that's PPE, or 'Philosophy, Politics, and Economics,' like Bill Clinton studied long ago, and Pete Buttigieg more recently, although I might be wrong about the latter chap's field of studies. I wasn't a student but a professor's wife, so my contact with students was limited. Frankly, Oxford is like Cambridge—a bit stodgy and elitist, if you ask me. They're like your Harvard and Yale."

"Is that the Labour Party member speaking?" said Ken. Kayla scowled at him.

"On the contrary, many Labour Party leaders have graduated from Oxford. It's often just the ticket for entry into His Majesty's civil service with a high position."

"What about African-Americans?" Kayla said.

Now we're down to it, thought Esther. "I'll confess I can't recall many handsome black faces from the time I was there, but I was there even before your New Jersey Senator Booker was in that program. I heard he did just fine. Times have changed, thank God. Your son will do fine too." Esther wasn't sure about that, but she believed it was what a mother and father might want to hear. And the son didn't seem to be a lazy oaf. "By the way, tell your son I wish him well and congratulate him for the scholarship. It's truly an honor. I should have said that earlier, and I apologize. It's not like we haven't been busy, though."

"No problem," said Ken. "We didn't know you were at Oxford until yesterday."

She winked at Bastiann before commenting. "I've had the privilege of being married to some fine men, but I don't talk about any of them much. I'm normally a private person."

After coffee and dessert, the festive atmosphere lost its sizzle, and people started leaving. The two couples remained as the room emptied. Ken was an avid reader of sci-fi, so he and Bastiann had something in common to chat about. Kayla was learning about classic art from Esther, and Esther was learning about American art, a subject where she was weak and needed to know more about because of the demand for it in London. But, after a time, the quartet also concluded they should call it a night. That conclusion started with Esther saying she was knackered. She had to explain the meaning of that word to the two Americans.

"A lovely evening," said Bastiann as they walked along the corridor toward their cabin. The American couple had to take the stairs down one flight. "Has your opinion of Americans improved, my dear?"

"Any Yank who loves curries earns my respect," she said.

"Maybe Ken loves spicy food too much. He did say his favorite curry dish was vindaloo, after all. I wonder how he'd make out with some of Amsterdam's fiery Indonesian dishes."

She chuckled. "Some of those even bring tears to my eyes." She paused at their door. "No chance they're involved in anything related to our investigation, right?"

"Absolutely not. They're basically innocents even, just a happy couple who are still in love."

"Quite an accomplishment these days." She took the door's key card from her purse and slid it into the slot. "I would—" She froze when she saw their room's interior.

Bastiann couldn't see around her. "What's wrong?"

"Someone's trashed our room." Esther stepped farther into the room, standing in the WC's doorway to allow him to enter. "What could they possibly be looking for?"

"My lists and notes?"

"You locked them in the safe, right?"

He nodded and went to the Apple monitor sitting at one edge of the combination desk and makeup table. He put his palm on the screen. "Still warm. They tried to break into my files. Let me see if they had any success."

"There should be nothing to see there, although I suppose security is not too much concern on this riverboat."

"They could learn something from just our emails. We've both sent them. And a good hacker might also be able to determine what databases I accessed."

"I see. Can you determine if that occurred?"

"I'm not a good hacker by any stretch of the imagination, but I created some special and unusual settings. Let's see if someone changed any of them." She waited. "No changes...and no sign of logging on to the email package. Maybe our intruder wasn't a good hacker, or simply assumed we'd leave the computer logged on to our account with applications open."

"What are we going to do about this mess?" Esther said, jerking a thumb towards the mess behind her.

He smiled. "We've already reported the break-in to proper authorities, namely us. Let's pile everything onto the little sofa and leave tidying up for morning. I know an activity that will help us forget this happened."

Esther badly guessed Bastiann's intentions. He only wanted to catch some of the floor show in the lounge. A Hungarian folk troupe was scheduled to perform as a welcoming party for Budapest, their final stop.

Unfortunately the captain was waiting for them. He'd cancelled the performance, yet the lounge was still full.

Chapter Thirty-Four

Wednesday Night: En Route from Bratislava to Budapest

"*Uram* Kertes has the floor," Captain Janssen said.

The Hungarian bigot Gazsi Kertes stood, turned to face the crowd, and folded his arms with an imperious scowl on his face. At that moment, he reminded Bastiann of someone, but he didn't know that many Hungarians. Perhaps a foreign politician?

"I think I speak for everyone," he said. "We require transparency. And if Agent van Coevorden can't do his job, captain, you should find someone who can."

"Agent van Coevorden, do you want to respond to that?" said the captain with a smile, his eyes twinkling.

Bastiann glared at Gazsi but rose and stood by the captain. *Gazsi needs to be in a straitjacket and locked in a padded cell!* The Interpol agent surveilled the crowd. At that moment, everyone there appeared hostile, except Esther, of course, who appeared to be amused by the confrontation as much as Sander Janssen. *Does she expect me to base my defense on mentioning Gazsi's past?* he wondered, recalling her notes. *That might not be wise.* He hadn't done that in the interview. To point a fine point on it, Gazsi hadn't given him the chance.

"I understand *Uram* Kertes and others' frustrations. I'm frustrated too. Running this investigation isn't my idea of an enjoyable honeymoon. But let me inform everyone that I'm doing my job, all behind the scenes, a task no one else wanted to do, either the local authorities or federal police in Germany and Austria."

He paused and forced a smile. *Are they understanding me?* He knew angry people sometimes weren't logical, the most egregious case being mob mentality.

"Investigations take time. You can't speed them up by adding more people. Perhaps you can build a brick wall faster by adding more bricklayers, but criminal investigations don't usually work that way. Most of you have gone on your tours and are otherwise enjoying your cruise vacation as I work behind the scenes. All that would have ended if the riverboat had to stay in dock so many criminal investigators could come onboard to poke around. Your lives would have had many more interruptions. Did you want that?"

There was a small chorus of nos in several different languages and accents.

"But, as a consequence of your working behind the scenes, we're kept in the dark," said Gazsi. "I want to know what's going on!" The yeses were now louder. "Is there any evidence the murderer is still onboard?"

"All passengers except the victim and the two murdered at Attersee are accounted for," said Bastiann. He winked at Captain Janssen. "Same for crewmembers, except for one waiter, who had a personal commitment requiring attention."

Bastiann would never say that commitment was to Marisol. The audience was full of gossips who would turn that into a scandal.

A woman jumped up and glared at the other passengers in the lounge. "Then someone on this boat is a murderer!"

Bastiann smiled at her brilliant deduction.

"Sit down, Liz," her husband said.

Bastiann nodded. "I'm afraid Mrs. Gross is correct. The Attersee murders and the onboard one might not be connected, which would make this situation even worse in a sense, but I believe they are. Also, the attempt on my wife's life is probably related. Is that transparent enough, Uram Kertes?"

Gazsi jumped up, shaking his fist. "I demand a squad from the Hungarian Federal Police be brought onboard to protect us, both passengers and crew. We should have had that protection early on. Security, van Coevorden, I demand security! If I don't receive that, I'll sue the cruise line."

"Your call," Bastiann said to the captain. "However, I don't recommend what he requests. We're already heading for Budapest. And, depending on its size, I don't know where you'd put that squad, before or now, but what *Uram* Gazsi suggests is a possibility when we dock. People would have to stay onboard and change their flight plans out of Budapest, though."

"We've already checked all movement in and out of the boat," Caitlin, the cruise director, said. "What do you want, Mr. Kertes? Police stationed along every corridor and on the top deck? I'm sure we'll have a fabulous time in Budapest with them onboard."

Bastiann smiled. Caitlin was one smart lady who also knew how to be ironic. Captain Jansssen was a lucky man. "And that's more than a squad," he said.

"Damn right," said the captain, "and it's a terrible choice. It would turn this riverboat into a floating prison. And, as Agent van Coevorden said, affect everyone's travel plans."

"I want my money back then," said the red-faced Hungarian. "This cruise has become a complete farce, if not a disaster."

Is that his motivation? wondered Bastiann. He wouldn't put it past the man.

Murmurs in the crowd indicated some of them agreed with that idea. The captain waved his hand for silence.

"I don't see the problem. All tours have taken place, and future ones in Budapest are still scheduled. Meals and entertainment onboard are still offered, except for tonight, at *Uram* Kertes's request, I might add. The cruise has continued and will continue as planned. Let's allow Agent van Coevorden to continue his behind-the-scenes investigation. Nothing has changed, and Budapest awaits us."

Now there were a lot more yeses. *This captain can handle a crowd,* observed Bastiann.

"Except we're still in the dark and not secure," said Gazsi.

"Oh, shut up, Gazsi," said Maja, Gazsi's wife. "You're always ranting about something. That's all I've heard for forty years. Rant, rant, rant. We're nearly home. People must think I've been feeding you a steady diet of bitter lemons. I want to finish this cruise!"

The mouse that roared, thought Bastiann.

***

"A near thing," Captain Janssen said to Caitlin and Bastiann after the meeting's participants cleared the lounge to return to their staterooms, some now grumbling about having missed the scheduled entertainment. "There was a lot of anger in this lounge."

"It's been simmering for a while with that Hungarian stirring the pot," said Caitlin. "Too much paprika, I'd say." Bastiann smiled and nodded. "Is there something more we can do, Bastiann?"

"You've both helped a lot. Caitlin, you know every passenger onboard. Your information complemented everything I've gathered from Interpol and countries' agencies. I'll continue my investigation, but I must warn you both, I most likely won't finish before docking in Budapest. Investigations are about hard work and lucky breaks, sometimes caused by a slipup an arrogant criminal makes."

Caitlin put her hand on his arm. "Do what you can in the time left."

"By the way, where's your wife?" said the captain.

Bastiann looked around the lounge. Esther was nowhere in sight. He made his apologies.

"She wouldn't have found this discussion productive. And we had a long day. But maybe she's even working. She's convinced there's something in Dragavei's past that will blow this case wide open. Out of many riverboats that cruise the Danube, even limiting the number to those going to Budapest and beyond, why did he choose this one?" He shrugged. "It's something to pursue in the time remaining."

He hadn't mentioned Robert Winston's encounter with Dragavei in London to Esther. He wasn't ready to mention it to Caitlin or Sander either. But he was wondering if Esther was the reason Dragavei had chosen their riverboat. *But why? What is their connection?* All his questions, including those two, remained.

Chapter Thirty-Five

Wednesday: En Route from Bratislava to Budapest

Days before, when Luynven had returned to her stateroom after a late celebration dinner with Viktor the evening Dragavei was killed, she realized her earring was missing. She searched for it the next day, but she couldn't retrace all her steps completely. Dragavei's cabin was either locked, or had the SOCOs or cleaning people inside, or Esther or Bastiann were working there, or he was interviewing.

Luynhen had rationalized and figured she'd lost the earring elsewhere. She also thought it might not matter. *After all, how can Esther or Bastiann trace the earring to me?* But she became nervous when Esther fixed her gaze upon her several times during the Hungarian's inquisition of the Dutch agent. *What was she thinking?* It had to be about her. And Esther rushed out near the end of the meeting. *Should I tell Viktor?*

She knew something was up. She also knew this day might come, although she never expected it to be on this mission. Her trainer in Sofia had told her not to become too cocky. Her slipup normally shouldn't have mattered, and it still might not have, but she was trapped on a damn riverboat! The thought of a prison term scared her. *And how will the others react? Will they forget me? Will Viktor? Or will they consider me only another casualty of the patriotic war against the West?*

That's crap, she observed. She'd never done anything out of patriotism, only to live a better life. *Putin and his cronies are neither patriots nor ideologues; they're not true communists. They're thugs who only care about themselves and exploit others to further their own agendas.*

She gave herself a hug. *A plan! I must come up with a plan!* Whatever Esther Brookstone was thinking, it couldn't be good for her.

She wasn't that good at planning, though. She mostly left that to Viktor or to whomever accompanied her on a mission. She was generally the bait, the woman men could take advantage of. *Older men, powerful men, men who needed to be killed.*

There had been many, most of them victims as unknown to her as Maxim Dragavei had been. The world hadn't known the true Maxim because he'd been in their same business. *We prefer to work in the shadows! The only problem with that is no one cares if you live or die. Not even people you work with, and certainly not the people you work for.*

***

Bastiann found Esther looking at his notes she'd pulled from the safe.

"I'm revisiting the notes on that Bulgarian couple. I was looking around the crowd and saw Luynhen wore silver earrings."

"So did Judith."

"But Luynhen's two were similar to the one you found. Maybe even made by the same jeweler." She waved the sheets. "And here's more confirmation for what I surmised. Remember, you declared that residue on the earring could be cleaning fluid left by one of the boat's staff who had missed finding the earring earlier. You didn't want to send the earring for analysis as a result. You even supposed it might be a previous passenger from another trip on the riverboat. But why not Luynhen?"

"I remember all that. And? Is this just another case of women's intuition?"

"Don't be a sexist. It doesn't become you. It's not intuition to ask, what if the residue is a bit of propofol? Maybe there was a tussle between Dragavei and his assailant. Or what if she lost the earring at the time she was administering the sedative? They're clip-ons, by the way, so there'd be no blood, but also they'd be easy to dislodge."

Bastiann pondered Esther's theory, smarting a bit from the sexism complaint. "I suppose it's possible. Ronaldo thought it was only cleaning fluid. Maybe even his. Maybe we should have that residue analyzed in Budapest."

"Too late. She could be long gone by the time we obtain lab results. We need to confront her now! Either confirm or kill my theory. I'll look for her in the lounge. You look for her in her stateroom. Are you with me?"

"Of course. After that meeting, I'm on adrenalin. I can think of better things to do in moments like that, but why not go after Luynhen? That should at least calm your suspicions."

"I would be terribly surprised if they aren't valid."

***

Luynhen, like some other passengers, had used the riverboat's approach to Budapest as an excuse to revisit the lounge and see the bridges—the Szechenyi Chain Bridge, in particular, but also the Buda Castle and Parliament Building on opposite banks and casting their reflections in the dark Danube waters, as well as other sights of the twin cities at night. That was only an excuse, though, because she hadn't wanted to be trapped in their cabin. And she'd wanted to look for Viktor, even though

270

he never cared much about scenery. Her paranoia had taken over. She was sure Esther was after her.

Luynhen didn't exactly know if her lost earring that matched the ones she was wearing, or something else-- maybe the knife?—had set Esther off. In any case, she surmised the English woman had left to check on something to confirm a hunch. Ihrin's knife, for example, had been a peculiar substitute for the deadly poisons Luynhen often had to use, much to her dread, but like those unavailable poisons and unlike Viktor's gun, the knife had the advantage of being silent. She'd used wires to strangle people too, but she'd decided against using that on Dragavei because she thought he'd be too strong.

She had no idea where Viktor was. *Flirting with a woman or even a crewmember, most likely.* She'd lately lost all hope their fake relationship might become an authentic one. *I should have told him about the earring!* She'd been embarrassed by her slipup.

She saw Esther enter the lounge from the reception area, look around, and then move toward Luynhen with purposeful strides. *Too late,* she thought. *And Budapest's so near!*

Esther approached, and Luynhen waited, leaping to her feet and timing her blow perfectly so the English woman's momentum would add to its force. But the old hag was more agile than Luynhen could have imagined. The fist that would have broken Esther's windpipe and suffocated her was deflected. With her opposite hand, Esther struck back, staggering Luynhen. But she whirled and kicked Esther in the ribs, sending her to the floor.

Luynhen then dashed out the lounge door to the ship's prow. She headed for the stairs and climbed them to the top deck. She spotted Esther at the head of the stairs and kept running, cursing in multiple languages. *I'll go down the middle or aft stairs. Are we near shore?* She glanced to her side, but couldn't make out the river's banks. *Somewhere over by the lights. Can I make it?*

Cecilia and Maria were power-walking on the track and enjoying the Hungarian capital's night lights ahead of them when Luynhen ran past them. They then also saw Esther at the head of the stairs and not far behind.

"I wonder what this is all about," said Maria, turning to watch Luynhen run on. "Say, isn't that Bastiann?"

The Interpol agent was at the riverboat's other end at the head of the stairs coming from the Chef's Table. The twins waved at him.

Luynhen saw him too. She skidded to a stop, looked back at the twins and Esther, and then climbed onto the security rail.

"Oh no! Is she going to jump?" said Cecilia.

"Stop!" both Esther and Bastiann called out.

Luynhen smiled at the twins, and then she jumped into the dark waters.

Esther and Bastiann ran together towards the twins now, stopping every so often to look over the side. Cecilia and Maria were already doing the same thing.

"She's going to drown," Maria said.

Part Four: Hungary

"That one may smile and smile and be a villain." Hamlet, Act 1, Scene 5

Chapter Thirty-Six

Thursday Morning: Budapest

Even under Soviet rule, Budapest always leaned toward the West. It is the capital and most populous city of Hungary, as well as the ninth-largest city in the EU by population within city limits. Its eclectic mix of past glories and future promises often seem at odds. Evidence of the bloody 1956 revolution still remains. The revolt started as a student protest, which attracted thousands as they marched through the city's center and to the Parliament building overlooking the Danube, attracting more protesters by using a van with loudspeakers. A student delegation tried to broadcast demands and was detained. When the delegation's release was demanded by protesters outside, they were fired upon from within the building by the Federal Police. One student died and was wrapped in a flag and held above the crowd. As news of protests and fighting spread, disorder and violence gripped the capital…until Soviet soldiers and tanks moved in to stop it…but they only added to it over several days.

Viktor had gone to the lounge to find Luynhen only to see Esther Brookstone jump up from the floor to pursue his partner. Considering she held one hand to her side, the old hag was surprisingly agile. *Good thing Luynhen has a good lead! But what's going on?*

After deciding to follow and struggling to find his pass key, he pursued the pair as far as the prow in time to see Luynhen's body float by. *The bitch didn't know how to swim that well. She drowned. Damn! Something's not right.* Luynhen was a pro, so he had a hard time deciding what went wrong. He decided it couldn't be good.

He spun on his heels to return to the lounge. He was thinking at high speed now. *Plans! I need a plan.* A way out occurred to him. *I might have time to hide and then disembark after we dock!*

Tick-tock, tick-tock. He was running against the clock. He'd been doing that his entire life, fully conscious of the danger involved in his chosen occupation—he knew his time could be short when he was thirteen and made his first kill—but now even more so after seeing Luynhen's lifeless body float by in the river. *I was born to die early. The Soviets used me; Putin uses me.* Of course, the old KGB leader just saw them all as trained dogs, their Pavlov ringing the bells to make them kill.

Tick-tock, tick-tock. Can I beat the clock? He and Luynhen were on-again, off-again lovers. *On, off.* Playing the role of a married couple always had its fringe benefits. Making mountains of euros added a lot more incentive. Putin counted on the latter and didn't give a rat's ass about the former.

They'd had a successful mission, all things considered. *What went wrong?* There was the little hiccup with the other Bulgarian couple, not part of their group, when he'd momentarily forgotten they knew Bulgarian. He said something in that language to Luynhen, as he often did when wanting to be secretive. They possibly overheard and might wonder about it. Luynhen had caught that, and, to be safe, he'd eliminated the couple at Attersee.

Tick-tock, tick-tock. He looked at his watch, a solar Seiko, a gift from Luynhen. *Stupid bitch had enough money to buy me a Rolex, damn her!* The woman had wanted to make their pretend on-again-off-again marriage official. Silently the second hand moved around the dial. No tick-tock, but time was running out.

I have to leave the boat the moment they dock in Budapest! Will I make it?

His life had been one long casino trip where he'd played multiple games with Death, who always seemed to have the games rigged. He'd still won, or it seemed that way. Luck had always been on his side. Would it fail him now? *Is it now time to pay for those lives I've taken? Or could he cheat Death one more time?*

***

Robert was chatting with Caitlin, who had left the lounge right after the meeting with the obnoxious Hungarian, when Viktor ran up the stairs by the elevator, two at a time. He threw Robert aside and kept going along the corridor.

"Are you okay, Robert?" Caitlin said from behind her desk.

Robert picked himself up from the floor, mad at himself because his reflexes had failed to come into play. *In my early years with the firm, that would never have happened!* "I wonder what that fool's problem is! Maybe I should have gone to Gazsi's bitch-and-moan session to make the evening a complete disaster."

"You didn't miss anything significant, I assure you. I counted it only as more lounge entertainment, although it had some educational value. Bastiann and Sander put Gazsi in his place. But should we do something about Mr. Demyankov's actions?"

Robert's cold eyes were still following Viktor, who disappeared into the Bulgarian couple's stateroom. "I suppose I could lodge a complaint, but he didn't hurt me." He turned to Caitlin and smiled, his anger gone. "And do you think his damn government would care?"

"I suppose not." She came around her desk. "Are you clear about your airport connections then?"

He realized she was anxious to change the subject. He glanced at her well-organized board with all the passengers' departures and connections information. "I think so. Three legs to get to London. Who would have thought?"

"I'm sorry. That's all I could manage for you. You were very lucky to have only two before, but that Budapest to Paris flight cancellation ruined your careful planning. There just aren't that many flights to and from Budapest. Most go to Frankfurt, in fact."

"I know, but that Paris flight seemed to be the perfect solution. By the way, thanks for your competent organization on this cruise, Caitlin. It was truly a lovely trip, all things considered. Quite an experience."

She smiled. "In many ways."

***

Once he entered the stateroom, Viktor started throwing random things into a carry-on bag. He didn't know what to pack, what he might need, but he knew he wanted to travel light. All the while, he was planning his escape route for when he left the ship.

One option was to disappear into Budapest. He knew the city maybe better now than he knew Sofia. There were even abandoned buildings still with pock marks from the 1956 revolution, where bullets and shells fired by the invading Soviet army left a grim reminder of those days for all the city's citizens. But not for him. *The Hungarians deserved payback for that stupid rebellion!*

He could hide in one of those buildings for a while. It was ironic, what with the fascist and oppressive Fidesz beefing up the Federal Police, that doing so could present a problem. Budapest would be only a temporary solution...and perhaps a dangerous one. Traveling outside the city on public transportation with the Viktor

Demyankov documentation could be dangerous too. They all had alternate documentation stored in lockers at various train stations around Europe—none of them knew the others' real names—but if the Interpol agent put out a bolo, Viktor might never be able to use one of those alternate identities waiting for him at the Budapest station.

Tick-tock, tick-tock. He glanced at the small clock on the end table by the bed. Not being certain of what the safest option was, he gave up planning for the moment. *I'll leave the riverboat and then decide what to do.*

He was reading a text message on his mobile with one hand and throwing some more things into the carry-on with the other when there was a knock at the door. *It has to be either Esther or Bastiann! But what can they suspect?* He hadn't even been at that damn meeting with Gazsi. *Stupid Hungarian! Nothing discreet about him!* He had no love for that buffoon.

But Luynhen had done something that sent the whole mission down the crapper. *Are the others in peril?* He really didn't care. He'd always looked out for number one, that fellow sometimes called Viktor. *The others could go to hell!*

He tossed the phone into the bag, zipped it shut, and shoved it under the bed. He then opened the door and stared at the gun with its long silencer.

"No!"

***

"Much more dramatic than the old-fashioned tooth filled with cyanide," Esther said, staring at the far-off body floating behind them in the riverboat's gentle and decaying wake.

"I'm calling it in," Bastiann said, taking out his mobile. "Were you watching Luynhen at the meeting?"

Esther nodded. "How do you think I saw her earrings? Someone might have warned her after seeing me dash from the lounge."

"Maybe her husband? I don't remember seeing him at the meeting with Gazsi, though."

"We need to find Viktor. I doubt he's an innocent in all this."

"I suggest we first check their stateroom. It was empty before, but that doesn't mean anything now. And there might be some clue there to his whereabouts if he's not there."

Bastiann asked Ronaldo, who was across the hall cleaning another stateroom, to open the Bulgarian couple's door. "Can you find Captain Janssen and tell him what's happened and that we're here?" Ronaldo nodded and disappeared.

Esther and Bastiann started to search the room. It occurred to him they were doing so without a warrant, but Luynhen's death was a probable cause if anyone asked. The first piece of evidence he found was at the back of one of the desk drawers behind the transceivers used on tours. He held up the syringe and empty propofol bottle that had been wrapped in a washcloth. The search the Linz inspector had proposed would have discovered this, he thought glumly.

"I wonder where they obtained these?"

"Syringes are generally available as standard medical supplies throughout Europe," Esther said. "Who knows where they obtained the drug?"

They continued their search. She found Viktor wedged into one side of the smaller wardrobe, some blood oozing from a hole in his forehead.

"I'm guessing Luynhen didn't want us to interrogate the poor bloke," she said. "Or someone else who saw me go after her did some cleanup." She glanced at the bed where clothes from the wardrobe had been tossed. She spotted the carry-on underneath and pulled it out. It contained a mobile and a small pistol. "Looks like Viktor wasn't so innocent after all." She held up the newly found items.

The gun was the first item she examined. She sniffed it; there was no cordite odor. "Not recently fired, but two chambers are empty. It could be the gun used by the abbey shooter, who didn't resemble Viktor, by the way."

"We'll need to try to access that mobile," he said.

She examined it. "We won't need a password. It's still on. He was packing and must have been interrupted while he did so. Was he communicating with someone?"

"Something droll like 'Can't meet you for dinner in Budapest,' I suppose, which wouldn't ring any alarm bells. You told me once spies generally don't use ciphers that take time to code and decode; they only use ordinary language that has hidden meaning for them."

"That was in East Berlin in the days before mobiles, love, although I suppose you could send bland messages via text nowadays. A smart phone is a tiny computer, though, so they could even have a secret coding/decoding app."

"They have an app for that?" Upon seeing her frown, Bastiann said, "Sorry. Couldn't resist. Find anything on the mobile? Or do we need your friend from MI5 to bread into it?"

"Not encrypted. Viktor was in a bit of a rush, I dare say." She scrolled to the first text message. "The last message he received is in Russian."

"What's it say?"

"'Clean up!'" She pointed to Viktor's body. "Likely an order for him, but I'm guessing someone else also received that same message and interpreted it differently."

Bastiann's ringtone sounded. He answered, listened, and nodded. "They'll recover Luynhen's body," he said to Esther, "if they can find it. They'll also be waiting for us at the dock in Budapest."

"Tell the blues and twos they'll have another body to pick up here at the boat. I hope Ronaldo informed the captain. I bet he'll be happy to know this is all over."

"I'll also tell him when I see him we won't be going on any tours in Budapest. At least, I won't be. There will be too many details to tend to here. We both know the city well enough, right?"

She nodded. "I will be the dutiful wife and stand by your side in spite of the spears and arrows bureaucratic authorities throw our way..." She stopped when she saw his frown. "It was truly a smashing honeymoon cruise, dear Bastiann. We must do another one again sometime, one that comes with some sort of guarantee it will be more peaceful."

She gave him a hug but winced as pain from where Luynhen had kicked her turned the hug into an ordeal.

***

Budapest's police force had several units patrolling the Danube. All patrol boats were equipped for search and rescue, or SAR; only one helicopter was available.

Jozsi Matyas loved his exciting SAR adventures when they were called on to pluck persons from the river. It helped if they were drunk because they'd struggle less when strapping them into the stretcher, and also there'd be less struggling inside the heli where EMTs finished saving them. Some were saved, some died on the way up, some in the heli, and still others in the hospital. It was all still a thrill ride, one where adrenalin flowed because every second counted.

A floating dead body avoided the struggling, although the time crunch was still there. He had to pluck the woman's body from the river before it reached the first bridge if at all possible. His SAR experiences had also included some harrowing ones between bridges, of course—the heli was ideal for all river rescues because it could hover and often arrived before patrol boats could.

The woman was dead, though, so a lot of fun and motivation were removed from the rescue. But respectful treatment of the dead was still required, and rescuing the body was part of that. Still challenging, still necessary, but not as rewarding as saving a life.

His helicopter pilot was an expert too. He matched the current's speed even as Jozsi was lowered to splash down besides the woman's body. He rolled the body onto the stretcher, strapped it in, and grabbed onto a handhold with his right hand. He waved his left in an upward motion. By the time he and the dead woman were inside, the bird was over land and heading to the nearest hospital with a helipad.

Of course, that hospital couldn't do anything for the woman, but they knew what to do with dead bodies too. And the patrol cars would already be there waiting, lights flashing but with no sirens to avoid molesting the hospital patients.

The morgue will be busy tonight, he thought. The pilot had informed him there was another body onboard the riverboat. He wondered if the two deaths were connected. The police certainly would.

Chapter Thirty-Seven

Thursday Evening: Budapest

Esther loved Budapest by night. She and Bastiann held hands as they rode along in the minibus on their late-night tour of the city, a last romantic moment on their honeymoon before heading home. The investigation was now in the hands of Hungary's Federal Police, the *Rendörség,* although he still had to write his report for Interpol.

With all the bureaucratic details necessary to put an end to the investigation, something which made the captain, cruise director, and honeymoon couple happy, they had missed the "Queen of the Danube" tour during the day. Other passengers had made the Castle Hill hike. That night's land tour was a replacement for the nighttime boat tour up and down the Danube's shores, one resulting in that accident a few years earlier.

But even from the bus, the tour was still worth it. The Parliament building was as sparkling as London's, if not more so, because, without the fog, one could see its luminous finery much better. She couldn't help thinking of how Soviet butchers had squelched that 1956 revolution, though, some murders taking place inside that very building. That event and many other Soviet atrocities had motivated her to work for MI6.

Under the Soviets, the Politburo had been like a Russian mafia; under Putin, nothing had changed, except he was now the mafia's capo. Russian-style communism was a dead and debunked ideology that always had been only an excuse to destroy personal freedoms and rape a large percentage of the eastern European and Asian continent, continuing now under Putin without any ideological pretensions whatsoever except "Make Russia great again." His plans for world domination were now helped along by internet propaganda filled with lies and conspiracy theories spewed out across the globe and world leaders who coddled him, democratic leaders included.

"You appear pensive, my dear," Bastiann said.

She wiped away tears. "I'm just happy we're together, old man. But I've realized that, after spending most of my life fighting the far-right and far-left, which are in the same pile of beans, fighting criminals and so forth, my successes don't amount to much. Everything's going to hell again. At least we'll have some time together. I don't want any more cases like this one. We need to leave it all behind. Are you with me?"

"Probably. No promises for immediate action, but I *am* considering retirement." He paused a moment to watch as their bus crossed a bridge. "I forgot to tell you. Hal Leonard informed me they captured Ernesto Felipe Lopez Diaz and will put him on trial for illegal international arms trafficking. That should cheer you up."

"It does. He was one scary son of a bitch." She grabbed his hand. "But it doesn't change what I'm saying. We're married now...and old. You should retire. I don't want to be a widow again."

"As I said, I've been considering it. This case put you in more danger than me, though...and it was my case. We need to change that. Retirement is an option I must plan for. But I must also do better at keeping you safe."

***

The next Friday morning, Caitlin caught Esther still in her nightgown.

"Oh, hello there, come on in. Don't mind the chaos. I'll make room for us on our little sofa."

Esther tossed some carry-on luggage and a makeup bag onto suitcases already stacked on the bed.

When they were both seated, Caitlin waved at the bed. "You don't travel light, Esther."

"I guess that's mostly mine. I normally do better, but this cruise was something of a surprise…in many more ways than I expected, as you know. Even packing, I didn't know what to bring, so I probably packed too much. We've traveled through several climes in seven days. And we were originally planning on going to Prague to start the tour, but bailed on that for lack of time." Esther shrugged. "Everything was rushed because we were married in Lyon, and I didn't have time to even look at a brochure or pay attention to your company's sound advice about what to pack." She smiled. "You're an old pro at all this. It was my first river cruise." She eyed Caitlin, realizing she was talking too much. "What can I do for you, my dear lady?"

"Nothing much. I'd add that this time of year can have changeable weather too, even in one spot, so one needs layers." Caitlin seemed lost in her thoughts for a moment. "I do want to ask you something important, though." Esther nodded. "Did you find it?"

"You have me at a loss, I'm afraid. Find what?"

"His tomb."

Esther was surprised; she hadn't expected that question. She carefully considered her response.

"You're Catholic, I suppose. Would my answer make a big difference in your life? I'd never want to destroy anyone's faith, or create a religious fanatic, for that matter. We have enough of those. They're a plague worse than that virus a while ago."

"Yes, your answer would greatly matter to me. Losing my Edwin shook the foundations of my faith. I went to confessional afterwards and asked the priest why God allowed such terrible things to happen. Can cancer be part of his plan?"

"No more than COVID-19, I'd guess. I'm not Catholic, so take my answer as a bit unorthodox: Don't let anyone tell you everything's God's will and part of his plan. First of all, He gave us free will, and human beings create enough of their own evil and problems for others to make the Devil often appear irrelevant. Second, I believe ye Olde Duffer doesn't have time to deal with the minutiae of His grand experiment." Esther leaned towards Caitlin. "I also find it the epitome of arrogance that human beings assume they're so damn special. The cosmos is so huge, space and time so vast, many others have most assuredly eaten their versions of the apple and left their Edens."

"ETs?" Esther nodded. "That's an unusual way to put it. Sounds like you're a sci-fi addict."

"Heavens no. Bastiann's the one for that."

Caitlin paused to digest what Esther had said. She seemed to refocus. "And your answer to my question about the tomb?"

Esther sighed. "You're persistent, I dare say, so I'll tell you. Yes, we found it. Ask to see Bastiann's wedding band sometime. I'm only guessing it was never used for that purpose and was simply a gift of friendship from Mary Magdalene to Christ. There's an inscription in Aramaic inside implying that."

"Oh my God!"

"Precisely. And, before we depart to return to the London fog, I'd like to see your engagement ring. I'm going to try to convince Bastiann to make a little detour to Antwerp once we arrive in Paris. I have a friend there who's a jeweler. We can always stay overnight at his place in Amsterdam and then travel on to London."

***

Esther dressed, expecting Caitlin to return wearing her engagement ring. Before she arrived, Kayla and Ken, Amy and Judith, and Arthur and his wife dropped in to bid adieu. All polite hugs and kisses, so she was glad Bastiann was off chatting with Sander Janssen.

Much to her surprise, Maja and Gazsi stopped by too.

"No bad feelings, Esther? You and Bastiann caught the killers. Good show. Quite an accomplishment."

From Gazsi, Esther knew that was a compliment. She kept the expression on her face neutral, though. *Never trust a fascist!* "Thank you, *Uram* Kertes." She nodded at Maja. "Help him mellow out. His blood pressure will thank you."

He frowned, but Maja hooked her arm into her husband's. "Gazsi will be fine. And I was able to enjoy my tour for the most part."

Gazsi shook his head. "Women and their damn holidays and tours." He saluted Esther with his free hand. "Treat that husband well, Esther Brookstone. You have a sharp tongue, so go easy on him."

"I feel no need to apologize or take your advice after how you treated him. I'm afraid I didn't hear the conclusion of that meeting. I wish you no ill, only peace."

Fortunately Sander made an appearance before the situation became more tense, and the Hungarian couple left. *Is Gazsi embarrassed by the trouble he caused for Bastiann and Sander? I hope so!*

"Any problems with that obnoxious fellow?" the captain inquired, watching the couple disappear along the corridor. "I just left Bastiann. We talked about him a bit. Too bad we couldn't get anything on him."

"We had our *kumbaya* moment. He was on his best behavior, which isn't saying much because it's like a sour pickle in brine. And how are things going between Caitlin and you? I'm waiting for her to return to show me her engagement ring, by the way. Bastiann owes me one."

"Bastiann gave me a little lecture. Seems like he wants me to lose my freedom like he did."

"Oh? I'll have to talk to him about that. I mean, about men losing their freedom. That works both ways." She thought a moment. "There was once a song Janis Joplin popularized, although I liked Kris Kristofferson's version better. He wrote it, after all." Sander raised an eyebrow. "I know. You mightn't consider me a country and western fan, and you would be right. So much of it now is only rock with a twang. But on my piano I play popular songs and sing along when I know no one is listening. Kristofferson wrote poetic lyrics. I interpret his 'For the Good Times' as a celebration of life with my first three husbands, for example, a life of good times I hope to continue with Bastiann. The chorus of that other song in question is also poignant and *à propos* in your case, to be taken as advice."

"Quite the sermon. I was thinking you had strange musical tastes for an English woman, so I thought you might be an imposter, but your using words like poignant and *à propos* squelched that."

She recited the chorus. "Do you understand the message?"

"You and Bastiann are a pair. You think I'm dragging my heels and she'll slip away?"

"I've known cases where a woman will wait forever, even a stunner like Caitlin—I might have been content to wait with Bastiann—but why take the risk of losing her, Sander?"

"You don't understand. She wants me to meet her parents!"

"In Dublin?" Sander nodded. "That would be a nice trip. Ireland is a beautiful country. Be sure and take a side trip to Killarney."

"Did you have to chase down an art thief there? A case for the Yard?"

Esther winked. "Let's call it that. Long ago."

"I won't tell Bastiann."

"Tell him what?" she said with a wink.

Five minutes after Sander left, Caitlin appeared. She was wearing her ring. Esther took a photo of it with her mobile.

"The photo is for reference. I'm still working on Bastiann about Antwerp."

Chapter Thirty-Eight

Friday Morning: Lyon

Hal Leonard had known Bastiann van Coevorden for years. Many investigations had sealed their friendship, he'd been his best man, and he'd met Philippa at the wedding. *But there is no sugarcoating this news!*

He smoothed his Hawaiian shirt and prepared himself. He'd been feeding his friend information gleaned from various sources, some not exactly legit. He owed Bastiann at least that much, if only for saving Philippa. Fate had been kind to Hal; he needed to help Bastiann.

He pushed away from his desk in Lyon, leaned back in his chair, and took out his smart phone. Bastiann was on speed dial. Three rings and his Interpol colleague answered.

"Bro, I have some bad news. Dragavei is an alias, as you might have expected. Every good assassin has a few aliases, I suppose. Goes with the job."

He stopped talking, waiting for Bastiann's reaction.

"I don't care about aliases. And we already have good evidence for his being an assassin from the Interpol files and elsewhere. But why was he here on this riverboat? Who did he work for? And who killed him? No, forget the second question. I suppose he killed for anyone who paid him, and pissed someone off in the process."

"It's hard to confirm that in all its gory detail. But his real name's John MacDonald. And that's important, bro!"

"Could be Scottish. Or American? Why is it so important?"

"He's Angus MacDougall's nephew, which makes Esther a distant relative. Second cousin, maybe. Whatever."

"I see. You do surprise me sometimes."

After some pleasantries, Bastiann hung up.

***

As Bastiann walked from Dragavei's stateroom toward his own, he reviewed everything about the case. He concluded that finding Maxim's murderer didn't provide complete closure. Moreover, they'd been lucky. Without the earring, dagger, and Esther's persistence, Luynhen would never have been caught. That had been a mistake, a critical error on her part.

But what triggered the murder of the Bulgarian couple at Attersee? He couldn't imagine. Was that couple part of a cadre who had second thoughts? *And who shot at Esther in the abbey?* The gun belonged to Viktor; his prints were all over it. But Esther believed the shooter was a smaller man than Viktor. The theory the shooter had also been Luynhen made some sense, but they'd likely never know for sure.

And who killed Viktor? Unless done before Luynhen went to the lounge, the timeline indicated the killer couldn't have been her. Was there someone else among the riverboat passengers working with the Bulgarian couple?

Possibly there was work still to be done. He hated an untidy case.

And then there was Dragavei. Why were they after him? Some things were falling into place: Robert's seeing Dragavei at Esther's gallery might only mean he wanted to make contact with Esther, his relative. *Did he just find*

291

out about their relationship? And did that have anything to do with why Luynhen and Viktor were after Dragavei?

Maybe he should discuss these things with Esther, still without mentioning Robert's comment about Dragavei. He'd hold that card close to his vest for the moment. He didn't want to worry his wife.

***

Esther rubbed her eyes and stared at the report. Her friend Jeremy Brand at MI5 had emailed her some more interesting information. Sources were overwritten with X in the plain text with MI5's "For Your Eyes Only" watermark, but she could read through them well enough. *You took a chance, Jeremy,* she observed, mentally thanking her friend.

Maxim Dragavei wasn't Romanian at all. Sighi?oava's infamous son hadn't taken possession of his body either. *That will teach my girls at the gallery another lesson! Dracula indeed!*

But Jeremy's message had created another mystery. Maxim Dragavei was an alias for another alias, Edward Morgan. But after seeing the picture in the media, Edward's family said that hadn't been their son's corpse on the riverboat, and that possibly he was John MacDonald, Edward's boyhood friend.

The report discussed the motor accident involving John MacDonald and offered the theory that Edward Morgan had also been in it, and John had stolen Edward's identity. They had no way to confirm that, so Jeremy insisted it was only a theory.

There was nothing secretive about that. But the report also mentioned that, as a contract killer, Dragavei had worked for both the CIA and SVR, the latter all overwritten with X. His last contract had been *with the*

CIA, with a partner, *Linda Santos*, whereabouts unknown. Their last target had been a Russian oligarch.

Jeremy wouldn't have had that information at MI5, so he must have learned about it from an MI6 contact. Esther knew that information would be Top Secret, although not labeled as such. She'd have to delete the email and hope for the best. Permanently. She'd query Bastiann about how to do that well after he also read it.

Jeremy offered another theory Dragavei's murder was payback ordered by "P himself." *Without X's, and not an effective code,* she observed with a smile. *The CIA*—the X's had returned—knew a team of *Bulgarian and Romanian* assassins were looking for Dragavei. The latter's disappearance had coincided with losing track of the *SVR-financed* team.

Esther observed, *Good old CIA, mucking up things as usual!* Not that MI6 was much better. From installing the Shah in Iran to Pinochet in Chile, many of their actions were questionable. She knew about their arming the Taliban to combat al Qaeda. How that backfired!

She assumed the CIA had changed a lot in the last decade or so. *Maybe like Jeremy, but even more worried about terrorism?* she wondered.

"All very intriguing," Bastiann said after arriving and reading the report. "We now know who Dragavei wasn't and have confirmed how he really made a living. The question, my dear, is: Who is John MacDonald? And why was he on this boat heading for Budapest if Putin's minions were searching for him? He only exposed himself, even more so by returning to Eastern Europe."

"I guess Luynhen and Viktor were part of the team."

"We can't prove that, but it's a logical hypothesis. But your friend mentioned a Bulgarian and Romanian team. We have the Bulgarians. Who are the Romanians?"

They lapsed into thought for a moment.

"The Culianus!" they both said at once.

"Ihrin said they recognized Dragavei when they came onboard," said Esther. "I'll bet they were afraid he recognized them too, so the team had to act in haste."

"We must find Ihrin and her husband Razvan then, and question them. They could be part of the assassination team. All conjecture, of course. There are other Romanians on the riverboat, after all. I wonder if the Culianus are still in Budapest."

Chapter Thirty-Nine

Friday Morning: Budapest

The Romanian couple had exited the boat at an early hour with the many passengers who had early flights, leaving the fateful cruise and the meddlesome Interpol agent behind. They were supposed to catch a bus to the airport, but Luynhen and Viktor's demise made them change their plans. They wouldn't be heading back to Dresden. The long train ride to Moscow would be their best bet.

Ihrin might slow me down, Razvan thought. *But we're a team.*

He glanced at her. He was dragging both rolling suitcases, and she steered two carry-ons—standard luggage for a plane trip. They had a plan for that too. They loaded it all onto the bus headed for the airport, but instead of boarding that bus, they simply walked up the quay's steps and into the city.

They both knew Budapest well. Both trains and buses left the country from the Keleti station. It was often busier than the airport, so they would be safer among the crowds there.

They found a taxi. On the drive to the station, Razvan recalled the events of the past week. He decided they'd had mixed success. He also decided it wasn't only the Interpol agent who had ruined their chances for complete success. They'd even contributed with their own mistakes—he still didn't know the exact points of failure—but Esther Brookstone aided Bastiann van Coevorden a lot. *Possibly in ways we'll never know!*

He wished they'd had time to eliminate both the busybodies. They'd been a huge nuisance. Like buzzing wasps fixated on stinging their victim, Esther and Bastiann were pests. In a way, he admired their competence, but the two deserved to die. Meddlers like them only stood in their way.

"We'll have to pick out some new luggage where we change trains," he said to Ihrin.

"And some new clothes," she said with a smile.

"The luggage will only be for appearances, my dear. One suitcase, one carry-on. Nothing more. Once we're safe, you can buy anything you like."

"Anything?"

"Anything within reason. It's your damn bank account, after all. You can't touch mine."

***

"Where are they?" said Bastiann.

The Romanian couple hadn't appeared for their jaunt to the airport, which confirmed Esther and Bastiann's suspicions. There had been a hurried search of the riverboat, but they concluded they had chosen to disappear into the city. Maybe that was the plan all along, and Luynhen and Viktor hadn't made it. TBD, Bastiann observed.

Esther, who was somewhat taller, spotted the balding head and monk's tonsure of the Romanian. "I have eyes on him. They're heading for the trains. There's a woman beside him, most likely his wife."

Bastiann waved the Budapest police toward him, and they moved to surround the couple, not an easy task with the mass of humanity at the Budapest-Keleti station. Yet they managed it.

Razvan recognized Esther and Bastiann.

"Esther and Bastiann, what a pleasant surprise!"

"Arrest them," Bastiann told the police.

"You have failed," said Ihrin.

Bastiann was wondering what Ihrin meant by that when his peripheral vision saved him. Razvan's blow had the steam taken from it as Bastiann partially deflected it. *I'll have a sore forearm to match Esther's sore ribs!* Before he could do more, Esther put Razvan down by destroying his kneecap with a well-placed kick. But Ihrin fell too, without a blow. *What?*

He saw their eyes glaze over, likely not even seeing all the guns pointed at them. There were some shudders from the Romanian couple, and then they were still.

"Back!" Esther said to everyone. "Don't touch them! Clear the crowd!"

One of the Hungarian agents said something in his native language containing the word "Putin."

Apparently Esther knew enough Hungarian to understand his meaning. "Indeed," she said. "A Putin special, gentlemen."

She must have been afraid that whatever the fast-acting poison was, any drop of it could be lethal for others as well. *That old KGB member likes his poisons.*

"We need the biohazard unit!" the police sergeant called out, as if he were answering Bastiann's thoughts.

When they arrived, the bodies were put into tight plastic bags. Then the rest of them were checked for any symptoms.

"Now we'll never know for sure who killed Dragavei or the couple at Attersee," said Esther after a handsome man had checked eyes, nose, and throat and then recommended she change her clothing as soon as possible.

"Or who shot at you in the abbey," said Bastiann, slightly annoyed by all the aftermath. "There might be more members of this murderous cabal. If so, not even the CIA knew about them!"

***

Ezster watched coroner's assistants remove the bodies of the Romanian couple. She shook her head and couldn't tell whether Janos was sad or frustrated. They were both upset. Partial success, partial failure. Would they be paid?

She was the sharpshooter in the family. Yet Luynhen was given the assignment in Melk, and Esther Brookstone had dodged two bullets in that abbey! The English woman had spotted Luynhen in her disguise as a young man. She knew Janos was unhappy about that result. On the riverboat, it would have been hard for either of them to go after the Interpol agent, the two often seeming more like reporters than detectives, but Janos had believed taking Esther out of the picture would end the agent's investigation long enough for them to disembark in Budapest.

Maybe the critical point of failure, if indeed they had failed. They killed their target, after all. *Did any of the rest matter?*

"We lost four of six," she said. "Sixty-seven percent. That seems quite a loss just to pay back that pathetic amateur assassin. Will they give us their pay?"

"Ha! Not likely. Success is always relative. Maxim was successful, and Linda too, because they were amateurs and completely under the radar. Until they became too greedy. The old era those six belonged to is long gone. We are the new blood the Kremlin needs."

"Not literally, I hope." She sighed. She was thinking of the other four. Not friends, but comrades they had often worked with. She looked at her watch. "I could go for a nice glass of *Egri Bikaver*. I wonder what my mother is preparing for dinner."

"Not a bad idea, love. When they say 'Bull's Blood,' I always think of drinking the Ottoman soldiers'. I wish Putin would take Turkey away from Erdogan's little mafia like he took Crimea from the Ukrainians. But yes, we need to have at least a small celebration. Shall we go and find out what dinner menu is being offered?" Janos looked at his own watch. "We'll only be fashionably late."

Chapter Forty

Saturday Morning: Budapest

In a quiet moment after settling their delayed return plans to London—they had to be off the riverboat because it would soon begin its return trip upriver—Esther called her old boss, George Langston.

"It's good to hear from you, Esther. How's the new Mrs. van Coevorden doing?"

"You know I'll be keeping my own name, right? I did that with my first three husbands."

"And I suppose you have many aliases, my dear."

She smiled. *Maybe more than Dragavei?* "I have no idea what you're implying, George."

"It's just that someday you must tell me about MI5. That chap Jeremy, who's been very circumspect, seems to hold you in high esteem."

"He'd better," she said, remembering how he had heeded her warning about the London terrorists. "And he used to be MI6, but that's all I'll divulge."

There was a pause. "I see. Then someday you must tell me about your time in MI6. Cold War, I suppose, before we met?"

"You're guessing now. And forget the chin wagging. I'm calling to see if everything is running on an even keel at the gallery."

"You should have no worries there. I do have a letter, though, from that Scottish barrister George Cearrach who oversees your castle, keeping you honest. Anna thought I should mention it to you."

"A nice bloke. He's approved all my repairs. Does the letter seem important?"

"How would I know? We only recognized the name. I don't open your mail."

"If it's his office stationery, I suppose you had better open it and read it to me."

"Very well." Esther heard rustling noises in the background. "Here we go: 'Dear Mrs. Brookstone, I must inform you that we have discovered another relative of Angus MacDougall who has closer kinship than you do, his nephew John MacDonald. Because of the property's entailment, he would have normally inherited it, so we will have to sort that out once again, at your convenience. However, if you are willing to pay his burial expenses, there should be no problems with continuing your ownership of the castle. Please contact me as soon as possible to chat about resolving this issue.' It ends with some pleasantries about some dinner you and your husband had with the solicitor and his sister. I wonder if you can write those burial expenses off as repairs to the castle."

"Only if I can bury the bloke there, which likely isn't possible. He could already be buried. But Lord knows who finally ended up with the body, and who buried him, but the old barrister seems to have information along those lines. And you just tied up a tiny loose thread for our case here, George. Say hello to your wife. Bye."

***

Esther used her mobile to search for a number she had buried in a text message, not in her speed-dial list, like Langston's.

"Ophelia, this is Esther."

"Oh, hello, how are you? I heard about some of your escapades. You took a while to get back to me."

Over a year ago, Esther had found Sylvia Bassett, the thief of the Bernini bust, at the castle she'd inherited from Angus MacDougall. At the time, the poor, abused woman was at wit's end. The text message Esther had received while waiting for her flight in Lyon after her wedding gave her a sense of accomplishment: Sylvia AKA Ophelia, Esther's pet name for the woman, had turned her life around.

Once in a dream, Esther had been intimate with her distant relative Angus; in real life, she'd been conflicted about her one night of intimacy with Sylvia. Back then, she had questions about her relationship with Bastiann. Sylvia's own questions had been driving the young woman mad; she nearly killed Esther. They had reached out to each other, both of them looking for answers that couldn't be found in one night. *Sometimes dreams are better than real life that way,* Esther observed.

She sighed. "My dear, getting old isn't made any easier when you're dealing with evil types out to do you harm. I suppose one escapade you heard about was my little run-in with your abuser's son."

"Indeed. Which reminds me: I want to thank you for putting his father away."

"And, to change the subject, how are you doing, my saucy lass?"

"Splendidly. My new job is very fulfilling and I have— how shall I put it?—maybe she's best described as a girlfriend."

"That's wonderful. Love is wonderful no matter how or where you find it. If we ever meet in London—I now own a gallery there—please keep our little dalliance to yourself. It might upset my new husband. We're on our honeymoon."

"That's wonderful too! You must tell me all about it. But you caught me at a bad time. I'm at work. Can I call you back? We can set it up via text messaging so your husband won't know a thing. I'll use Ophelia, of course. No phone sex, I promise." She laughed. "And it must be a longer catchup chat, mostly you giving me details about your adventures and your new partner."

"Yes, but I might become somewhat jealous to hear about your girlfriend, although I'm curious to know more about her too. Let's do that. But a quick question before I ring off: In your little parties at my castle as a wild teenager, did you ever meet someone named John MacDonald."

"Of course. Angus's nephew. That bloke set up most of the parties. I was never attracted to him, though. He was a creepy sort, to be sure, if I remember correctly. It was a long time ago. Like he wanted to be popular but tried too hard, especially with those parties. Why do you ask?"

"I'll tell you when we do a chin wag on the phone. I don't want to hold you up, dear Ophelia. Let me only say I met him in a rather ghoulish manner."

"Now you have my attention. Why ghoulish?"

"When everything's resolved, I'll explain. Right now it's hectic here too."

"Where are you?"

"In Budapest, on the Danube."

"The river? On your honeymoon? How romantic! Now I truly am curious, but I have to go. Text me, love."

Nice girl, thought Esther. *Life can be so interesting.*

She rushed to find Bastiann, who had gone to look for a newspaper.

Chapter Forty-One

Saturday: Budapest to London

Esther and Bastiann ran into Sander Janssen at the airport.

"Not doing the return cruise?" Esther said after a greeting hug. Bastiann went with the usual handshake.

"Flying to Amsterdam for a week's rest, and then on to Paris to do the Rhine cruise. Caitlin's unfortunately doing the return, Budapest to Vilshofen. We'll meet in Munich later because she's not doing Prague the next time."

"Any progress in the romance department?" said Bastiann.

Sander looked around and then smiled at the Interpol agent. "We're still keeping it quiet for now. Caitlin will start wearing the ring, though. That will generate some questions, so news will trickle among the company gossips soon enough. It's all for the best, so I don't mind. The company doesn't have any explicit policy against company romances."

"Why should they?" said Esther with a smile. "Their company understands passengers take their 'Romantic Danube' tour for many reasons, including romance, so why should crewmembers be immune to Cupid's arrows? What about Omar and Marisol?"

"I explained the situation to the directors. They want to help and some of them talked to Omar." He cocked his head, hearing an announcement. "Sorry. I have to run. Have a safe trip. I hope to see you again."

"Same here," said Bastiann.

The newlyweds found seats in the crowded waiting area, and Bastiann left to find a WC.

"You look like the cat who ate the canary," he said when he returned, plopping onto the seat they'd be sharing while waiting for their flight announcement. They'd be flying from Budapest to Frankfurt and then on to London.

Esther had just received a call from Fritz Reiner.

"Your art detective can do her sleuthing at a distance, dear Bastiann," she said with a grin.

"That's such a mysterious statement that I must find out what it means."

"It means that while we were solving all those murders associated with our cruise, at least partially, Fritz Reiner was helping Professor Elise Mayer recover her painting. Not only that, one of Sergio's friends authenticated it. The professor is now the proud owner of an authentic Caravaggio. Isn't that wonderful news? Of course, now she has to worry about paying the insurance on the painting, unless she sells or donates it to a museum."

Bastiann shook his head. "You are a marvel, Esther. I can't wait to go on another cruise with you."

"Just make sure it's free of assassins. Oh look, here's Robert Winston." She waved.

"I see you were delayed too," said the dapper man as he found a seat beside Bastiann after the Interpol agent put a carry-on in front of him.

"We were scheduled to go to Paris and Esther on to London, but Air France cancelled our flight," said Bastiann.

"Likewise," Robert said, "only I was headed back to London via Paris, along with Esther, I suppose. I wonder if we'll still be on the same flights."

"And Bastiann's boss gave him two weeks off for handling the investigation on the riverboat." She hooked arms with Bastiann. "I have him for a while longer."

"Pray tell, Monsieur Poirot, how you solved the crime," Robert said to Bastiann.

The Interpol agent shrugged. "We had some friends who helped. Information is often the key to solving crimes. Plus a few clues." He winked at Esther.

"You're admirably modest and suspiciously circumspect. I like that. We must keep in touch so I can continue to ask that question. I need to know someday, just to satisfy my curiosity. By the way, my sister found Esther's ex-boss quite charming."

Bastiann shrugged. "She caught on then. Sorry, but I had to check your story."

Robert laughed. "That old chap caused quite a stir in the convent. I'd wager they'd never had someone from Scotland Yard visit them before."

Esther leaned over Bastiann. "George and his wife are both charming people. And he fancies himself as the chronicler of my and Bastiann's adventures in fighting crime, so it's only fair that he helps out a bit at times, like Dr. Watson did for Sherlock."

Robert nodded and handed her a business card. "Keep it handy. If one of your clients, Esther, ever needs to insure a painting. Or if you ever need help tracking down a stolen one we've insured. Cheerio, and good luck. I must go and confirm my flights again just to be sure. I don't trust the prats. They're always changing flights on me. Otherwise, see you on the plane."

"Nice chap," Bastiann said as Robert headed for the Lufthansa counter.

Esther examined the business card and then smiled. She recognized the insurance company's name. It had been used by MI6 for ages, one of many covers for its agents. Hardly anyone knew about it, though, including the producers and directors of the James Bond films, or Ian Fleming, for that matter.

***

"We'll spend some of my free days in Edinburgh and your castle, I suppose," Bastiann said to Esther once they were seated on their plane. Robert was in the back somewhere. "Part fun, part drudgery, I suppose. I'll be there for you."

She stared out the tiny window at a baggage handler below. "How does one become an assassin, Bastiann?" she said without looking at him.

"You're not talking about skills, I suspect."

"No, more about personalities becoming so warped."

"Everyone is different. Some people might like the thrill of the kill. Others might act because of patriotism. And for still others, the attraction is the money."

"Can good people still remain good and become an assassin?"

"With your background, which you've never told me about in detail, I would guess you know the answers to all your questions. Are you thinking of Dragavei?"

She nodded. And Robert Winston. *Was he sent to kill Dragavei?* She hoped Bastiann had remembered his fiches. She would have to take a peek at Robert's. The man was hiding something, and Bastiann had been circumspect after Robert's interview. Or maybe Bastiann had discovered he was MI6 and after Dragavei but wasn't the killer, so it didn't matter.

She had kept secrets from Bastiann. *Does he keep secrets from me? And does that matter?*

Chapter Forty-Two

Sunday: Vienna

Fritz Reiner knocked on the apartment's door, feeling like he was in a place he shouldn't be. *How can I have a conversation with an art professor and a cellist? Especially with Franz and all his verbosity.*

The door opened to reveal an older woman who reminded him of Esther Brookstone when he'd first met her at that dinner so long ago. Esther had always been a lovely woman and was like a fine wine, becoming lovelier as she aged. *Or am I only coveting another man's wife now?* This woman could give Esther some competition, though.

"Sorry. I must have the wrong address. I'm looking for Professor Mayer and her fiancé."

A lame excuse because he'd been there before. *But she might not know that.* The lovely woman had surprised him, a fellow who didn't like surprises.

"I'm Elise's mother, Anna. I'm guessing you're Inspector Reiner, my blind date."

"I-I don't understand." *Blind date? Another surprise! Maybe a pleasant one?* He'd never had one, though, and he wasn't sure he wanted to start. *I'm not a young man focused on making the next conquest.*

She laughed. He loved her laugh—an authentic one, not girlish giggles.

"I'm only kidding. I just returned from Africa, so they invited me to dinner as well. Do come in, inspector."

He entered and again looked around at what he could see of the small but tidy apartment. He hadn't paid much attention to the décor when he was there the first time, just locks and doors.

"Where are Elise and her fiancé?"

She crooked a finger and he followed her to the living room. She gestured toward a living room chair. She sat on the small sofa.

"They're buying wine. Elise favors my husband who passed away a few years ago. Like him, she forgets things. In this case, the wine. Austrians can't have dinner without wine, correct?"

"I suppose not." He smiled. *A widow! This could be interesting. Did I know that?* In spite of his prodigious memory, he couldn't remember. *You are getting old, Fritz!* "Were you on a vacation in Africa? A safari perhaps?"

"Nothing so adventurous or ostentatious. I spent six months there studying tropical diseases. I took care of some patients too, of course. I work at the Centre for Infectious Diseases here in Vienna."

"I see."

Not much I can say that will impress this woman! He figured this was one widow who wasn't looking for a man. *Not my idea of a blind date!* He wasn't quite sure what Yanks meant by that, though. He certainly wasn't blind to her charms!

***

"I probably ruined your dinner," Fritz told Anna in the dining room as Elise and Franz prepared dessert in the kitchen. He had to look sideways, but her profile was striking too. "My description of that gunfight was perhaps too gory."

"No problem," Anna said. "Elise turned a bit white, and she was the one who wanted all the gory details, but I'm a doctor. I've seen what Ebola can do to a patient, for example."

She patted his hand. The result was like an electric shock passing through it and up his arm to create in turn a pleasant frisson going down his spine and into his privates. *Easy, boy!*

"I'm not certain I could have acted as calmly as you did in that situation," she continued. "You are truly a brave man."

Is she toying with me? "It comes with my job, Anna. Mine isn't nearly as dangerous as other colleagues'." He smiled at her, forcing himself to maintain eye contact instead of admiring her breasts. She turned more toward him. *Lecherous old man!* "And what you did in Africa is much more courageous."

"As you say, it comes with my job. No advances can be made with tropical diseases if we don't study them in their places of origin. And, with climate change, it seems inevitable they will cease to be tropical and eventually become more prevalent here in Europe."

Wunderbar! At least she's not a climate change denier. He was tired of right-wing politicians and company CEOs who denied science and called climate change a hoax.

***

Anna knew her daughter Elise had parenting issues about her mother. Her daughter's loss of her father hadn't helped, and some of Anna's worries about fascism had also been transferred to her daughter—not that the worries were unfounded.

The main problem was rooted in Anna's not spending enough time with Elise in her teenage years. Anna had buried herself in her work, especially after losing her husband, neglecting her own needs as well as Elise's. The COVID-19 era hadn't affected Austria as much as Italy, perhaps helped by that great natural barrier, the Alps, but

Anna had worked overtime preparing for that pandemic, and then during it.

She knew she couldn't turn back the clock. During the return trip from Africa, though, she'd decided she'd spend more quality time with Elise and Franz and pamper herself a bit too. She wasn't ready to retire, but it was time to have some fun in life. She thought her husband might want that for her.

She removed her hand from Fritz's and toyed with her necklace. It consisted of a simple gold chain with a single large pearl. Her action called attention to her cleavage again, and she knew her companion at the table couldn't avoid watching her long, delicate fingers play with the pearl.

"If you work in that center, were you involved at all with controlling the COVID-19 pandemic?"

"Of course. A bad time for all of Europe…and the entire world. We'll be better prepared next time, and there will be a next time. New viruses will surely come along, perhaps even worse than that particular coronavirus."

"I was a survivor. I hate to call it that, though. I wasn't very sick."

"You're not that old. It affected the elderly a lot more, but it was surprisingly virulent even among young people with predispositions, genetic or otherwise. In Italy, for example, where multiple generations live together. And most developed countries now have aging populations. The pandemic's data is still being analyzed."

Her nervous play with the pearl began again. He watched, and she was amused by his watching.

"I assume you're not married, Fritz. You have wandering eyes. Most married Viennese men are more discreet. Not at all professional on your part." She winked and then laughed as he blushed. "But I welcome it. Elise said you were quite the character. I hope you don't mind my being forward, but are you seeing someone?"

"Not at the moment." He jerked a thumb toward the living room where the Caravaggio now hung in its old place on the wall in its new frame. It would soon have a temperature and humidity controlled place of honor in the couple's new house. "That painting kept me busy lately. Some other cases too. They tend to come in waves."

"A circumspect answer." She continued to fiddle with the necklace. "I was seeing a doctor, a gynecologist, to put a humorous spin on the story, but he dumped me for a nurse half his age. I was able to put him out of mind while I was in Africa, but here—" She waved her free hand toward the far window where one could see the art thief's apartment building and the *Ringstrasse* beyond in its nighttime glory—"it often seems more lonely than Africa. Elise is so happy now, and I'm happy for her, but I feel I'm missing something in my life."

"I've never dated a doctor before."

Anna licked her lips and her eyes sparkled. "There are definite advantages for doing so. I know a lot about women and men's plumbing."

***

Because Anna had come in a taxi, Fritz drove her home. Her apartment was larger than Elise's and was farther from the city's center.

"Make yourself at home, Fritz, while I put on something more comfortable. There's liquor in the cabinet. I'll have a cognac, if you don't mind serving."

He watched her go. He thought he might be walking into a trap, but he knew there was chemistry between them. *A doctor and a police inspector? What a combination! But maybe Count Sartini was correct? Is it time, Fritz?*

He went to the liquor cabinet, poured them both a cognac, and loosened his tie before taking a sip. *There is a difference between cognac and brandy.* He didn't have words to describe it, but it was there. And that difference applied to Anna versus every other widow he'd met. *Well, maybe she's on a par with Esther, but she will be in London and unavailable, while Anna will be right here in Vienna.* And he wasn't going to consider her second best either, just different…and exciting.

When she returned in a sheer nightgown, his heart skipped a beat. *Must be the cognac.* He hadn't had anything more than white wine for weeks, and only two glasses with dinner.

She handed him a pile of folded clothes. "Only if you believe you need them."

It was a set of pajamas.

"We'll see," he said with a smile.

He handed her cognac to her.

Chapter Forty-Three

Monday: London

Esther left Bastiann in her London flat working on his Interpol report. She used the excuse of checking on her gallery to go for the tests she had scheduled back on the riverboat.

The first tech made another EKG to start, but the second tech wasn't too gentle as she poked and prodded with the ultrasound device used for the echocardiogram. Esther survived the torture, though, dressed, and returned to the waiting room, hoping the doctor wouldn't take too long. *I really do need to make an appearance at the gallery, if only to put the fear of God in Anna and Dorothy before Bastiann and I head north.*

"Mrs. Brookstone?" Esther looked up from her two-year-old magazine full of movie stars, many of them unrecognizable to her. "Come with me, please."

Esther followed the nurse into the little office where her chosen NHS cardiologist held court.

"Have a seat, Esther." She did, and he smiled at her. "I don't know why that Austrian EKG showed some irregularities. I saw none. Nothing from the ECG either. You're extremely fit for a woman of your age."

Normally she would fight with him about that last sentence, but her relief won the battle over her tendency to make her habitual feminist comebacks. "That's good. I was on my honeymoon, you know. It wasn't fun to imagine that my new husband could soon become a widower."

"Oh, congratulations." He examined some papers. "A riverboat cruise. How nice. I must suggest that as an alternative for my daughter." He sighed. "She wants a trip to the British Virgin Islands, of all places. I'd wager your trip cost less."

"The airfare there will kill her. Or you, paying for it all." She laughed. "But Daddy might have to give in." She refocused. "So I have nothing to worry about? What caused the irregularities?"

"Assuming the Austrian doctor's equipment didn't malfunction, there are many possibilities. Because you were on your honeymoon, maybe performance anxiety?"

"If I understand your meaning, I had none, have none, and shall never have."

"Maybe a fright? A good scare can send an old woman's heart aflutter. What were you doing before the dizziness attack?"

"I told the tech. Maybe she didn't believe me and didn't jot it down. You likely won't either if I tell you, which I won't because she should have recorded it."

"Let's consider it a false alarm then. I want you to make an appointment for a stress test, though. At your convenience. That will truly tell us what's going on, if anything."

She gathered up her coat and purse and stood. "I'll do that. And you should worry more about your own sex life. You have lipstick on your cheek."

As she walked by the nurse, Esther noticed the doctor's nurse-receptionist had the same shade of lipstick. *Like hell I'll do a stress test!*

***

"Welcome back, Mrs. Brookstone," Anna said. "Did you have a good trip?"

Esther looked around the gallery. "Interesting might be a better word. Or deadly. Where's Dorothy and Harry?"

"Both took an early lunch to do some errands."

Esther nodded. She didn't like to leave only one person in charge of the galley. Harry had been there when the thief attacked Anna. Afterwards she had done some sleuthing herself, putting herself in danger, when she trailed the art thief who stabbed poor Harry. Anna was a brave soldier.

"I don't suppose our friend, Dracula, made another appearance?"

She was only confirming what she'd already surmised. Bastiann had finally told her Robert Winston's story. Together with the MI6 data provided by Jeremy, they had a clearer picture about who Maxim Dragavei was. That still didn't tell them why he was looking for her at the gallery. They didn't even know why he'd picked their riverboat. *And I'm still betting Robert's in my old business, not insurance! Was he after Maxim for other reasons beyond what he'd told Bastiann?*

"No, mum, and I'm happy he didn't. He was creepy."

She smiled. "Turns out he was a distant relative."

"Was, mum?"

"Long story. And I have yet to learn how much of it I can tell. Did we sell any paintings?"

"There's an elderly woman who's interested in that 'Madonna with Child' you restored. She remarked it was in excellent condition. I explained how you're an expert at restoration."

"I wouldn't go that far. I see she didn't buy it. Was that the reason, that it was restored?"

"I'm not sure. She only said she wanted to talk to you about its provenance. Dressed well with gold necklace and earrings, too overdressed for most of London, I dare say."

"Some old earl's lady or duke's duchess, I venture, in from her country estate on her monthly shopping trip to London. That inquiry's worth following up, though. The painting has a hefty price tag because of its age, although the artist isn't well known. Mixing up those period paints wasn't an easy task. Do you have her contact information?"

Anna found a sheet of paper with name, telephone number, and address noted in Dorothy's small, neat handwriting. Esther went to her laboratory and made the call. When she returned, she was beaming.

"All she wanted was the history of the artist. I had that available in spades." She tapped her head but winced. She'd used her left arm, the same side where Luynhen had kicked her in the ribs. "That's how I knew how to mix the paints. She'll be in sometime this week to pick up the painting." She winked at Anna. "Don't question her bank check. I know her duke left her swimming in cash, stocks, and bonds."

***

When she entered her flat, Bastiann was at her dining table still working. He looked up and said, "You look like you won a lottery, my love. Good news?"

She didn't tell him about the doctor's news, which was also good, but she gushed about the sale of the painting. "The commission's equal to six months of my last Scotland Yard salary, tax free."

"That only says the Metropolitan Police, like Interpol, doesn't pay its coppers enough. Part of that will go to expenses, I'm sure, and some to taxes."

"Don't rain on my parade, Bastiann. What's left for me still pays for our little honeymoon trip and then some. I feel like celebrating with an early curry dinner."

"The earlier the better. We have to pack for an early start to your castle, unless you want to stay in Edinburgh. And we'll need to buy some things for the castle too." He paused to study her. "I suppose the trip will mess with your emotions."

She sobered. "Yes, the part in Auld Reekie won't be nearly such a joyous occasion as going home to the castle."

"Want to hear some interesting news about the investigation? Might even cheer you up. I was going to save it for dinner, but let's avoid talking about it there." She nodded. "The Hungarian federal police did a test firing of Viktor's gun as we'd suggested. The striations on the bullet match those on the ones fired at the abbey. Some other gun killed Viktor, though."

"Viktor is too large to be the shooter at the abbey. I'll place my bet on Luynhen."

"I thought it was a man."

"She could have dressed that way."

He nodded. "As maybe a small man. In addition, Passau police CID, with the help of the Dresden bunch, matched the knife to a lot received in a shipment to Ihrin's gift shop. She sold them there as a copy of the knife that killed Julius Caesar, although Robert was right—it's in fact modeled after a Venetian collector's item."

Esther smiled. "That's good police work. Establishes the case against the Bulgarians and the Romanians. I wonder if there's another gun the latter used to kill Viktor. It's most likely at the bottom of the Danube."

Bastiann shrugged. "Another addition to its history."

His thoughts had turned once again to the Romanians. He'd just realized an error he'd made: He hadn't queried that young Hungarian couple about the encounter they'd had with the jogger. He shook his head. *No one can have a cover that deep. Three generations!* He wondered how to express those thoughts in his report.

Chapter Forty-Four

Wednesday Morning: Moscow

Yevgeny Molchalin took the call from their Hungarian embassy and waited for the encryption to settle down.

"*Dobreya ootro, tovarishch.* You can see I'm your faithful servant, coming in to call you at this hour with my report. How are things with your old boss?"

"My boss is fine. What do you have to tell me?"

"Like many things in this peculiar business, the riverboat mission was a mixture of success and failure. But you already knew my concerns from our little drop in Vienna. And you probably know something from media accounts too. So I'll be brief: We eliminated him, and my wife and I escaped. That Interpol agent and his wife made total success impossible. One positive: Those of us who didn't make it can't talk. That's more success from the practical point of view. You won't have outraged simpletons calling to extradite agents like in some of P's other revenge missions. He should lose some of that old, smoldering KGB anger. The Rodina's success in this modern world needs calm, methodical thinking, not emotional desires for revenge."

"I might agree, but that's not going in my report. I have no missions for you right now, so enjoy a holiday with your family."

"We plan to do so," said Janos.

After hanging up, Yevgeny wrote a brief addendum to his own mission report, made some copies, marked them совершенно секретно, Russian for Top Secret, and filed them. One copy went into the red folder on his desk.

An hour after the call, Yevgeny left his small office with the red folder tucked under his arm. *A tie game between CIA and SVR,* he reasoned. *Only my point of view, of course.* He thought some more. *Maybe a few goals for MI6 too? How else could Brookstone and van Coevorden obtain so much information?* He wondered who her contact was. He also wondered if there was something in her past that would tell them.

His footsteps echoed as he walked along the long corridor of unmarked doors to the end. The only thing distinguishing the door there was its being at that end and somewhat wider, but the office behind that door was the one he visited most often. He walked in.

"Hello, Vladlena. How are you today? Is he in yet?"

"Is it urgent?"

Yevgeny admired her cleavage. *Someday I will be the boss and have someone like her as a fringe benefit.*

"I wouldn't be here if it wasn't."

As SVR director Mikhail Plotnikov's chief office assistant, Vladlena was smart enough to understand her place. She buzzed her boss. "Mikhail, Yevgeny's here."

"*Da.* I've been expecting him. Send him in."

Once inside, Mikhail gestured toward the brown leather chair in front of his large desk piled with paperwork, a desk appearing too small for that spacious end office.

"Our main operative in Budapest reports they lost four assets," Yevgeny said. He waved the red file folder. "I'll leave this with you to peruse at your leisure."

"If we'd placed our man as head of Interpol, none of that would have happened."

"One can only bully the UN so much, sir. It's not a great loss. There will be no exposure. And none of those lost received training here."

Mikhail raised his eyebrows. "Money, Yevgeny. These contracts are expensive. Mercenary-assassins are paid in Western currency."

"And provide complete deniability. It's only oil money, after all."

Mikhail pounded his desk, reminding Yevgeny of a leader from old Soviet times he'd seen in history videos.

"Which is all we have." The color in the old man's face faded to its usual paleness as he spun in his chair to look through the small window at the snowy street below. "Winter is coming early to Moscow. You know, Yevgeny, there must be a better way." He spun back to face his aide. "Are the Hungarians in danger? Somehow that old hag and her Interpol husband exposed the others. Do we have any idea whether they know about our little Hungarian cadre?"

"The older Hungarians are sly foxes, and they all have a strong anti-Russian history as cover. We would be giving too much credit to the Interpol agent and his bride to believe our Hungarians are exposed."

"Perhaps. But maybe we should do something about that pair of meddlers?"

"I recommend nothing for now. They were just lucky."

***

In Washington DC, Tom Bradford read the mission report summary, the entire report written by his two principal agents in the field. They'd been thorough, so he decided to leave the rest for later. A two-fer, he observed. *Or maybe a multi-fer?* He smiled.

He and the cultural attaché at the Moscow embassy, a clever fellow who was also head of station there, had come up with the plan. The brass had almost killed it, pointing out real and imagined risks, as always, but they finally okayed it because they liked the idea of possibly getting rid of the oligarch as well as some of Putin's mercenary-assassins. The latter had done a lot of damage over the years, and the former had been a favorite of the Russian leader.

The old Soviet Union had its KGB; Putin had his FSB and SVR and a multitude of helpers; and he still had KGB expertise, his own; so he could combine them all to make a formidable intelligent service. And that didn't even count all the special units designed to create havoc in the world's democracies.

Hiring Dragavei and Santos had started the dominoes falling. First the oligarch, then Santos and Dragavei, and finally that vipers' nest. Exposing the young Hungarians was a nice bonus, and they'd led his agency to the whole damn family. *Another nest of vipers!* He'd decided to keep them under surveillance for the time being, and move on them only when necessary. Or they could be used to pass lots of misinformation to Moscow.

It was good to be on the offense again.

The chess game never changed. Tom considered it job security. He wasn't sure about the cultural attaché. His old friend was closer to the action…and the danger. And he might be retiring soon.

"You're in a good mood," his secretary said when he returned the file to her.

"Come on. I'll treat you to an early lunch. I need to meet a senator at one."

"Where are you taking me?"

"Anywhere you like…as long as they have martinis."

***

With two martinis under his belt—he had desired but didn't want to risk a third—Tom felt he had enough liquid courage to meet the old man. The meeting didn't occur at the senator's office, though. That was too public...and Russian agents could be watching.

"You're late," said the white-haired survivor of many political wars, from long-forgotten local offices to the US House and Senate. He put down his copy of the Post. "I assume you have some news. How is your little plan proceeding?"

Tom smiled. "It's over for now. This business is like online gambling: Sometimes we win, sometimes we lose, but most times there's ambiguity."

"And there's ambiguity in your spook talk. So which is it?"

"I think we have a win. I believed in the plan. Maybe that's half the battle."

The senator sighed and nodded. "I considered it risky because of its complexity. I'll admit you and that Moscow head of station were clever to pull it off, though. Good thing you two are on our side."

"Thanks for the kudos. But you approved the plan."

"You know me. Putin's never our friend. Anyone who believes otherwise needs his head examined. That's not political opinion, Tom, just common sense."

"So you'll support subsequent plans?"

"We'll see." He picked up his paper. "This one was successful because you had the right chess pieces on the board." The senator stood. "I must get back to the office."

Tom didn't envy the senator. He wasn't getting any younger, and he had a lot of irons in the fire. He also had gone through that futile effort to impeach the sitting president, a lost cause considering the makeup of the senate at that time. He didn't know if recent presidents were any better, but it would be hard for them to be worse. And he always believed that guy was as surprised as everyone else in the US and around the world when he won. *I wonder if the movement to do away with the Electoral College will ever take hold?*

Tom stood as well and shook the senator's hand. "To continue your chess analogy, we didn't have that many pieces left, but the plan worked because we still had the queen and her knight. And that, sir, was luck."

The senator nodded. "Sometimes powerful men underestimate what strong women can do. They shouldn't be overlooked, my friend. You do so at your own peril."

Chapter Forty-Five

Wednesday Morning: Edinburgh

"You appear nervous, Bastiann," the barrister said.

Bastiann nodded. "One part I hate about my job is sometimes having to tell family about the death of one of their loved ones."

"This is somewhat different," George Cearrarch said. "You two will be giving this old couple some closure." He was interrupted by his old-fashioned office intercom. "Ah, they have arrived."

George ushered in Edward Morgan's parents. The father was eighty-one, a silver-haired man with a weathered face; the mother was seventy-eight, a black-haired woman with some strands of silver, her face wrinkled by the passing of time.

That's one more thing I'm not looking forward to, thought Esther. She hated wrinkles.

They all shook hands and everyone found seats.

The parents had few questions as Esther summarized what they had learned, keeping confidential information absent from her story.

"We realized something was wrong," the father said after Esther finished. "We knew the photo of the riverboat victim couldn't be our son."

"What we surmise," Bastiann said, "is your son died in that car crash and John MacDonald stole his identity. Remains buried in MacDonald's grave are most likely your son's. George will explain the next steps."

"Hmm. Yes, yes. There are but two options I can offer, and either one will have to be approved by a magistrate, I suppose. We can exhume the remains in the grave and compare the DNA to yours to be absolutely certain. Or we can simply change the gravestone. I'd recommend the former. That will give you more closure. In any case, Esther and Bastiann have agreed to pay all costs."

"Closure," said Esther, "and a complete solution to the mystery of who Maxim Dragavei truly was for us."

"But you said he's Angus's nephew," said the mother.

"And my distant relative," said Esther.

"But we didn't exhume Angus's remains to confirm that," Bastiann said. "And even that still wouldn't confirm the remains in John's grave are your son's."

The mother nodded.

"I also have a source who confirms Maxim Dragavei in that photo on the newswires looks like John MacDonald," Esther said, "but she's not completely sure. That's two opinions for that, at any rate. So the DNA test of Angus's remains wouldn't be a hundred per cent confirmation either without exhuming John, which is impossible because he was cremated."

Bastiann looked at Esther with eyebrows raised. She smiled at him. She'd kept Sylvia Bassett's participation private as well.

"Let's do it then," said the father. "The first option. Frankly, I don't care about John MacDonald, especially if he stole my son's identity."

"And I don't want to see any remains even if they're Edward's," the mother said. "How could John do this to us?"

Someone like Sylvia turns out okay, observed Esther. *Someone like John MacDonald doesn't. Both come from similar backgrounds. Life is strange.*

***

George Cearrach invited them to dinner at his house, but Esther wanted to spend another night at their castle. She knew Bastiann didn't want to meet the sister again either, but she couldn't say that to the barrister.

Before they left George's offices, the old man handed a bundle of some old letters to Esther. "The cleaning company found these when they prepared Angus's house for sale," he said. She took them but decided to peruse them later.

As she drove her Jaguar into a beautiful sunset, they chatted about the case. Several loose threads remained, but he believed they wouldn't be woven into the case history anytime soon. And he couldn't put anything in his report that would violate the secrecy of the information passed to them, especially that data received from Jeremy Brand.

The castle was cold, so he built a fire in the living room fireplace, as well as turning up the heat from the old furnace. Esther went to the kitchen to concoct a quick dinner. While her invention simmered and a cake baked, she examined the letters after opening them with a kitchen knife.

Some were love letters between Angus and a half-dozen women. The old boy was quite the ladies' man. The women's prose was filled with gushy verbosity expressed in an old-fashioned way that made her smile. His to them were more to the point, variations on the theme of "My dear, we had a good time, but I enjoy my freedom too much." *They should have known better! Curious that he made copies.* Was old Angus afraid of a paternity suit? Maybe Cearrach knew a lot of secrets about Angus?

Six letters were postmarked in as many capitals around Europe, addressed to Angus and without a return address. They were unopened. *Should I open them?*

She was a fast reader and read them before dinner was ready. The contents were all similar: *Dear Uncle Angus, I hope you're doing well, bla-bla...*and full of apologies and begging for forgiveness. They were signed by John MacDonald. No mention was made of the life John had chosen to lead, though. There were no copies of any replies, of course. *Angus didn't even read them!*

It was clear to Esther that John had loved and respected his old uncle, though. He wrote as a prodigal son might write to a father he hadn't seen for a long time. I've seen letters from soldiers like this, she thought. *Will Johnny be marchin' home again? Not this John.* As far as Esther knew, his ashes were still in Germany. She cringed. *Will I be receiving them?*

The business in Cearrach's offices and the letters made her maudlin. She hoped dinner with Bastiann would perk her up.

***

Bastiann soon detected the fragrance of her cake. Esther knew some recipes from memory. *She can make a good dinner when she puts her mind to it.* He put down the paper they'd purchased along with groceries in Edinburgh and headed for the kitchen.

"Now that the chill is gone," Bastiann said, "your castle seems quite comfortable, my lady."

She served the hearty stew along with homemade bread, and they sat down at the long oak table, one at each end, like they were the lord and lady of the castle...which they were in legal terms, perhaps more legally now.

"Our castle. Get used to saying it." He nodded. She took a bite of her slice of rustic bread and followed it with a spoonful of stew. She then looked around the dining room with its cold, granite walls. "Wouldn't it look better with some wood paneling?"

"A future renovation perhaps? You don't want to make it any darker."

She seemed to ponder his opinion, looking to comment, but her answer went elsewhere: "I wonder if Angus ever had dinner here with John."

"Angus didn't use his castle all that much. I suspect he considered the inheritance a white elephant. He left it in poor condition, to put it mildly. But didn't you say the lad threw parties here? He probably used it more."

"Sex, beer, and weed. Maybe other drugs. Who knows? I'm sure they didn't worry too much about the castle's condition in their state."

Bastiann eyed her. "How do you know about that? Your source?"

Esther smiled. "But here's another mystery: I'd like to find out more about this Linda Santos. How did John meet her? Where is she now?"

"Dead, most likely. Putin always kills those who he feels have betrayed him. How much longer for your cake?"

"Another thirty minutes. And then it has to cool a bit, although eating it warm can be nice."

"Then grab two snifters and find the brandy we bought and follow me."

He led her into the living room and linked his smart phone to their new Bose system. "I have some new MP3 tracks to play for you. I downloaded them while you were at NHS."

She glanced at him but could find no comeback.

330

He left her sitting on the sofa and approached the Bose. He tapped some icons on his mobile. A mellow baritone voice began singing Sorastro's aria from *The Magic Flute*. Bastiann turned and toasted Esther with a flourish but without saying anything. When the aria finished, he stopped the replay.

"John MacDonald?" Esther said.

Bastiann joined her on the sofa.

"The singer is listed as Maxim Dragavei, but yes, he's your relative. He has a nice range and a good feel for Mozart."

She took a sip of her brandy. "With a voice like that, why did he choose the life he led?"

"Perhaps because of Linda Santos? Or he found killing people more exciting than singing opera? Or maybe he liked the money too much? Jeremy didn't state how much the CIA paid him for the hit on the Russian oligarch. Multiply whatever that was by ten or possibly more, and he probably died a rich man."

"'Lord, what fools these mortals be.'" She was thinking of the letters as well. *Why hadn't Angus opened them? What could that hurt?*

"Indeed. Would you like to hear more?"

"Yes. It's creepy, but also interesting Also sad and beautiful at the same time."

She wiped away some tears as she listened, wondering if she had met John MacDonald, whether she could have turned his life around like she had with Sylvia Bassett. Churchill's old American WWII buddy had once said, "Men are not prisoners of fate, but only prisoners of their own minds." *Could she have changed his mind as she had changed Sylvia's, taking him from a dark place back into the light?* She'd never know the answer, of course, and that would torment her for a while.

She reached for Bastiann's hand.

Epilogue

George Langston walked to the front door of his Georgian-style house in the London suburbs and peered through the peephole.

"Mr. and Mrs. van Coevorden, I presume," he said to the two masked persons, one a barrel of a man, dressed in a tuxedo and black homburg hat, and the other a taller, elegant woman, dressed in a tweed suit and black felt hat.

"Miss Marple and Hercule Poirot for tonight, George," said Esther as he opened the door wide.

"Only for Halloween," added Bastiann, twirling his mustache.

"Stand aside, George, it's a raw night. I don't envy the children out and about."

George made a sweeping motion of welcome with one arm, inviting them in. "I bid you welcome, o famous sleuths. Follow me to the buffet and drinks."

"Sorry we're late," said Esther, "but we were just finishing up a murder case by participating in one of Dame Agatha's tell-all denouements."

"No problem," George said. "Fashionably late is right on time, madam."

In the large hall, a loud bash was underway. Esther heard spooky and macabre music, and some ghosts and goblins were trying to dance to it. All of Esther's gallery employees were there—Anna, as Margaret Thatcher; Dorothy, as that *Wizard of Oz* character with the same name, complete with red slippers; Harry, as a werewolf; and Harry's wife as someone's fairy godmother—*maybe Cinders'?* Besides George Langston, who was dressed as

Jean Luc Picard, those were the only ones she recognized because they all had on masks.

They started making the rounds, both she and Bastiann trying to guess who was whom.

***

"How's retirement going for you, Monsieur Poirot?"

Bastiann turned away from the railing back toward the hall. He knew that voice.

"Robert?"

"Good guess," Robert Winston said, lowering his mask slightly, although his eyes were still shaded by his deerstalker.

Sherlock Holmes, mused Bastiann. *Nice cape and pipe.*

"You're not the only one who can solve mysteries, Hercule. I was going at it when you were still in nappies." Robert smiled. "I observe you're also a fresh-air fan."

They were on the back porch, just out from the hall and through the French doors now slightly ajar to air out the room filled with so many people. In the dark, with only a sliver of moon, one could barely make out the garden and lawn that Bastiann had been staring at.

"George did well purchasing his house," Bastiann said. "I took a tour last Sunday when we were invited for tea. He still has packing crates in the basement."

"It's a stately old place, to be sure."

"Yes, and too bad he didn't own it earlier. I would have asked him the favor of borrowing it for our wedding."

Robert nodded. "You didn't answer my question."

Bastiann thought a moment. "I'm enjoying my retirement. It's splendid to have more time with Esther. I help out in the gallery, which does well enough to complement our two pensions. And we're often at our castle. It's becoming quite the nice getaway. We'll probably enjoy it more in summer, though. I'm also doing some consulting work with the Metropolitan Police, thanks to George."

"A bit drafty, those old Scottish castles, and winters in Scotland can be a bit harsh, so I understand your reluctance to be there over winter." Robert glanced inside the hall and then draped an arm around Bastiann's shoulder. "I wanted to give you enough time to become bored," he said in a low voice.

"I don't understand."

"My company would also like you to do some consulting work from time to time. That obnoxious American is already onboard."

"Hal?"

"What other obnoxious American could we possibly have in common?"

"Why would he work for your company?"

"He knows a lot about the illegal arms trade in Europe and the Middle East. And you yourself have participated in a variety of investigations when it comes to criminal activity."

Bastiann raised an eyebrow. "What does your company do exactly?"

Robert smiled. "Insurance. 10 Downing Street is one of our biggest clients." He handed Bastiann the same card he'd given Esther—Bastiann recognized it even with just a brief glance. "Give me a call when you're ready, and we'll set up an appointment. I'll make sure Hal is present." Robert looked at his watch. "I dare say it's been fun, but I must leave these festivities, I'm afraid. There's a huge hound howling on the moors of Baskerville Hall."

Bastiann studied the card again and then watched as Robert entered the hall, passing by Esther who seemed to be dedicated to a bit of tippling at her old boss's expense. *Did she wink at Robert?*

Note from Steve:

You have just finished *Death on the Danube*, the third novel in the "Esther Brookstone Art Detective" series. I hope you enjoyed it. Please write a review if you bought it online—only a brief review about the book suffices, one saying what you liked and disliked and why. Your review will help other readers and also provide me with important feedback.

Please peruse the preview of #4 in the series below.

And please consider these other mysteries and thrillers I have written:

"The Last Humans Series"

The Last Humans
The Last Humans: A New Dawn (to be published)

"Esther Brookstone Art Detective"

Rembrandt's Angel
Son of Thunder

"Mary Jo Melendez Mysteries"

Muddlin' Through
Silicon Slummin'…and Just Gettin' By
Goin' the Extra Mile

"Detectives Chen and Castiblanco"

The Midas Bomb
Angels Need Not Apply
Teeter-Totter between Lust and Murder
Aristocrats and Assassins
The Collector
Family Affairs
Gaia and the Goliaths

(Note: In several books in this series, Esther and Bastiann have cameos.)

For a full list of my books (including my sci-fi novels), see my website https://stevenmmoore.com. Special sales of my ebooks are only offered in my email newsletter. Sign up for it using the contact page at my website, where you can also download free PDFs of short fiction—see the list on the "Free Stuff & Contests" web page.

For book clubs and discussion groups, you will find below a list of discussion questions.

Around the world and to the stars! In libris libertas!

Preview of Novel #4 in the "Esther Brookstone Art Detective Series"

Chapter One

London, England

Reggie Fox set the alarm for Esther and Bastiann's flat and then exited. He made sure the key properly engaged the dead bolt and headed for the lift.

He'd completed his daily task: Adding to the mail piled high on Esther's counter. *She does her duty by His Majesty's postal service,* he thought. He wasn't about to sort it either. He had no idea what advertisements and catalogs she'd want to read. He was never discriminating—they always went into his bin.

He called the lift and took it down to the building's car park, essentially a stuffy, gloomy basement area mostly empty at that time of day. When the doors opened, he looked out.

Ever since that psychotic Italian had attacked Esther, Reggie had been wary of dark places where people parked their cars, especially their buildings. He stepped out and looked from side to side and towards the rear. *Reginald Fox, you old paranoid sod! There's no one here!*

Esther and he hadn't always got along, but he liked the old woman enough and had once imagined they might become an item…or at least one of his conquests. *After all, I'm a debonair and still sexually active old fellow with a pulse and plenty of money. For a widow, what's not to like?*

Bastiann, on the other hand, was a walking wine barrel, a Humpty-Dumpty shaped fellow, a man one might expect to be employed as a bouncer at some London night club. *She'd chosen him over me. Here I am, a witty fellow who can chin wag with aristocratic old ladies and young students alike, as long as they're attractive females!* Esther was a good-looking older woman who had resisted his many charms, though.

Can I even count her as a friend? He thought she might just tolerate him because she found him useful sometimes. If he was traveling, she'd look after his mail and check his flat; and she expected that favor to be returned. He thought she had the better part of that bargain. He had to admit her life was more exciting than his. His sporadic trips to the continent, long complicated by BREXIT, couldn't compare with her treks around the world.

He then realized he still stood frozen in front of the elevator, lost in thought like some senile old man. Embarrassed at his daydreaming, he looked into the dim recesses of the car park to find his BMW.

That's when they tackled him, one from each side. He went down.

***

One thug held him down while the other went through his pockets. Reggie saw the latter bloke stand and go through his wallet. *Common muggers!* Rozzers were never around when you needed them.

"You'll find nothing worthwhile in there," he said. "I was just heading for the bank."

The one sitting on him clocked him once, and Reggie spit blood. *Are they going to kill me if they find nothing worthwhile?* That happened sometimes on the telly.

The one with the wallet crouched again and found his BMW's fob. "Nice set of wheels, guv, but I hate Nazi cars. What's wrong with English-made, old bean?"

"Before BREXIT, most BMW parts were made here. Most motorcars are assembled elsewhere from parts—"

The other's fist slammed into his mouth again.

"My friend knows I hate blathering eejits too. Oi! Two sets of keys." The man kneeled again. Reggie could smell his whiskey breath. "Now, old man, we're going to play a wee game, we are. I'm guessing the ring with only two keys is the one I need to open Esther Brookstone's flat?"

Reggie spit out more blood. "You'd be guessing wrong. I don't know any Esther Brookstone."

The next blow broke his nose. The kneeling man grabbed his cheeks and stretched them.

"Listen to me, prat, my patience's not what it used to be. Why not make it easy on yourself?"

"I don't converse with dirty scrotes," Reggie spat, reaching back for language from his childhood he rarely used now.

The other's fist raised, but the squatting man stood and stomped on Reggie's abdomen.

"Beat the crap outta him to teach him a lesson," he said. "And make sure he don't wake up for a while, but don't kill him. Then meet me upstairs. One of these keys has to work."

***

Reggie went in and out of consciousness. When conscious, he empathized with Esther. He now knew how she must have felt when that psychotic Italian kidnapped her. It was a wonder she could later face that psychotic. *That woman has spunk!*

A long time later, the two thugs exited the lift and each one gave him a kick in the ribs as they passed by.

I tried, Esther, he mused. *I really did.* He lapsed into unconsciousness once again.

More time passed…and he heard someone approaching. *Did they come back?*

Chapter Two

Argyllshire, Scotland

Some years ago, Bobbie MacDonald was desperate and would have lived anywhere but New York City. She ended up moving as far away from there as she could. Argyllshire, with its lonely landscapes and brooding skies, seemed far enough from those who pitied her or might pursue her. Dr. Blake told her that would be good for her to get away for a while…and she did.

That while had become seven years, five at her secluded home on a bluff on Scotland's Atlantic coast. She valued her solitude. Even her weekly trip to the little village for staples still caused her paranoia, although the old gentleman who ran it was as nice as he could be. A typical taciturn Scot, but a kind, fatherly figure all the same. She attributed her agita more to leaving the house and making the three-mile lonely trip on a windy country road that rarely had any traffic.

She put the grocery bags in the back of her little Morris and opened the driver's door, eying the sky as a few clouds seemed to scud along the green hill tops. She'd seen on her laptop they were in for a storm, but for now the clouds only gave a hint of its approach. The forecast was Helensburgh's, and the biggest town in the area was twenty miles south of the village. The storm could stay south too, but there was no guarantee.

Maybe I can still get some painting done? Her house sat overlooking a small fjord where she could watch the waves from her living room. She painted in her studio around the corner from there where the soft northern light was optimal when the weather was good.

Her trips for groceries calibrated time for her. Without them, she wouldn't be able to measure its passage. Her idyllic existence now featured only a few major events beyond those weekly shopping: Her agent visited from time to time to take her paintings to galleries up and down the coast, even to London; and Dr. Blake occasionally called at random times from the US, which Bobbie found annoying. That woman was never satisfied. Bobbie liked her, but she seemed to believe Bobbie would go off the rails again. Sometimes she didn't even answer the phone when the psychiatrist's name came up.

As she drove by Scotland Police's substation, she tapped her horn. She didn't know if Rafael or Sam were there, but Dotty would be. Whoever was there would be worried if she didn't let them know she'd made her weekly trip to buy groceries.

Sam, the younger constable, looked like he'd just graduated from high school, but Dotty had told Bobbie he was twenty-eight. Rafael was Bobbie's age and a sergeant. Dotty, a good-natured woman, and Dan, the old owner of the grocery, were good friends...maybe more than friends? They were the only people in Bobbie's world now, except for the agent and Dr. Blake, who were more denizens of the urban world Bobbie had abandoned.

Rafael had installed her security system and taught her how to use it. With its videocams, motion sensors, and control panels, one in her entrance hall and the other in her bedroom closet, the high tech system always reminded her of the city she'd left. It also seemed out of place in her haven between the sea and the hills of Argyllshire.

Rafael and Sam manned the substation; Dotty was the dispatcher. At least one copper was on duty 24/7, but

Dotty was there only on weekdays from eight to five. She answered calls at home otherwise, and could dispatch Rafael or Sam, or someone from the main office in Alexandria. She was also the go-to person for fire and ambulance service, although the main hospital, Vale of Leven District Hospital in Alexandria, was about forty minutes away.

Dan, Rafael, and Sam were nice enough, but they were men. Bobbie had a problem with all men now. Dr. Blake hadn't said it directly, but Bobbie thought the psychiatrist wouldn't believe Bobbie was cured until she could relate better to men. She'd told the doctor several times, though, that she just hadn't found the right guy.

She sighed. Not going to happen anytime soon either.

***

Bobbie saw a strange car parked in front of her place when she returned with the groceries. Her knuckles turned white as she gripped the wheel and slowed down. *Should I park in the drive or run?* Dark clouds moving into the intense blue sky seemed to echo that thought.

She wasn't expecting any visitors. Her agent wasn't supposed to come until the following week. Besides, she had an older Mercedes; this one looked new.

In her panic, she could still note that Rafael's system had a serious flaw: The deck videocam would only reveal the person there if Bobbie was in the house. She went to the front porch to peek in. She could see all the way through the house and a back window to the raised deck attached to the kitchen.

Someone sat there, admiring the magnificent landscape. *My landscape!* Bobbie did that a lot, via her back picture window in winter and the deck in summer. Surprisingly the primeval loneliness of the vista calmed her.

She couldn't tell if her visitor was a man or woman, so she circled the house to where three steps took one to the deck's level.

"Angela? You gave me a fright!"

The woman turned. "Sorry. I tried to call. Is your mobile off?"

"Sometimes the reception isn't very good here. How long have you been waiting?"

Bobbie pulled a chair over and sat next to her agent. She gripped the arms of the chair to keep her hands from shaking.

"Are you having a panic attack, Roberta MacDonald?"

Bobbie nodded. "Did you come in a rental car?"

"No. New wheels. I decided to pamper myself a bit. I'm so often on the road. Why not travel in comfort?"

"I see." Bobbie tried to fold her hands in her lap but had to return them to the chair arms. Her knee started bouncing too. "You know me. Nervous Nellie."

Angela shook her head. "Can I get you some water or something?"

"I'll be okay in a moment." Her heart rhythm was reaching a more normal level.

Angela knew her history. Dr. Blake provided professional help; Angela helped in a less professional way...as a friend.

"I need to get back to Glasgow, so I don't have much time. I don't want to drive in a summer thunderstorm."

"You can stay here."

"I'd love too, but I have an appointment early tomorrow morning. Do you have anything—?"

"Oh crap! My groceries. I have two pints of ice cream."

"I'll help you bring them in."

***

The two pints were a slushy mix of ice cream and cold liquid. The two women finished them off on the deck in quick order, laughing about the mess they made.

"Leave it," Bobbie said, when Angela started to clean up. "Let's wash our hands and faces so I can show you what I've done since your last visit."

In a few moments, Angela stood with hands on hips admiring Bobbie's latest artwork. There was one of a saltwater marsh on the coast not far from there surrounded by a few trees decked out in their fall colors. She had done that from memory but she'd captured the reflections perfectly. Three others were lonely fjord and seascapes filled with sky and clouds. The last one was a portrait of the old grocery store owner sitting in his rocker and smoking his pipe.

"That fall one is lively and full of color," Angela said. "Your seascapes are more brooding than usual. Threatening, I should say. Are you having a relapse?"

"Of course not. They're all impending storms like today, only nearer. I guess they just matched my mood. They're a bit gothic, I suppose."

"I'll take them all. Suggested prices still on the back, I suppose?"

"Galleries can adjust accordingly as usual. Or you can. I have no idea how the market has changed."

"Let me get them into the car. I must get going, I'm afraid."

Before she took off in her new car, Angela hugged Bobbie.

"I saw microwaveable lasagna. Have that with a bottle of red to calm your nerves, girlfriend. I wish I could stay and be here for you."

"No matter how long you stay, you brighten my life." She patted her tummy. "And keep me in need of a diet. Where are you off to?"

"After my appointment tomorrow, I'll work my way down the coast as usual. There are five galleries before I even hit London. They've sold your work before. You're developing a reputation."

"All good, I hope. And not pitying."

"Even if they once knew, everyone's forgotten what happened except you. Take care."

Bobbie waved as Angela drove off. *Yes, why can't I forget?*

Discussion Questions for Book Clubs and Discussion Groups

Who's more set in their ways, Esther or Bastiann?

Who's the better detective, Esther or Bastiann?

What future does Philippa and Hal's relationship have?

What future does Caitlin and Sander's relationship have?

Murders aside, would you like to take a riverboat cruise on the Danube?

Esther and Bastiann seem enchanted by Austria's lake district. Do you think this is only because they're city dwellers?

Esther and Bastiann have strong opinions about geopolitics. Compare them. (Remember, the novel takes place a bit in the future.)

Even if you didn't read *Rembrandt's Angel*, it's clear Esther helped reform Sylvia Bassett. Do you think she could have helped John MacDonald?

What's your opinion of Angus MacDougall? If you read *Rembrandt's Angel*, did your opinion about him change at all after *Death on the Danube?*

The Elise Mayer - Fritz Reiner story shows Esther isn't the only art detective. Compare her to Fritz.

Notes, Disclaimers, and Acknowledgements

After *Rembrandt's Angel* and *Son of Thunder*, I had doubts about continuing the "Esther Brookstone Art Detective" series to a trilogy and perhaps beyond (several reasons are mentioned below). In particular, *Son of Thunder* was a tough act to follow, not only because it's an adventure story consisting of three separate but related road trips, but it also contains a lot of mysticism and religion.

In spite of those qualms, our own wonderful cruise down the Danube, similar to the one portrayed here (*sans* murders, of course!), inspired me to write this story. It's a road trip too, only on the waters of the most historical road in Europe. And romance and religion are connected even in the Bible, which is why Esther used the "Song of Solomon" in her wedding vows at the end of *Son of Thunder*, so a honeymoon trip for the two lovebird-sleuths seemed appropriate.

The inimitable Agatha Christie wrote two great mysteries that can also be classified as road trips, *Death on the Nile* and *Murder on the Orient Express*. In jest, Esther and Bastiann's colleagues have called them Miss Marple and Hercule Poirot, so it also seemed natural their honeymoon should become another Christie-style road trip. It's as simple as that. But the Devil's always in the details, isn't he?

For example, I wanted to make sure I didn't repeat Dame Agatha's stories except in spirit. And I still wanted to maintain the theme of "Romantic Danube" without writing a completely sappy rom-com or super-long cozy (if you don't know what those are, I applaud you). Fortunately, in the twenty-first century, there are ways to communicate "off the road" even while floating down the Danube, and Esther and Bastiann had a lot in their pasts I could use to do just that.

In fact, land action wasn't available to Dame Agatha in her two road-trip mysteries—the passengers on that steamboat and train were confined to their modes of transportation. Large cruise ships today often have the same problem, dropping anchor in a harbor far from shore and using tenders to take passengers to their tours on land.

In contrast, a lot of action in this novel takes place on land. Having the riverboat at a Danube dock where it can easily send passengers off on tours was a great help. The plot's settings could be varied, for example. I also used background material on Maxim Dragavei to achieve that effect (his story is essentially told in reverse, as a bow to and in the spirit of Garcia Marquez's *Chronicle of a Death Foretold*).

In the previous two novels as well as this one, I have focused somewhat on ambiguity. *Rembrandt's Angel* was ambiguous: Does Esther recover the painting she obsessively searches for? *Son of Thunder* was also ambiguous: Does Esther find St. John's tomb? Will the saint's bones be there if she revisits it, or will the Vatican still be discussing what to do about it? And here in *Death on the Danube*, it's assassins against assassins—a lot more serious than *Mad*'s "Spy vs. Spy," one of my favorite comedic critiques of the genre—and maybe Putin is the real winner?

Life is often ambiguous. Because fiction mirrors life, it too must be ambiguous. In that sense, this novel and the other two are not at all like Christie's, but perhaps they are akin to what she would have written if she authored twenty-first century crime novels?

Who's the better detective, Esther or Bastiann? I've added that question to the list for book clubs and discussion groups. Bastiann perhaps plays the more important role as a detective in this novel in contrast to the previous two, but that doesn't mean he's the better detective. So, while you ponder that question, let me emphasize they're always a crime-fighting duo to be reckoned with. Perhaps Dame Agatha is smiling because I have reincarnated her two famous sleuths, Miss Marple and Hercule Poirot, and transported them forward in time into the twenty-first century, where together they go after modern criminals, Putin and his cronies included.

With Google and Google Maps and many other online resources, it's hard to tell these days whether authors have visited the places they write about. In the case of this novel, rest assured I did. I especially want to thank the cruise line AmaWaterways and all their riverboat's competent and friendly crewmembers (some of which became dear friends—they know who they are) for our excellent cruise experience, during which I took the copious notes used to write this story.

All crewmembers and passengers in this novel are completely fictional, of course, and products of my own imagination, but the settings are mostly as I remember them, although some tours in my story were changed somewhat to better fit the plot. We even went to Prague, an experience Esther and Bastiann missed (although Esther visited there during her MI6 days).

I mentioned Google and Google Maps. I also used them and other sources to prepare an Irish stew of various descriptions of each riverboat port, and you'll see them at the beginning of appropriate chapters.

AmaWaterways's "Romantic Danube" brochure, provided to their riverboat passengers, was invaluable for getting all the timing right without having to know boat speeds, currents, and distances between ports.

Much of this story takes place in Austria, and Fodor's *Vienna & the Best of Austria* also helped me to remember the places we visited in our tours. The brochure on the Melk Abbey was also invaluable. I also consulted many other online and personal reference works, too many to mention here. Of course, I'm solely responsible for any errors I've made in describing the settings or timeline of the cruise. (Or the reader can write them all off as artistic license!)

Two short items that might interest readers: The novel that Esther was reading about WWII spies was Alex Gerlis's *Best of Our Spies*; that author has produced some excellent historical fiction in his spy thrillers. The novel Philippa was reading was my own *More than Human: The Mensa Contagion*. I'm sure neither author will mind me mentioning them here.

Like all books in any of my series, this third book in Esther's can stand alone. The reader need not have read *Rembrandt's Angel* or *Son of Thunder*, but if they did, there are some short references in this novel that will remind them of events and characters in those first two novels. Hopefully those readers who didn't read the previous books will now be motivated to read them. Esther is the same old but spritely sleuth in all three books, but her adventures in those earlier books are exciting too…and entirely different.

Some mention of the COVID-19 pandemic seemed appropriate and is made in this novel, but not many of the details are provided. I don't dwell on it because, as I write this, we're still in the middle of it—it's even ramping up as I start my final editing before sending it out to beta-readers and editors. For all I know, this book will be published posthumously! This novel is set a bit in the future, but it might be a future that never occurs. For example, river cruises might become a thing of the past (that would be a damn shame—ours was such a wonderful experience). In that case, the story here is one taking place in an alternate universe, one without extreme and disastrous consequences from the pandemic.

After organizing my notes and a bit of research, I started writing it around Christmas, 2019. It might be the last novel I write, but writing it allowed me to do something productive while self-quarantining. (Hopefully these words are completely unnecessary and everyone will have a good laugh when reading them. And hopefully AmaWaterways will continue to offer those wonderful riverboat tours. In any case, I'm leaving the mention of the pandemic in the text and these end notes so readers can realize the circumstances in which I wrote the novel.)

One related consequence of the pandemic was that I also read a lot. I've never been an ardent fan of TV except for a few PBS shows and the occasional drama series, so I did a lot of binge-reading, mostly novels I call British-style mysteries. As I explained in the notes to *Rembrandt's Angel*, fond remembrance of Dame Agatha's novels motivated me to team up Miss Marple (Esther Brookstone) with Hercule Poirot (Bastiann van Coevorden), but the *grande dame* of mystery writers has also inspired many other authors writing in the mystery genre. (I've also been influenced by America's hard-boiled school—hence the Nora and Nick Charles reference in this novel--as well as by Michael Connelly and a few others.) I started to realize those British idioms were creeping into my prose, especially when I was writing from Maxim, Esther, or other British characters' point of view.

Rather than eliminate them all, I decided to include the glossary you have found at the beginning of the novel. I hope British readers won't consider my use of idiomatic British English as nefarious cultural appropriation—they should in fact be honored—and I hope American readers don't find it too annoying. It's only the case of an author becoming too involved in his characters and his own reading, and admiring the varied culture of our friends across the Atlantic.

Needless to say, perhaps, but writing this novel was an entertaining experience. It was a lot more fun than just using all those notes taken on our tour down the Danube to create a new story. Now I'm in a real quandary: Do I go beyond the trilogy to a longer series? [Note added before press: I've provided a clue to the answer in the preview above.]

And now for some other sad words: While Penmore Press created the series title "Esther Brookstone Art Detective" for their two-book (at the time) series of my novels *Rembrandt's Angel* and *Son of Thunder*, I should probably explain why this third novel (and future novels in the series, if any) isn't published by them, but I'll forego giving details. I firmly believe in the independent small-press concept where, as a reader, I can still find interesting and exciting entertainment that the Big Five publishing conglomerates choose not to offer, and I hope my readers do too. If you are reading this, please support them, by buying their books, including the two in this series just mentioned, if you haven't already read them. I value the TLC I received from Penmore and enjoyed working with their staff, Michael James and

Christine Horner in particular. So I offer an effusive salute to Penmore's staff and authors, and bid them adieu…and wish them all good luck in the future.

Many people helped publish this novel: First, I send a hearty thank you to Carol Shetler for her beta-reading and editing—over the years, we have developed an online friendship that's more solid than most of my personal ones; second, Carrick Publishing and my friend Donna Carrick have done their usual excellent job of formatting this lengthy novel, and Sara Carrrick came through with her excellent cover art.

And there's one member of my publishing team I often forget, but never intentionally, so I apologize to Amanda Kerr of BookBuzz.net, who makes book launches as painless as possible for this nerdy author. I count all these smart and wonderful women as valuable friends who are much more skilled at doing many things that I couldn't begin to do.

And last, but far from least, I salute my wife. I recognize it's not easy to be married to a nerdy author, yet her patience and cheerleading over the years has been the foundation for the edifications my novels represent. Without her, my scientific and writing life would have been much less rewarding. And, to put a fine point on it, as the British would say, that cruise down the Danube wouldn't have occurred without her!

Steven M. Moore
Montclair, NJ
April, 2020

About the Author

Steven M. Moore was born in California and has lived in various parts of the US and Colombia, South America. He always wanted to be a storyteller but postponed that dream to work in academia and R&D as a physicist. His travels around Europe, South America, and the US, for work or pleasure, taught him a lot about the human condition and our wonderful human diversity, a learning process that started during his childhood in California's San Joaquin Valley.

Steve writes sci-fi, mysteries, and thrillers, short fiction, blog articles, and book and movie reviews. He has written many novels, including three for young adults under the pen name A.B. Carolan—his list of works includes six series. He also has published three short story collections. He has an active blog where he posts opinions about reading, writing, and the publishing business of interest to readers and authors alike.

He and his wife now live just outside New York City. For more details, visit him at his website https://stevenmmoore.com and follow him on Facebook, Goodreads, and Twitter, where he participates in many discussions with readers and writers. Steve is a member of International Thriller Writers.

You can learn more about Steve at his website: https://stevenmmoore.com. Use the contact page there to communicate with him…and to sign up for his email newsletter.